TUSCAN
DAUGHTER

TUSCAN DAUGHTER

A Novel

LISA ROCHON

Published by Harper Avenue, an imprint of HarperCollins Publishers Ltd

First edition

HarperCollins books may be purchased for educational, business, or sales
promotional use through our Special Markets Department.

HarperCollins Publishers Ltd
Bay Adelaide Centre, East Tower
22 Adelaide Street West, 41st Floor
Toronto, Ontario, Canada
M5H 4E3

www.harpercollins.ca

Library and Archives Canada Cataloguing in Publication

Title: Tuscan daughter : a novel / Lisa Rochon.
Names: Rochon, Lisa, author.
Description: Includes bibliographical references.
Identifiers: Canadiana (print) 20210154101 | Canadiana (ebook) 20210154136
ISBN 9781443463515 | (softcover) | ISBN 9781443463522 (ebook)
Classification: LCC PS8635.O295 T87 2021 | DDC C813/.6—dc23

Printed and bound in the United States

LSC/H 9 8 7 6 5 4 3 2 1

To my father, Joel,
for writing
and to
my mother, Mary,
for painting

Part I

1500–1502

I sought to raise myself on wings from here . . .
Defeating, I still live but loveless, lone
—Vittoria Colonna, sixteenth-century Italian poet

Chapter 1

Beatrice stirred and cast an arm across the straw mattress, seeking the warmth of her mother's body, listening hopefully for her breathing. Predawn, the sky was the color of river silt and the silence was deep; even the rooster slept. She pushed aside the rough linen blanket and pressed a hand to the stone wall, steadying herself against the absence. Only half-awake, she reached for her father's old quilted jacket and held it close, like a beloved friend.

Three months she had been making the journey to sell olive oil to the artists inside the city. It had become more difficult to gain permission to pass through the tollgates. But, then, measured against what her life had become, that hardly mattered. Her mother had disappeared, traumatized, her face crazed like the night's constellations. Her father—she would not think of it.

Alone, moving stiffly, Beatrice used her hips to guide the wooden cart down the dirt road, out of the tiny village of Settignano. One of the wheels wobbled, threatening to come off. There were no florins to pay an ironsmith. If she failed to sell her olive oil she would starve, and if she starved she would die. She pinched her thigh hard, giving herself a proper bruise for the self-pitying thought.

Kicking the wheel back onto its wooden axle with a naked foot, she walked on, imagining her feet to be padded like an animal's, her toes protected by bristled hair. The idea of loping through her village as a she-wolf buoyed her, and she started to trot down the hill.

The road leading to Florence had been pounded flat by heavy wagons pulled by men and teams of white oxen. The stoneworkers traveled from the local quarries, their backs bowed like willow sticks, hauling the *pietra serena* because the rich favored the calming gray-blue colors. "*Serena*," the cutters would joke about the name, a trace of bitterness lacing their voices, their bodies crippled by carrying the stone to the city so that the wealthy could raise monuments to God, to the Virgin Mary and to themselves.

A white cat, thin as a shadow, angled beside her and mewled loudly. Beatrice set down her cart and stroked its scrawny head, allowing the animal to crawl inside her wool gambeson. Before, even on hot days, her father wore the jacket like a noble soldier preparing for battle, though he was only a gentle philosopher and keeper of a few olive trees. Now he was buried deep in the ground. She held the warm cat and thought of a story she'd heard about prisoners in dungeons who befriended rats to keep from going mad. Being in prison might not be so bad if you were there with your *mamma e papà* and there was a portal to look out at the world. But her kin were gone, and without them, the joy in her land had run dry.

The air tasted of winter cold descending from the Apennines, and Beatrice knew there was more of that to come. She uncorked her deerskin and sipped wine. Her supply of olive oil was nearly exhausted. Only days ago, she had tenderly raked and sorted the olives from her modest family grove to have them inspected by the owner of the local olive mill. It was her first time representing the family, and she'd felt nervous and excited. He motioned her to the private yard behind the giant granite crushers. "You have money to pay?" Sweat clung to her skin from running her cart, heavy with her harvest, down the road to the mill. She had removed every twig and all the slender silver leaves from her autumnal haul and was bursting with pride at its glistening freshness. Now she was standing in olive muck up to her ankles.

"No money, no olive oil," warned the miller, his mouth twitching. He looked her over as if seeing her for the first time.

"I have no coins, but I can trade with you."

She watched his blackened fingers stretching and curling. They reminded her of short, pudgy eels.

"I have a pillow stitched with *tombolo* lace by my mother," she said, stepping toward him, pleading her case. "My father brought our olives to you over many years."

He leered at her. "Orphaned wench. *Tombolo* does not interest me." His fingers were suddenly upon her. He gripped her neck and clawed at her tunic. She kicked him hard between the legs and ran for it, dumping most of the olives from her cart by the time she had reached the safety of the road.

The attack had terrified her. Surely she had done something

to provoke his rage? Her parents had never raised a hand against her, so it was difficult to know how to gauge the customs of other people. Such an ugly man, with eels for fingers. She remembered how her father had taught her to hurl stones at the black night whenever she fell into a sour mood. "To the moon!" he had laughed, "*La luna!*" That was a game they had played together. She used to believe in its magic, but now she wasn't so sure.

She pushed her cart toward Florence, her feet now leaden and unsteady, her imaginary friend, the she-wolf, lying low in a tangle of juniper bush.

The sky was lightening to the gray of Florentine wool. She took two dirty lengths of linen from her satchel, wound them tightly around both hands, picked up the handles again and rolled forward, the wheels lurching down a steep pitch gnarled by tree roots and rocks heaved up from the earth. Her thighs burned with the effort and she felt a crack on her heel run with fresh blood. Her earthenware jars rattled against each other like broken bones.

The road dipped then flattened, and she saw the massive outline of the brick wall that protected Florence from peasants, the *popolo minuto*, like her. She watched as the outsiders pushed frantically toward the wall, three stories tall—villagers and shanty dwellers coming from all directions, a river of snakes with dull eyes and oily backs. Beatrice set the cart down and knotted her black hair tightly at the back of her head, the better to go anonymously into the crowd and avoid the unwanted attention of the guards at the city gates.

She pulled her hood down low and shifted her mantle so that her breasts were camouflaged, becoming less girl, more boy. Before the troubles, she was adored and coddled, presented as a jewel by her parents whenever they walked through the village. No longer. Now, alone, she carried a blade and kept her eyes down.

She pressed both hands together in a rough prayer to make ready for the humiliating inspection. A group of women hauling baskets of fresh-cut oak on their heads shouldered their way past as the chief sentry called out to open the thick wooden doors. Vendors scrabbled like cockroaches, using their carts and shovels to push their way forward toward the tollgates, ready to pay their meager coins to gain access to the great golden city.

Chapter 2

Outside the city walls, chaos all around, Beatrice hesitated to push into the massive crowd and retreated inside herself. Her hands clung to the collar of her father's jacket and she bent an ear, the better to hear his counsel.

"Do not hesitate. Be a Roman warrior. The goddess Diana. Walk without fear through each day. Head up, stand tall like the cypress."

She smiled at his love of the ancients, the way his counsel shimmered like a slab of Carrara marble.

"But I am alone now, and these people—"

He interrupted her thoughts: "Their suffering has corrupted their peaceful nature. You will discover those you can trust. Watch for them, reach out in kindness."

She gripped the handles of her cart and did not move, the better to hold on to his presence. He had been taken from her when all was right in the world. She knew she should not think of it, but it was difficult to resist going to that place of dark emotion. One year ago, when the sun was falling and pink and orange were stretched like yarn on a loom, the hens had set to shrieking in their enclosure and her father had walked off across the flats to scare off the fox that might be harassing them. Beatrice was at home, melting beeswax over a slow fire, preparing the slender tallows that the priest preferred for his church altar. Her mother bent over a piece of *tombolo*, her hands flying over wooden spools of thread, braiding lace to edge pillowcases for rich clients in the city.

It seemed, like so many of the evenings the family spent together, as if time was lifted up like an offering and held in a state of suspension. The wax melted slowly, the thread was braided, the sun went down, the birds shrieked, her father walked and then ran toward the henhouse. The wooden bobbins held the thread, the wax turned liquid, and a single lacy curve emerged on the *tombolo* pillow. From the inside of their little stone home, all was well. Still was the night. It seemed as sweet as the sweat rising on Beatrice's cheekbones and settling along her upper lip. Her mother's auburn hair swirled down her back, her eyes fixed on her work. The sweet suspension of time unraveled from the spool and floated in the air like gossamer wings. To interrupt it would be to deny a family's right to love, and so the mother and daughter continued at their work, lulled by the feeling, sated by the glorious Tuscan day, never noticing how long the man had been gone.

The war between Pisa and Florence had been a simmering feud where men fought each other among the cypresses and along the edges of rivers. Bands of Pisans knew enough to stay away from the heavily guarded battalion of Florence, but they enjoyed their share of violence in the villages that lay exposed and unprotected outside the city. Killing a hen was one way to lure an enemy outside. They waited patiently while Beatrice's father approached with anxious footsteps. To lose a hen to a fox represented half a month's wages, and so he went blindly toward the screams of his birds and the darkening olive groves.

The Tuscan earth was golden and fertile, without the weight of the clay soil to the south. But morning dawned and the land smelled of decay. There was a scent of poison in the air, the blood of her father, which the Pisans had smeared onto the hen hutch. Beatrice looked to the place where she had instinctively dragged the corpse, away from the cruel death by sticks and clubs, to lay him down on the earth in the benevolent shadow of the old olive tree. Her mind had gone numb. It was as if her eyes no longer saw in color, only black and white.

Now she needed to transport her father to the church, where the priest would clean the dead man's face with holy water, bless the body with frankincense oil, then bury him at the village cemetery. Without these rituals, her father would be in danger of wandering with evil spirits in the underworld.

In the distance, she could see a figure traveling toward her. He seemed to be walking quickly, without a hat, though the morning sun was fierce. Not the priest—he had already been to pray with the girl. While she stood by, he had closed her father's eyes with patient fingers, set two small stones over the eyes. Some neighbors had also come by, trekking from their homes in the village to heap bouquets of lavender and small sacks of their most cherished Etruscan grains at the front door to sustain the family in the coming months.

She was curious about who was fast approaching. Wary, she picked up one of the clubs the attackers had left behind. She watched as the figure cut down a path to walk alongside the creek before hiking up to where her father lay. Not an enemy. A young man with a serious face, a brow that looked permanently furrowed. She watched him kneel beside the body and bow his head in prayer.

She set down the club and gripped the handles of her family's wobbly wooden cart. The land was thirsty for rain, and puffs of dirt lifted as she walked toward the stranger, pushing the cart next to her father's body and keeping it between them like a rough battering ram. "I do not know you," she said listlessly, looking down on the bent figure. "Who are your people?" She listened to her voice and did not recognize it. She had taken on the sound of her mother, who was inside, curled on the straw mattress, unable to scream or even cry.

He did not speak at first but stood and offered a curt bow. His mouth was set in a straight line, and his eyes flicked gently to her. "My family has a farm on the other side of this grove. Di Buonarroti."

She shook her head.

"Mostly we live in Florence," he added, by way of explanation.

"I live here," she said. "And some of us are dying here."

He touched his right hand to his chest. "I'm sorry for your loss." She could tell he was uncomfortable, offering words he had heard others recite, but he stood his ground. "These troubles over the land will not soon be over." He hesitated, then asked, "Your mother?"

"She is not able to do this."

"I see that your spirit is strong."

Beatrice looked at his leather boots, broken and wrinkled. His hands were caked with white dust. "You are a stonemason?"

"I am a sculptor. Though I was taught how to work with stone here in Settignano."

She looked past him to the olive groves, listening to the gentle rustling of the silver-sylvan leaves, cooling her anger and the desire to seek revenge.

"*Scultore*," she said, clicking her tongue to express approval. The word had never been spoken to her before, and she chiseled its syllables with her tongue. The sculptures she had seen in Florence— mythical heroes, lions, angels and saints—transformed stone into things that could live alongside people. Somebody had made them, somebody like this man who stood before her. She wondered if he also drew from his imagination, as she liked to do. The question lay at the back of her mind, though she dared not ask it.

"My name is Michelangelo. Michelangelo di Buonarroti. You must visit me someday at my studio in Florence. If there is anything you need."

In the distance, the city's cathedral pushed its orange dome up powerfully, piercing the sky. She wondered how people could live confined to Florence. It seemed a punishment, even if a building like the Duomo offered a better relationship with God. As if that could be true.

"You are careless with your words," she said, curling her lip, pricked by rage. "I have no business in the city. You will not see me there." She said these words even as she rounded the cart and lifted her father's arms. Michelangelo quickly bent to hoist the dead man's legs. This artist, full of big-city presumptions, could not know the depths of her sorrow. Yet here he was, doing the unthinkable with her.

They heaved the body into the cart. Seeing her father crumple like a doll against the raw wooden boards, Beatrice let out a strangled cry. Weeping, she held her arms out wide and tipped forward toward him. "*Papà, papà!*" She was only thirteen. To live without her father was unthinkable.

Without hesitating, Michelangelo grabbed her and held her roughly in his arms. "You will see your father again, God willing," he said. His face seemed to be lifted to the sky. "Pray for him, and he will watch over you from Heaven."

He carried her back to the stone hut and set her down on the sacks of grain. She hid her face in her cloak, ashamed of her tears.

"You are young. Tomorrow will be easier."

He straightened and gripped her hands tightly in his. "Please come to see me in the city," he said, repeating the offer, taking care to speak with kindness. If he felt any awkwardness at their sudden intimacy, he did not show it. "Can I help you push the cart to the church?"

She hesitated and looked at the cloudless sky. Once, blue had been her favorite, the color of horizons and longing. Now its serenity, like her family, had splintered into shards of dispossession. From that day on, Beatrice would remember blue as the color of solitude.

"We will manage on our own," she said, though she doubted her mother would be able to help.

She watched him walk with a driven, athletic gait to the road, leaving her alone by the stoop of her hut. Michelangelo, sculptor, with a family farm in the olive grove beyond. He had left her with something: an imprint of stone dust on her hands. She rubbed her fingers together, testing the grit. Maybe he was honorable. Maybe he was a lie.

A woman cradling a freshly butchered leg of venison in her arms pushed past Beatrice, cursing her for standing in the way, wrenching her out of the memory. The smell of blood leapt from the deer to cling like sickness to the girl's mouth. She surveyed the crowd, seeking out the faces of the women, examining their figures, their shapes, the way they held themselves. Trembling, she willed her mother to step forward and show herself. She had disappeared and left Beatrice alone, but surely her *mamma* had meant no harm; she had been terribly delayed, that was all.

The crowd surged around her and her head filled with the noise of chaos. Next to her, gray rabbits had been upturned in their wooden cages, and chickens were clawing like madness to escape their woven bags. Clapping her hands against her ears, Beatrice looked to the gates and wanted desperately to be inside the city, where surely her mother would be waiting for her.

Chapter 3

"Step aside, ugly ones." A man with a woolen cap and dull gray eyes growled his command and shoved his cart fiercely into the crowd. Beatrice yanked her cart to one side to stay clear. She needed to sell the olive oil in her earthenware jars or go hungry another day. The priest in her village had advised her to begin trading in the city, sweeping the church steps with swift, angry movements while Beatrice stood with her head bowed, her stomach clenched with hunger.

"An orphan like you—"

"Father, I am no orphan," she had said flatly. "I am looking for my mother. She is lost, is all."

She remembered how her mother had rocked herself in a corner for days, sobbing and cursing the murderers of her husband.

"Mamma, can I send for somebody? The healer, the priest?"

She watched, helpless, as her mother paced their little manor like a caged ferret. Language had left her. She seemed incapable of forming words. With the passing of every day, her despair thickened into a fetid soup that no salve or herbal infusion could remedy.

It was when her mother started pricking her arms with her sewing needle that Beatrice finally reacted. "I cannot bear this anymore," she said. "You must go outside, seek counsel with the stars." She grabbed her mother by the hand and led her outside. She pushed her away from the door and watched her disappear into their olive grove, caressing every tree with her hands and her mouth. *I do not recognize her. This woman.* These were Beatrice's last thoughts as she closed the door on her mother.

"Your mother has fled," said the priest, averting his eyes from the girl. He was a stout man with a face that reminded Beatrice of a squash gone bad. "Like so many others."

"What do you mean, Father?"

"Women," he said, shaking his head. "They leave the village to follow the Devil."

Beatrice bristled. "My mother is kind and generous in every way. She loved my father—"

"Love?" He looked at her with disdain. "Well, then. Your mother will discover many variations of that in the city."

What the priest meant by that she had no idea. "Love" was a word rarely spoken aloud in her home, but Beatrice knew the emotion by touch and sound, the way her family greeted each other in the morning with gentle kisses on cheeks and, after sundown, the way her parents pulled the coarse blankets tenderly over her while saying a prayer and raising their eyes to the timbers. She would be astonished to discover that love could exist in the deafening, anonymous city, but the priest had provoked her to seek an answer.

And so Beatrice had hatched a plan to travel into the city, to recover her mother and bring her home. She would sell olive oil to make some quattrini, enough to survive, until her mother could return and life could be as it was. Head down, wheeling her broken cart to artists who would tolerate a barefoot girl in the dirt lanes behind the Duomo. One year ago, her life of hardship had begun.

Four crossbowmen stood guard high on the wall walk that encircled the city like a fortress, dressed in black leather vests with silk sleeves of white and gold. Another four men stood on either side of the monumental arched entrance. They were posted to check and frisk all vendors for weapons before allowing them to pass. They could take liberties, of course; pull anybody young and desirable from the crowd with a shout and a drawn sword, and pin her against one of the massive doors studded with iron nails.

A horse-drawn carriage took the crowd by surprise. Its riggings, oil-slicked and true, allowed the vehicle to glide noiselessly. The driver clicked his tongue at the horses, a black gelding and a silver-gray Andalusian, and the throng parted to make room.

The carriage pulled up next to her and Beatrice touched a hand to the ornate wrought-iron doors. Two men sat slumped against leather seats. One had a face framed by dark curls. The other passenger—his grandfather?—wore a silver-white beard. Bracing herself with both hands, she stood on her toes for a better view. The old man turned his head and Beatrice ducked. There might be a whipping coming her way. Anxious to escape the lash on her back, she rammed her cart forward, and the broken wheel resisted, causing her vehicle to lurch into another, stacked high with oak logs and an exotic caged creature whose feathers were as white as the moon. Beatrice had seen blackbirds, pheasants and guinea hens, but never this kind of fowl.

"May I purchase that bird?"

It was the old man from the carriage. He was now on foot and standing two carts away. His figure was tall and noble, and Beatrice admired the rose-pink color of his tunic and the summertime green of his velvet cape. It reminded her of cypress trees shooting into the air like arrows of hope.

"Market's not open," said the owner of the bird. She gestured toward the sky, still cast in gray though the horizon was washing up blue. "After the sunrise."

"With your permission, I'll take him off your hands."

His voice was soft, so unlike the sharp insults exchanged between those who lived poor and dirty in the hills beyond the city walls. The whiskery woman flapped her arms at him: go away. Her silky creature lifted its feathers and shifted restlessly in a basket that served as a makeshift cage.

"Here," said the stranger, smiling kindly. Beatrice watched him press coins into the woman's hand as the crowd pushed noisily past.

The bird woman quickly slipped the outrageous sum into her apron. "Just this once, signore." Seeing that Beatrice was staring, she snapped, "Little whore, with eyes big as a cow's." She tightened the band on her wimple cap. "Mind your own affairs."

The old man turned to Beatrice, an arm wrapped around the birdcage. "*Buon giorno*," he said, bowing slightly.

"My lord," she said, bowing low, amazed by the short cut of his cape and the pink hose on display above his boots.

"What elixirs might be on offer today?" He reached into her

cart and uncorked one of the clay carafes. "Olive oil," he said, breathing deeply.

Beatrice stared at the man, blank-faced, astonished by his brazen sampling of her wares.

"Reminds me of lying in a field of fresh-cut hay." He stepped aside to let a man hauling a pig on a rope go by. "Which I like to do far too often, according to my taskmasters."

A woman with a basket of bread balanced on her head moved next to them. He handed Beatrice the birdcage and reached into the baker's basket, handing her a coin for a round of Tuscan bread sprinkled with rosemary and oregano. He drizzled it with some of Beatrice's olive oil and stuffed it into his mouth. "My God," he said, raising a hand dramatically in the air. "It's good to be home."

He handed Beatrice a coin and reclaimed his bird. He opened the cage and held the creature against his chest. "*Vieni*, see how beautiful." The bird opened its curved black beak and gnawed on the man's fingers. Beatrice was unsure if he was speaking to her or the creature. His white hair and beard made him look as old as some of the monks in the city, but his eyes had a youthful radiance, and he smelled of cinnamon and rosemary. Country folk continued to move past them, cursing at the roadblock. She reached out to touch the bird.

"You sell in the marketplace?" he asked.

"No," she said, shaking her head, amazed by the way her hand disappeared into the depth of the bird's feathers. She could not afford to pay the extra coins to sell in the main marketplace. "To men working in the lane behind the Duomo. Goldsmiths, leatherworkers, painters, sculptors."

"The artists of Florence," said the man.

Beatrice shrugged. The studios she visited with her cart belonged to men named Lippi, Granacci. They made altar paintings adorned with gold leaf, mahogany chairs inlaid with ivory, naked bodies from slabs of Carrara marble. But there was never time for her to admire what they were making. That would show herself to be a slovenly villager. More than that, it might betray her interest in making art herself, something girls had no business attempting. "I should go now," she said.

"This beautiful parrot does not belong in a cage, or in Tuscany," he replied, as if she had not spoken. He buried his face in the downy feathers and stroked the bird. Then, without warning, he lifted it high in the air and opened his hands. The parrot screeched and took flight.

"He's gone!" Beatrice watched the sky, her heart lifted with joy even as she felt the dread of a crime having been committed. The man had freed the most beautiful bird, and it had flown like an angel into the heavens.

"*Amore*, Master, please, are you finished?" The handsome young man was calling from the carriage.

Beatrice impulsively pressed a carafe of olive oil toward the man called Master. His face radiated with peace. "For you," she said, then hoisted her cart handles. Somebody unseen pummeled Beatrice in the backside. She held tight to her cart, refusing to cede ground. "How long have you been away?"

"More years than you are old."

"I am fourteen, signore."

He nodded.

"With your permission, signore, may I bring you more olive oil?"

"You speak like a true Florentine merchant." There was the shriek of roosters and donkeys passing by. She stepped closer so as to catch his words. ". . . at the monastery?" he said. Then he retreated to the carriage. "Santissima Annunziata," he called over his shoulder.

"I know it," she said. She knew all of the streets in Florence. "Near to San Marco."

The carriage driver whistled sharply and guided the horses into the mayhem. Beatrice pushed forward on foot. At the tollgate, she bent her head low and extended her coin to a guard.

"Show your face." He ripped the hood from her head.

Sweat prickled on the small of her back. She bit in her lips, making them thin like a boy's. "The morning has gold in its mouth," she said, appalled by his smell and his rotten, broken teeth. "Can I pass? Here is my quattrino."

One of the crossbowmen on the wall shouted angrily down to the guard. It felt to Beatrice like all eyes were on her.

"Face down!" the guard ordered.

She braced herself for what was to come. It always felt like an uncivil war between the peasants and the guards. "Guard, may I pass?" she said.

"What's this? The village dog can speak?"

The other guards barked in excitement, bouncing in their boots, enjoying the humiliation. Those next in line went silent.

"Signore, gallant soldier of the state," said the master, suddenly there at her side. She felt his hand on her back, sweeping her away from the nearest guard.

Another soldier elbowed his way forward and brayed loudly, "Nearly winter, but here stands somebody in summertime green." His arms were heavily muscled, and his uniform was impeccable, the heraldic red lily stitched brightly on his silk vest. He shook his head in disgust at the man's pink hose and flicked the cape open with his dagger, revealing its sapphire silk lining.

"It was a present from Duke Sforza of Milan." The man looked at the guard with steady eyes.

"A likely story," said the guard, enjoying the mockery, "from an old lecher." Laughter all around, even from those who stood in line, craning for a better look at the interrogation of the man in extravagant dress defending a peasant girl.

"Indeed, signore, you are to be commended for your leaden mind. He who laughs last, laughs longest. As for this girl," the old man continued, "her clients are beloved Florentines."

The guard hesitated, looked at the man and back at the girl. "The dog can pass," he said at last.

Beatrice picked up the handles of her cart and moved beneath the soaring brick entrance into the city. Looking back, she could see that a third guard had joined the others, and that they were taking turns lifting the edge of her savior's evergreen cape with their daggers, flapping its edges like a sail cut loose in high winds. "Here's a sodomite all dressed up for dirty business." Their laughter was loud and malicious. A pair of guards were playing at humping the master.

"Christ watch over you," she muttered.

As she walked farther into the city, past artisan workshops decorated in olive branches and wool warehouses with facades of local stone blocks, a small red-haired boy appeared at her side; she recognized him from the squatter camp outside the gates. He seemed to be alone; nobody called to him to come back. His fingers sought hers and, still dazzled by the daring of the man called Master, she allowed it. Had she dreamed it, the flouting of rules? For she could actually taste his irreverence and kindness toward the bird as if it were wild honeysuckle in springtime. She felt the boy's little hand warm in her own, but he was gripping tightly now, whining for some bread, and the sweetness of the moment cracked in half.

Unbidden, a memory of her mother in the Piazza Santa Croce pushed into her mind. At least, she had believed it was her mother; her attire had been so strange, and it was difficult to be sure from where Beatrice had been standing, across the vast square. The woman who resembled her *mamma* had been with five other women, each of them wearing jingling bells around their ankles and yellow triangles stitched to the sleeves of their dresses. She had called out, but a crowd had surged forward to surround and heckle the women. "Crows! Crows!" they jeered, their own voices harsh like the black birds. Beatrice had picked up the handles of her cart and run as fast as the wobbly wheel allowed. The crowd had formed a nasty barrier between the girl and the dream of finding her mother. By the time she reached the far side of Santa Croce, the women had disappeared down a narrow street.

She swatted the boy away and spat an insult, "*Va' a farti benedire.*" Get lost. Go get yourself blessed.

Closing her eyes, she replayed the scene with the woman she thought was her mother parading past the grand basilica and across the piazza. The faint tingling of the women's ankle bracelets rang in her ears, and a feeling of dread came over Beatrice. That had happened many weeks ago, before the cold winds of the Apennine Mountains descended on the city. What had possessed her mother to leave that night? She might have stayed. Mourning the death of her father was too much for Beatrice to endure by herself. Stonecutters always worked in pairs, never alone, to lift the heaviest of stones.

She gripped the leather ties of her father's old jacket between her fingers. Her resolve to find her mother hardened. She was somewhere in the city. Then hunger—a miserable friend—forced her to keep moving even as her mood darkened.

She felt weak after the morning's walk, and her feet were numb with cold. Beatrice headed toward the workshops behind the cathedral, where she might find a place to rest, if only for a moment, away from the mauling crowds and city guards. The harassment at the tollgate had exhausted her, but in Florence it seemed she was condemned to days of constant motion. She looked up at the windows of the stone villas and spied three young noblewomen gazing out onto the streets. Oh, to sit in a chair as they did and live their lives for a single glorious moment. A carriage gilded in silver and gold rumbled past on the cobblestones; a woman in a heavily feathered hat stared at her with joyless, hooded eyes as the conveyance passed. Peacock, thought Beatrice.

The rich—the *popolo grasso*—loved to flaunt their wealth. Her mother used to say "The rich do not walk. They ride in their own arks and pretend they're Noah every day of the week." The girl half smiled at the memory. Her own people were castaways, Christian refugees from Constantinople, trekking to the terraced hills of Florence after the Ottomans had invaded their birthplace. Her grandparents had watched as the Muslims had scarred the wooden bridges with their spiked boots, pushing their invasion across the mighty Bosphorus to take their beloved city. Her father had relayed their stories of the defacement of the Hagia Sophia church, the scraping away and painting over of the angels' faces high up within its interior domes. "All of it a sacrilege!" her father would shout with bitterness, sounding every bit the philosopher and peasant farmer that he was.

Beatrice bowed her head to show respect as the carriage rolled briskly down the road, the woman in her fancy ark swinging a scented pomander on a chain.

Closer to the Arno, the air spiked by the rank smell of the river, she spied a canopy of trees that hovered above a stone wall. The garden likely belonged to the woman. Walking to a fig tree, Beatrice tore off her mantle and unlaced her father's gambeson. She pried away the wooden cap of the cart handle and teased out a narrow dagger, the one found buried in her father's body, which she herself had extracted and washed in the brook running below the olive grove. She placed one foot on the mortar of a stone wall; there was an iron ring for harnessing horses, and she slid her bare foot into it, then hoisted herself up. She reached into the branches and cut several figs, stuffing one into her mouth as she eased herself down. The fruit, shriveled by the cold, tasted like leather, but it filled her stomach.

She took stock of her situation: her supply of olive oil was running low, and there would be no more deals from the miller in Settignano. The inconvenience was that she would have to barter with her neighbor and pay handsomely for more of his oil and his terracotta jugs. Pay with the last of her family's copper pots. She had already traded the one her mother used for melting beeswax. If there was a God, why did he bless rich men's olive groves and turn their harvests into ever more gold florins?

Bending down low, she fished a stick of charcoal from a pocket and curved her fingers around it. Within a moment, she had tattooed the base of the garden wall with a drawing of a raging angel, its wings hunched up as if a falcon preparing to land, its heart pierced with the long stem of a peacock feather. She knew this to be a dangerous act—defacing the city—but it felt good to make her mark. Let the *sbirri*—the cops—throw her in the gallows for being a warrior girl starving for food and some parchment paper. She stooped to emphasize the huge eyes of the angel staring as if in horror, clutching the charcoal tightly in her hand. Satisfied, she blew the black dust off her fingers.

She set off again, and when she reached the fountain carved with three lion heads, she unwrapped the bandages from her knuckles. Sturdy houses, one and two stories high, surrounded the fountain on all sides. She could hear iron pots banging against stone floors and the scolding of children by exhausted mothers. The lions spat thin streams of water into the basin. Beatrice bent over the fountain and scrubbed her hands, then splashed water over her neck, her arms, and loosened her hair. She placed her crown of olive leaves on her head and pinched her cheeks to draw color, to impress on her city clients that she embodied all that was good from the country. Let the Florentines enjoy the lie; she was happy to pretend to be fed on goat's milk and fattened pig if it brought customers.

She bumped her cart down the dirt road and into the back lanes where guild artists kept their studios. Traffic on the path was growing to a frantic morning pitch. Two finely dressed boys wrapped in matching peach velvet capes passed by; Beatrice felt a silk merchant's sleeve decorated with pearls graze her naked hand. She walked on to discover a group of ironsmiths kneeling over a fire and, traveling in the opposite direction, a young man, reeking of red wine, who cradled a framed canvas in his arms. Its protective woolen shroud was poorly arranged, allowing Beatrice a glimpse of a woman in a Greek tunic who looked horribly old-fashioned— why paint something from so long ago? Next, several laborers, thick woolen tunics stained with sweat, forced her to the side of the road. They carried a church altar, their hands wrapped around its fat wooden legs, each elaborately carved with bunches of grapes and lilies.

Her first client was Filippino Lippi. He was stiff-necked, with lecherous wet lips, as if he'd just been released from a long stay in a damp prison cell. The right wheel groaned, filling her with bitterness; the stolen figs weighed heavy in her belly. She had not forgotten all of her Christian teachings—she would repent and ask forgiveness for stealing. God would smile down on her, and she would blow him a kiss from the dirt road.

Beatrice selected jars from her cart and approached Filippino Lippi's studio, passing his healthy lemon tree, eyeing its golden fruit. Before her father was killed, her mother often made a salad with thin strips of lemon peel mixed with olives and parsley. Sometimes she sprinkled violets on top, but only to inspire her husband, who would scratch a rapturous poem in the dirt about their meal and erase it when it was time to teach their child her letters. Beatrice learned well, and this pleased her father and even her mother, who worried that there were never enough florins to support the three of them. Though they owned very little, Beatrice always thought they were wealthy.

The door burst open before she knocked; Filippino was an early riser and moved with frantic energy. He was not an old man, but he seemed to Beatrice not long for the world. His skin had a leaden sheen to it, and his eyes were cavernous. She hoped he would not die too soon, as she needed his business. He waved her inside and shut the door.

She moved delicately away from his hands and placed the olive oil on the table, next to his drawings. Laid out was a sketch of the Virgin and the baby Jesus, drawn in loose strokes of brown ink. Angels and men stood nearby, all of them looking and gesturing at each other.

"It looks like they're talking to each other," said Beatrice.

"It's an experiment," said Filippino, studying his sketch. "Artists have always painted the saints doing nothing. Just standing and staring."

"And you?"

"I'm trying to paint a sacred conversation between saints about the Holy Child."

"A *sacra conversazione*." Beatrice considered this piece of news, bending closer to the sketch to seize the details. "Where did you learn how to draw like this?" She gazed at the charcoal sketches on the table, the half-finished altar works propped against the studio wall.

"With Botticelli. I was apprenticed to him."

"Who is that?"

"Oh dear, you truly are an olive oil girl. He's only one of the greatest painters ever known to Florence. We painted for the Medici and their wealthy circle of friends. *The Adoration of the Kings*, a vast work we painted together. He did the crowd on one side. Insisted on including a white horse rearing up and a man wielding an axe. Tempera on wood, the usual technique."

"What is tempera?"

He looked at Beatrice and let out an exasperated sigh. "Egg yolk, pigment and water."

She knew she was testing his patience, but she needed to ask: "Were there girls studying with you?"

"Girls? Of course not. Too distracting." He stepped closer to her and slid his hands inside her quilted jacket. "Like you."

"With your permission," she said, her eyes turned cold like the angels in his sketch, "I would like payment for this month's olive oil." She paused, looking again at his artworks, absorbing lessons from his technique that she might apply to her own rough sketches. "I would also like three of your lemons." With the fruit she could make ten jars of lemon oil and sell them for a handsome price.

"Your skin reminds me of copper dipped in gold. One lick of my tongue," he murmured. She stepped away from him, his hot, sickly breath on her neck. From a safe distance, she held out her hand. He sighed, rummaged in a leather purse and, unsmiling, dropped four quattrini into her palm while motioning her out. "It will take me hours to focus again on my art. Don't come back next week!"

Outside, she climbed high into the artist's lemon tree, balancing against one of its magnificent branches and selecting three perfect fruit to toss down into her cart. She took another lemon for herself and bit hungrily into it, enjoying the shock of the sour taste and the yellow flesh dripping all over her hands. It was glorious to be up in the leafy greenery, away from the dirt of the alley. Another bite and she felt brighter than she had for days. She counted on her fingers to make a cold calculation of her world. Finger number one: Father was dead. Finger number two: Mother had disappeared. Finger number three: She was starving. Finger number four: Not everybody can be trusted. Her thoughts thus enumerated on sinewy fingers, she looked down on her misfortunes as if inspecting tongue, tripe and other innards spread out raw on a butcher's block. But, this morning, there was something else to add to the hardened facts of her world. A great man had defended her at the city gate. She felt a series of knots coming undone around her mouth, possibly, even, the hint of a smile. Perhaps there was reason to feel less alone. She felt something warm—a tiny flame flickering inside her. She cocked finger number five, which was actually a thumb: Survive.

Chapter 4

His humiliation at the city gates continued until the guards eventually tired of the game and turned back to processing the peasants clamoring to pay their tolls and come through.

"Step to the side. Let me see your papers," said one thuggish guard delegated to handle him. He waved a reassuring hand at Salaì inside the carriage and allowed himself to be shoved below the towering arch of the gate. He stood tall and would not look at the ripped edges of his cape. Somebody's pig, escaped from a wagon, hurtled by. Above the noisy squeals, he heard a voice ringing out: "Maestro! Maestro!" A priest in a long black cloak hurried toward him, waddling as quickly as his fat body would allow, like an old, broody hen. "We are delighted, all of us, all Florentines—" said the priest, anxious to launch into his speech, a beatific smile printed on his face.

The guard, recognizing the Servant of Mary crest emblazoned across the front of the priest's cloak, lowered his dagger.

"You know this person?" He tipped his head toward the man in the velvet cape.

"*Idiota.*" The prior shot the guard a look of disgust. "This is Leonardo da Vinci, a genius come home to honor us with his presence." He grasped the master's hands and bowed low, kissing each of them.

Another pig and a pair of donkeys pushed past. The maestro looked at the cart driver as he sped past, mesmerized by his remarkable chin, as if two beets had been permanently stacked there. The Tuscan face, he thought, sculpted from the gifts of the earth like no other.

"Master, many long years have passed," said the prior, interrupting his thoughts. The priest was quite obviously dismayed to see how Leonardo had aged. His auburn hair had turned white and his erstwhile jawline was now covered by the curly beard of a prophet. Still, he knew he possessed a regal bearing that was missing from most dukes and governors lording over their small, feuding Italian states.

"The messenger informed me of your decision to leave Milan and return to Florence. We have prepared your lodging," the prior said. "I hope most fervently that you will find my monastery to be hospitable."

"You have to pay the toll," the guard interrupted, cocking his chin at the carriage. "Triple for the wheels and the horses."

The prior dug into his satchel and produced a piece of heavy bond paper. "An invitation, stamped with the pope's seal," he said, waving the document at the guard and offering a look of apology to his honored guest. "Can you read, soldier? Of course you can't."

"Pay the toll. It's the law."

"Prior, allow me," said Leonardo, bowing slightly at the hip and producing the coins in one elegant sweep of the hand.

Cursing at the guard, the priest stepped up into the carriage, sending it rocking on its wheels. "Now, then, let's get you to the peace of our monastery."

The master climbed in reluctantly, but not before gazing back at the crowd, wonderfully wretched as they were. Every face a unique portrait of raw, pure emotion. He would rely on this picture of humanity for a future commission; the memory would fuel his imagination.

"Prior, how kind of you to welcome us," he said, settling against the leather seat. "Let me introduce my assistant, Salaì, an artist of much talent."

Salaì ignored the introduction and looked out the window.

"The honor is mine," said the prior, inclining slightly forward. "I had hoped you'd miss the flood of people, but I fear they are arriving earlier and earlier. All of them God's creatures, but given to such terrible manners and smells. More animal than human. Born to sell their simple wares, I suppose, and bask in our sunshine."

The master smiled, unlacing his velvet cape to allow for air. He was accustomed to the elites bashing the downtrodden. "My hometown has changed, it seems, from the little city I once knew."

"Indeed, the old Roman settlement has grown in population and wealth. And notoriety," agreed the prior. "What other city can boast the presence not only of a genius such as yourself but Michelangelo di Buonarroti besides, whose *Pietà* in Rome causes people to fall to their knees and weep?"

Leonardo turned from the prior as if absorbed by the ongoing chaos outside. He had barely cleared the gates of Florence and already Michelangelo's name was slipping easily from local tongues. "By all reports he is a fine young sculptor," he said, turning back to the prior. One who was recently commissioned by the monied Wool Guild to sculpt the biblical David to sit atop the Cathedral of Santa Maria del Fiore. Word that Michelangelo was being considered by the Arte della Lana had reached Leonardo months earlier, in Milan. The duke had mentioned it at a dinner, wiping his mouth with linen. "This young Michelangelo assigned to sculpt David from the Old Bible? I wonder they did not ask other talented ones, such as yourself? But you have been busy, Master. Tell me, is your fresco of the Last Supper nearly, finally, complete?"

Past the tollgates, Florence unfurled like a sail, and Leonardo inhaled its architectural magnificence under clear Tuscan skies. The marketplace was pumping with energy, and it seemed that the squalor he had witnessed outside the gates had been dissipated and softened within the grand civic spaces where buildings had been demolished a century ago to make way for inspiring views of the city's monuments. He watched, amused, as boys gathered at the base of the Campanile tower, selling bundles of beeswax tapers wrapped in garlands of gilliflowers. A clutch of women he was sure had deliberately crashed their carts against each other outside of the gates sang in unison to beckon customers, scooping black olives into wooden bowls. The chill air was fragrant with the sweet smell of bread being pulled from a stone oven in a *panetteria* tucked down Via dei Martelli, across from the Baptistery of San

Giovanni. The baker's son sold the bread to a lineup of customers, digging into the pockets of his apron to make quick change for overworked servant girls. The master leaned forward in the carriage to take in the dazzling pattern of the white Carrara and green Prato marble of the holy monument glowing in the morning sun. He wondered if the local gossips still occupied their place in the square. Right on cue, he spied them: a trio of old men sitting on a long wooden bench with their backsides next to the golden eastern doors. He watched as they watched him, imagining what they might be saying about him.

"Is it he?" the man with a bulbous nose would whisper, elbowing his companions. "His body has not shrunk. But what of his mind?"

Ah, yes, recalled the Master of Arts, the gossiping bench-sitters, known locally as the *sersaccenti delle pancacce*.

He looked their way. Then he glanced to the north doors of the baptistery, where his eyes lingered on the panel depicting Abraham, sword drawn, preparing to kill his only son to satisfy God's wishes. His own father might be equally inclined, though not because of a desire to please God.

"Those are his eyes," another of the gossipers might murmur. "Always hunting for something, like a hawk."

He watched as the gossipers squinted and pointed at him. One of them had attracted a crowd and was speaking loud enough for everyone to hear, even the subject of their gossip.

"I tell you. That is Leonardo da Vinci, riding by in all his finery. The talented, beautiful one. Arrested for sodomy, as God is our witness. When his hair was freakishly red."

They were right. He had been accused anonymously, unceremoniously hauled from a late-night party to the gallows behind Florence's city hall, the Palazzo Vecchio. Accusations, true or false, were easy to make. Scribble something on parchment and drop it into one of the city's *tamburi*—letter boxes, or holes of truth—placed conveniently around the city, and let the Office of the Night and Conservers of the Morality of Monasteries do the rest.

He considered himself lucky. He might have been flogged to within an inch of his life if he'd been discovered with other sodomizers in devout Venice, where the doge fancied himself as significant as the pope. But in Florence, money talked. If you were privileged enough to have florins in your satchel (which he did) or friends who were wealthy (which he had), you were forgiven your wickedness after a few nights sleeping rough in stone cells underground.

The horses pulled the carriage quickly over the cobblestones, up the Via dei Servi to the Piazza della Santissima Annunziata, where the congestion of the city was suddenly interrupted. Leonardo breathed his thanks to Brunelleschi as the carriage rumbled through the square. They had never met. The architect had died a few years before he was born. But his belief in lifting people's spirits through ennobling architecture and grand, edifying public spaces that framed the heavens lived powerfully on. Those squatters on the wrong side of the gates? Brunelleschi believed they had a right to the city and clean air to breathe. On the east side of the square stood his stone arcade fronting the Ospedale degli Innocenti. Leonardo observed every detail—the blue glazed terracotta sculptures of babies in swaddling clothes gracing every one of the archways of the loggia, every column topped by a capital decorated with thick foliage. To him, they were offered like harmonies in a long, sustained chant. To the north, in sober contrast, the Basilica of Santissima Annunziata presented a meditative dome to allow worship in the round.

He gazed out the window of the carriage, and a prayer floated through his mind, words written long ago by Saint Francis of Assisi: "Most High, glorious God, enlighten the shadows of my heart, and grant me a right faith, a certain hope and perfect charity, sense and understanding."

The driver pulled the carriage below a grand arch and down a narrow lane alongside the church before coming to a halt.

"I'm starving," said Salaì, the first words he had uttered since crossing under the tollgates.

The prior bristled at the girlish whine. Leonardo knew what he was likely thinking: Italy might be shaped like a womb, but the population of Florence was dwindling thanks to the sodomizers wedged in the carriage next to him.

"Not long now," Leonardo reassured Salaì, though he was uneasy about their arrival. Shifting house and home from the princely accommodation within the duke of Milan's monumental castle to a few rooms at the Santissima Annunziata monastery was unsettling. And the scourge of being named a dirty sodomizer more than twenty years ago had never left him. Now the gossipers had thrown his shame back out to the public. He stroked his beard and tried to calm the feeling in his stomach.

The prior heaved himself out of the carriage; the master jumped down easily, the bird basket in one hand, the carafe of olive oil in the other. Salaì followed, stretched his arms and yawned loudly. "Looks a bit of a dump," he said, leaning over to Leonardo. "Send a message to one of those fancy merchant families. Or the bankers —they must have palazzi with room to spare?"

"Apparently not," said Leonardo, looking at the two-story compound, its courtyard garden dusted with November pallor. He had memorized the plan of the monastery from a drawing sent to him in Milan by messenger, and his eyes searched for a secret entrance across the commons.

The men ascended a narrow stairwell, white stains of mildew at the edge of its stone steps. Nothing like the Sforza Castle, where he and his assistants had thrived among musicians, dancing masters, military men, servants and dwarfs. How he had delighted in painting a fantastical forest to cover the vaulted ceiling in the magnificent Hall of the Axis, weaving branches and leaves together and then knotting them with a sinewy rope burnished with gold. He scanned the long, low corridor of the monastery and its plain plaster walls. "Icarus descending," he said to himself.

The prior stepped around a young monk who was sweeping a pile of dirt into a corner. "We have been waiting a long time for a new altarpiece, the great sacred themes, double-sided," he said, turning to Leonardo.

A painting. Sketching, drawing—he would happily abandon them all. Flight was what excited him now. But he had just arrived, must not speak his mind.

"Prior, I aspire to your expectations," Leonardo answered, returning his gaze, cradling the empty birdcage in his arms.

"I only ask that you bring your utmost attention to this commission," continued the prior, driving home his point. "Your time will be monopolized by the wealthy in this city. They are greedy and ambitious. They all want something—"

"And none will interfere with your commission."

"I look forward to seeing the altarpiece come springtime." The prior clapped a firm hand on Leonardo's shoulder as he moved to leave them at their new lodgings.

Leonardo set the cage down and leaned against the doorframe. "An altarpiece," he sighed. "Two sides. By spring."

Back in Milan, he had no deadlines. He attended to the challenges of the day as if they were flowers brimming with nectar. He would create decorations for a castle ball, then work in isolation to conquer a mathematical equation. As chief military engineer, fire-throwing machines had absorbed him, though his patron never manufactured his weapons of mass destruction. Sometimes he'd paint a royal portrait and, even—oh God—figure out a way to flow hot water to the bath of the duchess. In the Sforza court, there were no clients to haggle with, no fees to negotiate. When inspiration eluded him, he would settle into a velvet chair next to a roaring fire and play his silver lyre for the entertainment of the court. He and his retinue had been clothed and fed. The duke had given him the gift of time to explore whatever fancy floated into his mind.

And now?

Salaì threw a leather satchel on a straw mattress in the corner of a room. "In Milan they looked after us."

"Until the French invaded." Leonardo turned and carefully set the carafe of olive oil on a long oak table. He was not content with any kind of religion, did not believe in the wealth or the words spouted by the clerics—all their threats of Hell or promises of Paradise. But he was grateful for the free space, the ample natural light in the room.

Looking up, he surmised that the timber ceiling was of sound construction. No rain would damage his work. "When are the others expected?"

Salaì was pulling silk stockings and big-sleeved linen blousons from his bag. "Paolo should be here shortly. The others, day after tomorrow. Ferrando and Giovanni packed too many brushes and pigments and will blame their delay on lame horses."

Leonardo scoffed and Salaì waved a feathered cap in the air, caressing the long peacock feather back into shape. "Or frequent stops at taverns. Zoroastro and Raffaello will likely be even later. They could sleep past any invasion."

"Did you notice, as we rode past the Palazzo Vecchio, the copper ball atop the lantern of Santa Maria del Fiore, the Virgin of the Flower?"

"You mean the Duomo? Careful, Maestro, old names serve old men. You have told me this story many times." Salaì crossed the room and unlatched the deeply recessed oak windows. He kicked at a pile of ashes left behind in the room's modest hearth.

"It was too massive to be handled at the forgers. I was a youth at the time. A hot-blooded *giovane*, game for anything. My teacher, Andrea del Verrocchio, reined me in, taught me to bend sheets of copper into segments, sealing each of the seams with hot welds, using concave mirrors to catch the rays of the sun. We were working to Brunelleschi's design. I remember it like it was yesterday;

we soldered together the ball of the Santa Maria del Fiore, the two of us. Verrocchio was from the old school, an artist, a sculptor, a goldsmith. He was my master."

Salaì turned from the hearth, agitated. "You promised there was money here, a city of wealthy patrons, but the Duomo's facade is still unfinished, and it smells"—he waved his hand toward his nose—"like everybody pisses in the river."

"Florence is a village of fifty thousand souls with big-city ambitions." Leonardo picked up the basket and set it in the middle of the empty room. "There is beauty below the roughness. Like that girl with the olive oil. She smelled of rotten eggs, but what a face! Let's see what we can create here. As I used to."

They might have gone to Venice, he thought, to that splendid Byzantine city of islands; Salaì wanted to, but Florence pulled on Leonardo's emotions. There he had grown from a boy to a youth; there his father still lived, or was very nearly dead.

Ser Piero, grown feeble in his mansion on Via Ghibellina, could read any legal document in Latin, but he had never impressed much of anything on his son except for his illegitimacy. It was Verrocchio, not his father, who had taught him to sit with a problem, refine the answer through many tests, to fail and fail again before finding the satisfaction of a solution. It was because of Verrocchio that he had learned how to still his mind and focus, how to harness the energy of the sun, how to catch the rays and feel the pleasure of invention.

"And now we are here, it is incumbent on us to create a new social order. We will invite artists to gather—"

"No loggia for our parties," interrupted Salaì, sticking his head out the window. "How do you expect Ferrando and Giovanni to enchant pretty boys and the rich lovelies of the *ottimati*?"

"In the monastery courtyard, then. We shall invite Lippi, Rustici, Botticelli—"

"It feels airless. My God, I will suffocate in Florence."

"Here, take these coins, dear boy," said Leonardo, handing him a dozen quattrini. It was what a female silk weaver might make in three days. Salaì flipped them into his purse, looking disappointed. "Go to the market and buy us some bread and sweet cheese. Some wine," instructed Leonardo. "I have missed the bounty of Chianti all these years."

With Salaì gone, he allowed himself to close the studio door and lean heavily on the table. Had it been a mistake to come back to Florence? This Michelangelo—his star power was everywhere. He felt it in his gut, saw it now out of the edge of his eye. Seventeen years he had been away. He was nearly fifty years old. The commission for the sculpture of the *David* had been given to the young Michelangelo, not him. A hand drifted to his stomach, not for consolation, but to check whether he was running to fat. Still, he longed for a wedge of unsalted Tuscan bread and that girl's olive oil to sweeten his arrival back home.

Chapter 5

❧

S narl," said the servant girl. "Like a dog."
The girl leaned forward to inspect her work, the painting of her signora's teeth in lead white to prepare her for another round of society parties. The adornment required precision and careful drying time or risked being ruined. Servant and mistress understood that adherence to the rules mattered. Artifice was a sign of status, a way to garner invitations to grand events thrown by the oldest and wealthiest families. No kindness was to be indulged. "Three coats on each tooth," hissed the girl. "Now for the second. Stay still. No crying."

They had started after breakfast with the sprinkling of rosewater into Lisa Gherardini del Giocondo's hair. Adornments were necessary evils, something you agreed to when you married into wealth: a woman's public face was the measure of her husband's worth. Francesco del Giocondo was fourteen years his wife's elder. His temperament was often brutal but, because of him, she had escaped a lifetime in a convent among all the unmarried girls. God have pity on them and the women forced to work in the brothels.

Instead, fortune had smiled down on Madonna Lisa! She would do whatever it took: paint her teeth with yellow, pink and blue paint, powder her eyes with crushed gold—she could manage, with aplomb, whatever Florentine society required. If she suffered, she would do so in silence. Francesco expected an obedient wife. Tuscan law required as much: compliance and a payment after a satisfying wedding night. Pay extra to show your appreciation for the gift of virginity.

Agnella della Francesca stood in the corner of the bedroom, observing. She could tell that Madonna Lisa hated this, the decoration of her teeth, her servant's face unbearably close, hot breath poisoning the air between them. She imagined the pain that would be shooting up from the signora's jaw to her temple, the throbbing of her jaw muscles. Feeling the sensations of others came naturally to Agnella. Her job as a healer required it. She could fix broken bones and stitch gashes, but often her work required going inside the pain of her clients. The wealthy required plenty of that kind of healing. She watched as the servant girl narrowed her eyes and dipped the brush into the pot of white lead paint. The room suddenly darkened, and Agnella felt the clouds sitting down on the sky. Lisa was gripping the wooden sides of her chair with both hands. It would be impossible for her to eat until tomorrow. Agnella said a prayer for all the women who had tossed their pearls in front of swine.

Lisa's family owned land in Chianti, and Gherardini was an old, honorable name. She had been fifteen and unsullied—handsome enough, too—when she and Francesco had walked through the city for their wedding parade. She told Agnella it had felt as if she were the belle of Florence. Agnella had seen it countless times: how everybody lined the streets, bowing to the newlyweds, even old women waving olive branches from their windows.

From the steps of San Lorenzo church, Agnella could hear the troubadours: she strained to pick out a flute, a viola and somebody thrumming on a hand drum. The cool, wintry breeze caught and banged a shutter against the marble wall and brought her thoughts sharply back to the room.

"Can I close?" Lisa asked, sounding the words at the back of her throat.

The servant girl considered, then leaned forward and delicately pressed a finger to the signora's front teeth. "Seems dry," she said, wiping her nose on the back of her arm.

Lisa bowed her head and quietly moaned her thanks. Agnella moved deftly to her side and rubbed the signora's temples gently with her fingers to ease what she diagnosed as a throbbing head-ache. "*Va bene*," she soothed, moving closer, smelling Lisa's breath, like cheese forgotten in the cupboard. Laudanum would ease the pain and send her floating. But it would spoil her teeth, so Agnella would instead have to help her endure the suffering.

"Now for the easy part," she encouraged, nodding at the servant girl.

She knew that Lisa enjoyed the caress of the horsehair brush, the feel of the bristles, the strangely sensuous sensation when the wet paste was applied over her shoulders and down to her breasts. While her olive skin was transformed to bright white, she would drift off and listen to the musicians in the street. The paste reeked of vinegar, powerful enough to kill the roots of hair. Agnella would never submit to such abuse. But among these *ottimati* women, following the styles of Milan required strict devotion. She had witnessed servants use the sharpest blades to prune the roots of hairs and enhance a woman's high, shiny forehead. Lisa did not go to such extreme measures, but she agreed to the shaving of her eyebrows, to please her husband.

The servant began unlacing the signora's silk dressing gown. Agnella stepped forward to inspect her body, running her fingers over Lisa's shoulders and down her back, looking for lesions and signs of poor fluid flow that might discolor the skin. In spite of the burden of carrying multiple children, Lisa possessed a fine, athletic figure. Agnella knew that her client had spent years playing with wooden horses and chasing balls through the back lanes of Oltrarno, on the south side of the river. Unlike the Medici and the Rucellai, or even the Pazzi women, she had known more freedom than the pedigreed girls who sat quietly at home, stitching *tombolo* and plucking at harps and lutes.

The dressing gown slid to the ground. "Hurry up, girl," Lisa snapped, not willing to flaunt her immodesty. "Be quick."

Holding the clay bowl of paste, lips set against the toxic odor of the lead paint, the girl slid the brush down Lisa's nose and across the high planes of her cheeks. She covered her mistress's neck in a few deft strokes and set the brush back in its bowl. The clouds had cleared, and the room glowed golden. Quiet suffused the room. Lisa looked cut in two. Above her breasts, the painted skin took on the gray sheen of a Greek sculpture. Below, she looked like a peasant drying in the sun after bathing naked in the river. The girl lowered her eyes and looked at her signora's wide, serviceable feet. Made for foraging in the forest, Agnella reflected, watching the girl's glance. A patchwork of dark bruises darkened the toes, which explained why Lisa howled her thanks to God every time her narrow leather shoes were pried from her feet.

The other servants whispered to Agnella about Madonna Lisa: that she had grown up rough and dirty across the River Arno, and had only a tumbled-down manor in Chianti for her dowry. They could not know for sure; two of them were Moors from North Africa, bought by Francesco to serve as household slaves. Still, they gossiped. About how she loved to dance. How she had cried in the birthing bed when the nursemaid took her babies away to breastfeed.

Agnella watched Lisa jiggle her feet to the sounds of the street musicians, lifting her heels instinctively as if to spin across the floor. The servant cleaned the paintbrushes with almond oil and set them back on the toiletry tray. The signora had been blessed with five children: Piero, a strong lad; Marietta and Camilla, her three- and four-year-olds; her *bambolina*, Piera, just two; and a new baby son, Andrea. An experienced midwife, Agnella had been at her side to deliver all of the babies. Bartolomeo, Lisa's stepson, was a big brother to the others, though he was too rough whenever they were allowed to play at horseback in the courtyard.

"Go fetch Piera," said Lisa. "I need to kiss her rosebud cheeks." The words surprised Agnella. Piera's rosy complexion had become dangerously sallow these last days, and she was better left in the nursery to rest.

"She is still coughing, Madonna Lisa. Let her enjoy her *riposo*," Agnella advised.

When she had lifted Piera into the light at her birth, her complexion had bloomed like the most delicate pink rose; everybody had agreed the newborn bore a resemblance to the luminous angel painted by Leonardo da Vinci in Verrocchio's *Annunciation*. The baby had been bathed in warm white wine and swaddled in linen starched with rosewater. That was the tradition. Though there were plenty of other children in the mansion, Lisa and Piera had formed a unique bond. During the afternoon *riposo*, the signora would insist that the little girl be brought to her so that they could sleep together, Piera's body draped over her mother's chest, her blond curls interlaced with Lisa's long brunette tresses. Long after the other children were dressed for the evening meal, the two could be overheard playing games with finger puppets stitched from scraps of silk and wool.

The signora clapped her hands sharply. "Bring my sweet *bambolina* to me." It was as if she were addicted to her child and needed her badly, many times a day, to feel whole. Agnella stepped back, understanding that, when it came to Piera, her advice was not welcome. She watched as Lisa recovered her gown and tied the ribbons around her waist with resolve. "And some chestnut pie. Make sure it's thick with honey."

As the servant rushed from the room, Lisa, with deference to her friend and sage, said: "Agnella, come, hold my hand, give me strength."

The healer drew near and together the women looked into a hand-blown glass that Lisa had raised in front of them. Their reflections wobbled and then sharpened. Lisa opened her mouth and saw her chalky white teeth. Something to deploy along with her starch-white bust when her friends gathered later today in her salon, thought Agnella. They had been invited—Tomasia, Nannina, Lucrezia—to admire Lisa's new bowls, the ones crafted in Venice and galloped by courier just days ago. Agnella had seen the vessels, appreciated them, too. Each with a portrait painted on the opaque white glass; tiny dots of gold making a circle around each child's face at the bottom of the dish. The women would be sure to admire the ceramic, yodeling their approval like river birds. Lisa had told Agnella that the women had gathered at Lucrezia's villa to coo over her fine turquoise goblets, also from Venice—though Lisa thought they tainted the taste of the afternoon wine.

"I know you must be in pain from the painting," said Agnella.

Lisa nodded. She looked off into the distance, as if wanting to escape her bedroom.

"Would you like me to speak to the doctor about Piera?"

A sharp shake of the head. "She has a fever, is all. And I need all of your attention."

Agnella touched her fingers to Lisa's temples and made tiny circular motions to soothe the woman.

A long silence fell between them.

"Remind me why I am doing this?"

"Doing this?"

"Yes, this." Lisa gestured to her painted self and rolled her eyes.

"Oh, that," said Agnella, allowing her many jeweled bracelets to slide down her arm. "So that none of your friends can accuse you of being from the wrong side of the river."

"Yes, my darling, beloved friends. All of us with frescoed teeth." Saying this, Lisa smiled wide and started giggling.

"No. Don't," warned Agnella. "You'll crack the paint."

"I can't help it." Lisa was laughing loudly now, pointing at her teeth, her face and her neck. She wrapped her arms around her stomach to quiet her outburst. Recovering, she said, "I married a silk merchant for a husband. We have six children. A grand palazzo to call home. I'm adored and pedigreed!" She looked with admiration at Agnella. "Yet you possess all the elegance in the world. Just look at you. Your natural beauty, your ornaments, your wisdom."

"Well, I'm sure the elite *ottimati* wouldn't have me, even if I aspired to it."

"You are far too grand for all of them. But remember, I'm the one with the big feet!" She raised her arms and stomped on the wooden floor to the quick rhythms of the flute.

The servant walked tentatively into the room with Piera, interrupting the women's banter.

"Madonna Lisa, she is very hot. Shall I call the doctor?"

"No, she needs her *mamma*, is all."

Agnella was alarmed to hear the toddler wheezing heavily. She stepped forward to examine her, but Lisa waved her away, seemingly oblivious.

"*Salve*, my precious jewel! Shall we have some pie?"

Piera coughed and reached for the sweet pie. Would she be condemned to be a sickly child? Agnella had witnessed this with other families. Some toddlers sickened in the winter months, seemingly unable to bear the wood-burning fires. Others caught a cold that grew from something benign to a terrible inability to draw breath;

then their lungs gradually shut down as they became too fatigued to go on. And she was powerless to change it. Her only role was to support mother and daughter and try to avert a tragedy.

She watched as Lisa lifted her daughter to the sky, heard the quickening of her voice, saw the manic smile on her lips. "God must see His marvel, this angel on earth!"

Chapter 6

Beatrice arranged her clay jars of olive oil before lifting the handles and heading down the lane in the direction of Francesco Granacci. He was not to be feared, though she wondered at how a grown man could doubt himself as much. It seemed he was unable to find his own artistic style. Once, he had even asked her if his painting of the Virgin Mary looked like a copy of an old master. Shaking her head at the petty obsessions of such men, she slapped a hand over her nose as she walked briskly past a makeshift latrine, marked by wooden boards framing a hole in the ground. Rats rushed across the dirt path and disappeared.

She knocked on Granacci's door, once, and a second time. No answer. A group of men shouted for all to make way, and hauled across the square a large painting of three angels, their wings textured in gold, each of their faces individually, subtly human.

Instead of entering uninvited, she turned her cart toward the

Santissima Annunziata monastery and the man who had freed the white bird.

A monk in a black cloak looked her over, examining her ragged *guarnello* and patched jacket. Only when he saw the carafes of olive oil did his face soften. Females were considered an enemy of men on their spiritual journey unless they were bringing food or medicine. Grudgingly, he pointed to a dirt path off the cobblestoned road.

Rising up next to the road, the stone walls of the monastery were tall and formidable, rounded windows punched into the facade. The monk was staring hard at her, gesturing past the arched entrance—wide enough for two carriages to pass—to the far side of the compound. She nodded and followed his directions, traveling alongside the monastery wall. When it turned a sharp corner, to her surprise there was a side entrance across the inner courtyard, a secret one that looked abandoned, as if it were a tattered cape left on the side of the road.

Within the vast courtyard, two monks disappeared into pear trees to prune the branches. Chickens wandered, pecking at the grass, skittering clear of two grazing cows. She had expected chanting men, prayers. Or the shuffling of feet, the sound of linen cloaks trailing on stone floors. Yet here on the ground, the hush of winter had erased all sound. Midmorning—had she come at the wrong time? She left her cart at the discreet archway and breathed in the absence of the crowd. It was at times like these when she felt she could make a patch of the city her very own. She found a stick of charcoal and withdrew it neatly from one of her pockets. She bent and dragged the black stick against the white stone wall, drawing two curving arcs—the shape of a bird's wings lifting effortlessly. A mess of brutal lines to define the bones of the wings and, more brutal lines, the poetry of flight. There. She stood back and cocked her head to the side. Her bird finding freedom had been etched in less than one minute. Quick and raw, the way drawing in secret required. Satisfied, she wiped her hands on the grass to rub the charcoal from her fingers and started climbing a flight of stone stairs as the monk had directed, clutching a carafe of olive oil in her hands.

Another flight of stairs and the silence was broken. She heard the crack of laughter and clanging pots. Somebody shouted, and before she had time to turn away, she saw a young athlete running full speed toward her. She watched, astounded, as he turned a somersault before landing lightly on his feet, hands on his hips.

"A girl?" His eyes glittered with mischief. "What kind of a monastery is this?"

From down the hall, a man with a shock of black hair appeared, wiping his hands on a rag. "Girl, what's your business?" he demanded.

"A few weeks ago, a man with a white beard—" started Beatrice. "At the gates he tasted my olive oil." It sounded like she was lying, a desperate attempt to get inside the hallowed halls of a monastery. "He said I could meet him here with more—"

"*Good* oil, from the hills outside the gates?" the man interrupted, wiping his sweaty face with a linen pulled from his pocket. "Is that what you're selling? I'm not interested in anything watered down," he warned.

She handed the bottle to him. He uncorked the vessel, inhaled deeply.

"That's the stuff!" Waving her forward, he led her into the kitchen. The room was lit by a large window with a deep sill crammed with earthenware pottery and pewter plates; copper pans hung from wooden beams and, within the stone-hooded hearth, an iron pot balanced from a chain above the lively fire. A long-handled pan set on a trivet next to the fire contained a massive omelet. The smell of basil and garlic wafted in the air, and Beatrice could see a copper bowl where a bean soup was cooling. Her stomach cramped with hunger.

"He'll see you," said the man. "He loves to meet with the local"—he hesitated, looking Beatrice over—"people," he finished, with a definitive nod.

She watched the man lift a patch of cloth from a bowl and look inside. He pulled a perfectly formed mound of mozzarella onto a large ladle. "Now, this is a work of art!" he exclaimed, looking for her approval. She looked away, unsmiling. Her belly growled angrily.

"Not everybody has the honor of meeting him." The cook was stirring beans, pulling fresh marjoram from a pot on the windowsill and sprinkling the soup with her olive oil. "Court artist for the duke of Milan. Come home to Florence. For now," he said, cutting basil on a small slab of white marble, then the cheese and a hunk of bread. "This is a recipe for white soft cheese, more common in the south," he confided, eyebrows raised in delight. "As for introductions, I'm Paolo, chef, studio manager and dispenser of free wisdom." He gestured for her to remove her father's old gambeson and hang it on a hook by the door. "We don't just serve farro soup here," he said, assessing her bone-skinniness. "Here, try this." He handed her his freshly made creation.

She bit ravenously into the bread, stuffing the cheese into her mouth without shame. "Beatrice," she said, through a mouthful of food.

"Welcome to our humble home," he said, smiling with gratitude at her obvious appreciation of his food.

A door opened across the hallway. Beatrice braced for the worst. A great artist who had worked for the duke of Milan? She had made a terrible mistake following him here. She had presumed the man at the gates would be glad to see her, but now feared he would not remember meeting her. Worse, he might have her thrown out into the street.

She could hear the swish of velvet and silk. And then the man with the beard of a prophet was leaning against the doorframe. The cook handed him bread with cheese and nodded toward Beatrice. "Seasoned with olive oil from a Tuscan hill town."

"So you have come," he said, bowing gallantly. "Leonardo da Vinci." He touched his hand to his rose-pink tunic. "Honored to meet you here." He smiled. "In quieter circumstances."

She took a step back into the kitchen and lowered her eyes. Leonardo da Vinci? The name gathered force and threw its power at her thin body. Her father's voice sounded in her head, the time he told her of the magnificence of Leonardo da Vinci and the portrait of Ginevra de' Benci, the way he had captured not only her flinty teenage eyes but her inner self-possession. "Look," her father had said, calling to Beatrice one afternoon from the modest stone hut. It had been when she was still innocent and young, maybe twelve years old. "The sun lights the tree from behind, as in Leonardo's painting." And he posed her next to their juniper bush, which had turned shiny black in the afternoon shadow. "There," he said, stepping back to admire his daughter, his only child, given to him by the grace of God. "The tree of chastity. It becomes you." She remembered every detail of that day, the way he pressed his rough, land-worn hands to her cheeks.

It seemed impossible that she was standing in front of Leonardo da Vinci, the mythic maker, who dared to paint women looking directly out into the world, not meekly in profile.

"The honor is mine, Maestro. Have you come to Florence to make another painting?" she asked shyly.

Somebody gave a loud shout from down the hallway. The gymnast—whose name, she learned, was Salaì—leapt into the room with arms outstretched, and hugged the old genius, then ran at full speed in the opposite direction. The master took a bite and chewed. Paolo handed him a linen cloth. Wiping his mouth, stroking his beard, he gazed down the hall as Salaì leapt into the air once again. Turning to Beatrice, he spoke with a confidential hush: "What I want to discover is how to fly like a bird."

"Like the white one?" Beatrice whispered back.

"Like the white one, like the brown ones, like the ones with speckles of white on their black tails." He extended his arms wide and powered them slowly up and down.

"But, signore," she said, finding courage, "if they are frightened, like the white bird, they beat their wings like this." She pumped her arms with childish energy. "Desperate to escape."

"And are you escaping from something?"

"The castle up on the hill," she said without hesitation. "All day they want me to work on my *tombolo* and playing"—she did not know the word for "harpsichord," so she played her fingers in the air—"music, but I have escaped its walls with my olive oil so that I may see new people." She wiped her mouth with the back of her hand, and her heart leapt with the daring of her story. It was better than saying her father was killed by Pisans, that her mother had vanished. "All the artists want to paint my portrait. I refuse, no matter how many florins they offer."

Beatrice saw the great master glance at her dirty feet and sun-baked legs. Her toes looked nearly black. He could guess, no doubt, that she had been born to refugees who had eventually come north to live in the hills above Florence.

"Selling olive oil to pass the time?" he said gently.

"Anything to escape the castle." She shrugged, wishing she had shoes on her feet.

"Ask your duke to buy you some boots, and come see me again in a week's time."

He ripped more bread from the loaf, piling it high with mozzarella. "We'll need more of your hobby by then," he said, handing the food to her, "to keep us in good cheer."

The wintry days blurred into weeks of being hungry and alone. Beatrice began to curse her parents for their kindness, for making her feel that their family was whole and unshakable. Her father completed every poem he scratched in the dirt. Her mother finished every *tombolo* pattern, every cotton thread wound into place and snipped tight to the cloth. Their love might have been imperfect—Beatrice wondered at times after they argued passionately—and yet it thrived just as the cypress and olive trees did. Now the covenant had been broken. Their lives ripped apart.

With nothing to do and nobody to talk to, she often cried her bewilderment, hiding her tears in the feathers of her rooster, even howling her rage without shame, without fear that other villagers could hear. Exhausted, her throat sore, she would drop onto the patch of land where once her father's body had lain and claw at the dirt below the great olive tree, turning her fingernails black.

She had always been protected by her parents. They had never taught her how to protect herself. She knew she could find food and good company at Leonardo's studio, but without a pair of boots to wear on her feet, there was no way she would return and humiliate herself.

She made the long journey to Florence twice a week, sometimes three times, depending on the condition of her feet. Mornings, if her hunger was bad, she would stop at a small manor in a hamlet not far from her own and ease her cart into a juniper bush. She knew the boy who lived there—at least, she used to. Noiselessly, she hoisted herself over a low stone wall, her body light and her arms sinewy with muscle. The henhouse was an abandoned water well with a pitched roof and a narrow wooden door set between two crumbling columns. There was a warmth and peace to the cramped interior, with its pine shavings on the floor. Steadying herself, she would feel her heart pounding inside her rib cage, racing with the birds' tiny heartbeats. She would stretch her hands toward the bed of straw, lift one of the birds quickly and slip an egg out from the warmth. Sometimes she dared to reach below a second bird. Then she would turn away, rolling over the wall and back to her cart. Standing alone in the predawn dark, she would crack the eggs on her head and suck the sweet liquid into her mouth. The yolk and the white ran as sweet as freedom down her throat.

At the end of one particularly difficult day, she pushed on up the hill toward her empty home. The narrow road twisted sharply, and stone huts pressed their facades among the rose and cedar bushes. The smell of peas and hock brewing over a fire salted the air. Ahead of her, she could see the village healer, Agnella, chopping wood while chickens rooted for grubs in her yard. The road pinched in hard next to her manor, but Agnella seemed a woman of bounty, never poverty. She was wearing fine leather boots, and her long blond hair was tied back with a bow. Rumor had it that she worked often for the wealthy merchant families in the city.

Beatrice slowed her pace, aware of the sweat clinging to her back even as her breath blew puffs into the cold air. She felt the wolves of loneliness driving hard at her. Seeing Agnella chopping wood in her garden patch cut her breath short, for she could not bear to witness somebody else's peace with themselves and their little patch of domestic comfort engraved on the earth. She felt she must be close to death, for what was the point of surviving without a home, without people who knew everything about you, even all the stupid things you said and did? She rested her cart, unsure of what she wanted, wary of showing any weakness.

Agnella was considered by some to be a witch. At least, that was the dark gossip of the village. Taller and fairer than most Tuscans, with eyes flecked with violet and hooded like a secret, she enchanted Beatrice. Her mother had exchanged candles with Agnella for tinctures of oregano and each time returned with stories to tell. When she had been little, hair wildly decorated with gilliflowers and silver olive leaves, Beatrice had pressed her mother with relentless questions about the woman. Did she come from another place, a faraway land or distant stars? Did she travel sometimes on the backs of bears? Were her eyes real or made of colored glass?

Beatrice's mother had explained that Agnella was an acquaintance, somebody from the village, cursed by being barren. That her late husband was a stonemason and lime-burner whose lungs gave out far too young. She spoke of this to Beatrice with a shake of sorrow at a time when their own family was free of troubles and birds flew clean through their carefully pruned olive trees. But if Agnella had known terrible personal pain, it never showed. She cracked her whip against the backside of anybody who stood in her way. Beatrice had always admired her for being a woman of few words, and tough—possibly even as tough as a man.

She stood her ground, feeling herself tremble, and waited for the chopping to finish.

"This winter has been hard," said Agnella, finally looking up, letting the axe swing loose in her hand. "Though summers do their Tuscan best to suffocate us all." She had been one of the villagers who had paid her respects after the murder of Beatrice's father, setting a mass of red roses wrapped in a wool blanket down on the front stoop.

"Everything is hardship," Beatrice replied. She held her head up high as if to ward off the dark humiliation of being abandoned by her mother, with a murdered father buried in the church cemetery. Her throat felt dry and parched.

"True. There are more wolves than asses in Florence." Agnella looked at her for a long time and finally added: "Beatrice." Then: "Are you coming from the city?"

"These last months I've been selling olive oil to the artists."

"They pay you well enough?"

"They are not silk merchants. They pay what artists can."

The woman shouldered the axe and considered. "Their hands on their paintbrushes, not on your young ass?"

"I can handle myself." Beatrice shrugged. She examined Agnella's hair, its golden-blond length cut through with dark streaks, likely dyed with walnut oil, and tied with black leather. Such luxury—the leather stitched with gold thread—a sin for this time and place.

"Signore da Vinci has come back home, which pleases Florentines well enough."

"I met him. At the gates. At his studio. An old maestro in fancy shoes. A great painter, as you may know."

"Have you met Michelangelo?"

Beatrice wondered at the lines Agnella was drawing between people, like traces between the stars.

"You mean the sculptor? With the farm on the far side of the village?"

"He is an ugly man to look upon," said Agnella, raising the axe and swinging it down hard to cleave an oak log in half. She kicked the wood into a chopped pile and set another log on the block. "But he has a kind and generous heart."

It was true that Michelangelo did not possess a noble profile. Wrestler's cauliflower ears, a brooding forehead. He had smelled like vinegar, as if his sweat was brining in his woolen underclothes. Beatrice remembered it all from when they had loaded her father onto her cart. But there was an intensity she had liked about his face. And his body had looked as if it were made from stone warmed in the hot sun. There was something to *that*.

"Is there gossip in the market about him, his work?" Agnella tightened her grip on the axe. "Michelangelo is like a son to me, from years back."

"But he lives in Florence."

"He still hikes from the city to see me, and afterward to visit his family farm."

"Dolce, the root vegetable vendor, says his *David* will have a massive sweet potato hanging between its legs," Beatrice offered. It was a village custom to exchange gossip with your neighbors, and she warmed to the conversation.

"I know the woman," said Agnella, chopping another log clean in half. "Has a growth the size of a rat on one side of her neck. No doctor would ever go near that."

Beatrice laughed loudly, hissing like a hyena. She wondered why Agnella was looking at her with concern clouding her face.

"How long have you been living alone?" Agnella asked.

"That is not your affair."

"Six months? Ten?"

"I don't know or care," said Beatrice. "My mother will be returning soon enough."

"I see." Agnella hesitated, then went back to chopping oak. She waited before speaking again. "Your mother and I were not kin, but we knew each other well enough."

"But not enough to care about where she has gone."

The woman narrowed her eyes as if sheets of rain had closed them. "We had a bond, as women often do. I wish we had spoken more often."

"I asked her to go see you, or seek counsel from the priest. When she was—" The memory of her mother cutting her arms with the lace needle came flooding back to her. She needed to choose her words carefully so as to not humiliate herself, her family name. "When she began her wanderings."

Agnella turned her face to the road, and back to Beatrice. "The priest is useless."

"As is the man at the olive mill."

"An ass in a man's skin." She raised the axe and cut another log clean. "I will do your bidding for you from now on."

Beatrice felt her mouth crack open into a half smile. "Why do you want to help me?" She suspected that Agnella wanted to use a girl from the village to enchant some of her wealthy clients in the old ways of healing. Beatrice had heard of how healing women— even beauties like Agnella—lay down with the Devil. If this was the wicked secret that Agnella was hiding, she would run from this place and condemn her to the village priest. "Are you a witch?"

"No," said Agnella. She looked startled by the question.

"Can you heal broken bones?" asked Beatrice, taunting.

"Yes."

"Bleeding?"

"Sometimes. Not always. For sick stomachs, I make elixirs, poppies mixed with bitter almond oil and fresh river water."

"I have a pain in my gut, too," said the girl, hunger clawing at her insides. Agnella set the axe into a log and gestured toward the house.

"Come inside."

Beatrice walked with her, feeling fresh with power now that she had gained the woman's attention. Inside, the roasted chicken cooling on a long wooden table was a miracle. Agnella nodded. Using both hands, Beatrice ripped a leg from the bird. She bit into the taste of rosemary mixed with fat; she closed her eyes and fell into a time little more than a year ago when her parents were alive and together they enjoyed a simple, rich life. That boy with the henhouse she stole from; his smiles would warm her for months. They used to swim in the river together and lie on sleeping pigs, giggling, to dry their skin. Once his fingers had touched hers and they had held hands. But when his voice had changed, he'd walked out of the village and gone east. Maybe, like so many others, he'd joined Cesare Borgia along the cliffs of Romagna. They considered themselves mercenary soldiers, though their mothers called them lost boys and watched for their return every day from the olive groves.

When she opened her eyes, Agnella was sitting across the table from her. "I see you have a great appetite. You could earn enough money to have chickens of your own. In time, I could teach you some of my remedies," she said. "Maybe you could live here for a while." Her tone was coaxing.

"I like the comforts of my home," said Beatrice, thinking

darkly of her loneliness. "I have some birds. They're my family now." How easy it had become to spin golden cloth on her rotten loom. She chewed and considered this healing woman, sitting with her head held high, shoulders thrown back, as if she were some kind of Medici princess. Once, it seemed a very long time ago, Beatrice had stood at the base of the church steps with her parents, and she'd heard Agnella say: "The true way to go to Paradise is to learn the road to Hell." The air had been hot and thirsty, and the sun had turned the gray stone of the church fish-belly white. Beatrice remembered everything about that day, especially the way Agnella flicked her eyes wide, saying: "Learn the road to Hell so as to avoid it."

She wiped her mouth with her sleeve, looking restlessly at the roof timbers and polished stone floor of the woman's house. It was glorious to feel nourished again.

"Here," said Agnella, handing her a cloth she had soaked in a pitcher of water. "Your face. Wipe off the mud."

"Mud?"

"Do not listen to city folk and their fear of bathing. Make a habit of it in the village river—even cold water will do you good."

Beatrice pressed the linen against her face and rubbed. "My mother said the same." She inhaled. The cloth smelled of lavender and lemons.

"Tomorrow we'll go to the city together," said Agnella. She pulled the long leather ribbon from her hair and offered it to Beatrice. She had noticed how it had attracted her attention. "I'll knock at sunrise. No walking. The donkey will be pulling the cart."

Beatrice accepted the ribbon and nodded, and together they stepped back out into the garden. She glanced at the Duomo in the distance. Once, she'd thought of the domed cathedral as an orange blossom rising miraculously in the valley. Today, the Duomo assaulted her senses. She thought it resembled a turnip. Turnips belonged in the ground, not bursting into the sky. If God was interested in meeting her, he could come down to the banks of the River Arno or find her cradled in the branches of her old olive tree. He would not find her in the hallowed halls of the lofty church.

"I've been learning all about the road to Hell," she said to Agnella. "Though I can't say I've avoided it."

As she walked to her cart, Agnella called after her. "We will bring fennel soup to Michelangelo. He has been suffering from stomach pain."

Beatrice laughed. She felt unhinged, like her old wooden wheel. Agnella was trying to make a match of her and the sculptor, she realized. The man who had prayed over her dead father. Who had invited her to visit him in Florence. Michelangelo was no fool. He did not desire her. She was nothing to him.

"*A domani*," she said, wiping her greasy hands on her skirt, remembering the touch of his hands. The light dusting on her skin. The way he had been, the way he had held her, the way he had taught her a new word: *scultore*.

Chapter 7

"D amn them to Hell." Michelangelo half walked, half ran along the back alley behind the Duomo, released from an elaborate dinner thrown by the Rucellai family in their Renaissance palazzo by the River Arno. Their wealth came from wool, and Giovanni Rucellai had financed the completion of the marble facade of the Santa Maria Novella church in exchange for having his family name emblazoned on the front. Rumor was that he was happy to pay for grand architecture in order to serve God, honor the city and commemorate himself.

The party had been crowded with women dressed in several layers of taffeta silk edged with gold and silver brocade, all of it made across the river in the San Frediano silk district. Their husbands, mostly bankers and cloth merchants, wearing expensively dyed crimson coats lined with the fur of foxes' breasts, had patted him with their gloved hands, whispering urgent requests that he sculpt their garden fountains and tombstones, that he join them at their estates in Chianti for the spring deer hunt.

Their sixteen-course dinners, their wine stewards, their sugar sculptures of baby doves, all of the pretension of the fat *popolo grasso* made him feel alone and drowned, washed up on the banks of the river. "Damn them to Dante's Inferno," he muttered.

He turned into a narrow alley and spied the glow of a burning torch. "Attilio!" he called to the guard of the Duomo alley. "Waiting for the stars to touch the River Arno?"

The barrel-chested man, wrapped in a horse blanket, looked up and smiled. "And you, my brother. Riding the women like a good horseman?"

Michelangelo laughed loudly. He had been celibate for years, though male models obsessed him and fantasies about making rough, evil love to the goldsmiths and woodworkers down the lane haunted him. Always, there was the memory of that kiss in the monastery. He clung to its softness, its passion. Would there ever be another like it? He pushed away the thought, rubbed his crooked nose. "It was a prenuptial party tonight," he said, banging his boots together as a cooling wind swept through the laneway. "The women painted bright white, even their teeth, the fashion of Milan. They looked unreal, like ghosts at a funeral." He hoisted himself up to sit on the stone wall next to his friend.

"You arrived late, ate little and hid so nobody could find you?"

Three men dressed in colorful jester costumes and silk hats appeared in the alley before Michelangelo could answer. A ferret clung to the shoulder of one of the men, who was staggering and gripping the sleeve of one of his companions. Another man blasted a horn twice and threw a bottle to the ground. He attempted a third blast, but one of the buffoons called for silence. In front of Michelangelo, he bowed deeply.

"Blessed are we," gushed the man, pointing to the moody sky, "to encounter a great artist tonight. This night of celestial"—he paused to find the right word—"embellishments."

"An artful night!" bawled his fellow entertainer, brandishing his horn.

"Away with you," Attilio said, pushing the men forward. They clapped arms around each other, bowed low and doffed their hats.

"God's grace. And we are away to the Buco," said the one with gold ringlets framing his handsome face. He slapped his companions hard on their backsides.

"Salaì, oh, Salaì, harder, and harder!"

"More of that at the Buco!"

"The place for men with hungry appetites!" called the jester.

Michelangelo knew the Buco—it was known to locals as "the asshole"—a tavern near the Ponte Vecchio that attracted sodomites. He had been there himself, had tasted enough flesh to know his craven desires needed to be repressed or they would govern his life. He watched the men as they stumbled away. The pull of the Buco was strong; he felt himself physically resisting as their drunken song echoed in his ears.

The alley grew quiet again.

"I hear that Leonardo da Vinci came home," Attilio said, caution in his voice. "Dressed and decorated like a true court artist. Hosting parties below the lemon trees at the monastery. Indulged, of course, by the Servites."

"I've heard the same," said Michelangelo, shifting on the stone wall. "He'll expect to be handed the grandest commissions. Taking work from the rest of us," he added. "Given him free rooms, have they?"

"At least half a dozen is what I heard."

The men trained their eyes on the sky, observing the moon flicking silver behind the clouds. Attilio pulled a tall crock of hippocras from his leather satchel and handed it to Michelangelo, who uncorked it and raised the spiced red wine to his lips. "Ginger?" he asked.

The guard nodded.

"Cinnamon?"

"Ginger and nutmeg."

They passed the liquid between them, and Michelangelo felt the warmth of the wine liberating his soul. He toasted Attilio, his long-time gentle friend, older, silver-haired, happily married for two decades. "To my night guardian," he said. "Thank God for the wise men of Florence. I have abandoned all hope, you know."

"Agnella came by today."

"Agnella. Here?"

"Yes, with a girl. Maybe fourteen or fifteen. Marrying age." Attilio laughed and stuck an elbow in Michelangelo's side.

"Did you get a name?"

"Interested?"

"I could be."

"Somebody from your village. Wears a black leather ribbon in her hair. Unusual girl. Lots of fight in her." He looked over at Michelangelo, enjoying the lightness of the moment. "A real beauty, by the name of Beatrice. Mean anything to you?"

Michelangelo sniffed, scuffed the wall with his boots. "I met her a year ago. Her father was murdered by a sick band of Pisans."

"Those people living outside the city walls are sitting ducks."

"But it's great Tuscan country. I still go to visit my father's farm and the people—Agnella—who raised me there. It's where I escape when I need some peace."

A moment of silence passed between the men. "Is it the marble that once defeated di Duccio that troubles you?" said Attilio, changing the subject.

"Sculpting it, that massive rock. I believe the colossus will eat me alive."

"Michelangelo—make the move and God will look after the rest," urged Attilio.

"Seventeen feet," murmured Michelangelo, shaking his head. "You're right, of course, but . . ."

The stone had secrets of its own. He had discovered bubbles and stains, crystals reflecting like snow on the surface, and black seams of iron hidden like traps below.

"Sculpt *David*. Give him life. Give the city a great new symbol."

"I say as much every day." Michelangelo looked down the alley, toward his studio. The work haunted him.

"Here, my friend, something for you," said Attilio. He rummaged through a potato sack on the ground and pulled out a narrow length of deer hide, its fur smooth-stitched to a backing of fine gray wool. "From my wife. To keep your body warm when the women have run away."

Michelangelo wrapped himself in the fur and surfaced from his melancholy. "Attilio, before I came upon you tonight, I was condemning people, the ones who demand so much from me. I was condemning them all to that place in Hell where all flatterers spend eternity. You have given me great comfort." He gripped the deerskin in his hands. "Please give my thanks to your wife."

He draped the fur around his neck and walked down the back alley; umbrella pine trees rose from a neighboring courtyard, their trunks creaking in the coolness of the evening above a low stone wall. Soon the alley widened, and he passed a small sheep corral. Against the darkness, he saw black shadows, possibly the veils of a thousand Virgin Marys dropped from the heavens into the dirty street. What sacrilege! Praying to God for forgiveness, he crossed himself and kissed his fingers.

Michelangelo turned right and walked toward a clearing where slabs of white Carrara glowed in the dark. He ran a hand over the largest, acknowledging the marble, then drew a large key from his pocket and unlocked the iron bar extending across a thick wooden door.

Inside the studio, he swept a hand into the blackness, like a blind man, knocking aside a roll of parchment and a butt-end *culo* of bread as hard as the stone he liked to carve. He muttered obscenities until he seized upon a candle of goat's tallow affixed to a leather strap. He pulled it onto his head and lit the wick with his flint.

The cavernous room warmed to the candlelight; walls of buckling plaster and high ceilings of cypress wood came into view. On the floor was a straw mattress heaped with worsted blankets; he'd left his trussing-bed in Bologna or Rome—which it was he no longer recalled or cared, such was the extent of his fatigue and despair. Sleep was best shunned, like sins against God. He sat on the mattress and pulled one of the blankets around his shoulders. Attilio was right. The pride of Florence depended on the new work. Hunched over, he muttered a prayer, his voice half-strangled in the dark: "Oh, God, forgive me my sins, for I am imperfect and unworthy of your love. Bless me, in the name of the Father, the Son and Mother Mary. Help me to sculpt the *David*, for I am merely a man with little value."

He stared at a samite tablecloth—silk interwoven with gold threads—rolled into a heap and splattered with marble dust. The Medici had given it to him with instructions to use the cloth often for festive gatherings. In five years, he hadn't used it once. Half smiling, feeling his mind relaxing, he reached for a stick of coal. On the wall he drew from memory some sacred angels he had seen earlier at the Palazzo Rucellai. He sketched these putti, giving some lively attention to their chubby bodies and their angelic curls.

Now his mind turned to the girl in Settignano. He hesitated, then set the sharp end of the coal on the wall to draw Beatrice from memory, her arms spread wide as if flying above a gaping hole in the ground. She seemed to him a girl on fire. An angel resisting death. Leaning closer, his nose almost touching the plaster, he brightened the shape of her neck, her full lips, defining the light glowing from her large almond eyes.

Satisfied, he doused his light, returned to his mattress and pulled the deer hide over his body. He wondered whether she might visit him. Thinking on this, he turned onto his stomach and slept.

Chapter 8

In the milky darkness, Leonardo blinked awake. Late to bed, up twice to piss. The smell of his own urine wafted over to him from the clay pot in the corner of the room.

There was a time, he thought, admiring the strokes of the broad axe on the oak beams, when he cared not about the quality of slumber but about what he had enjoyed the night before. He glanced at the naked body of beautiful young Salaì, his *bell'uomo*, asleep next to him. This exquisite creature who cost him a small fortune: a black leather jerkin with a blue silk lining, pink velvet hats, all the leather boots he had ordered immediately upon arriving in Florence. Without Duke Ludovico Sforza to cover his expenses, money suddenly mattered to Leonardo.

He propped himself on an elbow and sat up, feeling for his velvet cloak on the stone floor. Wrapped inside it, soothed by the luxurious fabric, he moved to the long oak table, flipped open his small leather journal and read his latest entry about the movement of air, written right to left with his left hand in a style he had developed as a boy to keep his thoughts safe from his father's judgment:

revir a ekil sevom ria Eht
ti htiw sduolc eht seirrac dna

He snapped the book shut. Lifted his arms and stretched until his shoulders ached. It had been an intellect's paradise to work for the duke of Milan. The French invasion had brought his time there to a swift, dramatic end. He had been indulged by his patron while in Milan, but Florence was a city where commissions were won by cockfighting among rivals. A place that pitted talents against one another, dating back nearly one hundred years to when Brunelleschi won the contest to design the massive brick dome soaring over the cathedral.

An old man playing at a young man's game. That's what he had become. Winning commissions required all kinds of tricks. Ghiberti had won the prize to create the monumental doors at the baptistery. How had he impressed the forty-three citizens who sat on the design jury? By recommending the hollowing-out of the backs of his panels, allowing for an impressive saving of expensive bronze. Leonardo had to be street-smart to be competitive in Florence. Was he too old to enter the fray again?

He walked to the window to take stock of his situation. The prior had kept quiet about his flamboyant style of dress, about his sharing a bed with a young man, even averting his eyes and apologizing after discovering Salaì—buck naked, drunk, desperate to suck on a lemon—in the monastery garden. Leonardo felt a twinge of guilt—he did not wish to devote a moment's thought to the altar painting, the only thing the Servites had asked for in exchange for this free studio space.

He eyed the iron bar holding the velvet curtains against the window. Ten chin-ups, he thought, to show that he still had strength. He gripped the bar with both hands, stomach muscles clenching. Once he had bent an iron bar into a horseshoe with his bare hands. How long ago was that? Years? Decades? He hauled himself up, shoulders shaking, chin barely grazing the top of the bar.

Lord of the Arts. That's what they had called him on the streets in Milan. When his mane of white hair was a mess of auburn-gold ringlets. He forced his body up again. Two was his limit. Further evidence that his body was disintegrating back to the earth.

Rubbing his arms, he thought of the heartbreaking poetry of Genesis: "In the sweat of thy face shalt thou eat bread, till thou return unto the ground; for out of it wast thou taken: for dust thou art, and unto dust shalt thou return." The Bible always delivered. Simply, poetically, with excruciating honesty.

The sharp sound of hooves clattering across the pavers of Piazza San Marco reached his ears—donkeys hauling carts loaded with squealing pigs to market. He turned from the window and sat down on a narrow chair, observing his great oak bed and Salaì, mercifully, still sleeping.

Morning declared itself, turning Salaì's torso bronze, the light deepening his biceps in color, turning the *linea transversae* and *linea alba* of his stomach into a ladder of muscle. The woolen blankets were at his pelvis.

There was a gentle tapping at the door. "*Permesso*, signore?"

"Paolo, come in, come in, the door is open," said Leonardo. The cook carried a brass tray laid with a blue and white flask of spring water and a carafe of red wine. The two porcelain cups, featuring a flowing, arabesque design, had been gifted by a rich merchant of gold—a Muslim—whom Leonardo had met in Venice. With the reverence of a priest about to baptize a child, Paolo lifted both of the vessels high and poured a stream of intermingled liquid into the cups.

Paolo bowed, then hesitated at a small round table where scraps lay scattered; Salaì had ordered capon and a *berlingozzo* late last evening but had been already too drunk to do more than throw the fruit from the cake at imaginary ghosts.

"Let it wait. *Va bene*," said Leonardo, waving Paolo off. Sunrise was to be enjoyed in silence.

The cook departed, and Leonardo pulled from his cloak a notebook in which he could observe, calculate and consider. In Milan, he had books filled with lists calling for the measurements of the duke's palace and the need to see the master of arithmetic to determine how to square a triangle. In the glow of the Florentine morning light, Leonardo wrote a fresh to-do list: *Walnut oil, linseed oil, resinous plaster and wax*, he wrote, from right to left. Then, *Calisthenics every morning. Horseback riding. Walks into the mountain.* He looked at the bar suspended above the window. *Throwing large rocks*, he added, pressing the nib of the goose quill hard into the page.

The salon was a fine space to work. The other rooms also carried the promise of discovery, but one was accessible only by the bedroom, which overlooked the courtyard. That was where he would keep the tiny carcasses of lizards and rats, or baby falcons, if he found any dead in the monastery's garden. He had once dried and purged the innards of a castrated sheep; it had been a hefty size, yet the bladder had reduced, over time, to a tiny inflatable sac. With delicate movements, he could still pump it up with a miniature smith's bellows and launch it as a tiny flying machine.

Something else could happen in that private room: dissections of cadavers. Monks who died of sickness or old age could be delivered from the monastery's infirmary; nobody needed to know. The prior claimed he supported the advancement of the sciences. Some monks might be distressed by the slicing open of their cellmates, he'd said, and had asked only that the work be conducted discreetly for the peace of his community. Leonardo thought it might be simpler to perform dissections a few blocks over, at the venerable old Ospedale di Santa Maria Nuova.

Dissecting and painting were exercises in problem-solving and discovery. Both required technical skill and extraordinary patience. Neither was truly enjoyable.

Swimming in a river after a long afternoon's hike—that was something he considered delightful. He found immense pleasure in gathering the latest wisdom from other expert minds—*Get Maestro Fazio to teach you about proportion* or, in another earlier notebook: *Ask Maestro Antonio how mortars are positioned on bastions by day or night.* He also delighted in bringing the most advanced methods to his studio. "The best colors, wrought from nature," he muttered. As Pliny the Elder once described in exquisite detail. He scribbled in his journal the colors that currently inspired him: *purpurissum, indicum, caeruleum, milinum, orpiment, appianum, ceruse.*

There were times he enjoyed painting very much. A client settled into a softly padded chair, a breeze floating through the studio, a musician playing the lyre.

Painting Ginevra de' Benci had been like that. When she looked up from her embroidery and stared at him with daring and fierceness—

A knock on the door startled him out of his reverie. Paolo appeared and motioned to a messenger standing breathless behind him.

"An urgent message by order of Francesco di Bartolomeo di Zanobi del Giocondo," the messenger said, bowing low. "Apologies. It is still early." He glanced at the wildly colored clothes thrown over a mattress, leather bags half unpacked, the table cluttered with drawings and little dried-up bats and mice, acorns, thistles, cockleshells. That night, Leonardo was sure, the messenger would tell his mother and sisters that artists were a curious breed, strange thinkers, not to be trusted.

Leonardo noted the heavy gold lettering on the parchment scroll—no expense spared—and saw the youth puffing out his chest, making ready to deliver the message in his most grandiloquent voice. He quickly wiped his hands on his purple silk hose and took the scroll. "So it begins," he muttered to himself. Summoning his energy, he read it aloud: "F. Giocondo would be delighted to make your acquaintance and requests a meeting at Piazza della Santissima Annunziata."

The messenger gaped at Leonardo, seeming astonished that a mere artist—even the Master of Arts—could read. "Prepare yourself, master," he said, bowing. "You will receive all kinds of invitations from the *ottimati* to paint their wives. They like to make a show of their wealth."

Leonardo stifled a snort, pretending to be distracted by the collection of dried artifacts on his table. He picked up a conté, offered a curt bow to the messenger and dropped a coin in his outstretched hand.

"Naturally," said Leonardo, "the pleasure would be all mine."

As the messenger took his leave, the great bell in the tower of the Palazzo Vecchio sounded, like the lowing of a cow. "*La vacca mugghia*," said Leonardo. "Seven in the morning."

He looked at Salaì's sleeping face. Without willing it, he saw the structure of his skull. He walked to the bed. Bending over and stretching a hand over the young man's throat, he muttered: "At a distance of two fingers, the uvula, where one tastes the food, lies straight above the windpipe, and above the opening of the heart by the space of a foot."

Salaì shifted and moaned with the pleasure of a long and satisfying sleep. "You are more animal than man," said Leonardo.

"So you have always said." Eyes still closed, half slurring his words.

Leonardo joined him on the bed. They had been together for a long time—ten years. The dukes, the priors, his own father, all of them raised their eyebrows. But there was this . . . always this. He could feel Salaì's breath, still sweet with wine, warming him, his mouth kissing him on the neck. Leonardo felt himself relaxing. He had discovered Salaì, a boy living rough on the streets of Milan, all manic energy and yearning. Had glanced at him and continued walking, then felt himself returning, pulled back by the force of an angel. "Come with me. Do you like chestnut pie?"

In those first years, Salaì had been given to fits of anger. He would climb the walls, scratching frantically at the plaster, his eyes rolled high into his head. "Be still," Leonardo would say. "You are no longer a runaway."

Theirs was a carnal union, to be sure, one that had developed long after Salaì first came into his house. Leonardo had enjoyed other boys, and the game from behind, as it was known in Florence. With Salaì, though, it was different. What started as master and orphan had grown into a mutually dependent love affair. It was passionate. Even now.

He pulled Salaì toward him and traced his luscious mouth with his fingers, exploring his lips with his tongue, sliding down to his stomach. The morning sun danced over the room. He tasted the sweetness of youth on Salaì's skin, and thought of a new drawing that he had started of the Virgin Mary and Child, seeing every line in his mind.

Chapter 9

Agnella jumped from the cart and entered Michelangelo's studio without knocking, kicking open the old wooden door with her boot. This was the boldness that marked her as a witch with terrible powers, thought Beatrice, pinching her thigh as a reminder not to cross the woman.

"I brought soup," Agnella called into the murky void. She took the clay pot from Beatrice and sat it loudly on the table.

The studio was shrouded in the dull light of dusk, and clouds of dust seemed permanently suspended in the air. Beatrice noticed how the oak plank floors were charred and there were stains of brilliant blue from the woad plant; likely the previous renter was a wool dyer. On the wall, there were scribblings in black, too numerous to make out, and drawings of angels and a girl who looked like she was flying.

Without a word, Agnella cleared some of the ash from the cooking fire and set to work preparing a fresh one, all efficiency.

"At last you're home," she said. "Come and greet my young friend from the village."

Behind her, Beatrice lifted the canvas dividing the room. A naked youth was standing on a wooden pedestal, a leather thong wrapped like a snake around his torso. She watched mesmerized as the thong pressed into his waist. Even though the boy was slim, the pressure of the leather against his flawless skin created gentle swells of flesh. Such was her surprise that it took her a moment to realize that the hand pulling the thong tight belonged to Michelangelo. His other hand stroked the curves of the youth's perfectly athletic ass. She dropped the canvas and looked away, feeling herself begin to shake, even as Agnella walked briskly toward her.

"Is he here? Michel? Michelangelo?" Looking quizzically at Beatrice, she strode across the studio room, heels clicking loudly on the floor.

"Agnella, I am working. This is not a good time." Michelangelo stepped in front of the canvas, letting it drop behind him. He held the leather strap loosely in his hands, his face burnished, sweat gathering at his temples.

"When are you ever not working, my dear boy?" Agnella set a kiss lightly on his cheek and took him by the arm. "Put it away for now," she said, taking the leather strap from his hands and setting it on the far side of the table. "Beatrice"—nodding to her—"brought you some soup. Sit, eat, feel better."

Michelangelo sat at the table, head down, avoiding Beatrice's eyes.

He had prayed over her dead father, she thought. He had invited her to visit him in Florence. She had believed he could be trusted. Had even dreamed of his hands upon her. She pushed her wretched disappointment to the bottom of her stomach where everything else forbidden and painful was left to fester and roil.

"Beatrice, it would please me if you would water the donkey at the well." Agnella walked across the room, ripped open the canvas and hauled the young man out into the open. "Take your leave," she hissed.

Beatrice glanced at Michelangelo, the hunch of his shoulders, both hands gripping the table, and though it made no sense to her—he was much older than she was—she felt strangely drawn to him, unspeakably so, as if what she had witnessed behind the canvas made him more beautiful to her.

She hurried out to the well, clutching her arms to her sides, regretting the shame he must be feeling, the way she felt every day for being an olive oil girl from a hill town. Abandoned. Cast off. She stepped back across the cobbles to the studio.

From outside the door, she heard Michelangelo kick over the heavy wooden bench. "Agnella, *you* need to leave. You know nothing of my art. I need male models for my *David* to make the stone come alive."

"And you know nothing of your life," she heard Agnella shoot back. "It might not be worth anything to you, but it's worth a lot to me. Sodomy can get you killed in this city."

"You and your judgment. Go back to the village and leave me alone."

"Michel, you need to resist your hungry ghosts, or they'll devour you. Push away your obsession with"—Beatrice leaned closer—"before the Officers of the Night knock down your door and charge you with it!" She imagined Agnella's eyes darkening. "This vice that plagues you can destroy you—it will."

"What nonsense you speak. Have you gone mad?"

"My boy, you do not see with your own eyes. People are talking in the market. The naked giant you plan to carve with a *cazzo* as big as the legs of their children. How ignorant you are, and naive. Michel," Agnella said, "I have *always* been by your side, since you were a motherless child."

Beatrice heard a chair being thrown down, the sound of Michelangelo's heavy boots walking across the studio. Was this why Agnella wanted to introduce her to the sculptor? To secure his safety by way of marriage?

"I want to be alone. Without you and your idiotic ideas."

"You, who are devoted to God," she shouted back. "Remember what is written in the Bible: 'He who walketh with wise men shall be wise: but a companion of fools shall be destroyed.'"

Beatrice heard something heavy—a rock, a shard of marble—being chucked, connecting, splintering against a wall. There was a long silence, and clouds of dust, she imagined, thickened the air. Finally, she heard Agnella speak in her low, commanding voice: "Protect yourself. Allow yourself to experience a girl."

Without thinking, Beatrice heaved the door open and stood to face Agnella and Michelangelo. She had no idea what to say, but words came out of her mouth: "You squabble and threaten and command," she said, striding across the studio to pick up the overturned chair. "Throwing water on his wings, Agnella, to stop him from flying on his own."

She left the airless room before finishing, unable to speak any further. But he, a hard-nosed loner, had lifted his head and looked at her as she stormed past. She had caught his attention, and this gladdened her heart.

Chapter 10

Beatrice imagined her *mamma* coming home. She rehearsed her arrival, the ceremonial walk along the dirt road, her figure cutting up to the trail that led to their family home. She would look happy—that is something that Beatrice would notice immediately—with a healthy shine on her cheeks and some extra flesh on her hips. Likely she would be singing an old Italian folk song, the one that ends with a curious line about the girl who throws apples at the cows. She would be holding roses in her arms that neighbors had offered to her as homecoming presents, and her eyes would be fixed on the girl sitting on the stone step at their front door. That was the cue for Beatrice to notice her mother. She would look up, and exclaim, and they would run and leap into each other's arms. A blissful reunion with roses falling to the ground. Life would resume and the clock would rewind to a time when the sweet smell of beeswax rose from the pot hanging over a gentle fire and it seemed possible to believe that darkness would steer forever clear of their lives.

It was a stupid dream. Beatrice knew that in her heart. But she held on to it anyway. As the months slipped by and her loneliness and hunger deepened, she became fiercely attached to the dream and looked forward to playing it out when she had crested the hill and turned her cart into her family patch next to the olive grove. She would call to the rooster and the hen and their two newborn chicks. She adored them completely. They would zigzag from the hutch, taking their time, easily distracted, pecking at anything that looked like something other than dirt, and eventually arrive by the front step of the stone hut, lured there by the clucking of the girl and the promise of a few kernels of corn.

There were some vegetables to pick from the garden, some cabbage and chard, mostly onions and herbs, not much to sate her hunger. Chewing on fennel, Beatrice would scoop the chicks into her skirts and sit with them on the stoop to deliver her monologue. Sometimes, if she was resting for the day and not in Florence, there was time to cut triangles from a cabbage leaf and put them on the birds as sun hats. Even when she was worn down to the bone, she still found the energy to wave her arms to begin the drama: "Few in the village believed it possible . . ." and "Nobody believed her to be alive, and yet . . ." She would lean close to the chicks to whisper the exciting part when her mother's footsteps could be heard approaching, and would nuzzle the tiny birds to her cheeks, feeling their beating hearts, while sharing her joy about how well her returning mother looked and describing the bouquet of roses: "Every one an exquisite crimson, deep and lush, and perfumed in a way that could never be fully captured in a bottle."

With the chicks still in her skirts, she would pick up the wooden stick by the stoop and draw something in the dirt. A cupid, an angel, a crowing cock with a magnificent fleshy comb on the top of its head. Someday, she thought, instead of a stick and a piece of dirt, she might come by some parchment and colored pigments to make her art. She had glimpsed the abundance of tools at Michelangelo's studio: the chisels and hammers, the clay and brushes, the sheets of paper and the countless stubs of conté in red, black and white. She wanted to start drawing the women who, like her, lined up outside the city walls, to capture the hollow-eyed girls and emaciated grandmothers carrying sacks of farro on their backs. She wanted to convey their wounds and abuse, but also, somehow, that they were clinging to their dignity like wild ivy to a stone wall.

Her visit with Agnella that day had gone all wrong. Delivering a pot of fennel soup as a way to get herself formally introduced to a man who was in the middle of seducing another man! Since then, Agnella had made herself scarce—something about treating women at a Florentine convent where her healing was badly needed.

There were advantages to being abandoned, thought Beatrice. Since nobody was watching, or cared what she painted, she was free to live according to her whims: climb a tree whenever she pleased, eat an onion when she was hungry and avoid being taught how to draw by an old man in a stuffy Florentine studio. She decided then and there to give herself permission to be in charge of her life and her art. Yes to transferring the sunset onto the wings of her angels and the bodies of her cupids. Yes to heaving the rules aside and drawing the *popolo minuto* the way they deserved to be drawn.

The sun blazed a final glory and dropped hard into the horizon, leaving the sky looking bruised and sullen. She picked herself up and shepherded the birds inside her hut, guiding them into an old wooden crate for the night. Michelangelo—where was he now? Did he sleep with his models or stay awake alone on his mattress? His kindness at the scene of her father's murder had left a sweet taste in her mouth. His shuffling shyness, his passion for his art, his hurling of rock against his studio wall—all of it provoked her. Though she knew there was little hope for a match, she committed to seeking him out, the *scultore* with dust on his hands.

She bolted the door shut and slid the iron rods across to hold it fast. The chicks turned circles around each other and warbled their trills of pleasure. Beatrice smiled and found comfort in believing that everybody inside was safe. She tumbled down a long shaft toward uneasy sleep, then woke abruptly in the morning, cold and alone, refusing to give in to regret for what she had become.

Chapter 11

The bells from the medieval tower of the Palazzo Vecchio rang out. Fourteen heavy booms. Excellent. He still had time to enjoy the piazza before meeting this Francesco, the cloth merchant of considerable means whose summons he was answering.

Summer had deepened to a shimmering heat and Leonardo was glad to remove his ocher-colored cape and relax on the stone stairs. He pulled some parchment and a red pencil from his leather bag. Across the piazza, children shouted as they ran toward a man rolling a cart of fresh baked bread with black olives.

The arcaded Ospedale degli Innocenti sat directly behind him, its loggia punctuated by gracious white columns. Baskets provided for unwanted babies sat at the hospital's grand wooden doors. He looked over at the woman sitting next to him, her tousled hair, her eyes glossy and ringed with darkness. A swan ravaged by time. Gently moving his left hand, drawing from the lower right up, he applied a fine layer of hatching, deepening the hollow of the cheek.

He moved his pencil over the paper to her right eye, pressed there, and left a tiny patch of white to allow the iris to glow. He drew the curve of the neck, capturing tenderness and grief in one stroke.

He felt her fingers pinching him. "You stick out," the woman said, and nodded to his luridly colored stockings. "You from here?"

"Yes," he said, caught off guard, catching sight of the yellow triangle stitched to the arm of her dress. Her eyes, the bones of her face, her unpinned auburn hair—there was a certain quality, but here she was, this whore, cast into the street like a piece of rotten fruit. She seemed to be speaking through a haze. Cheap wine or opium? "Though . . . there have been times when I have felt like an outsider," he added, feeling exposed by declaring it to a stranger.

It was not just the return to Florence at his advanced age. He had to admit to being an outsider even as a child. His mother, Caterina, had been impregnated one spring evening when she was fifteen by his father, ten years her senior, enjoying his privilege as a lawyer fresh out of school. Leonardo was born *non legittimo*. Given shelter as a young school-aged boy by his grandfather, not his father, down the road from the blacksmith and the parish priest. Banned from attending university or pursuing medicine or law. Whenever he thought of it, of his mother's humiliation, he felt the cruelty of the world, a place abandoned by decent humanity.

"Rain is coming," the woman said loudly, interrupting his reverie. She straightened her back, the tiny bells on her ankle bracelets jingling softly. "The olives are thirsty."

"Rain only dampens the spirits of city dwellers," he said, observing her shining eyes and wondering if she had been crying. With the overcast sky, the light on her skin was radiant.

"Good for the farmers," she said. "The summer has been dry."

He followed her eyes as they examined his velvet cape, richly decorated with gold brocade.

"You are not a farmer," she said, waving a finger at him.

He smiled charitably at her and shook his head.

"Let me guess," she said, her voice raspy. "You are a goldsmith."

"Not at all. Though I was taught well by somebody who was." Leonardo detected a slight accent in her *volgare*.

"Wearing too many colors to be a notary."

"True. I am not my father's son." She might be Greek or Turkish, he thought.

"You draw a pretty picture of me," she said, gazing at his buckled velvet shoes. "I will call you an artist," she ventured.

"What if I draw instead an honest picture?" he queried, returning to the sketch, deepening the shadows around her eyes, emphasizing the long line for her lovely neck. Then he saw that it was badly bruised. What man had abused this woman as his plaything, he thought, stiffening.

"Harder to sell," she said, as if she had repeated that phrase often. "People don't want suffering. They want something sweet to distract them from war and disease. They don't want my troubles."

Pointing a finger at him, she gestured to his long, curled beard. "I like your art." She leaned suggestively toward him, breasts bulging from her tightly cinched *gamurra*. "My lips are for hire. Big, blooming roses, not the mean stick lips of rich woman."

Leonardo laughed out loud. "I appreciate your candor. May I know your name?"

She narrowed her eyes. "La Riccia," she said, finally.

"La Riccia, it is a pleasure to know you," said Leonardo, turning to his parchment. He looked up to see a knot of men gathered in the piazza. A man charged up the stairs where they sat, swerving to kick at the howling cats. The drunkards were still fighting; the similarities between humans and animals could not be ignored. *Passioni dell' anima*. A fierce desire to survive. To find food and drink. To lust, to mate, to procreate. To establish dominance. Leonardo had seen the alignment countless times in his dissections. The bear walked on the soles of its feet; the flexor tendons of the beast's toes were remarkably similar to that of a human.

"God make you joyful," he said as a goodbye.

"You paint me and rob me of my soul." Her tone was cool. But Leonardo ignored her, turning his focus to the arrival of a large walnut coach pulled by a pair of elegant horses. The driver stood up on the footboard and whistled loudly to clear some room; children playing with ribbons and ropes bolted out of the way like startled rabbits. Some of the men and women sitting nearby on the steps shuffled to their feet to show their respect; the sight of flamboyant wealth stirred their Florentine pride.

The driver slowed the horses to a walking pace, but before he was able to jump from his post, the passenger wrestled the coach door open himself. A short, stocky man emerged into the public space, pulling an enormous velvet cap festooned with a peacock feather from the leather seat behind him. He adjusted the hat to offset his perfectly coiffed bob of hair. His beard was thick, a sign of virulence, and Leonardo felt a tinge of jealousy. His own beard had thinned in the last couple of years.

"Must be my man," murmured Leonardo, brushing his beard

upward, giving it some lift with his fingers. He stood so that he might be recognized.

"You may have talent, but not so many smarts," said La Riccia, standing several paces away and turning to laugh at him.

She had his cape! This woman was a prostitute *and* a common thief, he decided. She was becoming a nuisance.

He looked over at the walnut carriage and waved at the man with the preposterous hat.

She pressed his cape under her cloak, thumbing its gold brocade, and walked breezily down the stairs, swaying her hips.

Leonardo tucked his sketchbook under his arm, unsettled by the woman   a trickster, he thought grimly. There was no time to go after the wretch. He looked at the man approaching with considerable speed. "My lord." Leonardo bowed, and rose with a gallant sweep of his arm.

"I am but a humble trader of silk," replied the man, removing his hat with a flourish. He bowed deeply in return. "My lord, it is an honor to meet you at last."

"Brother of Florence," replied Leonardo. He estimated the man to be well into his forties. He had pearls stitched into his shoes and was stuffed into a green damask cape decorated with a collar of squirrel fur that said its wearer did indeed have the means to commission a work of significance. Still, the man's deep-brown eyes, like rich, fertile soil, communicated something to be relied upon. There seemed to be a wounded history in his furrowed brow. Deep pools of personal loss. Leonardo decided he liked him. He shook the stranger's hand. "I am Leonardo da Vinci, painter, a member of the Guild of Saint Luke."

The man seized Leonardo's hand and shook it vigorously. "Your name is celebrated. My name is ridiculously long and yet my fame is short." He laughed good-naturedly. "I am Francesco di Bartolomeo di Zanobi del Giocondo. Francesco del Giocondo, if you please. My family owns a chapel at the basilica." He gestured to the Santissima Annunziata.

The flaunting of wealth made Leonardo wince—how unlike Milanese aristocracy.

"I supply the church with the finest of silk for their sacred altar cloths," Francesco added, sitting heavily on the stone steps and motioning to Leonardo to join him.

Leonardo watched as Francesco removed his shimmering cape to reveal a shirt of silk sleeves decorated with gold thread. From behind one of his cuffs, he pulled a piece of expensive-looking linen, likely imported from Reims, France, to vigorously wipe his face. It might be that the linen enjoyed a pedigree greater than the man. And such was the sorry truth of the Florentine. Newly rich, freshly cultured, considered usurpers in cities beyond its historic walls. Florence was a merchant republic without a king, without the necessary historic weight. Even its ubiquitous symbol, the fleur-de-lys, had been borrowed from the French.

Leonardo felt the man's hand press his arm. "I am a man of no great culture. Do not be deceived by the pearls stitched into my shoes," he said, as if intuiting Leonardo's thoughts. Francesco looked around the piazza. "My wife, Lisa, has a noble spirit. Her family carries an old name: Gherardini. I believe many arrows flew true from the battlements of their castle in Chianti." He paused and wiped his face again with the linen. "In the old war against Siena."

Leonardo noted the smell of garlic and lavender wafting from Francesco.

"We have been blessed with five of our own children and a son, Bartolomeo, from my previous wife. But"—he shifted on the steps—"our little girl has taken ill. This has been difficult for both of us." He stared at his pearl-rich shoes; calf leather, Leonardo noted. "Lisa's acceptance has been . . . is taking longer than mine. I believe that our sweet Piera will pass from this world. May God bless her."

"Death often comes too early," said Leonardo.

"True," agreed Francesco. "My last wife passed during child-birth. May God bless her."

The men looked out at the piazza, offering a silent memorial.

"*Il filo*," said Francesco, breaking the silence, catching a thread from his coat and holding it in the air. "The wool thread made Florence rich. Such a tiny thing—so much easier to understand than life and death, and what might make us happy."

Leonardo looked at Francesco, warming to him and marveling at the human condition, what it required of people, made them endure. "In Milan," he offered, "I was painting colors and shadows evaporating like smoke, from darkness to light. Something new. Full of risk and the possibility of failure. Sfumato."

"Sfumato?" Francesco pressed a fist to his forehead. "If only Lisa's pain, and our daughter's, could evaporate like smoke."

"Perhaps your child will be cured."

"We pray most fervently for her to heal. But she has the cough. Every day she struggles to breathe a little more."

Leonardo nodded and bowed his head. "The loss of a child

creates a void inside," he said, reaching over and pressing his hand to Francesco's chest. "And all around," he added, gesturing over his head. "No lines, no angles, but a part of everything."

"No lines, no borders," said Francesco, nodding, showing he understood. "Will you meet my wife? I should be honored if you would paint her portrait. We have moved into our own home, next to my parents, and are arranging the furniture and art. Via della Stufa—"

"Behind the Basilica of San Lorenzo, yes, I know it," said Leonardo. This silk merchant would surely pay handsomely for a portrait of his beloved, troubled wife. "I would be delighted to meet her." He would prefer a commission to equip warlords with giant crossbows, and yet here he was, agreeing to paint a portrait. But that kind of client was in short supply and his account at the Ospedale di Santa Maria Nuova bank was dangerously low. Even with free accommodation at the monastery, Florence was expensive.

The man looked as if he had won a cockfight, and he made fists of his hands and pounded them against his knees. "Will you come to Via della Stufa?"

"Have her come to see me at the studio," said Leonardo lightly.

Leonardo saw the man's face cloud over with concern. Noble women rarely traveled by themselves, and Francesco did not wish to sully his wife's reputation. Leonardo touched the man's arm gracefully: "A portrait of this kind is not only about art—my art—it might also serve to heal your wife's sorrows. The distance from your home will cleanse her mind and do her tremendous good."

The man considered. "I shall send her in the carriage with a driver. I believe the honor of your company will indeed lighten her melancholia. All in good time. And payment will be honorable. I will provide florins by messenger, every month."

Leonardo allowed a small laugh and placed his hand on his heart; the artist indebted to the patronage of a wealthy merchant. "We can discuss all of these details another day. For now, we might enjoy the humanity on parade in the piazza." He swept his hand forward to a farmer struggling to drag a reluctant hog across the cobbles. Children scattered, racing after their balls and hoops, while vendors sold olives and bread. Butchers lay back on the steps, shining their bloodied aprons up to a sky turned back to jewel blue. The rain would have to wait for another day. "It, too, is a work of art," he said, delighted that Francesco had not insisted on a deadline.

He stood to go and regretted that his cape had been stolen. At least he had the sketch of the woman, with her long, tragic neck, and new work to replenish his coffers.

Chapter 12

Being abandoned felt like having a broken candleholder and, besides, no candles to light. There were shadows moving inside her, and she knew she needed some kindness today after walking the streets for hours, looking for signs of her mother. Beatrice needed to go back to Michelangelo and start again. He was a sullen mink, but he was decent and kind—she had seen that in his eyes and in his hands back in Settignano.

The afternoon dripped with heat and humidity, and she was glad to set her hand on the coolness of the iron door handle of Michelangelo's studio. "*Buon giorno?*" She nestled an olive oil bottle in one arm and heaved the door open with her shoulder. It was possible the young model would be inside, or they might be together on the straw mattress. Instead, she found Michelangelo with his back to her, naked to the waist, fully absorbed in sculpting. She watched the muscles on his shoulders rising and flexing with every thrust of his arms. A small model of a naked young man was emerging on the table. The weight of his body was supported by the right leg, the other stepped lightly forward. Michelangelo was sloughing off clay to reveal the model's calf muscles. She could see horsehair and sheep fleece; he'd mixed it into the clay for texture and body.

She held still, not wanting to interrupt. The model was roughly hewn, with ragged, muddy edges, so unlike the polished marble statue of the Virgin Mary looking down at her with sad, perfect eyes inside her little village church. This model seemed to be testing the limits of balance. How much weight the right foot could take. She lifted her eyes from the model's legs to the genitals. It seemed Michelangelo was also testing how much masculinity to sculpt. He wasn't holding back, she thought, stepping forward to have a better look. "*Dio mio*," she whispered.

Michelangelo turned, rubbing his face as if he had been roused from a deep sleep. "You, there," he said, looking at her. His mouth shifted into a tense smile, and she noticed the way his eyes darkened at the same time. He was likely upset by her unexpected arrival, the interruption of his work. He crossed his arms and motioned with his head. "This is called a *bozzetto*," he informed her.

Encouraged by his voice, she nodded and stepped closer. "Is this the beginning or the end? I mean, is somebody paying you to make this?" The torrent of questions spilled from her mouth as she gestured with the olive oil bottle to emphasize each one. "It looks rough. Do you want it to look rough, or will you be polishing it? And he is little, so little compared to that other *David*. I think it used to be over at the Palazzo Medici. It stood for a while in front of the Palazzo Vecchio. Do you know the one I'm talking about? It is brown, and David stands on the head of Goliath."

She stopped talking and waited. He seemed slightly amused and taken aback by her unbridled tongue. "Yes, I know it. That's the *David* by Donatello. He cast it in bronze; that's why it looks brown."

"Well, he looks like a girl and he slays a giant. That's one of the reasons I like it."

"I like it because he stands without any support. No trees or columns to lean against. A first since antiquity."

"He or she," said Beatrice.

"True enough," he said, cocking his head to the side, considering. "I like the way you think." He took the olive oil from her and placed the carafe on the long studio table. "Thanks for coming back, especially after the last time, with Agnella." He looked again at Beatrice and may have seen the concern on her face. "Don't worry, I'm not using a live model these days."

Beatrice stole another look at the *bozzetto*'s hair matted between the legs. Those tiny curls—was that what Michelangelo looked like below his own intimate wraps? She felt a rush of feelings that revolted and amazed her.

"This little man will be my teacher," he said. "I'm testing my ideas on this *bozzetto* before starting the sculpture."

As he spoke, his mouth relaxed. He glanced at her again. Maybe he didn't mind her visit, she thought.

"Is somebody paying you for this little man?"

"The Wool Guild. They asked me to make a giant *David* for the Duomo."

"I bet they're paying you in gold florins." She felt happy, truly happy for him, and yet demolished by her loneliness, her insignificance, the fact that she was paid in coppers, never gold.

There was a long, uncomfortable silence. "No fennel soup today!" she said, changing the subject. "I mean, I was sorry we just barged in on you that time. Agnella knows how to kick down doors with her boots." She stood looking at her naked feet, regretting her words. "I hope you like the olive oil, though, from my— our—village."

"You and Agnella are neighbors," he said, over his shoulder, as he stepped back to the *bozzetto*, hands pressing against the clay. "She looked after me when I was a boy."

Beatrice had heard this. "Was your father at war?" she asked; she had wondered if this "Florentine" was truly from outside the walls.

"My father has always been at war with me. From the time I could draw," he said. "He thought art was a low thing. That sculpting was the same as being a stonecutter." She saw him narrow his eyes, wipe the sweat from his brow with the back of his hand. "Lower class. Beneath the name of our old, noble family. He put me in grammar school and I ran away. I took a lot of beatings for that."

She wondered if she should confess her own attempts at making art: her pathetic stick drawings in the dirt, her primitive charcoal drawings on the city's walls, for which she was paid nothing. Standing in his studio, inhaling the wet, loamy smell of mud, she hardly felt worthy as an artist. "Is this *bozzetto*, as you call it, like a sketch before doing the real painting?"

"Exactly right." He seemed content to have her next to him

while he worked at shaping the clay. She waited and observed, mesmerized, keeping her words inside her mouth.

"Have you ever sculpted anything?" Michelangelo turned and looked at her.

"Just headdresses made of leaves and grapevines."

"I was thirteen years old when I started my apprenticeship with the artist Ghirlandaio. We spent our days practicing how to draw. We drew with silverpoint or conté, sometimes on white sheets, sometimes on colored paper. We made our own paints with natural pigments—yellow ocher or indigo—mixed into crushed animal bones. We would copy drawings by the masters and learn how to draw space and buildings with perspective, how to draw the body with anatomically correct knowledge. After one year I was accepted into the Medici Free Art School."

She was listening carefully to what he was saying while also studying the muscles in his arms, the smoothness of his chest.

"Here," he said, picking up a mound of clay and shaping it into a ball. "Make something out of this—whatever you like."

Beatrice screwed up her face and went silent. Michelangelo recounted his story of apprenticeship as if it were as easy as fishing in the Arno. But she knew better. To be picked as a protégé of the Medici was a rare honor. There were hundreds of artists whose studios she passed during her olive oil runs, and they were typically dark bottegas, hardly grand villas surrounded by vast gardens.

"I wouldn't know how," she said.

"Pick something, anything at all."

"I don't know . . ."

"Forgive me if I have been too forward," he offered. "I usually

don't talk so much. I usually ban my friends when I'm working."
He looked over at her kindly. "Trust yourself. Give it a try."

Tentatively, she touched her hands to the ball and was instantly
repulsed by the cool, wet texture. "I'd rather draw," she blurted
out, confessing, "Sometimes I do drawings on walls."

"That's good, really good. Look, I'm working on one over here."
He walked to the plaster wall of his studio and picked up a stick
of charcoal.

"A putto," she said, following him and seeing a half-dressed
cherub on the wall.

"Unfinished, though. I need to deepen the folds of the drapery."

"Or something else. Something beside it?"

"What are you thinking?"

She looked at the ground and said nothing.

"I was raised by a stonecutter and his healer wife. I'm most
comfortable with simple people, the *popolo minuto*, telling stories
around the hearth. It's rare that I trust anybody else."

His encouragement was difficult to resist. She thought back to
the time he left her sitting on the sacks of grain after lifting her
dead father into the cart for burial. When he had offered to stay
and help her, when she had wondered if he could be trusted.

"You should try putting a bird on the wall. I like to draw them,
and cherubs, or angels looking wrecked and sad. Maybe a goldfinch?" There. Done. She had dared to speak it.

He pushed aside some of his hair—curly, unbrushed, fallen
over his eyes—and looked at her sideways. "A goldfinch . . ." He
didn't sound convinced.

"Not a tame, unmoving thing like artists around here do.

Something with some life. Wings out, about to fly. The way Leonardo likes to see them."

"Leonardo? Da Vinci?" Michelangelo looked directly at Beatrice. Now she had his attention. "You know him?"

"He sets birds free. I saw him release a big white one in the line outside the city gates. We were both trying to get in." The words tumbled out of her, and her eyes grew wide with the telling. "He buys birds and releases them so he can watch them fly and escape into the sky."

Michelangelo smiled, and she watched him as his eyes flitted from her face to the timber ceiling to the dirt floor. His brain was working, she could see that. The way his mouth was tensing again into a straight line, it was as if he were talking to somebody in his head. Not her. Maybe God.

"Why don't you draw the bird yourself?" He held out the charcoal.

"Me? I'm no artist!" She laughed one of her shrill hyena laughs, the way she did when she was nervous—or lying, as her mother used to tell her.

He held the charcoal and waited. She noticed that the tips of his fingers were cracked and bleeding. "What happened to you?"

As if noticing for the first time, he dabbed his hands with a patch of linen, staining it with pinpricks of red. "It's nothing. There's so much moisture in the clay. It cracks open the skin of my fingertips."

She took a breath in and exhaled long and slow. Reluctantly, she took the charcoal from him and bent slowly toward the wall. A few deft lines and she had defined the delicate head and the body of the goldfinch. She backed away from the wall, considered her drawing and bent in again. This time, she loosened her grip to express something quick, like movement. "I want the wings to beat fast."

He reached over and touched her hand. "More here," he said, guiding her fingers to crosshatch the lower section of the wings.

She moved toward the wall and deepened the curve of the wings. She liked the feeling of his rough, hard hand on hers. There was nothing lecherous about it, not like the groping fingers of other artists in the laneway. The tenderness of Michelangelo's touch came as a surprise, and the moment she felt it she wanted more of it, more of his sweaty, wet clay smell. Clearing her throat, coming back to her senses, she stood back, amazed that by darkening she had also freed space for more light on the wing tips. The bird looked like it was moving fast toward the open sky.

"There," said Michelangelo, nodding at her work appreciatively. "I like it. Feels primitive, very direct, almost Etruscan."

Beatrice looked over at him. She liked the way his low brow pressed toward his crooked nose when he spoke. Was it possible to love somebody for a misshapen nose? "*Grazie*," she said, looking at him and the table with his drawing tools.

"You will visit me again, bring me more olive oil?" His voice was serious and raspy, as if veiled in stone dust. "Are you safe?" he asked. "Do you feel you're safe living in Settignano? The Pisans are warriors. As you know."

"Yes, I am fine. It's not just me. I have a family of birds." The words were gushing out of her mouth again. "We sleep together at night. My constant companion is the sun. And the moon when I walk down the hill to Florence before dawn." She spoke of her life as if it was pure bliss.

"Birds?" he asked, without moving his eyes from his drawing on the wall.

"A rooster and a hen and baby chicks. The rooster is called The Pope. We all get along. And the city isn't far."

"It's two hours by foot," he said, smiling gently at her.

"Sometimes Agnella picks me up in her cart and that saves my feet from the walk. Mostly I . . ." She stopped talking and peered closely at her drawing of the goldfinch on the plaster. It really did look like it was beating its wings fast.

"Keep working on your art," said Michelangelo, scrutinizing their wall paintings. "Remember, you're an artist, too."

"I'm not like you," she muttered.

"Why is that?"

"I'm just an olive oil girl."

"Maybe." He flicked his eyes to the roof timbers and down to the goldfinch. "But look at what you've drawn right now on the wall. Not just a bird, but something else." He shifted on his feet and found the words: "A feeling called freedom."

"I like that. When I am walking, I will think of your words," she said. "For I hate climbing that hill home."

Chapter 13

Michelangelo had gone to the other side of the river to perform a human dissection on an old cleric named Antonio. He had worked all night in a private room within the Santo Spirito monastery. It was a privilege to learn about human anatomy, but every time he cut into a dead man a feeling of dread came over him, as if he was trading his humanity for knowledge. After dissecting, he would retreat to the church—a masterwork of symmetry and serenity by Brunelleschi. This morning, exhausted from his night's work, he lay down on a wooden bench and was about to fall asleep when the prior of Santo Spirito interrupted him.

"That dead man," said the prior, shoving Michelangelo aside so he could set his own sprawling body down. Prior Bichiellini maintained strict discipline among the Augustinian order, but was himself fat, rude and wickedly intelligent. "Tell me, did you have to pull his head out of his ass?"

He was ten years older than Michelangelo, but they were comrades whose bond had been forged from a secret: Prior Bichiellini provided him with the cadavers.

Officially, the church outlawed dissection and warned that anybody who abused a dead body was committing a mortal sin, punishable by death. The prior felt, in this case, that the pursuit of knowledge outweighed the decrees of the pope. Michelangelo was an exceptional artist—he had earned that reputation by carving the *Pietà* for Saint Peter's church in Rome—and Bichiellini believed his decision to grant dissection rights to the young man was warranted. There would always be grandiose dictates from the Vatican. Most high-placed cardinals were careerists in search of worldly gain, not enlightenment. Perhaps they might learn from some of Michelangelo's investigations into how muscles were woven throughout the body or, his most recent interest, whether the brain was more powerful than previously thought.

Michelangelo rubbed a hand over his eyes.

"A delicate man," added the prior, gazing at the east clerestory of windows. "Antonio preferred undergarments in the finest silk. Couldn't stand rough linen. But a dandy in bed, if you could persuade him."

"His brain showed various shades." The dissection had been long and difficult—extracting the jelly from the vessels and pulling the sections apart. "Light gray at the front lobe, and darker purple matter toward the back." Michelangelo had suspected the brain was divided into lightness and darkness, but it took him more than two hours to remove the sticky layer of blood so that he could see for himself. Then it was as obvious as the white and dark meat of a turkey. "People don't place value on the brain, compared to the heart. A year ago, I wondered that a brain could have such complex—"

"Inner reflection, dreams, motives?" suggested the prior.

"Ambitions, animal desires, poetry and evil. Why shouldn't the brain consist of more than one shade?" He looked down at his hands, his nails rimmed with blood.

The prior folded his arms over his rotund middle and nodded, considering Michelangelo's words. "Shall we?" he said.

The men rose, walked to the western corner of the church. They made this pilgrimage often, for the pleasure of staring at the cross hanging in the octagonal sacristy. Michelangelo had carved it from limewood when he was eighteen years old.

His Christ depicted more of a boy than a man. The mouth full and sensual, the calves softly defined, as befit a carpenter's apprentice; his arms, stretched wide, were lithe and innocent, as if only days before they had embraced his mother and father at sunrise. After cutting himself on a thornbush, Michelangelo had painted a path of blood from Christ's ribs all the way down to the right hip; the loins he covered discreetly with a cloth made from wood and plaster. He'd fashioned Jesus' hair from human hair braided into sheep wool. A few novices at the monastery had donated their locks after having their heads tonsured. Michelangelo had tried to carve a life that had been robbed. Once there was a man, and he was a carpenter, and he was good and decent, but none of that mattered compared to the need to satisfy the aspirations of others. The crucifixion was the only one of his works he could stand to view over and over.

"This interest in distinguishing light from dark in the brain," said the prior. "It goes well beyond Leonardo's notes on the skull. You recall his observations?"

"Of course."

"He was obsessed with proportions. About the cavity of the eye socket and the cavity in the bone that supports the cheeks; that the nose and mouth were of equal depth." The library at Santo Spirito was among the most sophisticated in the land, and the prior had arranged for some of Leonardo's works to be copied.

"And each is as deep as the third part of a man's face, from the eyebrows to the hairline," recited Michelangelo.

"So you have memorized his anatomical studies?"

"At the Palazzo Medici—like everybody else," came the curt reply.

Michelangelo owed a huge debt to Lorenzo de' Medici for choosing him, an awkward, obsessive boy, and taking him into his palatial home; his shyness could sometimes be confused for belligerence. The manicured gardens of the Medici palace, the orange and lemon trees framing naked figures sculpted during antiquity, had made a profound impression on him. Lorenzo had once lovingly placed a rose-colored velvet mantle around his shoulders. And then the Medici family was run out of town. Was that nearly ten years ago?

"What everyone hasn't noticed is that there's a problem with his notes," Michelangelo said. "His treatise on dissection was limited to aesthetics. The old man's attempt at solving the ideal proportions of man was simple-minded—"

"Simple-minded? You miserable piece of shit," roared the prior, in mock despair. "Leonardo da Vinci is a genius."

"I merely speak the truth."

"That *old man* was the first to explain the workings of the womb and conception. And there was nothing simple in his explanation of the physical properties of joy, sadness, labor . . ." He tapped his forehead. "Forgive me, I'm forgetting one of them."

"Emotions associated with killing," said Michelangelo. "Flight, fear, ferocity, boldness, murder." He shook his head. "I want to prove that emotion—all of what we feel as humans—shows up in the *brain*."

"If you discover the truth about the light and dark regions of the brain, you will have leapt well beyond Leonardo's work," admitted the prior. "And if you make that discovery, you must paint it, the separation of light from darkness. Take that moment from the book of Genesis and paint it so large that all those who see it will be forced to believe."

"Light from darkness," said Michelangelo. "Joy from terror."

"Leave aside your feelings of jealousy, Michelangelo. You are an original, as well. Think of your *Pietà*."

Michelangelo felt a wave of euphoria at hearing such praise. He had carved Mother Mary's arm to fly unsupported into the air, each finger curled to express a different level of anguish. Others copied from the ancient Greeks. He had placed his Mother and her Son at the base of an oak, in the hope they might endure for as long as there was human suffering and trees on the Earth.

The prior put a hand on Michelangelo's shoulder. "Leonardo is to be admired, not feared. Look to him for ways of seeing."

Michelangelo felt his mouth grow tense. He was anxious to change the subject. "Are there others who might be passing?"

"One of our pastors is gravely ill. His skin has turned yellow and the doctors are at a loss. And another local man, a stonemason, can barely breathe; he's not long for this earth."

Michelangelo nodded. He hoped the men would hang on for another month at least; this latest dissection had left him exhausted.

"Get some rest. And remember my counsel," said the prior, hugging him gruffly. "Leonardo can teach you more than you can imagine." With that, he released the sculptor from the basilica.

Michelangelo went first to the fountain within the cloister and splashed the icy water over his face. Drying himself with his tunic, he heaved open the great wooden doors and stepped out to the piazza, his gaze yanked upward by a gaping blue sky.

He knew that Oltrarno had been settled long ago by outsiders obliged to put down roots across the river from the protected northern part of the city. This was where the *ciompi* wool workers were forced to bend their backs, where the Flemish and German weavers plied their messy trade, boiling dyes in tin and copper containers along the Street of the Boilers. Today, like every day, the pressed, dyed cloth made from English wool was hung out to dry, a riot of color flapping against sober earth-colored houses and shops. He liked the evidence of hard work fluttering gaily like festival pennants. He greeted the locals gathered on the steps of the church with a polite nod, then walked toward the river, heading to his studio on the other bank.

His fatigue was clearing and he turned briskly from the laneway onto Via Maggio, the widest boulevard in the city. It was being transformed, workers' housing knocked down to make room for big houses owned by the burgeoning merchant class.

His boots made footprints in the construction dust that coated the black stone walkway, disguising its herringbone patterns. The prior had called him an original. He felt the gladness rush up from his stomach.

He quickened his pace. The prior had also recommended Leonardo as a friend. Friendship between competitors? Perhaps in Milan. Or Venice. Not here, he thought grimly; there were too many talented artists. If he was rich enough to support his father and brothers without working, then he could afford to seek out Leonardo as a wise mentor. But the roof needed patching, his brothers were complaining, his father made insufferable demands, and he needed to provide for them.

He came upon two girls begging for food. They appeared to be ten or eleven years old. Michelangelo stopped to study the scrawny girls with deltoids as round and hard as crabapples. He had seen girls like these begging for unsold food or rotten fruit from vendors once the market closed at Santo Spirito. This pair looked like sisters, and they walked with their arms linked, their faces grimy from the day's heat. Somehow, he felt a kinship with them, for he had been their age once and had learned from Agnella and her stonemason husband how to work as hard as an animal. This was before his father had taken him home to Florence, before the start of grammar school. When times were lean, they would lay up stone walls for villagers in Settignano who could pay: the priest, the olive grinder, the stone agent. And even when there was little to eat, they would share their harvest with those in greater need. Agnella walked at the front of their procession, a basket of bread, onions and honey balanced on her head.

Michelangelo examined the neatly trimmed beards of two men standing nearby and guessed that they were landowners or guild members. They were deep in conversation:

"Via Maggio has the advantage of great width. Surely that alone would attract those willing to pay," said one.

The perfectly symmetrical entrances and arched windows of the new palaces pleased Michelangelo well enough. What he regretted was the bullish invasion of new money. The half-built palazzi looked ridiculous towering over the ramshackle wooden houses of their *ciompi* neighbors.

"But on the filthy side of the river?" countered the other man.

"The river offers a welcome buffer from the meddling politicians! You watch, my friend, the Palazzo Pitti will someday be finished to lord it over Oltrarno."

The men slapped the girls' hands away from their capes, and one threw a quattrino to the ground. The girls scrambled to collect the coin from the dust.

"You live here?" Michelangelo asked the beggar girls.

"Yes, signore." They looked up at him shyly. They stood and led the way to the rickety front door of the shack behind them. A veiled woman appeared, and the girls stood at her side.

"These girls are yours?"

She scrutinized him, his rumpled clothes and broken nose. She did not invite him inside, but spoke from the doorway: "I am their guardian. Their mother died in childbirth, their father in the war, killed by a Pisan, *testa di cazzo*, may God curse his family." The woman spat on the floor, then crossed herself.

"They beg like this for what purpose?" asked Michelangelo.

"Not for what you may think, signore," protested the woman. "I provide them with shelter. They beg for food, some coins they gather for their meager dowry. God willing, they will marry by the time they are sixteen."

"Do they read?"

"A little, thank you, signore. And some math."

"Then they go to school?"

She laughed bitterly. "Mainly they are trying to survive."

Michelangelo looked back at the girls. So much was unfair; there was so much he wanted to repair. The older girl was retying the knot of the younger one's hat. It came to him then, unexpected: his mother tying a straw hat onto his head. He could feel the tenderness of her hands. She wanted to protect him from the hot sun. Not long after, when he was barely six years old, she died.

"They have the blessing of the prior at Santo Spirito," the woman said, fearful now that he meant to order the girls off the street and impose a heavy fine.

"And mine, too," Michelangelo reassured her. He reached into his leather pouch and pulled out a handful of gold coins. "Here are some florins. With this you can buy enough food to last several months, and extra for their dowry."

The gift was sizable—he was being paid four hundred gold florins by the Wool Guild to sculpt the biblical David. He knew nothing about this woman or these girls, yet he could not contain himself. To give away ten florins was an act of generosity that would surely merit the favor of God. Besides, it buoyed his spirits to help others, especially the poor, the marginalized, the girls. "See to it immediately, so that they no longer must beg on the streets."

The woman stared at the coins and then buried her face in her hands and started weeping.

As he walked away, he felt that the spirit of God had touched him—of that he was certain. How many times had he passed by the beggar girls and failed to do anything aside from recognize their miserable existence? He cringed at how his own pain blinded him to the needs of others. At least he had pulled himself out of his artistic obsession to listen to the girl, Beatrice. He thought back to her drawing of the goldfinch on his studio wall. Her ease with making art, without the obsessions he knew all too well, was like an offering of peace. He looked at the drawing every night before falling asleep. The wings alive and beating like hope. Sketched by a village girl. Maybe he could make a match with her, as Agnella had advised, and bury his longing for men.

By the time he set foot on the old stone bridge, he was in a state of near ecstasy. Bounding across the Arno, he threw his arms above his head and pretended, as he once did with his younger brothers, to slay the monster that lurked at the bottom of the murky river. He felt cloudless and pure, and time slipped by invisibly as he leaned over the narrow balustrade and watched the water flow slowly by. The river had created the city, he knew, and the city had created the river. Smiling like a child, he felt glad for all of it.

Suddenly, a heron lifted from the riverbank, floating over his head like a black veil and snapping him out of his reverie: "Release me!" It was David, trapped in marble, shouting at him from a workshop arranged by Governor Soderini and the Opera del Duomo, the cathedral's public works committee. "Release me from this stone!"

Immediately, he felt sweat prickling the back of his neck. "What do you want to be?" he muttered back in frustration.

His thoughts circled around the massive block of white marble, landing on the rough outline of legs, badly blocked out by the previous sculptor, Agostino di Duccio. The feet were stiffly rooted, the legs static instead of moving forward into possibility. They might be impossible to repair. Then there was the long crack in the marble to solve, running where the heart side might be defined. That fool Duccio had driven his chisel in to indicate something—a knot of drapery? But he had not completed the blow. Had it been fear that stopped him? Indecision?

Directly across the bridge, on the Via de' Tornabuoni, a handsome boulevard of simple, elegant austerity, a crowd was gathered. There were twenty, possibly thirty men. Michelangelo could now hear their shouts and laughter. He recognized some of the faces: Botticelli and his brother Simone, Raphael, and Filippino Lippi, as well as Piero di Cosimo—all talented artists. And there was Granacci, in a peacock-feathered hat. Rustici stood next to him— he could always be counted on to boast loudly. Then Michelangelo saw, at the center of the crowd, Leonardo, holding court.

"Michelangelo, *vieni*! Michelangelo, *vieni, vieni*, Michelangelo!"

It was Rustici. The bastard. He was waving his arms as if he had been set on fire.

The crowd went silent. Leonardo seemed to have inspired an aura of reverence. Even Raphael, who had visited him only a week ago to study some of his drawings, stood there indifferent to Michelangelo's arrival.

"Join us in some enlightened conversation," said Granacci. "We are honored to be here with Leonardo da Vinci!" He hoisted a jug of wine in the air.

"Come, my friend," enthused Rustici. "Or has Oltrarno worn you out?"

"Pay them no mind." Botticelli motioned to him. "Come to me. Kiss me, my son." He lifted his arms.

Everybody knew Botticelli's sugary painting of the naked Venus floating on a golden shell had bought him financial security. The canvas had been sold for a handsome fee, then rolled up and sent to decorate the country seat of a nobleman. Out of respect, Michelangelo received the elder artist's bony embrace, felt gnarled fingers on his back.

"You promised you would visit. Why have you not come?"

Why indeed? Botticelli was a genius of perspective. But *The Birth of Venus* had marked the end of his serious career.

"My work keeps me occupied," Michelangelo declared. The smell of piss wafted from Botticelli; the longer he stood next to the old man, the more his status declined.

It was Leonardo who broke the awkward impasse. "You are the youthful Michelangelo? You add extra gravitas to this already distinctive crowd," he said, voice booming. "We were only now discussing the philosophy of science and art." He waved a page of parchment in the air. "You're familiar with Dante?" He began to read: "'Art, as best it can, doth follow nature, as pupil follows master.'" Michelangelo recognized the passage instantly: Canto XI of Dante's *Inferno*. He had been tutored at the Palazzo Medici, had written madrigals and sonnets himself. He had dined at the table of Lorenzo de' Medici with Cristoforo Landino, who had translated Pliny, Horace and Virgil into the local *volgare*. He eyed

Leonardo, his beautifully curled silver beard, his purple cape with its velvet hood. The old Master of Arts thought him stupid.

"The honor is mine," he said. "Master," he added gracelessly, feeling ridiculous. "Master of *painting*," he added, to clarify.

"A master of painting?" Leonardo repeated. His mood seemed to darken. "Am I to be content or disturbed by this modest compliment? I am not entirely sure." Uneasy laughter from the crowd. "I shall endeavor to be optimistic about the worth of my talent"— he gestured theatrically to Michelangelo—"to this, this wonderfully . . ." He stroked his beard as if to facilitate the search for the right word. "*Young* artist."

Rustici immediately turned his body to Michelangelo and gestured with his hand as if releasing gas from his behind. A wave of laughter went up. Granacci caught Michelangelo by the sleeve and whispered, "He makes fools of us all. But remember, you are among friends."

"There is plenty of time before the sun sets. Dante can wait," announced Leonardo. "I wish to weigh your assertion: that I am a master of painting. For it is true that I do spend some of my days painting. Though if you were to speak to my good and generous clients, you would know that I am also preoccupied by the rigors of mathematical calculations and the invention of military arms. And the drafting of maps, as if from the viewpoint of a bird looking down on the land."

Lippi spoke. "To be called a master of painting is a high compliment." He had been apprenticed to Botticelli's workshop some thirty years before. "On this we can all agree. It is what many of us—myself included—have devoted our lives to."

The crowd murmured in agreement. Lippi's exquisitely colored frescoes in the Strozzi Chapel flashed in front of their minds.

"A compliment, yes, true enough," conceded Leonardo. "Fellow guildsmen, compliments are as easy and cheap as olives. Are they not?" He laughed and looked at each of them in turn. "Painting is a noble pursuit—with this, I am in agreement. Michelangelo, you have demonstrated a fine talent for sculpting stone. I believe you make proud the stonemason and his healer wife who raised you."

Michelangelo was stunned by the old man's audacity. His childhood—how his noble father had put him out to be reared by Agnella until he reached school age—had just been laid out like a dissected heart for all who stood on the public square.

Leonardo was still speaking. "Having observed the arts for more than forty years, I have come to the conclusion that painting is the more noble, greater than sculpting."

Michelangelo felt his face burn. "I cannot agree with your contention—"

"Let us speak of specifics rather than of whether we agree or disagree," interrupted Leonardo. "The life of a sculptor relies on relentless pounding, the waging of dumb strength against nature's densest, hardest stone."

"You know it is more than that." Michelangelo scrambled in his mind to find an argument that might usefully serve him. He felt unhinged; the great Leonardo, twice his age and admired by all, had targeted him for public ridicule.

"I know that sculpting covers a man in white dust, like a baker."

"And I know that your bitterness comes from failure!" shouted Michelangelo, his face twisted with rage. "Your equestrian monument in Milan. You were unable to cast it, and to your shame left it in the lurch." The prior's earlier instruction fully vanished. "Behold the truth! Your sculpture was seventy-five tons of failure!"

Breathing hard, he scanned the faces of the crowd. A few seemed mildly amused. Granacci looked away. Most of them regarded him with embarrassment and disbelief. "Everybody knows the story," he continued, unable to rein himself in. "You make fantasies, mathematical nonsense and designs"—here, he flipped his hands in the air dismissively—"and those Milanese capons believed in your ability to do it!"

There was an uneasy quiet.

Then: "You speak the truth, my son," Leonardo said, his voice a velvet baritone. "The duke of Milan asked me to raise a great monument to honor his father. He was an excellent patron. I wanted very much to please him. I owed him that."

The crowd held still, as if paying respect to a lost friend.

"I labored over that giant horse statue for nearly twenty years. I visited the best stables in search of the finest horses, made countless studies. I wanted to show the beauty of the free, noble horse," he said. "In the end, I could not find a way to cast it. The French were invading. The duke needed the bronze for cannons." He paused and looked up to the heavens.

Then Leonardo did something nobody expected. He laughed—without any trace of bitterness, but genuinely, as if the folly of man stupefied him. "To no avail! The French marched into Milan. My clay model? It might have been the biggest equestrian monument ever. But it ended up being destroyed during target practice by French bowmen. That is the awful truth. My dream was destroyed and I came home," he concluded, lifting his chin. "Here I am."

The crowd murmured in agreement. Leonardo had won the vote of sympathy, had shown Michelangelo to be petty and brutish.

Botticelli attempted reconciliation. "Leonardo, we hold your opinion in high esteem. But we recognize, too, the extraordinary talent of Michelangelo."

"I saw your *Pietà* at old Saint Peter's church," said Raphael, turning to face Michelangelo. "Your sculpture of the young mother holding her dead son on her knees. My God, love and forgiveness are alive in that work."

"And we know it's yours, since you engraved your signature across the front," cracked Rustici, rubbing his nose; it was red and inflamed from excessive drink.

"What of it?" countered Michelangelo, still enraged. "My family comes from ancient nobility." He looked accusingly at Leonardo. "I have a first and last name. I will sign my full name on my works when I please. My family lineage pleases me."

"Did you include your address, too?" Rustici asked, laughing. The crowd broke into hoots of delight.

"Rustici hasn't had work for months," said Granacci, to soothe Michelangelo. "Let's go. Now." He bowed low to Leonardo.

Michelangelo followed, aware that the face of a coward is the back of his head.

Chapter 14

Brilliant red feathers. Sharp spurs on the back of his legs. One eye that was permanently shut. Her rooster was a magnificent bird. A fighter with more wins than losses. Gleaming with health, so unlike the lumpen fowl of Florence that luxuriated on shit-stained saints of marble and ate whatever garbage was thrown their way in the city's streets and piazzas. Her bird had driven away the foxes and the badgers. He was the king of her stone hut. At night before sundown, when the sky was misted over with loneliness and regret, Beatrice would crouch on the ground next to him, stroking his plumage, the bird tolerating her caresses while standing guard against predators. She would tell the story of her mother's grand return, treating him as a treasured confidant, though he refused to look her in the eye and she found herself losing interest in the truth of the story.

Tonight, she lay exhausted on the depleted sacks of grain outside her front door after having walked the streets of Florence in

search of her mother. She had dared to roll her cart into the courtyards of some of the grand mansions, imagining that her mother
might have found happy employment as a servant to a noble
family. At midday, under the hot Tuscan sky, nobody was around.
She drew her mother's face—what she remembered of it—on the
foundation wall below the massive rusticated stone facade on one
of the palazzi, and was deepening the drapery of her gown when
she was set upon by a guard. Short and stocky, he lifted her easily
off the ground by the back of her gambeson and kicked her in
the backside. She sprang to her feet like a cat and hurled abuse
at him. "Old toad, may you be dragged through the streets on
your ass." He smacked her head against an iron ring extruding
from the wall, used for harnessing horses. Stars clouded her eyes
and she unleashed a feral cry. It was delicious to scream her rage
about what she had lost and could no longer find. He unsheathed
his dagger and lunged at her, and she sent her nails into his eyes,
crumpling the man and allowing her the chance to escape. Limp-
ing home with a throbbing headache, she'd heard herself grunting
from the effort of pushing her broken cart up the hills from Florence, and was disgusted by her new life as a shoeless donkey.

Grace came from her birds, the way they seemed delighted by
her arrival at the end of the day. She and the cock walked toward
the terraced grove in search of some olives decent enough to eat.
She shared whatever she found with her birds, a few kernels of
corn, a maggot scratched from the ground. Then she climbed
one of the trees and waited in the crutch of two branches. "*Vieni!*
Vieni!" she called to the cock. The hen and the baby chicks scattered and wandered idly back to the front step. The rooster stood

still, head in perfect profile, body balanced on twig legs, finally trotting toward her. She called to him again, praising him—it was stupid, but Michelangelo had done the same with her—and he flew up into the branches to sit next to her, his plumage piled high on his tiny head, looking like a pompous ass. "*Il Papa*, here you are. King of the castle."

From her perch in the olive tree, she looked at her little stone hut. Once it had been a place of family joy. "*È romantico!*" her mother would shout, arms flung wide, face lifted to the sky. Beatrice remembered the annual tasting of fresh-pressed oil with her *mamma e papà* at her side. Usually in late November. They would gather under this very olive tree, her parents smiling at her timid dipping, urging her to soak the flatbread in the golden-green liquid. The sound of their laughter, the smell of fresh-cut grass filling her nostrils. "*Su dai*, Beatrice," her father would say, pushing more of the goodness of the oiled bread at her. Her mother, leaning forward, hands gripping the arms of her husband and daughter, would say, "*Ti voglio bene*," eyes filled with tears, ever thankful, ever dramatic. And Beatrice, mouth stuffed to overflowing, would wave her arms, eyes bulging, finally exclaiming, to the delight of her parents: "*Buonissimi!*"

Now the olive groves looked threatening, unknowable. In the shadows, she imagined the trees taking on the bulky shapes of monstrous bears, the bark crawling with spiders, the branches twisting like snakes. She hated living in the hut by herself, but was determined to make herself scarce in the village to avoid the possibility of being labeled an orphan and turned over to the authorities to live out her days in an asylum or convent. She had stayed clear of Agnella these last weeks, growing armor as strong as iron to harden her heart.

Nobody would know of her fears.

"*Il Papa, vieni e vedi!*" She dropped out of the tree and picked up a tattered linen sheet left on the ground. She waved it impatiently at the cock. The Pope stood looking off into the distance, one eye open, the other shut. "*Il Papa, vieni!*" This was their version of a bullfight, something the Spanish liked to do, something she had heard artists joke about in the back lanes. She shook the sheet again, willing the bird to charge like a proper bull and make her think less about her loneliness.

Beatrice was aware of her own smell, and her menses had flowed between her thighs a few days earlier. Despite what Agnella had advised, it had been weeks since she had bathed. The river was a long walk away, and it was shrouded in forest ivy and willows.

The sun spread a final wash of pink across the horizon, the color lingering before the sky deepened to black. A waxing moon. The promise of stars. And no bullfight. Beatrice pulled the length of linen wide behind her back and flapped her arms, generating a cool breeze. She thought of a song her mother would sing to her during the olive harvest: "You feed among the lilies, surrounded by a choir of virgins." As she sang the song aloud, she turned a slow circle in the dirt, head down, eyes closed: "A bridegroom beautiful with glory and giving rewards to his brides."

That night she took the chicks in her skirts and set them down in the crate in her hut. The hen considered coming inside, but finally turned and wobbled away to the hutch. But the cock took up his watch, as he often did, from the foot of her bed. Beatrice toppled onto the straw mattress and pulled the blanket of hemp beside her thin body. Her thoughts drifted to sketching on the wall, with Michelangelo standing next to her. The feel of his hand, his gentle coaxing as she drew her little bird. She missed him. But his studio had been locked the last two times she had attempted to visit. Leonardo, too, had been absent, gone to work as an engineer for Cesare Borgia, the new duke of Romagna. Paolo had told her that Leonardo was assigned to make maps of territories to conquer.

Her legs cramped from the day of walking, and she bounced them on the mattress to offer rough comfort. It was too hot for a blanket, and its scratchiness reminded her that it was the one her family had used as a net to capture olives shaken from the trees during harvest. The other blankets had been bartered away for food—even a wool blanket given to her by Agnella. Settling her legs on the bed, she thought about Leonardo: the artist who freed birds was also somebody who worked for warlords. It seemed strange to her. "But we live in a time of war," enthused Paolo when she impulsively visited the studio that day. "Leonardo sometimes works in his own dream world, sometimes for the real world. He has a great talent for inventing war machinery!" He stirred the pot of beans and garlic and did not offer the ladle to Beatrice. "Come back in two or three months. He'll be home then. I'm away now to the market." And he shooed her away with his hands, as if she were a mouse come to spoil the baking.

She felt the weight of the day crash upon her like the felling of an ancient oak. The chicks had gone silent. The cock stepped fretfully across the bed. Finally, when the moon rose high, the bird tucked its head deep into its feathers and slept.

❖

She was awakened by the sound of footsteps outside the hut. Many footsteps, moving around outside. Male voices urging further action. Something heavy and blunt pounding on the door.

She opened her eyes and watched the cock watching her, warning her from his one good eye. She felt her body trembling and found it impossible to move. There was another crashing against the door, and she listened with terror to the groaning of the iron rods that braced it shut. She looked again at *Il Papa* and heard her father's words: "Do not be useless to yourself." Heeding his words, she rose soundlessly and pulled the rooster tight to her breast. There was only one window in the hut, a small square carved high on the wall, inaccessible except by ladder and barely big enough to fit a man. There was no way to escape but down.

Soundlessly, the hemp blanket tangled around her legs, she lifted the chicks into her skirt pockets. She opened the cellar door and descended gingerly down the ladder steps with The Pope nestled against her. The blanket snaked behind her and she yanked its length down into the cool, muffled depths. The cellar was a storehouse for barrels of vinegar, wine and a salt box. Once there had been jars of oil, but Beatrice had sold them. The rooster adjusted its feathers and cooed softly. She pulled the trapdoor down and tightened her grip on the bird. She could feel the depth of its feathers, tracing her fingers along a raised scar from a cockfight.

Wood splitting apart. It sounded like a fork of thunder, right there, overhead. The cock shifted against her. He must not crow. He must be invisible, like her.

A memory came to her of a time when she and two of her friends became invisible inside the thick, rugged branches of a cypress tree. They had decided to climb the tallest one in the valley, and they scaled its interior until their hands were raw and their thighs shook with the effort. But none of them would stop until they reached the top. How beautiful it was—to sway on the thinnest of the branches and see the valley stretch in dimensions far beyond what they had ever known. How quietly enlightening it was to be suspended above the ground and realize that the earth, like people, had a soul. Though they were terrified of falling, there was comfort in bearing witness together.

If you were loved, people would go to you, be your companion, hear your story, she thought, her hands buried in the bird's feathers. Jesus was never alone. Even on the crucifix, his Mother was with him. If you were going to suffer, it was better to be with someone. Not to share the pain with that person, but to learn from it. If you showed people your pain, you were also showing your weakness. That you were a fallen star. Nobody wanted to witness that. Stars belonged up high in the sky.

The cock escaped and flew to the top rung of the cellar ladder above her, ruffling his feathers and preparing to crow. Without hesitation, she grabbed for the bird and slammed him against her chest. There was nobody to bear witness, she thought, nobody to help her with what she had to do. She felt the bird's jagged breastbone, and the pulse of his heart, his body vibrating with the need to crow. She listened, thought she heard the growl of men directly above her, and others with their fists on the door. She located The Pope's throat with a hand and squeezed. The bird kicked back its long spurs, dragging them along her chest and ripping open her skin. He pounded against her grip, tearing at her, bloodying her clothes.

Her father had not fought the Pisans hard enough, and she had never forgiven him for this. She refused to succumb. Death would not claim her today. She twisted the bird's neck and heard it snap, and still the spurs kicked back. Dear Pope, dear Pope. My God, forgive me for this. They fought against each other until his claws went limp and the vibrations stopped. Silence descended. No sound of footsteps. No crowing.

When she reached Agnella's home in the village, dawn was breaking the face of the dark. Beatrice held the dead cock in her arms, blood from her wounds pasted onto her chest and splattered on her face. She walked stiffly through the garden, its lavender shining with dew, and registered the clatter of a copper pot, the smell of freshly baked bread. She kicked the door with her naked foot and cried out. Agnella heaved open the door, a knife in one hand, a thick stick in the other. A pounding on the door never brought blessed news.

Beatrice's body was convulsing and she could not speak. She held the bird up like a sick offering, her hands gripping its wrinkled neck. "I'm sorry," she said at last, dropping to her knees. "I'm sorry. But I have no one."

Without hesitating, Agnella pried the cock away from her and set the bloody mess down in the garden. "You are here and alive," she said, kneeling, holding Beatrice close to her, whispering in her ear: "You and I, we will survive together. Promise me that."

Beatrice nodded, her face blotched and gray.

"We are all alone at times," Agnella said. She took her knife and punched it into the heel of her own hand. Without flinching, breathing a prayer, she pressed her warm burst of blood to the gash in Beatrice's chest. "There," she said, holding her wound against Beatrice's body until she could be sure their blood had intermingled. "I'll be your witness."

Chapter 15

Beatrice agreed to stay with Agnella while she recovered from the trauma of the home invasion. In truth, she had only imagined them breaking into the hut; the iron security rods were still intact when she emerged from the cellar early that morning. But the men had wrecked the hutch and taken the hen. Thankfully, they had not found her cart in the shed. Agnella brought it back to her manor in the village.

Life took on a rhythm of its own, though an undercurrent of anxiety haunted Beatrice day and night. She refused to step outside to chop wood or feed the chickens. Instead, she sat curled next to the hearth inside and made bread with Agnella, adding rosemary, olives and garlic from the garden for taste and texture. They even, in an act of defiance, threw a teaspoon of salt into the mix, knowing they were offending the Tuscan gods of saltless bread. "Love over rules," said Agnella, brushing wisps of blond hair away from her face. "That's how you make an interesting life—and good bread."

"Am I safe living here with you?" Beatrice asked this question several times a day, drumming her fingers on the table, looking around nervously. "You're not a witch, are you?"

That was another of her regular questions. Agnella shot her looks, half-ironic, half-exasperated, and would go outside to feed the chickens, or continue braiding her hair. She knew this was part of Beatrice's trauma, that the girl's mind was a jumble of terrifying thoughts.

Her third most favorite question was about the origin of Agnella's bracelets, which rang like music whenever she moved her arms.

"This thick gold one was gifted to me by the governor for curing his daughter of excruciating stomach pain."

"What ailed her?" asked Beatrice, kneading the bread on the wooden table.

"Nothing more than her first menses. She was cured with a peppermint tisane, some spinal twists and me listening to her story of unrequited love."

"Typical girl," said Beatrice. "I wish I'd had sisters to talk about all of this when I was growing up."

Agnella screwed up her face and shot a hard look at her. "You're still growing up."

"I'm sixteen!"

"This one with the emerald jewels on silver was given to me by a duke," said Agnella, ignoring her response.

"Duke Cesare Borgia?" Beatrice asked, naming the duke Paolo had mentioned during her last visit to Leonardo's studio.

"Long before his reign. No, this was a duke who was part of the Medici family. That was a glorious time. Dining on pheasant stewed in berries, dancing in fountains." Agnella poured herself a glass of Chianti from the wine carafe and another, watered down, for Beatrice.

"Sounds romantic."

"It was, for a while. But affairs with married men never really work out." She splashed some olive oil onto the bread dough, and Beatrice continued to knead. "These three with the quartz nuggets were made by my dead husband." She hesitated before adding flatly, "He loved me more than I could love him." She sighed and continued, "This one with the inlaid ebony and ivory was from an Arab silk trader who wanted to bring me back to his homeland."

There were also two bracelets carved from jade. "From a Florentine navigator who needed to be cured of scurvy, and a Portuguese adventurer who had brought sugar cane from an island called Caribbean."

When Beatrice had collapsed on her doorstep, Agnella had lifted her into her arms, shocked by how thin the girl had become, and carried her inside. At first she was inconsolable, screaming about how she had murdered the cock, shivering badly and rocking her body against the bed. A girl living alone outside the village was a public invitation for early death. Agnella knew Beatrice to be a stubborn and fierce fire spirit, but to honor the memory of the girl's mother, she insisted that Beatrice move into the village with her. Agnella believed Leda had traveled into her own private Hell, the way Eurydice lingered in Hades. It wasn't enough that women were beaten up by men and condemned to life with the same rights as cattle. Their trauma inspired them to punish themselves further—it only seemed natural—and so they ran from the children they loved to commit themselves to other, hideous forms of life. Leda was her friend and Agnella was determined to find her. But Leda would stay hidden until she was ready.

When Beatrice was done raging at the world, Agnella brought warm compresses and washed the girl, easing her into some fresh wraps. It was only then that she discovered two chicks buried in the pockets of Beatrice's old skirt. She pulled them out and set them against the girl's cheeks. They stayed there for much of the night, reviving her beyond what any of Agnella's elixirs might have done.

The women ate and tended the garden. Beatrice slept deeply. But on her fifth morning with Agnella, her mood changed. "I want to find my mother," said Beatrice. She was staring out across the hills toward the Duomo. "I want to find her. Mamma is in the city. I know she is."

Agnella set down the slop pail for the chickens and turned quietly to the girl.

"Somebody has her. I know they do!" cried Beatrice, and she pulled away from Agnella when she tried to comfort the girl.

Agnella detected in Beatrice's strangled voice the same desperation she had felt when Michelangelo was taken from her at seven years old, a bright, warm-hearted boy with a serious brow that held the wisdom of an old man. She had spoon-fed him home-made chicken broth whenever he caught a cold, taught him about the moon and the seasons, and her husband had showed him how to chisel stone. Abruptly, without warning, Michelangelo's father had trotted his horse-drawn wagon to the modest stone house to pick up his boy. Michelangelo had reached the age, in his father's words, of "sufficient civilization."

Agnella's husband died not long afterward, and she was gutted by grief so strong it broke down the walls she had long since built around her heart. Agnella had never revealed to anyone, not even her husband, that she had escaped from a village north of Florence (measured by a distance of two weeks of running), close to the Swiss border. The region had been slow to convert to Christianity and some of the old pagan ways hung about. Harmless rituals—performed by Agnella's mother and her friends—such as waving wispy-green fennel branches in the air to inspire fertility among people and their animals. But the church did not take kindly to such devilish heresy, and sought out the women who had, apparently, brought sickness to the area and caused thunder and lightning storms. Her mother and aunts were all burned at the stake for their maleficent deeds. To save her life, Agnella had been instructed to escape to the south. She had never been able to bury the wise, tender women who raised her, but she could hide the truth, like a walnut buried deep in the earth.

She had already learned to repair broken limbs and mend dagger wounds, and she offered these services quietly to her fellow villagers, eventually commanding decent wages for her expertise at healing the variously afflicted wealthy in Florence. The villagers suspected her of being a witch, but they never openly accused her—especially because she helped them birth their babies. Agnella liked the Tuscans well enough. They were taciturn and given to hard work in the name of "God and profit." But she never told them the truth about her past, or that her last name, della Francesca, was made up.

"Stand up, girl," she ordered now. "Stand up and be strong. The weakest of the flock will be the first to be devoured by the wolf packs."

Beatrice slowly got to her feet.

"Let me tell you something. The world is broken. People have gone mad. For those of us living out here in the hills, surviving is the only thing that matters, day after day, night after night."

Beatrice nodded and wiped her nose on her sleeve. "How do you survive?" she asked, her eyes large and watery.

"Tending to others helps me forget my own pain."

"Your clients in the city?"

"Yes. One of them, Lisa Gherardini, is rich with silk money," said Agnella. "But her child is failing to thrive. It's a miracle she has survived this long. I believe the mother suffers from a disease of melancholia."

"Only the wealthy could invent such a disease," said Beatrice.

Agnella knew what Beatrice was thinking: sickness was easy to understand; it looked like boils protruding from people's necks and legs weeping with rashes. Melancholia must sound as strange to her as breathing underwater. She looked thoughtfully at Beatrice and said, "She could benefit from the presence of someone young and vibrant. Will you travel with me to Florence to tend to Madonna Gherardini?"

Beatrice hesitated and looked at the ground. "I'll go with you," she said at last. "In exchange, will you help me find my mother?"

Agnella nodded. "I see you have become skilled at bartering," she said. "Well, then. Tomorrow we begin."

Chapter 16

"Move your hand in a circle—follow the curve of nature."

Beatrice slowed her hand as she continued to grind the leeks and peach-tree leaves with the pestle. She looked over at the woman lying on the bed, her eyes closed, her face defiant, her hair disguised within a black scarf.

"That's fine," Agnella encouraged, speaking in a low whisper as she poured an infusion of cabbage seeds into the healing paste, one drop at a time.

They had started the search for Beatrice's mother in the line where people waited restlessly to get past the monumental brick wall encircling the city. Agnella did most of the talking, using her honeyed voice to press people to pay attention, asking whether they had seen a woman with auburn hair and a long neck, like this girl's, in the line. And she would angle her head toward Beatrice. "Or inside the city? She would be wearing long linen skirts and a regular blouson."

"Sounds like every one of us standing around here," a woman cackled at them. "Unblessed slugs, too ugly to be adorned." The crowd laughed at the keen observation. They were all dressed in ragged clothes—natural fabrics—without the luxury of colorful dyes.

The hunt for her mother had given Beatrice fresh purpose, made her mind gleam with focus, but here, in the private boudoir of Agnella's patient, she grew impatient. This Madonna Lisa woman's home was a spectacle of texture and color. How could a woman not bother opening her eyes when she was surrounded with such visual riches? Silk taffeta hanging from wooden posts, pillows covered in burgundy and pink velvets, portraits of the Virgin Mary haloed and glowing behind thick golden frames. Even the water carafe was vividly colored, a floral pattern cast in a luminous blue.

A servant carrying a tray of food entered the room. Beatrice eyed the food hungrily: bread coated with crushed olives, medallions of partridge arranged among plump orange sections. Beatrice knew she was meant to feel sorry for Madonna Lisa, mother of a four-year-old daughter who was slowly failing to breathe. Unable to bear the impending loss, Lisa had surrendered to a dark humor— an immobilizing *malinconia*—that left her incapable of comforting her child. A heavy sheet of black wool hung over the bedroom window, blocking out the sunshine, signaling the mourning that had already descended for the imminent loss of Piera.

The signora waved the servant away, not bothering to look at the food. Agnella took the healing bowl from Beatrice, who had ground the herbs to a satisfactory pulp. She took a pinch of the poultice into her left hand and rubbed it across Lisa's forehead, then unlaced the strings of the woman's nightgown and rubbed the plaster over her chest.

"Agnella?" said Lisa, her voice hoarse.

"I am here," said the healer, her bracelets jingling against her skin. "Give me your hands."

The woman lifted her hands limply in the air. Agnella coated each with paste. "*Segnalo qui*," she said, taking a short willow stick and etching the sign of the cross over the back of the woman's hands and into the paste on her forehead. She signaled to Beatrice to light the candles encircling the bed: thirty-three votives, representing Christ's age when he died. Next, she placed fennel seeds in a basin and added a small wooden cross. "*Erbe medicinale*," she said, pushing the basin under the woman's bed. "*Erbe medicinale*," she said louder, throwing a handful of fennel into the fire. Her arms moved in sweeping circles as sweet-smelling smoke drifted across the room.

Agnella bent over the woman. "Have you had any flows this month?"

"No," whispered the woman, a look of shame on her face. "Nothing."

"May I see for myself?" The woman nodded slowly, and Beatrice watched Agnella press her hands gently, deeply into the woman's stomach. "The belt," Agnella instructed, holding out her hand.

Beatrice removed a thin leather belt from a pouch. Agnella had told her the belt had been worn for a week by a virgin boy and inscribed by him with a prayer of healing. Something from the old religion, with words like "mirth," "Diana" and "Mars." She looped the belt behind the woman's back and buckled it securely at her waist.

"Will it cure me?" asked Lisa.

"It contains powerful ingredients, a recipe handed down to me from my grandmother. But the belt's magic depends on you. You must want to heal yourself."

Agnella moved her hands slowly in a circular motion on the woman's stomach. She watched as Lisa's shoulders dropped and relaxed against the bed. Some of the pain creased on her forehead softened. "Beatrice, would you take some quattrini and fetch fruit for Lisa?"

Beatrice took coins from the table and walked out of the room, closing the heavy wooden door behind her. She stepped onto the marble floor of the grand hallway and looked up at a skylight made from colorful patches of glass; rays of red and pink reflected on the floor. She slid her freshly washed bare foot forward and watched as it turned the color of a pomegranate. The same thing happened when she reached her hand below the skylight. She removed the wreath of flowers from her head, the one she had made at Agnella's, whistling softly as the white lilies became red as roses.

She heard the woman groan inside the bedroom. Agnella had told her that to lessen the grief and hysteria that were poisoning Lisa's body, she might be required to induce her female fluids. Not by using cups to draw blood out of her body; rather, she might draw out the woman's creamy white liquid by massaging the lips between her thighs using a technique shared by the sisterhood. It sounded mysterious and unpleasant. Jumping lightly down the grand, spiraling staircase, Beatrice was glad she had been excused.

Outside, reaching her cart, she eased her knife out of the handle and slid it inside her shoulder pouch. She could walk to the old marketplace in front of the Basilica of San Lorenzo, but instead, she pocketed the copper coins and headed in the opposite direction, to the trees she most preferred. As she walked through the streets, she watched the crowds with special attention, tuning her eyes for the profile of her mother, the square of her shoulders, her gentle, brooding face framed by auburn curls. She stepped around chickens pecking at a large patch of grain left to dry on the road. Then she arrived at the familiar stone wall and started to climb, balancing on the top of the wall and leaping into a robust fig tree. Landing safely, she twisted her body to secure a handhold on the branch above and slipped her blade from its pouch, placing it between her teeth.

"Thief!"

Her hand froze in midair. She looked toward her accuser, heart pounding, prepared for the worst: time in a dungeon or a public flogging.

It was Michelangelo. She stood motionless on the branch, staring down at him. Eyes never leaving him, she threw him a ripened fruit.

"I'd come down from there if I were you," he warned, biting into the fig. "The owners might have you beaten."

She deposited figs in her pouch, slid her knife back in and dropped lightly to the ground, a touch of color rising to her face. He was wearing a green silk tunic that emphasized his black curls and deepened the rugged blush of his cheeks. He seemed relaxed, even boyish. Not like a man suffering from personal doubts and fears.

"You look fine," she said.

"Haven't seen you for a while. Not a drop of your olive oil is left."

She wanted to tell him how much she had missed him, about the men who had surrounded her home, about the rooster she had killed with her own hands. It was strange and unsettling to meet him outside of the studio. "My work, my other friends keep me occupied," she offered, revealing nothing, preserving her dignity.

"Too busy for an old friend?" He smiled and shook his head.

She dipped her head, grateful for their encounter. It seemed she could count on his friendship.

There was a peal of laughter and Granacci and Rustici appeared from around the corner, jostling each other. "Brother!" called out Granacci. Michelangelo clapped him on the back, allowing Granacci to pull him into a bear hug.

"Excuse us for interrupting," said Rustici, elbow jutting into Michelangelo's side.

"Who do we have here?" prompted Granacci, wagging a finger. "Wait, I know you."

"Indeed, you are one of my finest customers," said Beatrice. "You buy my oil, my lemons, even my lavender."

"She's a beauty for a slut," said Rustici to Michelangelo.

Beatrice looked at Michelangelo, hoping he might come to her defense. He had praised her sketch of the goldfinch on his studio wall. Perhaps he would introduce her as a fellow artist.

Michelangelo said nothing. His eyes were flitting in his distracted way from the sky to the stone cobbles, no doubt feeling uncomfortable with his friends meeting her in the street.

"Best to ignore Rustici," Michelangelo finally said. "He's one of those too young to get married, too old to be called a baby. And it's easy to hate him."

"Remind me of your name?" added Granacci.

Beatrice still bristled from Rustici's comment, but she had always enjoyed Granacci's company. He was a gentleman whenever she made deliveries to his studio.

"Beatrice," she said, dipping her head.

"An honor to know you," enthused Granacci, bowing low. "I believe you deliver to many of us in the laneway. And over by the Santissima Annunziata monastery—to Leonardo, too?"

"I do," she said.

"Have you seen his flying machine?" said Rustici. "Amazing mind, full of fantasies, though nobody will pay for that."

"Somebody with a bottomless pit of riches might," said Granacci.

A bottomless pit of riches. *Ricco sfondato.* Beatrice's mind flashed to Madonna Lisa lying in her splendid bed, rank with the odor of the unwashed.

"Yes, olive oil girl, tell us what you know." Michelangelo demanded this as if she were the lowest of servants. "He's not painting at all?" he pressed, stepping closer to her.

"There's no need to pry," said Granacci.

"I want to know," he insisted. "What is our friend Leonardo painting?"

Beatrice shrugged and bit into a fig. Birds flying free danced in her mind. A man suspended in the air, arms strapped into monster wings. At this moment, she hated Michelangelo, every aspect of his being. She thought about taking her knife from its pouch and cutting out his poisonous tongue. Gentle as a lamb one day, abusive the next, he made Florence rusty as a nail, not golden.

"Leonardo has been working for Duke Borgia these last months," she said, happy to impress with her knowledge. "Mapping, machinery of destruction. Serious projects—not pretty sculptures of naked men." She looked hard at the men standing around her.

Michelangelo observed her, no doubt noting the angry curl to her lips.

"He is to paint a portrait of a lady," she added.

"A portrait always pays," said Granacci, leaning into the conversation.

"Will she hold an ermine, or a bear in her arms?" said Rustici, laughing at his awkward joke.

"You insult the brilliance of Leonardo. Have you any portraits to better his?" Beatrice felt a flush of anger rising to her cheeks.

"And you, village girl?" said Rustici, puffing up his chest. "Come from the hills to fill us with your opinions?"

"My father was a poet," she said, ignoring him. "Probably more literate than you. He taught me about Greek philosophers, Euripides, Aristotle. That we should avoid being boors. And avoid the trap of vanity," she continued, eyes sliding over to Granacci. "Being truthful is what Aristotle wanted for us." She met Michelangelo's eyes again. "This is not always easy." She smiled bitterly, thinking of Constantinople, the stories of the epic city she had heard from her parents, huddled around a fire in their village outside the little city of Florence. Of killing the cock to save herself from the home invaders. "But now my father is dead. So is Aristotle."

The men stood still, chastened, and nobody spoke. Michelangelo stared at Beatrice, intrigued.

"Something else I know," she said, face lifted, shoulders thrown back. "Olive oil. Mine is requested by Leonardo da Vinci himself."

She added, "He pours it over bread with mozzarella. His cook creates art with food. I have tasted it myself."

The return to da Vinci and art soured Michelangelo's mood. "So now cheese is art," he said, raising his voice to a high nasal pitch to mock the formal language of the newly wealthy in Florence. "And I should become a cook, not a sculptor."

Granacci and Rustici hooted in appreciation.

"You look like a baker most times," she shot back. "All covered in dust—it might as well be flour." Beatrice looked directly at him. "My lords," she said, with a short curtsy and irony lacing her voice. "I must take my leave. *Salve.*"

"Beatrice?" Michelangelo called after her. "Tell the old man that while he wastes his time on fantasies and flying machines, Michelangelo is creating a new hero for the city."

His friends pounded him on the back and then hoisted him up into the air, but she ignored them and turned the corner, eyes lifted, searching the crowd for her mother: a head of auburn hair, curls caressing her neck.

The sun was high in the sky by the time Beatrice returned to Madonna Lisa's mansion on the Via della Stufa. She bounded up the marble steps to the woman's private quarters.

Agnella was not in the room. Beatrice looked around, uncertain about her role. Confirming that the signora's eyes were closed, she stepped past the blacked-out window to a dresser adorned with a washing basin. Her fingers touched the ivory handle of Lisa's brush and caressed the blue glass bottles, each one curved and shapely, like a woman's body. After a quick glance to make sure Lisa's eyes were still closed, she dared to uncork one of the bottles. The perfume was a sweeter, purer version of the incense priests burned in church. She doused her wrists in the magical liquid and inhaled deeply. Except for the steady whisper of the client's breathing, the room was a tomb of silence.

"Were you born so rich?" she said, her voice low, stepping to the bed. The woman's face had gone pale. Maybe death would claim her, as well as the child. She felt a flare of anger rise up in her, that the world was ugly and unjust.

At that moment, Agnella appeared. She shot Beatrice a warning glance, moving efficiently to check the pulse of the silk merchant's wife. "Beatrice," she said. "Did you purchase fruit for Madonna Lisa?"

Beatrice took out a fig and twirled it between her fingers. Agnella nodded and sat down on the bed, her eyes shadowed with sadness.

"What happened?" asked Beatrice.

"Piera's cough is bad. Even clapping my hands on her back to encourage the phlegm to clear was useless."

Beatrice reached out and gripped Agnella's hands. They were not given to displays of affection and had not touched each other since she had clung to Agnella after the killing of the cock. But now she held the healer's warm hands in her own.

Agnella's voice was laced with doubt. "There is not much more I can do, except for some cooling cloths for Piera. She's burning up with fever." Agnella looked at Lisa. "Try your best to keep her calm."

"How?"

"Be inventive," she said. "Remember to concentrate. You can't run after two hares at the same time."

Kneeling there, alone with Madonna Lisa, Beatrice looked up and discovered a fresco of dancing angels painted in light, frothy colors, as if Heaven were something sweet to eat. In each of the high corners of the room were sculptures of cupids. Compared to her own human versions of putti, they looked overly fleshy, with bodies fattened on goose fat, ill equipped for flight.

From outside the room, she could hear music approaching. It was one of the ways Florence mesmerized her—the range of instruments that musicians would play in the streets, producing sounds lush and beckoning, far beyond the thin, reedy sounds made by the penny whistlers in Settignano. In one leap, she was at the window to listen. The shawm—how wonderfully delicate its sound was! She preferred it to the loud fifes and drums played at carnivals as sing-along catches. The latch on the window was easy to release, and so Beatrice found herself suddenly bathed in the brilliant light of the day and the spritely melodies played on three shawms. She leaned out the window to see the musicians. They were wearing red velvet hats adorned with crests of the Florentine lion, and they beckoned to her with their woodwind instruments. Without willing it, she was suddenly dancing lightly on her feet, her hands raised delicately by her head. By the time she had finished dancing through three more songs, sweat had pooled on her lips and between her breasts. A breeze floated in from outside, refreshing the morbid room.

"You came here to dance in my room?"

Beatrice turned to face the woman, whose eyes were now open.

"Madonna, I am sorry. I did not intend to wake you," she said, quickly closing the window shutters.

"No," came the order. "Leave them open so that I may see it is not always night. Come here, girl. Tell me your name." Lisa spoke in whispered, halting tones, as if testing the timbre of her voice.

"I am Beatrice."

"The object of Dante's love." The patient looked steadily at Beatrice, challenging her.

Beatrice dropped to her knees and leaned in closer to the woman in the bed. "Can you believe that Dante waited nine years before daring to speak to her?" she said, delighted to engage. Her mother and father had told her of the love story many times.

"The fool. Wasting time, the life they could have enjoyed together." Lisa picked up Beatrice's hands and pressed them against her nose. "You smell like my perfume."

"What do you call it?"

"Frankincense mixed with myrrh and lavender."

"It's beautiful."

"You're a girl born to be carefree. It's beautiful on you."

"Is anyone truly carefree? I think not," said Beatrice, eyeing the pillow, the lace that her mother might have made with her *tombolo* spools not so long ago. She remembered her station, Agnella's instruction. "I brought you fruit. May I cut you some slices?" She pulled a fig from her leather bag and peeled back the skin with her knife. Realizing that Lisa was unable to feed herself, she cut a small piece and pushed it gently between her lips. Lisa chewed and considered. "It tastes good enough," she said at last. "Fresher than most. Which market did you find it at?"

"Oh, it's not purchased. The best figs come straight from the trees of your neighbors."

Lisa looked at her quizzically and said nothing.

"Shall I rub your feet?" Beatrice asked awkwardly, anxious to fill the silence. She set to doing so, massaging the insteps with her thumbs as her mother had taught her years ago. "I find it relaxes. By the way, you have a nice face. Naturally handsome." She was happy to talk, even if her tongue might run away from her. "My mother would say: 'You are blessed with all of the female perfections. Three long: hair, hands and legs. Three short: teeth, ears and breasts. Three red: cheeks, lips and nipples.'" She tugged some of the coverlet into her hand, making a ball with the fine silk. "She liked to tease me," she said, eyes cast down. "I miss that."

Lisa turned her head slightly, a flick of concern showing in her eyes.

"If I had a gold florin in my pocket, I'd buy myself boots," muttered Beatrice, "or that flying machine Leonardo wants to create."

Lisa looked up to the ceiling and pressed her hands against the silk sheets, smoothing them below her neck.

"I am looking for my mother," added Beatrice. "Maybe you have seen her? Auburn hair, long neck, simple dress. She might have sought work here?"

Lisa shook her head slowly.

"Have a slice for each of your toes," encouraged Beatrice, cutting another fig wedge. Lisa rolled her eyes and accepted the food. "The best thing when you're hungry is to crack an egg on your head and let the liquid slide down your throat. I do that whenever I steal an egg. I mean, borrow an egg from a hen. The bird looks at me, I thank her for the egg and pay her back by feeding her a bit of the shell. City people do not know this—that way, she can make another egg."

Lisa offered a tentative smile. A flush of rose was beginning to brighten her cheeks.

"*Va bene.* That is fine," said Beatrice. "I can tell from your eyes, and your feet."

Lisa nodded and looked directly at her. "Tell Agnella to bring Piera to me. And all of my children." The clarity of her voice surprised Beatrice. "They need their mother. Piera is not yet dead, and neither am I."

Beatrice grasped Lisa's hands and squeezed them tight. "With pleasure. I'll go straightaway."

"And Beatrice, let us not waste time as Dante did," said Lisa. "In the armoire." She motioned with her chin. "Go ahead. Try on my boots. Most of them have never been worn. Find a pair that pleases you."

Chapter 17

By the time they left Madonna Lisa's home, the sun was beating down mercilessly on the city. Agnella clicked her tongue and urged her donkey to manoeuvre slowly through the busy streets, finally arriving at the Duomo. Beatrice sat beside her, head held high, toes wiggling with delight inside the Madonna's lace-up ankle boots. She wished she could brandish a pomander to ward off the evil smells of the streets, as a wealthy Florentine might. And the ride—it was a blissful thing to be pulled by a donkey rather than pulling a cart herself. She set her face to stone, giving nothing away, not even her delight at seeing Madonna Lisa blissfully surrounded by all of her children.

Agnella was still a mystery to Beatrice, less of an evil force than she had feared, more a woman of the earth guided by both intelligence and female intuition, her remedies culled from the land and proffered, Beatrice had to admit, with motherly kindness.

Besides all of her bracelets, Agnella wore three golden rings on her left hand: one from her dead husband; another, she said, for the lovers she'd had; and the third for the lovers to come. "Here," she said, slipping one of the bands from her finger. "It's a pretty thing, like so much within Madonna Lisa's palazzo. Wear it for a while." Beatrice hesitated, cradling the ring in her palm, enjoying the weight of extravagance, before finally slipping it onto her right thumb.

They rode together in silence, past the Basilica of San Lorenzo toward the monumental Duomo, its orange tiles turned to shards of silver by the unforgiving rays of the sun. Anybody who lingered in Agnella's path received a lick of her whip and curses strong enough to make aspens shiver. Leaving the shadows of the Duomo, Agnella guided the cart down the lane of the artists' guild, allowing her body to move in concert with every bump in the road.

The late-afternoon heat soured Beatrice's mood, and she turned to look at the woman sitting tall in the cart. Agnella seemed oblivious to the heat, except for beads of sweat gathering delicately at the highest planes of her cheekbones. Like jewels, Beatrice thought, scowling.

"Can I keep this for a day or two?" Beatrice hoped to wear the ring to impress Michelangelo during her next visit to his studio, to trick him into believing she was worth more than a simple village girl.

"I think not," said Agnella, looking straight ahead and extending her hand. "But did you enjoy wearing it?" She signaled to her donkey and the cart rolled to a stop.

Beatrice set the ring back on the woman's outstretched palm. Agnella slipped it over her knuckle and took up the reins again.

Beatrice felt the heat of the day claw its way down her neck to the small of her back. She longed for the shade of a tree, or to dive into the river, the way boys did. Something twisted in her gut. She needed to confess to Agnella.

"Wait," she said. "You have been good to me. I don't know why I did this." She swept a hand inside her father's gambeson and fished out a silk square, embroidered at each of its corners with a purple lily. She allowed Lisa's handkerchief to drift through the air onto Agnella's patient hand. "Madonna Lisa required a silk, and having none myself . . ."

"That is sufficient, Beatrice. One lie is enough of an annoyance."

"But she called out in the heat!"

"Two lies smell like meat boiled twice. Besides that, you dishonor your chance to be a woman of virtue. Daughters, wives, mothers, sisters—we hold up half the sky."

Beatrice gripped her knees below her skirts and tried to stop the overcrowded thoughts populating her head. It seemed her ability to be good and virtuous was swirling in tight, treacherous circles, caught in a river's eddy, threatening to rush away. Then she felt clarity again.

"Please, can we ride to the Duomo and Piazza della Santissima Annunziata to look for my *mamma*?"

Agnella narrowed her eyes.

"I know: it'll be dark by the time we start for the hills, and it's dangerous," said Beatrice, resigned to going home.

Agnella softened her grip on the reins and walked the wagon past dozens of tiny shops, set cheek-by-jowl, that sold plush crimson velvet and squares of gold leaf to those able to pay with florins.

She watched as Beatrice feasted her eyes on imported berets that shone with tightly woven silk, while strings of silk flowers swayed high in the breeze. The privileged girls would expect the *sarti* tailors to sew the flowers on their head garlands. "Silk is the future of the city," she said. "More and more women will become artists, weaving exquisite gold and silver threads into baudekin brocade and sendal silk." She gestured to the festival of color and craft, inhaling the smells of freshly pressed cheese and bouquets of lavender. "The city is a great creation, and the artists never become wealthy."

"None of this matters to me," said Beatrice impatiently, jabbing a finger into Agnella's side. "My *mamma* is not here."

The bells of the Leone and the Podestà were tolling powerfully in the city to signal the end of the day. Agnella lifted her chin and inspected the thinning crowds on the street. She snapped the whip above the back of the donkey and turned the animal and the wagon down a narrow back lane. The stench of an open latrine made her lift a scarf against her nose. Looking over at Beatrice, she gave her commitment: "We'll search until sundown, and tomorrow we'll start again."

Chapter 18

"You're back!" Beatrice appeared at the door of Leonardo's studio, out of breath, as if she had run across the city to see him.

He was playing his violin, a lira de braccio, the wood of the instrument glistening in the sunlight. "Only love makes me remember," he sang, drawing the bow over the strings, ignoring the girl. "It is the flame of my fire. Of the time we met before."

She was no doubt familiar enough with the way musicians sang their poems while accompanying themselves on their lutes or liras da braccio. Leonardo knew he had a fine voice, deep and sonorous, but she was clearly anxious to get his attention, and it was true, the *frottola* song-poem could go on for a long time.

Shrugging off her father's old quilted gambeson, Beatrice sighed loudly. "Signore?"

He lifted his bow and set the instrument down. What game might she be up to today? What lie might she tell? This abandoned girl with a look of daring etched over her face. He nodded for her to come in. She burst into the room and bounded over to his side. "I was counting the days. I was hoping you would come back to Florence. How was it with the duke, over in Romagna? Were there battles to see or were you safe in a room, making maps?"

Not waiting to hear his reply, she leapt onto fresh topics: "I told Michelangelo and Granacci and his horrid other friend that you had returned. I brought you something." She pulled a twig of juniper from her leather pouch. He motioned to her to come closer. "This is for you. I don't know the name."

He held the greenery in his hand and looked closely. "In Italian, *ginepro*. In English, juniper. In French, *genévrier*."

She looked curious, allowing herself to slow down. "Like the Ginevra you painted once?"

He nodded solemnly.

"In your portrait, you set her against a tree like this to show her with nature, a good person." She mimicked the posture of the girl's portrait. Also known as the filthy rich girl's portrait, she recalled, amused. "Master da Vinci, you selected a big, powerful juniper tree!"

"To symbolize her virtue." He was interested to know where she was going with this.

"See this?" She waved the juniper twig gently in the air. "Little people, little trees." She pointed to the tiny spikes on the twig— miniature trunks and delicate branches, all adding up to exact replicas of a larger tree. "We are one tree, no?" She smiled at him. "You are my father, like this—" she pointed to the spine of the twig. "Michelangelo is your brother." She extended the twig toward Leonardo. "Here. For you." He took the twig and placed it on the table.

"Did you bring olive oil?" He feigned interest, looking longingly back at his lira de braccio sitting idle on the table.

"When I was a little girl, I had friends to play with," she said, ignoring his question and seating herself at the table next to him. "Our stupid little games kept us busy for hours. Making homes for rabbits at the base of trees. Throwing olives at old women walking through the groves. And sometimes we were mean to each other. But nobody else could say mean things about us. That wasn't allowed."

Leonardo nodded and reached for one of his notebooks, full of sketches and rough ideas. He was meant to be working on his altarpiece for the Servites, panels to fill in a big, carved wooden frame. The prior had requested a Deposition of Christ from the Cross for the front and an Assumption of the Virgin at the back. This did not interest Leonardo; after hearing from Francesco Giocondo about his dying child and his wife's refusal to accept the tragedy, he had become more interested in creating a scene about love between mothers and their children. One that would celebrate intimacy and tenderness, flesh pressing against flesh, without any formal stiffness. How good it was to return to drawing scenes of love and humanity—he had seen too much blood and suffering during his time in Romagna working as military engineer for Duke Borgia.

Florentines revered Anne, the mother of Mary, so he'd decided to feature Anne prominently, providing a safe, hallowed lap on which Mary could sit while holding Jesus. The Child would be wrestling out of her arms to connect to Saint John and Heaven above. Using his chalk lightly, rubbing his finger into the darkness, he was attempting to create *il concetto dell'anima*—human feeling—a moment that was always evolving. Emotion is contoured, after all. It is never one straight line.

He weighed the chalk in his hand, considering. Remembering himself, and the girl standing expectantly beside him, he turned his chair toward Beatrice. "Was somebody mean to you?"

"Michelangelo talks about you all the time. He always wants to know what you're making. I think he might be jealous of you."

Leonardo wanted to ignore the girl's comment, brush it away with his hand, but instead he was listening carefully. The governor had asked him to be part of a committee of distinguished Florentines. Their mission was to decide where to place the *David*. Michelangelo was not to be part of their discussions. He would be furious when he found out.

"I tried to tell him about all your important work," she said, chin lifted, surveying the many drawings on the long wooden table. "Portraits and inventing war machines and wanting to fly—and working for Duke Borgia."

"You are a sponge for details. I might have to hire you as my new assistant."

"I'd like that very much," she said. He saw her eyes shimmer with hope. Maybe she could come along with him to some of his meetings. He could make her part of his entourage.

"Michelangelo thinks you can't be trusted, that you'll steal commissions from him." She bent over the table, a hand pressing against her stomach. "Paolo forgot to feed me," she muttered, picking up one of Leonardo's drawings with her free hand. On the page were small studies, each one framed deliberately with pencil.

There was a baby boy reaching a hand across his body and a pair of women, Anne and Mary.

"Mother and daughter," said Leonardo, bending over the drawing with Beatrice. He had wanted to use intense lines and dark shading to unite the family as one.

"They look very close. Pressed together, woven together like rope or braids of hair."

"Do you like it?"

"The way their skirts are draped. I like that. Mostly I like the way it makes me believe again," said Beatrice.

"Believe?"

"The way Mary is sitting easily on her mother's lap, and looking with love at her son, Jesus. It makes me believe in family again."

"A picture is dead, even doubly dead, if it does not affect the viewer," said Leonardo, enjoying the impact his drawing seemed to be having on the girl. He rarely discussed his work with Salaì, and it was dangerous to invite opinions from clients, whether dukes, priors or the fantastically wealthy. They were never satisfied.

"Am I the viewer?" she whispered, still staring at the page.

"Always. Except when you're creating. Then you're the artist."

"Can you tell me what else you're working on? Have you solved the problem of how to fly like a bird? Or how to stop the guards from harassing us at the city gates?" She looked directly at him, and he remembered with sorrow the way his cape had been ripped by the guards.

He set his chalk down and looked over at the girl. "I've been commissioned to paint a portrait of Lisa Gherardini del Giocondo. The wife of a silk merchant. I don't know much about her. Not yet."

"Madonna Lisa. I know her!" shouted Beatrice, looking puffed up with her insider knowledge, as if she had been catapulted into the privileged circles of Florence. "Sometimes I go to her mansion with the healer Agnella. By the way, she is a wise woman, not a witch. If she were a man, she would be a doctor." She strode to the window and looked out, leaning dangerously beyond the windowsill, enjoying the view of the monastery courtyard, perhaps pretending it was her own. "Lisa's friends have made her vain," she said, coming back into the room. "They like to paint their teeth and pluck away their eyebrows. But Madonna Lisa is not like them. Not entirely. Her feet are simple, made for foraging in the forests and dancing."

Leonardo watched the girl clomp around the room in her fine leather boots. Delicately sculpted heels, laced up, likely made from the softest goatskin. Purchased or stolen?

"She requires healing?" He wondered what he was getting into. The women he had painted in the past were all complicated creatures.

"If your little daughter was dying, would you not need some healing, too?"

"I suppose so."

"You suppose so?" Beatrice shot him a look of disbelief. "You are a great artist. Surely you feel emotions? Can you not understand other people's pain?"

The accusation in her voice surprised him. She was part girl, part old soul. There was much that burned within Beatrice, a lot of pain with an undercurrent of joy.

"I create paintings to reflect harmonies. Harmonies of color, harmonies of form. Emotion needs to be calculated, as well as a system of logic. When you combine the two," he said, looking at her, "your portrait will find success."

"Emotion and logic, all perfectly harmonious?" The girl shook her head, doubt in her voice. "From what I have seen, Lisa is not ready to sit for a portrait. Her pain is too deep. I hope you can understand that," she said, bowing curtly to the great man. She turned her fine heels toward the door and muttered to herself: "Logically speaking."

Chapter 19

The river, slow and brown, the smell of stillness and silt; minnows jumping, kicking up silver reflections like coins skipping across the water. The sound of laughter—men jokingly pulling a velvet robe from a friend. Michelangelo looked up and spied the ancient Roman bathhouse, strong and noble as an old warhorse, its fluted columns chipped and calloused, the massive stone lintel spread across its front like a heavy brow on a weary face.

This passage, from nature to ancient architecture, under the cleansing sun, out on the banks of the river, made the destination seem less of a sin. His knees were sore from kneeling in feverish prayer for two hours on the stone floor at Santo Spirito. The river would make everything right again.

Scanning the crowd one last time to ensure he was among strangers, Michelangelo stripped off his boots and linen breeches and sat down on one of the wide stone steps leading up to the old Roman temple.

A group of men lounging near the shore were throwing dice. Others were vigorously dousing themselves in the water, splashing it into their mouths and ears, while perched carefully on rocks—most of them could not swim. A couple of teenagers stood naked in the river, fishing for small fry to bring home and make their mothers happy. Watching men at the public bath excited him far beyond observing a model in his studio. He excused his fascination as research on the movement of the body, allowed his eyes to rest on a stocky youth—possibly a woodworker—who was stretching both arms overhead without a care for sin. He turned, eyeing a man nearby with a noble profile. That one, he thought, painfully aware of his erection.

The nobleman had gray stubble in his beard, though he moved athletically, like a young man. "My workshops are in San Martino," he said by way of introduction.

"Not far from here," said Michelangelo. He was lousy at small chat.

"We make expensive cloth woven from English wool. Luxury—it's the only way to make money these days." He gestured toward the men on the bank of the Arno. "Still, there is nothing more alluring than the naked body." He took Michelangelo's hands in his own. "Old hands on a young body. I believe you are a serious sculptor?"

Michelangelo nodded. Leonardo had made "sculpting" a dirty word. But who was he to judge? His *Last Supper* was flaking off its wall in Milan, and his equestrian monument had been destroyed.

The man reached under Michelangelo's tunic, brushing his fingers over his stomach and thighs. "A full moon last night—did you see it?"

Michelangelo was ashamed by the man's hand, the weight of the sin, wanting it all the more. "I saw the stars and"—he recalled hearing the full-moon parades in the streets from his studio—"I heard the moon."

Smiling at the sculptor's distracted observation, the man brushed higher on the inside of Michelangelo's thigh, lightly touching his erection. "May I?" he said, moving closer.

There was a wave of laughter from the river. Michelangelo saw hands caressing the full, rounded buttocks of a man. The offer was difficult to resist, even though the jaws of Satan might devour him. A man of nobility and physical beauty had chosen him. That surprised him. He knew he was not handsome. His nose was misshapen, not patrician. He was a man who gave himself entirely to God, who wanted nothing but a life without sin—

"Feels good, doesn't it?"

There was no denying what he was feeling: a wave of dirty hunger.

"We could go inside," the man said, touching a hand to his belt's silver clasp, expensively carved with leaves in the antique style.

Michelangelo looked anxiously from the man's belt to the crowd. He might be seen giving himself over to the darkest of evils, exposed for a second time in a public square. Homosexuality was no secret in Florence, the city of sodomizers, where older men often took young males from behind. Still, the coin that honored Savonarola, the Dominican friar, flashed through his mind, its vengeful dagger descending from the heavens, warning against the sin of indulging the body.

He had prayed until his knees were blue with bruises, but his desire for sodomy always surfaced; he observed it with disgust from a distance, a snake gorging on the shit deep inside a latrine. And he felt it in his gut, the kind of desire that devoured your senses and made you want to grunt and sweat like an animal. At times it haunted him up close and all around him. Leonardo surely knew about this desire. That old man had been caught out by the Office of the Night and publicly humiliated, yet after all those years toiling in Milan, here he was, returned to Florence more of a dandy than before, strutting around with his rose-pink tunic and matching cap. Michelangelo admired him—for his brain and his abilities, of course, but especially for having courage. Which, apparently, Michelangelo did not possess. He lacked the balls to follow his animal desires. God wouldn't allow it.

"I'm not sure," he said, though he wanted badly to go with the nobleman. Somewhere dark, away from prying eyes.

"Michelangelo! Out of your studio and lounging at the public baths?"

It was Lorenzo della Volpaia, the clockmaker. Everything about the man was annoyingly precise and loathsome. Michelangelo wanted to punch him in the face.

"Join me in the bathhouse." The nobleman touched a hand lightly on his back.

Michelangelo watched his seducer tighten his cloak and take his leave.

"The latest commission is consuming all of my time," Lorenzo said, oblivious. "A new one, along the lines of the astrological clock I made for Lorenzo de' Medici, may he rest in peace. This one is without all the planets. The Pazzi asked for a simple timepiece—"

"You've told me—a few times."

"A complex mechanism, extremely complex."

"I'm sure you're right," said Michelangelo, and rose to walk up the steps. The sound of water splashing, of buckets being filled from pools and emptied slowly over men, grew louder as he approached the bathhouse. He had dedicated his life to his art, to God, and he wanted at that moment to be washed clean, even as he entered a place of sin.

It was a relief to disappear into the near-darkness of the ancient inner rooms, to settle in a quiet niche. Where had the man with the silver belt gone?

Attendants glistened with sweat and moved silently. One, naked save for a white loincloth, threw a bucket of water on a pile of burning wood, sending a cloud of steam to the ceiling. Another, carrying a clutch of thin olive branches and a large ceramic pot, gestured for him to turn onto his stomach. The attendant struck him gently, to invigorate the skin.

Michelangelo raised a finger, and the man hit harder, thrashing his body. He turned his face toward the simmering fire and saw, across the domed room, his would-be seducer sitting with his back against the wall. Hot steam rose, causing the man to disappear.

Michelangelo turned his face to the wall. "*Forza!*" he ordered, and succumbed to the beating. Swallowing the pain, he felt his commitment to God renewed. "*Forza!*" he ordered again.

He wondered at what he had become. In childhood, he had nicknamed his young friends the Stick, the Basket, the Friar, the Woodpecker. The names stuck because they were honest. He was a serious boy, known for his loyalty, for his Florentine *virtù*.

"You'll join us at Maiano," his comrades would say, lounging under the shade of cypress trees whenever he visited his family's farm in Settignano. Michelangelo would always deny it. He hadn't feared the harsh, dirty work of cutting and dressing stone in the quarries of Maiano. But his dream was to liberate what was trapped inside the stone.

He grimaced as the olive branches struck him—and cursed himself for being a sinner. He had almost given in to his hungry ghosts. That's what Agnella had called them that day at his studio. He had nearly succumbed to the very desires that Savonarola and all the priests shouted must be repressed. His back throbbed. Sin and shame and injury. Agnella said he needed a wife.

He longed for the innocence of an earlier time, dry-laying stones for Agnella's wall with his father. Her stonemason husband had died of white dust poisoning in his lungs, and they had wanted to lend a hand while she walked and keened in the gorsy valley below the village. Or when he sculpted a snowman in the Medici gardens during that bizarre storm when the entire city lay blanketed and hushed by the snow. Then he had been merely a wild-haired youth who enjoyed playing and running races with boys his age, who loved wrestling them to the ground until somebody would cry out to Archangel Gabriel or San Giovanni to release them from a strangling grip. Whether he was more attracted to boys or girls never bothered him then. Though he had to admit, his feelings were aroused most often by the boys. And he would call on God to help soften his *cazzo* when it would grow hard during early-morning swims in the creek with his friends.

The olive branches came down hard on his back once more. He

winced and saw the face of his almost-seducer push forward again in his mind. Why was it that a man could arouse him more than the fearless olive oil girl, Beatrice, who stole figs and understood his obsessions?

He resented Agnella for exposing his sexuality, forcing him to think about marriage. All he wanted was to be left alone to work in his studio.

What good were any of these thoughts; they only distracted him. He must pick up his chisel and begin the sculpture—the savage taking away. Energized by this thought, Michelangelo gestured to the bath attendant to leave him. He dressed quickly and left the bathhouse. "Stop thinking about *David* as a slab of marble," he muttered to himself, jostled among throngs of churchgoers released into the freedom of the streets. He must instead think of the colossus as a monument to the will of a man. Under his touch, the bare left leg would angle up from the pedestal, brazen and unprotected, and reach out toward an imaginary Goliath. The right would take the weight of the body, flexing every muscle, exposing veins in anticipation of the kill. Michelangelo would create a youth in motion, turning to face the enemy. God could see all. God would bless the work and forgive him for his sins.

Lost in his own thoughts, he was suddenly knocked off his feet by a horse being trotted in the opposite direction. His temper flared as he recovered himself enough to grab the reins of the great white horse, forcing it to a standstill. "You ride with your balls, not your brain," he shouted, pulling down hard on the bit in the horse's mouth.

"Step lightly or I'll have you arrested," came the voice from the saddle. The man peered down, and they recognized each other at once. "Michelangelo, you would do well to keep your hands for sculpting rather than for fighting in the streets."

The argument had drawn a crowd, ever hungry for blood and fury. Michelangelo released the horse, his ego bruised, his backside freshly throbbing. "Forgive me, I am not myself, Chancellor. Please, let me clear the path." He gestured for Niccolò Machiavelli to go ahead.

He knew as well as any Florentine that Machiavelli would rather suffer the boils of syphilis than have his days restricted to a desk in the confines of the Palazzo Vecchio, where city officials toiled. Urgent acts of diplomacy were what he preferred. It was often told that the chancellor had ridden post for days, sometimes covering hundreds of miles, collecting a fresh horse at every inn and roping himself down hard in the saddle to keep from falling over from exhaustion. He once rode seven hundred miles, chasing down the French court for the Republic of Florence, mud caked on his leather boots, climbing the grand sweep of marble stairs to meet Louis XII. The rumor was that his job advising Governor Soderini had become focused on ensuring that the talents of Leonardo da Vinci made Florence the envy of the other Italian states.

"Your impudence will be overlooked this time," said Machiavelli, casting his eyes down at Michelangelo. "I must not delay. You may be interested to know that I'm rushing to negotiate a new commission with the city's genius, Leonardo da Vinci." He lifted his chin, enjoying the admiring gaze of the crowd. "Someday, if you keep your stumpy hands off my horse, you might see some fresh work come your way."

One cheek, the other cheek, thought Michelangelo grimly. Humiliated once again in the streets. He endured the barbs as a man might bear the crack of a whip while strapped to a mast, without crying out for help.

Machiavelli stepped his horse as if to take his leave, but a man from the crowd, raising a muscular arm, shouted: "You pledged to create an army of real Florentine men instead of hiring mercenaries."

"Nothing has come of it," yelled another, whose teeth were crisscrossed over each other. "Florence remains undefended."

"These things take time, but I am working on a fresh plan of defense for our city," said Machiavelli.

"Birthing a baby takes time, but something always comes out," called an unseen woman, provoking raucous laughter from the crowd.

"Some of us work. Others push around paper and live a quiet life of inconsequence," said another man grimly.

"Today I enlist the services of the great Leonardo da Vinci," Machiavelli said loudly, interrupting the jeers, beaming from his saddle.

"At long last. Da Vinci has been in Florence for some time! Will he lead the army?" A wave of sniggering rose from the crowd.

"He is to paint the Battle of Anghiari for the Great Council Hall."

"For what purpose?" somebody asked.

"We must celebrate our triumphs if we are to believe in the greatness of this city. We laid waste to the Milanese in that battle. Four thousand Florentines fighting together with four thousand papal troops. There were twice as many soldiers from Milan, but we beat them badly," the chancellor instructed the crowd, high color cresting his cheekbones.

"Though Leonardo rarely finishes anything he starts," shouted someone Michelangelo could not see—someone obviously well educated and well traveled. "Everybody knows that. His *Last Supper* was badly frescoed. Master of the Arts? It's already showing stains."

"Leonardo is far too loved," a young woman yelled. "Stop fawning over his talent. Let him fear you instead."

Machiavelli turned his attention on Michelangelo. He appeared to have endured enough from the crowd. "Show your worth and make something fine of the *David*. We are all waiting to see it." With that, he gathered the reins in one hand and whipped his horse with the other.

Michelangelo put his head down and pushed his way through the crowd like a young, ornery bull.

Chapter 20

Agnella rushed along Via Ghibellina on foot, her long hair twisted back with leather and gold silk ribbons. Her bracelets jangled, her sleeveless *giornea* fluttered in the wind. She pushed past guildsmen and old market women with sour, yellowed faces. "*Per cortesia,*" she called. "*Posso passare?*" Everybody from the highest to the lowest rank had a right to move about the city, and she was thankful for its straight, broad streets; she could not be late for the baptism. She turned right on Via del Proconsolo, then went left, skirting a small flock of sheep to be sold at the wool market, then took another right before emerging into the grand Piazza del Duomo. The cathedral's dome always dazzled her. What an act of architectural daring in a city of low-slung buildings made of golden-brown sandstone. Most of Florence looked tethered to the land and shaped by the sand of the Arno. The dome? More like God had floated the round mountain of Fiesole on top of the cathedral.

She could see a crowd gathered outside the baptistery and a monumental table being set by attendants. Agnella slowed her pace, admiring the massive orange dome and, beside it, the tall marble campanile, designed by the artist Giotto, which, she figured, soared as tall as sixty women standing on each other's shoulders. Across the piazza was the octagonal baptistery, smaller than Brunelleschi's *cupolone*—more of a circus tent in white marble—but still magnificent. Between all of these architectural chess pieces spread a public square that gathered the laborers, merchants and craftsmen responsible for the riches of Florence. There was no doubt the Florentines were all about work, not play; they were known for spending little, and always driving a hard bargain, except when it came to baptisms or weddings. As she squeezed her way between two carts pulled by oxen, she thought of the joke that was often told of Florentines: how a couple shared an egg and looked to see how much they could put away for another day.

Today was not that day. Layers of starched linen tablecloths washed in the Arno had been set with dozens of pewter plates, candlesticks, carafes of wine and water. Many babies would be baptized today, and she absorbed the people's happiness, the way they looked lit up and delighted to be dallying. She had personally delivered some of the babies into the world, pink-skinned, swaddled and bawling for their mother's milk. No expense would be spared for the celebratory feast. Agnella expected there might be sixteen courses following the afternoon baptism and the dousing of the newborns into a fount of sacred water by a huddle of priests. The squatters outside the city gates still ate off bread trenchers, but at this party, there were square crystal glasses with gold trim at each place setting, and she could see two roasted pheasants and a peacock on separate platters, their breasts painted with gold leaf, their glorious feathers reattached to their tails. She loved it all: the banquet spilling into the public commons, the violet blossoms floating in silver bowls of water for handwashing, the autumn grapes, pears and apples hanging from a white canvas ceiling, the whole banquet surrounded by large earthenware pots planted with lemon trees.

Celebrating the birth of a child was just what Agnella needed. She needed to believe in the gifts of the land and its living creatures, in the simple pleasures of cultivating white autumn roses, of eating *cena* late because the sunset was too spectacular to leave behind, of witnessing a babe survive childbirth and then, against all odds, thrive. That happiness did not come often enough. But Agnella also had a gift, like the Delphic Sibyl, to see into the future. Standing there at the bronze doors, waiting to enter the soaring golden interior of the baptistery, she felt herself in a liminal state, like a fish with a hook in its mouth before being pulled from the water. Something needed her attention. She slipped from the crowd, moving reluctantly away from the fragrance of the baptismal banquet toward Via della Stufa. Her pace quickened and she started to run.

The Giocondo courtyard, like so many Tuscan gardens, was divided into outdoor rooms distinctive for their scents and textures. Agnella found the women not in the orange room, nor the lemon room, but standing in a small field of Roman chamomile that ran below pear trees. Madonna Lisa was cradling Piera in her arms, the cool October air allowing the child to take her final breaths more easily. Beatrice was there, stroking the girl's head and singing a Tuscan folk tune very slowly.

Piera was wrapped in a fine wool blanket, her head swaddled in a linen cap. Agnella could see from the blue tinge of Piera's lips that, deprived of oxygen, she was quickly slipping away.

Huddled there, the women looked as if they were hiding from the world, from the noise of the commerce in the street, the exchange of goods, the scrutiny of legal documents, the demands of the artisan workshops. Stepping nearer, Agnella saw that they were both weeping. Beatrice reached silently for her hand, and the three of them gathered around the child. Nothing else mattered; only the certainty that they were there together, as sure as the cypress tree that stands tall no matter how harsh the wind that blows.

This was how Piera died, before the priest and the doctor insisted that she be ushered inside, the covenant of love broken by official duties.

Francesco was waiting for them, grim-faced, without words. He divided the women, separating his wife from her attendants, and Agnella and Beatrice retreated to the child's sick room. Beatrice looked at the stone floors and sobbed openly.

"There is little comfort to be found at times like these," said Agnella. She cast her eyes around the room, trying to find a measure of hope among its wealthy refinements and wall hangings.

"I would curse any street musician who dared to play now," said Beatrice bitterly. "Or any jester who would dance. There is sickness and evil in this land."

Agnella placed an arm around her young friend, feeling sad for the loss of Piera and the disappearance of Beatrice's mother. "There is more than that," she said, thinking of the joy of the baptism and the raucous gathering of people in the streets.

Beatrice drew a linen patch from her sleeve and wiped her eyes. Taking a breath, she lifted the edge of a wool tapestry away from the stone wall. Agnella stepped forward and saw a drawing of Piera being pushed in a cart by her siblings, the folds of her tunic spilling out from the edges, a bonnet nearly sliding from her head. Agnella followed Beatrice around the room, watching intently as she lifted another tapestry to reveal a conté portrait of the same little girl twisting to face out, smiling gently while playing with her hair ribbons. There was another of all six of the children lying happily intertwined on their mother's bed, as they had done when Madonna Lisa told Beatrice to fetch them. The last sketch on the wall was darkly shaded and showed Piera lying peacefully in her mother's arms.

"You have captured so much tenderness and innocence." Agnella bowed her head and reached for Beatrice's hand. "Your drawing reminds me, somehow, of Michelangelo's."

They were quiet for a while, and Agnella felt the spirit of the child moving through the room.

"This little girl lived and she was loved," said Beatrice. "That is what I wanted to draw. In the end, it's all any of us might wish for."

Part II

1502–1504

There were giants in the earth in those days; and also after that,
when the sons of God came in unto the daughters of men,
and they bare children to them, the same became mighty
men which were of old, men of renown.

—GENESIS 6:4

Chapter 21

The rain punished the city for days, causing raw sewage to overflow in the streets, robbing citizens of light, the sun nailed into the gray skies like a single spike. The roof of the Hall of the Pope—the Sala del Papa—where Leonardo was to work on drawing the cartoon for his fresco, started to leak badly and, while repairs to the slate tiles were undertaken, he was asked to make an inventory of the books in the convent of Santa Maria Novella. The governor had already started paying him and wanted him to toil for his keep; he estimated that an idle genius would risk fleeing to another, more industrious city.

On the other side of town, Beatrice pushed her cart from one covered storefront to the next, finally arriving behind the Duomo at the far entrance, the one used by builders and masons hired to keep the monument in good repair. She was drenched. Stomping the rain from her boots, she opened the narrow wooden door and walked down a hallway. The air was perfumed with frankincense. She moved slowly, breathing hard, the color drained from her face. She was hungry again. But she had not forged through the rain squall to find food. She wanted to escape herself, her existence living in despair in dark woods, with nobody, not even a rat, for a playmate.

At the door of Michelangelo's studio, she heard the harsh sound of a mallet being pounded against a chisel. Granacci was waiting down the hall, leaning against the wall. "He won't open the door."

She felt awkward standing there with this friend of Michelangelo's.

"No olive oil today?" he said, smiling, looking at her empty hands.

She wanted to flee. She stood still in her wet clothes and looked at the ground. The dull, hollow tapping from inside the studio slowed the racing of her heart. Looking over at Granacci, she could tell that his thoughts were turning inward.

"I used to think he hated me," said Granacci. "Michelangelo was tough. I was soft, coddled at home by a bunch of sisters. He wouldn't talk to me. Do you swim?" he asked suddenly, looking over at Beatrice.

She shrugged her shoulders. "I won't drown."

"It was like I was swimming across a wide, deep river to get to him, to make him see me and trust me. Something to swim for."

"He likes silence," said Beatrice. "He told me it's ennobling."

"I thought it was rejection, like he was cutting me with a blade of machismo."

"You apprenticed together?"

"At the Medici Sculpture Garden. He wasn't like the rest of us," said Granacci. "Michelangelo's reputation preceded him before he even arrived for the first day of class. Word spread that imperial blood coursed through his veins—"

"He likes to boast," said Beatrice. "He told me he comes from Canossa nobility."

This was when Michelangelo had caught her graffitiing the base of the stone fountain in the laneway not far from his studio.

"What the hell are you doing?" he accused, pulling her sharply to her feet.

"It's public property and I need to practice my drawing," she said, wrenching her arm away from him.

"We don't need you to impose your, your—"

"What, my art?"

"On the city, forcing people to look at it."

"What do you mean? You're making a massive naked monster of a man to hang off the Duomo." She remembered feeling both angry and amused by the turn of their conversation. Michelangelo did that to her, made her feel like the center of his world and a loathsome stranger, too.

"Remember who you're speaking to, olive oil girl. I am Michelangelo, descendant of Canossa high blood."

And then they both started laughing, really hard.

"We finished the portrait I was working on together, a woman draped in a Roman-style toga," she said now, looking over at Granacci. "He's been showing me how to draw somebody twisting slightly from the waist—*contrapposto* is what he calls it."

"I hope he gave you some paper."

"He did, but honestly, I prefer drawing on walls."

They stopped to listen to the pounding of the mallet and the beating of the rain against the corridor windows.

"When I was young, I thought of Michelangelo as the prince of sculptors and painters," said Granacci, smiling wide, relishing the memory. "We left him out of our *calcio* games rather than risk breaking his fingers."

"He must have hated that."

"A couple of the boys in the studio—lesser talents—liked to provoke him, see if they could get him to react," said Granacci, leaning toward Beatrice, confiding in her. "When our teacher, Bertoldo, stepped away, they taunted him a little more. 'Prince! *Lo scalpello! La mazza!* Catch!' and somebody would hurl a mallet across the room. Michelangelo was oblivious, always obsessed by his work. One time, the taunting went to a new level. '*Lo scapezzatore!*' somebody growled. It was a hefty pitching tool with a broad, blunt edge that could split stone. The tool sailed through the air, just missing Michelangelo's ear. He didn't even look up."

"He goes into a different world when he's sculpting. He needs to, so he can trust his intuition, but it means shutting everything and everybody out." She walked to the door and knocked with her little fist. "Selfish man, bring yourself here! *Idiota!*" From inside, she heard the unmistakable sound of a sculptor hard at work. She kicked the door with her boot this time. "Michelangelo, I brought you some sausage," she shouted, lying.

The hammering stopped. There was a long pause, then the shuffling of feet. The click of a latch and the door swung open. Michelangelo appeared, his face haggard and drawn. Beatrice could see a cloud of dust hanging inside the studio. She could taste the dryness, feel the grit on her tongue.

"Got any tallow?" asked Michelangelo. "The light is no good."

"Sculpting by feel?" she asked. "That's got to be stupid."

"Touch and feel," said Michelangelo. He reached out for Beatrice's arm, as if seeing her for the first time. "*Amici.*"

"I know, don't tell me. When you're sculpting, you forget all about your friends."

"Though your friends don't forget about you, Michel."

Beatrice rolled her eyes at Granacci. There was no need to be a bootlicker.

The studio at the back of the Duomo was enormous and grandly arched, though it looked like a storm had blown through. Heaps of dusty blankets and linens lay thrown into a corner. A half-eaten chicken had fallen to the ground. One of her jugs of olive oil was leaking onto a pile of knives and chisels. It occurred to Beatrice that the perfume of frankincense had been overwhelmingly replaced by the smell of rank, rotting meat.

"I can't take it," said Granacci, moving to a window and pulling the sash open. Outside, the rain was bucketing down on the terracotta rooftops.

Beatrice gazed at the colossal sculpture, her mind flicking back to the rough *bozzetto* she had seen over a year ago at Michelangelo's small studio. *David* had certainly grown up.

"It doesn't look like David from the Bible. More like a giant boy pretending to be a man."

"He is whatever a person needs him to be. A duke. A soldier. An artist. A shepherd. A warrior ready for war."

"Give me some coins and I'll go buy some food," she said quietly. Her leather boots were soaked through and she was chilled, but seeing Michelangelo's face helped to revive her spirit. That much she was able to admit.

"I brought some food for us," said Granacci.

Michelangelo shrugged, looking back at the *David*. Beatrice watched him rub his hands and bend his fingers back. She was sure his hands were sore and cramped from hours of using the chisel and something he called a riffler-rasp. With its shaped end, the tool could access tight, complex areas. He shook his arms and a cloud of dust went up into the gloaming.

"So, I convinced a stonecutter from Settignano to pose," he said. Beatrice noticed he was telling the story to her and the timber rafters of the workshop. "His body was good, but a little thin. For the clay model, I expanded his waist and chest to be more athletic, more heroic."

Beatrice wondered if she knew the stonecutter. There were plenty of them in Settignano. But she didn't want to interrupt Michelangelo. He rarely spoke more than a few words at a time.

"And then you started on the marble?" Granacci stood close, eyes wide with the telling of the story.

"I cut away from the parts that projected the most to show the head, the left hand, then the left knee, before cutting deeper into the marble. From there, it's easier to know where I am and where I have to go with my flat-blade chisel."

Granacci was pulling food from his leather bag. "*Pane? Salame?*"

"Not hungry."

Beatrice was. Very. But she held her tongue. No amount of *pane* and *salame* was worth trading away this conversation, this golden moment in art.

Michelangelo strode over to the colossus and looked up at it. "You can see that the head and the upper body are starting to come out of the rock. The consuls of the Wool Guild are paying me to make a shepherd—"

"To guard the sheep," said Granacci.

"Not a lion, or an ancient Roman," continued Michelangelo.

Beatrice stepped to Michelangelo's side. "The marble has streaks of blue and gray running through it. It reminds me of the river coming down the hill in Settignano, the way it changes color when the water runs over the pebbles. Do you know the place? In the clearing without the shadows of the willows."

"I do not. But you can take me there."

"They say this marble slab lay untouched for twenty-five years," said Granacci, arms folded across his chest, keen to be part of the conversation.

"I want nakedness. I want a boy warrior," said Michelangelo, ignoring him.

"You could give the people, the *popolo minuto*, a hero that belongs to them," said Beatrice. "The people standing outside the city gates. They have nothing. They have no one."

Nodding his head slightly, Michelangelo went back to work, and Beatrice slumped against a wall, peeled off some of her wet outer clothes and watched him knock off unwanted chunks from the marble. A miscalculation of force would mean scarring the slab of stone badly. She watched as he set his point chisel and struck it with a heavy wooden mallet; then he reset the chisel and struck again, connecting the wedge of the tool to the stone. With every second came another precise blow. The stone was neatly pitched off, like unwanted fat.

Granacci slid down the wall beside Beatrice. They watched and did not breathe a word as Michelangelo sent the energy down into the stone, then cocked his wrist to twist the chisel. Hammer, twist. Hammer, twist. Hammer, twist. Michelangelo's eyes flashed with the intensity of the work. His shoulders and arms thrust back and forth with the exacting rhythm of a *scalpellino*, rising up again to make another strike.

Granacci rose to move around the studio, cleaning. He threw the chicken into a pail, along with mildewed cheese and figs. Beatrice picked up a large jug and held it up in front of Michelangelo. "Wine?"

Michelangelo shook his head, dragged a hand through his hair. He stepped toward the *David* and touched the right, forward leg. Beatrice drank, wiped her mouth on her sleeve and drank some more. It was a strong, full-bodied red, the kind she could not afford. She noted *David*'s piercing gaze, as if he were greeting an Olympian. She wished Michelangelo would look at her that way.

"I can see you're letting your *David* move forward out of the stone."

"I started by defining the high planes first, the nose, the forehead."

"Why is movement so important to you?" She was still sitting with her back against the wall, trying to ignore her hunger.

"Remember when you were drawing your mother in the toga? On the fountain outside my studio?"

Beatrice looked at the stone floor. "I never said it was my mother."

"*Allora, va bene.* I thought it might have been her. As a memory."

"I asked you about movement."

Michelangelo jumped from the scaffold and sat down beside her. "To show that life evolves. That we can change ourselves. That humans can own ideas and their beautiful, God-created bodies."

"I'd sell my ideas if I could earn a florin."

"Beatrice," he flirted, "you're on to me."

"There have been some arrests," Granacci interjected, holding tight to a broom. "The Office of the Night brought in some men, apparently sodomizers."

Ignoring him, Michelangelo unwrapped a packet of food and bit down on some spinach and anchovies heaped on Tuscan bread. Beatrice walked over to the *David*. She longed to be alone with Michelangelo, just the two of them in this darkened hall.

"Michelangelo, you have to listen," continued Granacci. "Two men, a jeweler and a goldsmith, were arrested last night while leaving the Buco. Drunk, of course, loud—and the *sbirri* were waiting to crack their skulls. Machiavelli is getting ideas from Duke Borgia and his sick love of discipline among his men."

"I don't go to the Buco. You think this place stinks?"

"Nobody is accusing you of anything," said Granacci. "But don't you see?" Panic etched his face. "This beautiful creature, this naked man—"

"This is not some kind of sickness, if that's what you mean, Granacci. Some call me Il Divino. But here you are, my friend, thinking less of me."

"Michelangelo, I'm worried somebody will denounce you. Go to Settignano, take some rest, until this passes."

"Remember those days at the Medici Academy?" said Michelangelo, his face darkening. "You were always trying to protect me. I don't need it. I don't want it. Get out!"

Beatrice stood up. The Angelus bells announcing sundown were ringing loudly. Walking past Michelangelo, she hesitated. "Your *David* is . . ." She was looking for the right word. "He is courage."

Granacci took his leave, closing the door softly behind him.

"Beatrice," said Michelangelo, looking over at her. "I forget myself when I am working."

"I know that."

He handed her some bread and anchovies. "Please stay. I need . . ." It was as if he was incapable of finding the words. His eyes moved all around the cavernous studio and back to her. "You are a lark escaped from its cage. I need your spirit to help me through."

"Well, then," she said, looking from him to a pile of rag paper on one of the studio tables. "You sculpt. I'll draw." She reached for a sheet and paused. Here she was, sitting beside Michelangelo. And now there was something other than a wall for her to draw on. With paper, she could practice telling the truth about what many suffered during their lives. More and more these days, when she drew a childlike putto or a person, she tried to evoke emotion, even if it meant disfiguring their angel wings or hanging rags of pain across their faces. Give her the kind of luscious oil paints that Leonardo used and she would color the face of Madonna Lisa with streaks of purple and red, like a warrior.

"Try this," he said, handing her a piece of *sanguigna*. "It's the color of flesh."

Without speaking, she set the chalk aside and took his hands. She felt their rough, dry texture, his palms turned hard from gripping cold chisels and receiving the shock from the mallet. She saw that his fingertips were as smooth as glass from testing the surface of his marble sculpture when the light went bad and his eyes no longer served. She turned his hands over and bent to slowly kiss his knuckles, every one of them swollen and enlarged.

She picked up the reddish-brown chalk in her hand. "Looks to me like dried blood." And her heart leapt at the gift from Michelangelo.

Chapter 22

Salaì watched from the monastery as the woman stepped from the carriage, wrapped in a heavy black dress. She brushed away the outstretched hand of the driver. A dry wind lifted her veil off her shoulders, and still she stood like a tree in winter. He glanced at Leonardo, hunched over his drawings of horses' heads, a heating brazier set for his comfort below the worktable.

"Madonna! Madonna!" shouted Salaì, leaning dramatically out the window. He beckoned to her with both hands.

Leonardo was already at his side. "Is that her?" He turned away from the window. "Paolo! Paolo!" he called. "What is her name again? Her name?" he hissed as his studio manager rushed into the room. He gestured to the window, and Paolo pushed in next to Salaì.

"She is Lisa Gherardini del Giocondo, of Gherardini nobility. Madonna Lisa—*vieni!*" Paolo called, daring to address her with a term of familiarity.

From beneath her black silk, Lisa raised an arm tentatively. A flash of white—her hand. Then another figure emerged from the carriage, someone moving with a muscular grace. A servant? No, it was Beatrice. She leapt to Lisa's side and took her arm. Bending to the woman, the girl seemed to be providing counsel. The woman listened, waited and gave her approval. Then, as if pulled by a string, they walked with deliberate, stoic steps toward the studio.

Leonardo hustled down the hallway toward the side entrance. Blocking his way was a jester in garish stripes with a monkey sitting on his shoulder—the animal wearing the striped uniform of a sentry and nibbling a large apricot—and a second jester with a baby monkey clinging to his arms. Paolo often hired jesters to entertain clients during portrait sittings; it always put them at ease, relaxed their shoulders, brought a smile to their eyes.

"Paolo," scolded Leonardo. "Her little girl died. A messenger informed me. She's in mourning. No jesters today."

He could see that grief had robbed the woman of her vital spirit. It was as if her red, sinewy insides had been replaced by wool batting.

The jesters pulled sad faces at Leonardo, stretching their mouths with their fingers into ridiculous frowns.

"*Va bene*," replied Paolo as he motioned the jesters away down the hall.

The troupe started a charade of bawling. The baby monkey escaped with high-pitched squeals, and his mother leapt from her perch and followed at a gallop.

Leonardo waved his hands at the scene, willing it into oblivion. Then he descended the stairs to greet Lisa Gherardini and her companion. At the second-floor landing, he slowed his pace and offered both women a deep bow. He kissed Lisa's hand, icy to the touch, barely brushing it with his lips. Her skin had the sickly pale patina that comes from being shut inside for too long.

"Maestro. It is a pleasure to meet you."

"Signora Gherardini, I am honored to receive you. Please accept my deepest condolences. I am entirely at your disposal if the tragic circumstances are—"

"She is well enough, though still grieving deeply," interrupted Beatrice, stepping forward. "We will proceed with caution, as pleases the signora."

"I see you are in good hands with our wise Beatrice."

"My husband speaks often of your reputation," said Lisa stiffly, a mix of formal speech and informal *volgare*. She pulled her hand away from Leonardo and back to Beatrice's grasp. Her breath shallow, she added: "I have not seen *The Last Supper*. He describes it as a work of great devotion and—"

"Humanity. That was my intention, signora."

Her brown eyes flickered briefly to life. He gestured toward the next flight of stairs. She leaned against Beatrice and walked cautiously, as if on borrowed legs.

"You are living here with the Servites," she said, a statement rather than a question.

"Yes, with the grace befitting the Servants of Mary. These private rooms are given to my assistants and me."

"How many assistants do you have?"

"Five. And Paolo, our studio manager and cook, who tries to

manage our many appetites. We are all busy enough. I'm painting for the Servites. An altarpiece." He nodded along with his words, as if to emphasize his enthusiasm.

"One painting in exchange for five rooms?"

"Correct."

"Well, then," she said. Leonardo watched how she stopped to catch her breath, as if she were an old woman. "The Servites are property-rich."

Weak of body, he thought, though there is still a boldness about her mind. He bent his head and watched her from the corner of his eye. She betrayed nothing. Her teeth appeared to be without lead paint, though it was difficult to know for sure because she spoke without fully opening her lips. Her eyebrows were plucked clean, with a thin line of something arching mid-forehead—likely mouse hair, he decided. Sorrow darkened the curve of her neck. She stared down the corridor and then at him, her eyes solemn, seeing him with unblinking intensity. They passed one of the studios, walking so slowly he became acutely aware of every step, every burst of color that greeted their passage: a crabapple tossed in the hallway, a shard of late-afternoon winter light streaming across the wooden floors.

"*Buon giorno*," said Ferrando, his youngest assistant, looking up from his work. He was holding a piece of sapling over a pot of steaming water, bending it slowly.

"My assistant from Spain. Ferrando, please make the acquaintance of Signora Gherardini del Giocondo."

Ferrando de Llanos stepped forward and made a short, athletic bow graced by a wave of his right arm, as befitted a gifted artist from Madrid.

"Of course, you are already acquainted with Beatrice."

"*Salve*, Beatrice! Come visit me and I'll show you my experiment with wood."

Paolo reappeared from the kitchen, holding a tray of exquisitely prepared stuffed Damascene dates. He followed them toward the studio Leonardo had decided Lisa would pose in. An ink map of Imola, a fortified town that he had personally walked and measured, the better for ambitious usurpers to attack and conquer it, hung from the wall. He had been to war. Sinking in mud up to his knees, breathing in the stench of rotten grapes, their juice mixing with blood on the ground. As Duke Borgia's military engineer, he had witnessed carnage with his own eyes—"Ah, yes, the *pazzia bestialissima*," Borgia had said to him, his face masked to hide the ravages of syphilis, sweat-slicked and grinning: horror tickled his fancy. A stone-walled villa outside Imola had become the invaders' headquarters; Leonardo remembered the massive circular towers, but also the violations by the thugs, their crimson and yellow uniforms stained in blood. What did the duke call him back then? "Family architect and general engineer." How quaint, he'd thought, but not nearly as quaint as the duke's own nickname, Il Valentino.

At the threshold, Madonna Lisa and Beatrice stopped abruptly. To Leonardo, it was as if they had planned their choreography from within the plush confines of the carriage.

"We are taking a moment," said Beatrice, eyes surveying the room as if she were seeing it for the first time. "Tincture?" she inquired of the signora, holding aloft a small jar of green liquid produced from a pocket inside her jacket.

Lisa nodded and swigged from the bottle. "*Grazie*, Beatrice. Yes, that feels very helpful."

"With your permission, signora, I shall leave you to make the acquaintance of the great Master of Arts," said Beatrice, speaking with an eloquence and formality that surprised Leonardo. "I'll be in Ferrando's studio if you need me for anything at all."

Leonardo took Madonna Lisa's hand. She was not pretty. She could not be depicted like Cecilia, the young mistress of the duke of Milan, who was as lithe and watchful as the ermine he'd painted her cradling. But still, there *was* something about this Lisa Gherardini. Something about the lift of her chin, the pride in her shoulders. She personified a greatness that did not end with the city but began with the earth. He had anticipated that the merchant's wife would be a lady of the *ottimati* class. He'd imagined she would require a phalanx of servants to accompany her to his studio. But she had caught him off guard. Perhaps, he thought, this signora was not so very different from himself. And how her body shifted with uncertainty, how heavy with sorrow she appeared! As she slid the black veil slowly from her head and arranged her dress, he wondered if the weight of her grief would sink them together. He was troubled by loss, too: of his reputation, of his youth, of his status in Florence.

Leonardo looked at her sideways. The layers of black—the brocaded overgown, the bodice stitched with shiny beads, the diaphanous head veil—all of it clothing to indicate the depths of a person's *virtù* as well as grief. There were times when he grieved

---

a little for his own failings, for what he had become. He wore purple capes and boots to show off the curve of his legs. But more and more, when he dressed in the morning, he felt that his flamboyance was a disguise.

"Madonna Gherardini—"

There came the sound of paws pounding and an unholy shriek. The two monkeys hurled themselves down the hallway, screaming with wild abandon.

"Our monkeys!" The jesters appeared, wild-eyed, then ran after them.

"Delicacies for the monkeys!" yelled Paolo, chasing the group with the tray of dates held aloft.

Turning, Lisa watched the departing monkeys as if hypnotized. The owner clicked his tongue and beckoned to them. The larger of the two nibbled tenderly from his hand. The baby scrambled up her mother's back and reached for a date, resulting in a small shift of Lisa's mouth—the suggestion of a smile. Leonardo was stifling laughter, a hand clapped against his mouth, tears springing to his eyes. It was all too much, the cavorting monkeys in sharp contrast to his client's deep grief. He wondered why she had turned up, yet he admired her formidable strength.

Her hand grazed his elbow. "Later, with time, I will laugh along with you," she said, nodding at him, providing reassurance, acknowledging his face gone red from suppressed laughter.

They went into his studio, past the indigo-blue velvet curtains that fell from the oak rafters, hiding the bed where he slept with Salaì, past the long wooden table heaped with his notebooks and sketches, to a heavy wooden chair, arms of thick oak, cushioned at the seat. He suggested with the wave of an arm that the signora should sit. She stood next to the chair, looked to the window as if searching for an escape, then finally nodded and sat. It was chilly in the studio. The fireplace heaped with oak logs managed only to take the bite out of the winter air held in by the stone walls of the monastery.

Leonardo pulled his heavy velvet cloak around his chin and stepped several paces away to an easel that held a poplar board. The easel provided a safe haven for him and, hidden from her gaze, he rubbed his cold hands together, curling and uncurling his fingers. He felt stiff as a runner after too long away from training. Painting? For years, he'd been sketching and making engineering calculations; mostly he'd been managing the affairs of his studio in Florence. But the poplar board helped to steady his mind. It was cut from the heart of one of the great trees that grew fast and high in Lombardy, near Milan, and it had dried to perfection over years in storage, waiting for the right commission. All these years later, it still smelled like the freshwater springs of verdant valleys. True, at 30 by 21 inches, it was large for a portrait, and he'd known he was taking a risk when he set it on his easel that morning.

He looked over at Lisa, sitting rigidly in the chair, though her eyes flitted like restless moths over every object in the studio. A jar of lead white sat on a mixing table next to him, prepared as instructed by his most reliable assistant, Giovanni. He dipped a thick brush into the jar and began spreading a thick primer coat onto the board. He moved slowly and felt a moment of regret that the tight grain of the poplar was being erased. With half the plank painted white, he looked again at the signora, observing, making notes in his mind, with no intention of beginning her portrait.

"Would you look directly at me?"

"Are you painting already?" she asked, her eyes sliding over to him, down to the floor and back to the window.

"Not yet," he said, smiling at her, thinking he would start by sketching with paper and pen after she had gone.

"*Permesso*. May I?" Beatrice was at the door of the studio, sending a reassuring smile across the room to Madonna Lisa. Leonardo waved her inside, "*Avanti*," but she had already stepped to Lisa's side.

"Is that enough?" inquired Beatrice, easing Lisa to standing.

"For today, certainly," said Leonardo, setting his brush down, glad the session had come to an end. "We can meet again at your leisure."

"Will I always have to sit?" said Lisa, her voice tired and querulous.

"On the contrary," said Leonardo. "My portrait depends on you not always sitting down, but moving around, both of us. With time, we will come to know each other, to listen to each other's stories, to see each other truly. Only then can I begin to paint in earnest."

Chapter 23

Inside the massive studio, standing on the edge of his scaffold, Michelangelo dropped the buffing pad and picked out a rounded pumice stone. He pressed his chest lightly against the sculpture, a reluctant lover, and rubbed gently into the curve of the neck, coaxing with careful strokes. Running his fingers over the *fossetta*, he selected a pad layered with abrasive emery from his pocket to heighten the polish. He wanted to work the marble to the point of porcelain transparency, that people might imagine a pulse beating in the hollow of *David*'s neck.

It was like this every day: morning became afternoon, afternoon became night. The hours were swallowed whole by the art of careful, patient work.

"Under order of the Florentine government!" A man's voice, unexpected, shouted from outside his studio. The oak doors were thrown wide and three men stepped inside. Michelangelo immediately recognized Soderini, a friend of the family and the republic's governor, who heartily supported the Wool Guild. He knew the governor's footman and, to his chagrin, he recognized the third man as Machiavelli, the second chancellor, who had nearly run him down on his horse.

"Gonfalonier, welcome," said Michelangelo, addressing Soderini by his formal title, though he wanted to order the three men away so that he could continue to work in peace. The governor stepped toward the *David*, all business, ignoring the greeting. Experiencing art unsettled Soderini. Michelangelo had heard stories of the man wiping his brow furiously with a silk cloth, overwhelmed by the luminous frescoes of Giotto or the brilliant perspectives of Brunelleschi. Once, Michelangelo had been sitting quietly inside the Brancacci Chapel at Santa Maria del Carmine, sketching Masaccio's luminous depiction of Adam and Eve being banished from Paradise for eating the forbidden apple, and Soderini burst into the church with a loud, excited entourage. The visit was part of a civic itinerary to educate the new governor on the city's master works, but it had to be cut short. Seeing the fresco of the weeping, humiliated Adam and Eve, Soderini started pacing and muttering about the evil imperfection of man. It was the same when they made a stop at Santo Spirito to examine the crucifix up close. The limp body of a teenager sculpted by Michelangelo tore at the governor's emotions. Afraid of upsetting the day's schedule, his advisors guided him outside for fresh air.

There had been no warning that Soderini and Machiavelli would be visiting this morning. Michelangelo braced for an unpleasant encounter and a strange reaction to the *David*. Even from high up on the scaffold, he could see that the governor's forehead was already slick with sweat.

"We must determine where to put the thing when it is complete," said Soderini, to no one in particular.

"My lord," said Machiavelli grandly. "The advantage of our surprise visit is to see the colossus up close." He rubbed his hands in delight. "In advance of the public viewing."

"My trusted chancellor," said Soderini, wiping his face aggressively, clearly suffocated by the binding of his official woolen doublet, "you are a man of unexpected pleasures. Tell me, Michel, where do you keep your wine?"

The sculptor climbed down effortlessly along the scaffold rungs and jumped to the floor. Picking up a carafe of wine, he wiped a glass with the edge of his dusty apron. Soderini downed the drink in one gulp and wiped his mouth with the length of his arm, as if a common oarsman.

"Seems too big for the upper buttress of the Duomo," said Machiavelli, cocking his head and throwing his gaze to the rafters, as if imagining the cathedral. "Per the signed contract."

"Chancellor, I see your point. Worthy of an animated debate. Could we set the *David* on prime real estate in front of the Palazzo Vecchio?"

Michelangelo listened to the men discussing him as if he was no longer in the room. He detested the chancellor's authoritative voice, his need to declare a position every time he spoke. Here was a man trying too hard, with his black eyes and cropped hair wet with oil, likely from a class lower than Soderini's and Michelangelo's families. Status and class would always separate them—but

Machiavelli was making up for it, developing a hard love of the classics, of Plato and Aristotle, of the work of Botticelli and classical architecture and jousting.

"I see it more and more in Florence," said Machiavelli, rubbing his chin thoughtfully, pleased with another of his assessments. "We need to pay attention, you and I." He pressed a fist to Soderini's shoulder to emphasize his point. "The artist is no longer a creature. He is a *creator*."

"Michelangelo is a dear family friend. I've watched him grow—"

"No longer a child, grown into an artist with a mind of his own."

"If I may," interjected Soderini. "My God, the gaze of this *David*—it's overwhelming. Never before have I locked eyes with the eyes of a sculpture and felt my own mortality. I have to admit that my thoughts feel cloudy, a little messy. Michel, give me some more wine. It appears there is something amiss with the face."

Here it comes, thought Michelangelo, looking up to the timbers and back to the ground, shifting restlessly on his feet.

The gonfalonier tapped his nose. "Yes, indeed, the nose," he continued. "The nose appears too large." He scratched at his neck. "Anybody else feeling the heat crawling everywhere?"

For a long while, Michelangelo did not move as he tried to make sense of the man's meaning. Finally, as if struck by enlightenment, he reached into his leather pouch for a fine-tipped chisel, then, with the other hand, he dug into the pocket of his smock and pulled out a fistful of marble dust, kept for polishing. He climbed easily up the scaffold and leaned from the top platform, about fourteen feet in the air. His chisel tapped with expert precision, the notes echoing through the studio. He released the dust into the air; it was beautiful to behold, a cloud of subterfuge.

"Better?" he shouted, gazing without emotion through the scaffolding. Soderini tapped a hand to his rolled velvet cap to signal respect. Michelangelo gripped the block of extra marble he had tapped against, pleased with his duplicity. The *David* was beyond the comprehension of Soderini—or indeed any mortal—just as God was unrecognizable and ethereal. He, Piero Soderini, of a family with minor nobility, had no right to look upon this colossus, this monster-child of fearlessness, and attempt to improve it.

What now? Here was Machiavelli, climbing the wood scaffolding, hauling himself up like an Olympian!

"Signore Michelangelo di Buonarroti, you are an honored son of Florence." Machiavelli wiped his long-fingered hand over his closely cropped head. "The world will visit your *David*; long convoys and pilgrimages of people will worship your talent."

"If I can pay my rent with my wages, I am pleased," said Michelangelo, bristling at Machiavelli's sudden switch in tone from condescension to excessive flattery. His father and brothers had already laid claim to most of the four hundred florins for this commission, beyond what he had donated to the beggar girls. They were urging him to find new work. Repairs to the farm in Settignano and their villa in Florence depended on his salary. "The governor, or that prior you are so friendly with, the one at Santo Spirito, they must have money to spare," his father would harp every time they met.

The wooden platform creaked under the weight of both men as Machiavelli stepped closer.

"Should I come up?" It was Soderini. He lifted a foot as a hero might, prompting Michelangelo to picture Hercules slaying the Nemean Lion.

The men on the scaffold ignored him. Soderini put his foot back on the ground.

"You were born to sculpt," said Machiavelli, inspecting the statue closely.

"Some say I was." Michelangelo stared at the man who was now beside him. He had an intensity that was difficult to measure or trust. "My nurse, Agnella, was married to a stonemason in the hill town of Settignano. He would take me to the quarry when I was a boy and we would sleep on the marble at night."

"Bed of marble. Sounds uncomfortable."

"Even warmed by the sun, it never grows soft," Michelangelo admitted.

"With your art, you hold much power." Machiavelli allowed the flattery to flow out of him. "You might have been a governor," he said, waving a hand toward the ground and Soderini, who seemed to be stroking the feet of the *David*. "A prince. Or a tyrant. But this!" He clapped a hand on Michelangelo's bare back, breathing deeply as if inhaling the smell of his sweat. "This hits us mortals here." He pounded his heart. "This is the power of the artist."

"You flatter me, Chancellor."

"I am Niccolò Machiavelli. Advisor to the governor," he said, bowing low. "Admirer of princes such as yourself," he whispered, fixing his gaze on Michelangelo.

Machiavelli flicked his leather gloves up and down in the palm of his hand. Much like the flicking of a poisonous snake's tongue, thought Michelangelo.

"My lord, I am certain we can both agree that Florentines should be celebrated for more than the ability to turn out fine wool and silk brocade for gentlemen." Machiavelli clenched his hands behind his back. "Let us stand for a city recognized once again by Venice, Milan and Rome for the right of all people to think and create."

"You make a pretty speech, Niccolò Machiavelli," shouted the gonfalonier, his head twisting past the scaffold to look up at the men on the highest platform. "But Florence must be defined on its own terms, not as a city measured against another metropolis"— he looked at Machiavelli to ensure he was listening—"to borrow a term from the ancient Greeks."

Soderini now turned his full attention to the towering man-boy in front of him. The warrior's left hand held the pouch of the sling with wise self-assurance, but the right hand was cocked, veins pulsing, hiding the rock that would kill the enemy. The governor looked pale, and Michelangelo was moved to ask: "Gonfalonier, are you quite well?"

"It's just that I had not expected this. This colossus," said the governor, weakly. "He's much bigger than I imagined. I feel as if . . ."

"Go on," encouraged Michelangelo.

"To be frank, I feel my own mortality torn asunder and thrown onto the ground, a useless heap of ashes." He turned his back on the *David*, drawing a patch of linen from his vest. "A jug of water?" he said weakly to his footman. He slowly swiveled back toward the colossus, then away from it again.

"I speak for myself and the gonfalonier when I offer our congratulations." Machiavelli took a knee, inspiring Michelangelo to do the same. He waited, looking up at the timbers of the studio while his lips moved silently: *Hail Mary, full of grace* . . . The prayer lifted automatically from his lips, but he was unable to speak directly to the man kneeling in front of him.

"Could I entice you to consider another, even grander commission?" Machiavelli spoke in hushed tones, leaning closer. "You will be well compensated for your work."

"Chancellor, you are too kind." Despite the lure of money, Michelangelo was talking in platitudes in the hopes the rodent-headed man might disappear from his scaffold. "A man of your position, with many affairs to manage. The Pisans, whether Florence should go to war with them again." The Pisans had slaughtered Beatrice's father—leading to that tragic, bizarre moment when he first met her. The memory came hurtling back to him, leaving a sour taste in his mouth.

"All in good time," said Machiavelli. "A young man like yourself needs to be thinking about your next big work. Something grand, as grand as this commission." Lowering his voice still further, he confided, "I'd like to put you and a great master to a task."

"A great master?"

"You and Leonardo da Vinci. The pride of Florence. The only living rival worthy of your genius. Creating, dazzling, in the Great Council Hall of the Palazzo Vecchio."

"In the same room?"

"Frescoes on the east wall. You are our genius artists. Our best gladiators."

Michelangelo dipped his head and did not speak for a long while. Then he said, "This *David* consumes me. I think it might devour me whole."

He had no idea what Machiavelli was up to, but he wished more than ever for the chance to get back to the sculpture towering in front of him. Cracking a weak smile, he swung easily from one platform of the scaffold to the next and jumped to the floor. Michelangelo thought all government officials fat-kidneyed, especially when they showed up without an invitation. Even a visit from the pope would have annoyed him.

He pocketed his chisel and turned to Soderini. "I should get back to it."

"It's a miracle, your *David*," said the governor, extending a hand to Michelangelo's shoulder and gripping it hard. "Your father must be so proud."

"I suppose so," said Michelangelo, knowing it to be untrue.

"How old are you, son?"

"Twenty-eight." He looked shyly to the floor and up to the timbers. "Though I barely have time to keep track of the passing moons."

"Old enough to be thinking of marriage. Any prospects in mind?"

"Of course," lied Michelangelo again. "A man needs a piece of prettiness to put his mind at rest."

"Well, then, as an old family friend, here's to toasting you many times at your wedding!"

Machiavelli leapt from the scaffold and took a final appreciative look at the *David*. "This is the kind of greatness this city needs. You've done it, Michelangelo."

"Gentlemen, I bid you goodbye." Michelangelo bowed low. "My work awaits me."

He had already climbed to the top of the platform by the time the men walked out of the studio and closed the oak doors behind them. Slowly, with a deep breath, he bent to pick up his buff, but decided against it. Crouching down, he held his hands against his ears. The muffled silence soothed him. Oh, to be deaf, he thought, and avoid all of the world's endless useless chatter.

Chapter 24

"Your fresco of the Battle of Anghiari is the talk of the town," said Lisa Gherardini. Leonardo set down his cup of spring water and looked over at her. It was true that he had signed the contract enlisting his services as painter of a monumental fresco for the city hall. Machiavelli had arrived at the monastery last fall, pounding his heels down the hallway to Leonardo's studio, his brow shining with sweat, his eyes lit with a maniacal intensity. Soon enough, people had started asking about the commission. Leonardo would have to set his mind to drawing a preparatory cartoon of the historic battle scene when the Florentines triumphed over the Milanese army.

For now, he was surprising himself by being intrigued by the woman standing in front of him. She had emerged from behind the changing screen and was wearing the clothes he had chosen for her. Unconventional, of course, but she and her husband had decided to trust his vision for her portrait. Wasn't that why they had hired the great one?

Leonardo had decided to dress Lisa in typical Florentine fashion. She would wear a *gamurra* woven from the finest silk and dyed a rich, verdant green, with yellow velvet sleeves attached to the fitted bodice by ribbons. Her hair would be loosened below a transparent black silk veil, and there would be a suggestion, very discreet, of a linen *camicia* undergarment appearing at her cleavage. Sleeves discreetly rolled back at the elbow. No halo. No jewels at her neck. Her skin naked. Not even her wedding ring. Subtractions, reductions of color—all of this pleased him.

He stared at her, taking in the aesthetic of her garb. "Yes, this is fine, very fine," he murmured to no one in particular. He was weary of the brush. But Lisa was a woman of complexity. Her child had died. Even with an overbearing husband, there was something of a wild spirit that lurked deep within her. Here she was, enduring. He was thinking of the future, when he might add borders of embroidered braid, or drapery that shifted according to the slightest adjustment in her posture—even, perhaps, a gauze overgarment.

"Have you started the wall painting?"

It was their second meeting, on a day in May that had bloomed pink and exploded to radiant blue skies.

"Art begins in my mind. When the idea is complete, the sketching is quick."

"So you have not started it," she said, challenging him.

He looked up and saw something new in her eyes. Amusement, a flicker of light—more reflection, rather than all grieving. Time was slowly healing the woman.

"I wish I had such abilities—to conjure an idea and give birth to it," she admitted, surprising him again. "Beatrice told me it was the best feeling, to imagine a song or the shape of something— even angels—and offer it as an improvement to this." She waved a hand in the air. "The atmosphere."

"You are in possession of a brain," he said, picking up a sketch- book and a conté. He felt an irrepressible desire to help this woman feel less sorrow and more hope. "You are naturally predisposed to exercise its magnificent powers."

She pressed a silk handkerchief to her brow. "Women pos- sess many assets. Yet we are tutored to expect nothing from our thoughts."

"Leave some room for change," he said.

"I wish it could be so, but . . . your advice . . . I find it to be blithe. I can't explain it. But your words have upset me."

He set the conté down and looked at her. "I see." He wanted to understand. Perhaps his advice had been delivered with an air of higher authority, but he was unsure how to comfort this Floren- tine lady. "Shall I call the musicians back? The jugglers?"

"No, what use is distraction? Let me feel this darkness. Imagine a wave of despair crashing through me. Unbidden."

He waited, head bowed.

"I remember how the doctor hovered over my child's body. Her dead body," said Lisa, her cheeks glistening with tears. "The priest was there, too. I heard the rustling of silk, his hand pressing ashes in the shape of a cross on my little girl's forehead. I lifted her up, and kissed her cheeks. Her skin . . ." She looked over at Leonardo and he met her gaze. "Her skin was still warm. Such an exquisite creation, small eyes and nose. Even in death, she was a thing of beauty. My Piera."

"Her spirit will always be with you," he said, but immediately regretted the poor solace of his words.

She wiped her cheeks roughly with the back of her hand, forgetting her silk hankie. "I remember how the priest's bitter breath poisoned the air. He lit the coals in the holy thurible, lifted its chains and smoked the room with frankincense. Then he said: 'Piera has passed from this life, as pleased God.' I'll never forgive him for that."

Leonardo tapped his conté against the table to bring her mind back to the room. He realized that, despite the light he had seen in her eyes, the woman's mourning still imprisoned her. He reached forward to soften a piece of beeswax, producing a tiny cube, which he set down on the table. He gestured for her to leave off sitting and come closer. When she stood next to him, he pressed a thumb on the wax cube and flattened it into an oval. "People can change, too," he said, lifting the wax from the table and placing it in her hand. "A mighty flame followeth a tiny spark." He smiled gently at her. "Men, and women—there are many rules about how we should behave." Then he added, "Of course, your security and mine are subject to unpredictable displays of ego by men seeking to acquire more wealth and status." He plucked a pear from a bowl and handed it to her, and she gripped it in her hands. "Does it please you to be a woman?"

"Leonardo, what bedevilments spout from your lips! My husband would *never* utter such thoughts. Such candor. Honestly, I'd rather be a man. Women are sexual pets and property."

He looked over at her and shrugged. "Now I know."

"You were employed for many years as the duke's court painter, were you not? You must know what it is to feel like a pet."

The biting accusation pleased him. "Men invade foreign lands, plunder other people's castles, seize all the gold and melt down bronze that does not belong to us," Leonardo offered. He wanted to entice her to express more of her thoughts.

"Is this conjecture, signore, or do you speak of an experience lived?"

He had witnessed the ransacking of castles led by Cesare Borgia and his troops, husbands and wives dragged by their hair to slaughter in the public square. Not suitable conversation for a woman struggling with grief. He reminded himself that he must proceed carefully. Lisa Gherardini was a woman of shifting emotions, like water, like the moon reflecting the light of the sun. "I once painted the portrait of Cecilia Gallerani," he said instead. "In Milan. She was the duke's mistress. About sixteen." He gestured for Lisa to return to her seat. "She was known for her musicality and her sharp tongue."

Neither captured his fascination. What had intrigued him— what he wanted to paint into her portrait—was her face frosted with the ice of rejection. He had bound her neck with tiny dark beads and placed a sleek, creamy ermine in her arms, her long white fingers caressing the rodent. The animal was a signal that she was capable of plotting revenge. The duke had cast her aside after she gave him a child. In the portrait, she was a woman who looked but did not tell.

"I must admit to my penchant for difficult emotions—feelings of outrage and injustice that have to be repressed. To keep your husband happy, or your place in society."

"My tears shock you, is that right?"

"Not at all," he said, looking gently at her. "I am learning, is all."

"Perhaps, over time, you might admit to the importance of expressed human emotions."

He nodded and glanced at his work. In his sketchbooks, while she was away from the studio, he had established that Madonna Lisa would be sitting on a chair in front of a stone balcony. But what world should lie beyond still perplexed him. He'd considered a cityscape, buildings from Florence, possibly the Basilica of San Lorenzo from Lisa's own neighborhood. But he fretted about choosing architecture—replicating something that might soon enough be demolished. Maybe he should paint nature instead. The question was, which landscape? Lake? River? Craggy cliff?

When he looked up at his subject, he knew her thoughts were back with her daughter Piera. She was beyond time, edges blurred; there was an ambiguity about where her smile began and ended. The shadow of death had seeped into the room. He saw the sorrow, held her feelings, their weight and their feathered texture, as if a sparrow lay dead but still warm in his palm. He continued to gaze at the woman with the same attention he would give an acorn or a bat. He smelled her loss, its putrid odor, her sadness.

For him, the human experience was mirrored in nature. She was on a journey, feeling everything: the rain squalls, the shadowy caves, the bitterness of wormwood.

Chapter 25

Salaì burst into the studio. He had been playing *baletta* in the open grasslands of San Marco monastery. Hot, sweaty, he discarded his red beret and his purple tunic, hauled off his linen shirt with balloon sleeves, then pulled off his stockings, which clung stubbornly to his skin, finally hurling them into the air. Stripped to his underclothes, he lifted a carafe of wine and downed half of it, then stuffed a wedge of cheese into his mouth. "Artists against goldsmiths," he said, his voice muffled by the food. "It was agreed last night at the Buco. But just before the match started, a whole crew of silk workers showed up to play with the goldsmiths—"

"Representing the Arte della Seta," said Leonardo, looking with despair at the tossed clothing on the floor.

Beatrice was walking around the studio, looking at the drawings pinned to the wall.

"And Giovanni, who is supposed to be on our side—who works for you under this roof—agreed to the extra players."

"Were you inclined to rush out and recruit some doctors for your team?" Leonardo could imagine Salaì at the center of the mayhem, turning various shades of purple to match the rise of his temper.

"Exactly! Painters and doctors—all of us part of the same guild, so why not?"

"How about we invite them next to a dinner party and share food instead of *baletta* balls?" Leonardo rose, needing air, wanting more from his exchanges with Salaì, but unable to see his way clear to something sweeter.

"I'm exhausted," said Salaì, flinging himself down on the straw mattress, legs split wide, wiping a sheet over his sweaty torso.

Beatrice was lingering in the room, as she always did after making her olive oil delivery. "It seems your life of luxury exhausts you," she said, looking sideways at Salaì. She treated him much like an annoying older brother, one full of antics and rudeness, and it was clear she had no patience for the way Leonardo indulged him.

"Who's talking?" He laughed, still prostrate on the bed. "Didn't you say you lived in a castle up on the hill?"

Beatrice kept her eyes on a conté sketch of a woman with disheveled hair. Leonardo heard her murmur how beautiful and sorrowful the woman was, head bent as if she were succumbing to the weight of her life. He could see Beatrice taking in the way light played delicately across the face. "I'm still standing. You're the one lying down," she said, looking up at Salaì at last, her eyes flashing.

"Oh, the olive oil girl is getting high and mighty," sneered Salaì, sitting up on the bed, ready to spar. "Is it because you're wearing fine boots these days? Do tell—you're here among friends—where did you steal them from?"

"In truth, they were a gift from Madonna Gherardini. She is a beloved patron, and I owe a debt of gratitude to her."

Leonardo turned toward the girl, suddenly interested. "How is she?"

"I cannot speak to that, Maestro, as her interior thoughts are her own private matter."

Leonardo knew Beatrice felt fiercely protective of Lisa and did not wish to divulge anything of their relationship to her portrait painter—and especially not to Salaì, whom, he suspected, she thought a thuggish pretty boy. Though she was still staying at Agnella's, in the village, he knew she saw Lisa often, sometimes twice a week, mostly to listen to stories of Lisa's happy times in Chianti, her favorite horse, whose name was Dante, the harvesting of grapes to make glorious, rustic red wine with her family. Lisa herself had told him they usually talked in the courtyard garden while pulling weeds and pruning the rosebushes, allowing the children to spill over each other and make forts of old worsted blankets. There were many signs that Lisa was slowly coming back to herself. He could picture them in the garden. They would sit cross-legged on the grass and Lisa would braid the hair of one of her daughters while Beatrice did Lisa's, decorating the tresses with lavender and gilliflowers.

He watched as Beatrice sifted through his drawings on the studio table, turning over page after page, and wondered if her own troubles could be healed.

"Maestro!" A cry of anguish leapt from her throat. "Maestro!" she shouted at Leonardo, hands gripping her head. "This drawing— who is this woman? Where did you find her? Tell me, where is she?"

He registered her anguished cry, the intensity of her emotion. Raw, without the gloss of fine manners that belonged to the privileged circles he typically frequented. He needed to pay attention. Lisa had taught him to do so. He stood up and faced Beatrice. Looking over at the drawing she was holding in her trembling hand, he remembered: "In the piazza." The scene from the Piazza della Santissima Annunziata flashed through his mind—the woman's suggestive *gamurra* and long, graceful neck, but also the dull, vacant look in her eyes. He recalled the bells on her ankles, the yellow triangle on her sleeve, how she had stolen his ocher-colored cape. Maybe she'd come to the city from a hill town in search of a better life and ended up a prostitute instead.

"Tell me. Listen to me." Beatrice gripped Leonardo's arms hard. "What color was her hair? Was it—"

"Auburn, with curls," he said, nodding, wanting to be helpful. "But it was two years ago when I saw her."

"She looks like my . . ." Beatrice's voice was strangled. "I have been trying to find her. Oh, please, take me to her," she said.

He held her in his arms while she sobbed. Salaì stepped next to them, silenced by her anguish. He reached over and gently smoothed her hair back from her face.

"I think this is my mother," she whispered, all energy gone out of her body.

Chapter 26

That night, Beatrice refused to go home with Agnella. She twisted her arm away and ran as fast as she could to the Piazza della Santissima Annunziata, where Leonardo had sketched the portrait of the woman she believed to be her mother.

A group of men were cavorting in the square, drunk on cheap wine or, more likely, alcohol made from pine needles. One pulled hard on his companion's shirt and both crashed to the ground. The larger man ripped free of his tattered blouson, displaying a body muscular from stonecutting. He reared to pummel the other man, splitting his cheek open.

Behind the front arcade of the Ospedale degli Innocenti, feral cats hissed at each other. Beatrice cleared the animals and put her back against one of the hospital's Corinthian columns. She laced her father's gambeson tight around her neck and pulled her hood over her head, ready to watch for her mother.

Long after night fell and streams of people had passed by with no familiar face among them, her fervor had quieted. With the market vendors gone to make their suppers of trencher bread and sops over open fires outside the city, Florence became subdued and hushed. Beatrice gazed at the hospital's terracotta rondels of babies in swaddling clothes. For the first time, she noticed they were not all the same, each sculpture a different essay on an individual life, and she scoffed at the kindness of the artist, trying to pay tribute to orphans left in a basket at the hospital's front door.

Listless and cold, she watched as a distinguished-looking man rushed past her. She did not recognize him, but found his head remarkable for its resemblance to a rodent. As if heeding a sign from above—from Diana or the Virgin Mary or God, she did not know or care—Beatrice had a sudden jolt and decided to follow the man. Keeping a safe distance, she hurried along the cobblestoned streets in his shadow until they reached the Ponte alle Grazie. The Medici owned most of the brothels in Florence, that much she knew. Where else would a man be going at this time of night?

On a side street before the bridge, she watched as the man eased open a discreet door with a lily carved into its panel. The building was low-slung, without any windows facing the street. She wondered if her mother could be confined there without the right to look down into the street for fear of poisoning the people who passed. Did she dare enter such a place? When she considered her fear, particularly her fear of being flogged in a public square for invading private property, her feet stayed on the ground. When she considered that a flight of stairs and a stone wall might be the only barriers to a reunion with her mother, she felt invincible.

She pushed the door open. A guard blocked her way. "*Idiota*," she muttered, cursing her stupidity.

"It's late for a girl to be wandering the streets," said the man. "After the last tolling of the Angelus." He had an unhealthy, fish-scaled complexion, and eyed her hungrily. "Looking to pass the time?"

"No, I only hoped to know . . ." She tried to think of a lie, to no avail. Fighting to stand, feeling the animal weight of her exhaustion, she whispered the truth: "I'm looking for my mother."

"Aren't we all?" He chuckled softly in the grim light and stepped forward.

"She might be here. Curly auburn hair, a long neck. Her name is Leda."

"Nobody here calls themselves that. Though she sounds like a looker. Do you ever do tricks together?" He reached out a hand to grab her neck, but Beatrice ducked. Swiftly, he kicked her into the street.

"Please help me," said Beatrice, falling to her knees, hands clasped tightly in a wretched prayer.

"Go ask Machiavelli. He might know." The man laughed before closing the door hard in her face, thickening the air with his scorn.

For three days, Beatrice slept rough in the city, searching for her mother, finding no trace. She hid from the city's night officers and the *sbirri* with their daggers unsheathed. In the stifling Tuscan heat that plagued her night and day, she wandered the streets of the convents and circled back to the lane of brothels, finding peace from the harassments of men, young and old, near a small lemon orchard at the Ripoli convent. One afternoon, the heat twisted into an unbearable humidity—the promise of a thunderstorm that never delivered. She sat in a laneway behind Santa Spirito, using a stub of charcoal to draw an angel plunging upside down on a stone wall. Her clothes were damp with sweat. From a distance, a cabal of Servite priests walked slowly toward her, their black hoods pulled low over their heads, their tunics shifting slowly around them. Maybe her mother had quit the city to finally go home, she thought. She dropped the stub and struggled to her feet.

Love is painful and lonely, but it is also an exercise in hope. She picked up the handles of her cart and moved east, head down, passing through the city gates to trudge listlessly up the hills to Settignano. Her mind had fogged over with hunger, and her cart was empty. But the dream of her reunion with her mother kept her mind focused and her legs moving. As she passed the oak forests toward the towering cypresses, she convinced herself that she'd been a fool. It was obvious that her mother had been waiting for her to come home all this time. Pushing forward along the craggy path, she regretted the time she had wasted in the city. And staying with Agnella had been all wrong; she had come under her spell and grown soft in her warm kitchen with the aromatic smells.

She crested the hill and pushed through a final stretch of forest to the family clearing. At last, after waiting for so long, their time to reunite had finally come. She would be sure to celebrate by drawing a pair of birds alighting in their family nest, the mother feeding a babe from its mouth.

Years had passed since she had last seen her mother. What if the naked eye could see time, up close, in all of its dimensions, she wondered. Would it turn up as male or female, object or animal, rich or poor? How would it travel? Would it float as something delicate and rarefied, like a golden thread in olive oil, or swim like a fish blading its fin past an old rowboat?

She could not understand why the door to her home was swung open on its iron hinges, why the charred mattress lay brutally on the ground. She dared to look tentatively inside, but it was black with fire, scorched beyond recognition. Even the iron cauldron in the open hearth, where her mother would lovingly tend to stews and soups, had been stolen.

Beatrice walked to the pen where the hen hutch had once stood and found only a rat scrounging for forgotten kernels of corn. The sun had sunk low, shading the hills matte blue, and night fell over the olive grove. Crawling like an animal, she slunk to the base of the old olive tree. She took off her leather boots and hurled them into the darkness. Reaching into her satchel, she took out the piece of *sanguigna* that Michelangelo had given her. Slumping on the ground, she wiped the chalk across her forehead, below her eyes, down her cheeks. A girl without papyrus, without family, her home destroyed by marauders. Once a warrior, her heart shattered, she lay down and prayed she might never see the dawn.

Chapter 27

Beatrice's mother had washed her in the summertime waters of the river the day after she was born, immersing her fully. She didn't bawl, just lay there, floating happily in the shallows. Leda had told Agnella this, confiding in her when they were washing clothes at the river one day. They had walked past the willows and dark, shadowy ivy hanging from the tree branches to settle their laundry baskets at the edge of the river, where the water ran clear. Beatrice was young, maybe eight years old. She liked to stalk fish, amazed at their perfect symmetry when they were still, waiting for the tail to curve, softly angling to one side. "How easy it is to catch a brown trout," she would whisper, her body naked, and she would bring a fish back and silently drop it into the basket, delighted by the work of her bare hands.

❖

Now Agnella held Beatrice below her shoulders and watched the warm bath waters loosen her hair.

"Michelangelo, some more hot water."

She heard him set the iron cauldron above the fire as she bent over the large wooden tub, supporting Beatrice in her arms. The girl was immersed in the water, eyes closed in sweet resignation, lips upturned. All the anger and bitterness that had pinched down on her face had gone. Knowing Beatrice, she was probably dreaming that she was a creature of the river.

Two forest-green velvet curtains were draped around the tub, the better to keep the heat in and ensure privacy. She and Michelangelo had built the round basin from oak dried in her shed for two years, pounded into place through mortice and tenon joinery. Most Florentines contented themselves with bathing on occasion in large open bathhouses called stews. Agnella considered that a disgusting and unclean habit. To her, bathing was all about pleasure and healing, deserving of the most luxurious attentions. She shifted position on a thick cushion covered in white linen and allowed the girl to float on her own. What a beauty she was, still an innocent, though the wolves had been biting hard at her heels. Despite her skinniness, the sharp angles of her shoulder blades, there was a bloom to her lips and to her breasts rising above the water. Agnella stroked the girl's cheeks. Water dripped from her bangles, the gold and silver glittering in the morning light.

A neighbor in the village had sent word to her at the hospice that Beatrice had been seen walking in a state of distress to Settignano the night before. She had trotted her mule over to Michelangelo's studio, woken him and ordered him into the cart. They had discovered the girl at the base of the great olive tree in the gray predawn, stiff and seizing up.

Michelangelo parted the curtains, his face turned away, and passed her the cauldron and a ladle. "Careful now, pour it in easy, away from her," he said, his voice heavy with worry.

Despite her own concern, Agnella couldn't suppress a grin that *he* was instructing her.

"Pass me the rose oil—it's on the shelf above the fire."

He stuck his hand through the curtains again and handed her the earthenware jar.

Agnella caught some of the perfumed elixir in her hand and rubbed it gently into the girl's cheeks. "She doesn't want to open her eyes," she said, angling her head to try to understand.

"Wash her hair," he said, shifting restlessly. "You know, how you used to do."

She smiled that he remembered the times she had washed his hair when he was a small boy, her fingers lovingly massaging his scalp with her soap made from lavender and mutton oil. Later, when he was older, she would rub her poultice of olive oil and salt into his hands, dried and calloused many times over from days of working with the chisel without a break. And then there were the times when she would dress the welts on his small back, the result of beatings from his father for daring to dream of becoming a sculptor. He would wait patiently, never speaking a word of malice about Lodovico, while she applied linen strips cooled in a tincture of chamomile.

She reached a wet hand to brush away stray locks running across Beatrice's brow. "Stay with us," she said to Michelangelo, hoping to convince him to rest for a while. "You used to live here.

Remember?" She wiped a sleeve against eyes running with tears as she recalled their years together, when her husband was alive and Michelangelo was a little boy.

Together, she and Michelangelo would help set Beatrice back on her feet. And it would keep him away from Florence for a time—away from the naked colossus and the Office of the Night.

"Can you get the towels ready?" she said, her voice harsh to hide her emotion. "They're in the cedar cupboard."

He found a stack of linen towels and inhaled their sweet fragrance, made from the quince tree in the back orchard. Handing them through the curtains, he said, "Wrap one around her head."

"You know I will." She remembered wrapping his own freshly washed head in a towel and telling him he looked like a Medici prince or the sultan of Syria, though he was only five years old. Then she would kiss him on both cheeks and hand him a cup of rosehip tisane.

"Tell her she looks like a fair duchess," said Michelangelo. "She'd like that. I'll make the tea."

Chapter 28

A flash of color caught his eye and Leonardo bent to look out a window from the upper corridor. Just as he had hoped, it was Madonna Lisa leaving her carriage and crossing the inner courtyard of the Santissima Annunziata monastery, wonderfully, bravely alone again. Her red silk *gamurra* spilled like pomegranate juice onto the cobblestones. The monks had gone outdoors to pull weeds now that the heat of the day had lost its intensity. They tugged their hoods over their shaved heads and stared sideways at her.

Lifting her full skirts with one hand swept to the side, she traveled up the stone steps leading to Leonardo's studios. "A gift for you and your assistants," she said, setting the heavy basket of lemons and pears down and walking past Leonardo to the windows. "Do I look strange to you?" She was peering at the gardeners in the courtyard below.

"They mean no harm," said Leonardo. "Most are young, parochial and accustomed to women being kept behind closed doors."

"I feel their eyes burning my skin when I walk across the field. They are thinking strange thoughts, no doubt."

"Such as?" Leonardo was intrigued.

"'A woman. Alone. Outside at sunset. Scandalous! Will this harlot pose nude for the great artist?' Oh, and another thing: 'What's in the basket she's carrying against her hip like a peasant?'"

"You provide their only delight." Drawing at this time was his preference, when the brilliant, unmediated light of the day was nearly extinguished. That or posing his subjects against blackened walls.

"It's true. Their life must be one of excruciating monotony."

"Beatrice would chase them away."

"Yes, so true. I miss her."

"A villager at heart, our dear Beatrice."

"Given to the whims of a hot-blooded teenager," said Lisa.

"Never mind. I shall greet you at the carriage next time; we shall dance across instead."

Lisa clapped her hands. Without a moment's hesitation, she stepped lightly across the studio, quick on the balls of her feet. "Soderini will want to see our entertainments."

"I was thinking the pope," countered Leonardo.

Lisa turned a pirouette. "We will charge for the privilege."

"One ducat per person," agreed Leonardo.

"One golden florin," corrected Lisa. The currency common in Florence, not Venice. She stopped at the long wooden table and picked up a drawing of a machine with enormous wings attached to a man. "We need to fly like birds?" she said, looking at him from the corner of her eye.

"Would you like to try? I'm looking for willing candidates."

"Ask Salaì," she said. She went behind the screen and called out: "My feet are staying on the ground."

He could hear her unlacing her clothing, dropping the garments onto a wooden bench and stepping into the *gamurra* he'd chosen for her.

"It feels like a second skin," she said from behind the screen. "The silk is finely woven—Francesco must have helped you source the material."

"Not him, but his assistants did," Leonardo called back. "How do you feel about the neckline?"

"It's lower than I would normally wear," she said, looking down at her cleavage as she emerged from behind the screen. "The monks in the courtyard would be scandalized, no doubt."

Leonardo nodded, appreciating the effect of what was barely visible to the eye: a sheer black veil to define the edges of her face and her female, married *virtù*.

"How do you feel?"

"Exhausted and exhilarated." She tilted her head, considering. "As if a teenager after riding for miles along the valleys of Chianti. Beatrice has helped me retrieve those happy memories." She touched her ring finger to her forehead and tapped it. "I feel you, too, are touching my mind."

His thoughts darted to the dissection of the man's brain he had performed in the room beside his studio.

"Cleaving it open," she continued, "reminding me to believe again in my strength, the old power of the Gherardini family."

A long period of silence followed, with Lisa turning slow circles around the room while Leonardo worked. He encouraged her to move—it revealed so much more about her interior mind than sitting ever could. Looking at his sketches and working from the woman standing in front of him, he drew an underpainting of Lisa in charcoal, wiping away where he wanted to create shimmering highlights, going in and out with the black pencil to model the shape of her body, pushing and pulling to emphasize the body's contours, the angles of her face, the length of her neck. He needed to establish the ground before applying color, layer upon layer of translucent color.

"You have gone into the face of the deep," he said at last.

"As written in the Bible."

"It's a powerful book."

"I stayed in my dark place a long time. Unmoving in my boudoir, unable to eat, incapable of feeling. Beatrice and Agnella saved me. I would eat figs that the girl stole from my neighbor's orchard. They cared for me in ways my *popolo grasso* society friends never did."

"Those village women threw you the rope of life."

"Yes, they did. But I'm trying to understand my life before that, with Francesco." She pressed a hand gently against the side of her veil. "I spoke, but I was never heard." She considered, waiting. "You listen to me."

He looked up, encouraging her to go on. The bodice of her dress had turned the color of green hills darkened by the evening's gloaming.

"When I first came here, I was shaking with fear. I didn't know what to say, or how to impress you."

"But you're an intelligent being," he said, and he realized that when he read to her verses of love and humanity by Petrarch or heartfelt poems by Dante Alighieri, he savored them all over again because of her, because of the way her eyes glowed when he looked at her. Salaì had never warmed to poetry. Though playing *baletta* inspired him to no end.

"'A mighty flame followeth a tiny spark,'" he quoted, eyeing her.

"You know"—Lisa smiled—"that might well be my favorite line by Dante because when you first recited it, I felt that you saw me."

"There is much to see in you."

"My husband is ever occupied with his business—importing leather from Ireland these days—and he purchased a new slave the other day."

"Oh?" Leonardo hesitated, disturbed by this new information. The cruelty. The dehumanization. "Does she have a name?"

"He gave her the name Sophia. Though she has not been shown to me. I do believe he thinks me stupid. But you don't seem to mind my mind." She tapped her forehead again and smiled her half smile. "Your battle scene," she said. "Have you started it yet? My husband hopes to arrange a tour to impress his friends."

"War must be honestly captured," said Leonardo.

"When the idea is complete, the sketching is quick," she said, feeding his own words back to him.

He walked to the window ledge and looked up at the sky, now fully dark. He motioned to her to stand beside him, as a brother might beckon a younger sister. "See it there—the white specks way up high? I think of it as white sand thrown from a beach into the sky."

"Milk from a Greek goddess?"

"A nighttime path of souls traveling from Earth to the heavens."

"Why a path?" He heard her step next to him to look even more closely at the sky. "God transports the deserving souls immediately to Heaven."

"How do you imagine the specifics of the transportation?"

"God wills it and His command is granted."

"In midair appears a wooden carriage, a white stallion? Or Swiss fighters? Maybe somebody who can fly?"

"You are more scientist than Christian," she granted, her hand on his shoulder. "But how can any of us know the details of all that is unseen? You make a mockery of Him to imagine the mechanics of how a soul travels upward to Heaven."

In art, simplicity of line captivated him. In life? His relationship with the mercurial Salaì could be described as a series of sharply angled valleys and peaks. With Lisa, he felt their conversation carried them forward along a cobblestoned road that disappeared gently into the distance.

"My intention is not to rankle. Otherwise, I may be forced to throw my portrait on a great burning pyre." Only seven years had passed since the crazed Dominican prior Savonarola had worked Florentines into a frenzy over their hedonistic ways and an apocalypse to come, provoking them to burn their cosmetics and jewels, even their Botticelli paintings, in a massive fire at the Piazza della Signoria. Leonardo had been away in Milan during the terror. "Madonna, did you contribute anything to the fire?"

"We had to. It wasn't that I wanted to. The police were checking homes. I gave a string of pearls to a servant to throw onto the pyre. The apocalypse never arrived and I regretted the loss of the necklace, given to me by my most beloved grandmother, from the old Gherardini lineage."

He returned to his easel and she looked around the room, suffused with golden candlelight. The workday had long since passed, but Leonardo had no intention of quitting.

"Are you satisfied with my portrait?" she inquired. "So far, I mean."

"I'll likely have to start again," he said, shrugging and smiling kindly at her. "This one's not that good."

On hearing this, she ran to the easel. Leonardo blocked the portrait with his body. "Though I would hate to part with this fine piece of poplar board."

She threw her arms up in the air. "When can I have a look?"

"Soon enough, soon enough, my fine Florentine lady." He motioned to the chair in front of the table, placed his hand at the small of her back and, using his fingertips, propelled her forward. "Now, shall we try to make something of this portrait, Mona Lisa?"

She sat and pressed her hands down the flats of her bodice. She settled herself, straightened her back and arranged her sleeves like hills of ocher falling over the wooden arms of the chair, saying, "You place your faith in knowledge. I place mine in religion."

"True enough. As you have already observed, I am more scientist than believer." His mind wandered to his preliminary drawings for the altarpiece: was he right to place the daughter, Mary, on her mother's knee? He shook his head; he could settle that later. For now, he needed to concentrate on the task at hand. Looking at his palette, Leonardo weighed the steps necessary to create a shimmer of sweat: his assistants had ground white pigment, placing a small amount of the precious powder next to rose pigment and a dash of powdery cinnabar. Moving delicately, he transferred a mix of the pigments into walnut oil, one at a time, and stirred the ingredients slowly to create a thin glaze that looked nearly color-less, a rose-gold, approximating the color of damp skin. Oils were slower to dry than egg used to dilute tempera paint, and they pro-duced more subtle shades of color. That's what he wanted, what he needed to test, to paint lightness emanating from the wooden board—it mattered very little whether this experiment would take months or even years.

With a thin hog-bristle brush, he selected from powders of muted, earthy tones: blues, browns and forest green—the color of Lisa's *gamurra*. Using the blade of a small knife, he transferred the pigments into walnut oil held within a freshwater mussel shell. He stirred the liquid patiently until it registered as another almost colorless glaze.

"Where do the best pigments come from?" asked Lisa.

"Venice. Salaì fetches them for me. Cinnabar for reds, mala-chite for greens. The German blue comes from the mineral azur-ite. Sometimes I use Florentine suppliers, the Ingesuati and the convent of San Giusto alle Mura. The monks there have a labo-ratory with small furnaces." He wiped the side of his brush and tapped its bristles against the pestle. "They are suitably skilled in the manufacture of colors."

When he touched his brush to the board, she murmured that it was almost as if he were stroking the skin of her face, the transpar-ent glaze of walnut oil sticky and wet down her cheek. One stroke. Another, then another.

Thirty minutes into the sitting, she signaled with her hand, then rose from the chair. She stretched and walked across the room to the bowl of fruit. "Orange?" she asked boldly. It was not her place to handle food without the help of a servant. Leonardo remained bent over the portrait, concentrating intensely, and did not reply. She hesitated, then peeled the orange herself and handed him a dripping section. "I've never noticed before how sticky the juice is, and how pulpy the flesh. The textures of an orange are mesmerizing."

"I do place my faith in knowledge," he said, straightening, picking up the earlier thread of their conversation. "In ideas and theories and places still undiscovered. I am also unlearned and ignorant." He watched her lift an orange segment and bring it to her mouth. "I am an *uomo senza lettere*."

She dismissed this last assertion with a wave of her hand.

"I place my hope in my ability to imagine," he continued. "In my imagination there is a pair of glasses that you and I could place in front of our eyes, the better to see the moon. There is a machine that allows me to speak to the sultan of Syria without having to travel to see him. And another that allows us to breathe underwater. But please, don't misunderstand me. Like you, I am amazed and inspired by the way God works."

She returned to her chair. Her body appeared to be trembling.

Leonardo considered her face, the robust, full bones of her profile, a generous, wide forehead giving way to delicate nostrils. He could not read her now. She moved like a woman of wealth and good fortune, was shuttered from the world. And yet. A moment ago, peeling an orange by herself. How strange and remarkable.

Truly, her profile was inscrutable. A thought, unbidden, came to him: the old nobleman whose gnarled face he had sketched the other day, the one seated with his back against the baptistery. Who sat motionless for an hour, then stood and walked away without asking to see the drawing.

She was a woman of sorrow, but hers was a mind in flux. He knew what it was to desire, to despair, to regret. But to descend into darkness, as she clearly had . . . taken by surprise, he realized that he felt seduced by her capacity for emotion.

"For example, I believe you need only travel to a woman's bedroom," he said, lifting his brush nonchalantly, "to witness one of His greatest miracles: the birth of a child."

He needed to say this, to raise to the surface the awful thing.

Rising from the chair, she did a slow turn around the room, her gown brushing the wooden floor. He saw how she clenched her hands, how her face darkened, instantly stricken. They had both experienced loss. But he had buried his sorrow for a long time. Madonna Lisa reminded him what it was to feel pain.

"A miracle, yes, that is true," she said slowly, her back rigid. The orange peels curled in her hand. "Or a nightmare. Women die in birthing beds. And babies, too, blue in the face when they are brought into the world."

"Your child did not die at birth."

"No, not at birth," she whispered. "Piera was four years old. Her fever—her cheeks burned my fingers. She was limp and couldn't breathe anymore."

"And you have mourned the loss deeply." He thought of a sonnet Dante had written: *One day Melancholy came to me and said: "I want to stay with you awhile"; and it seemed to me she brought Sorrow and Wrath with her as companions.*

"I was not fully aware of her condition." Her face contorted for a second before she regained control. "Of anything, really." And then the wretchedness came hurtling across her face. "I was real before I started playing a role—this—" she said, waving her hand toward the city. "Before marrying," she clarified.

"Tell me the best memory of your childhood."

"How could I? There are far too many!"

"Tell me a story, Madonna. I am all ears."

She relaxed back into the chair, seemingly grateful for the way he had released her from the pain, and smiled. Finally, she spoke: "*Allora* . . . I would ride my horse through the hills near Caprese and my father would ride with me. Where the gnarled olive trees and terraced vines cut their shapely lines down the slopes and the cypresses point like feathers to the sky."

"Away from the city."

"Always. Our family—my grandfathers and great-grandfathers— owned much land, many manors in this area. Before they traded away their nobility and their claim to the land to become citizens of Florence. We liked to ride in the autumn, after the olive harvest. One afternoon the skies grew dark and the clouds curled into strange shapes. I remember they spread like juniper bushes in the sky. The wind picked up and the howling became so strong we could barely hear each other's voices."

"And were you frightened?" he asked, noting the shape of her body, its geometry, her torso ever so slightly twisted from the hips.

"We found refuge in a hunting lodge. It looked abandoned.

We crawled in through a window and I made a fire for us in the hearth." She inhaled deeply. "My father had dried boar in his sack. I fried our bread in garlic and lard, and we ate our *fett'unta* piled with the meat. He wrapped his gambeson around me and we slept there that night. That was when I felt the most love for my father. His name was Antonmaria."

Leonardo nodded. My own father is dying, he thought. He had heard whispers in the marketplace: "The notary is unwell." On his deathbed, a few streets away from this monastery. Had he ever felt love for his father, the way he did for his mother, who had likely ceased to exist long ago? His father had told him it was better to think of her as one of the unlucky peasant girls who died young, as was so often the way.

Against the shadows of the studio, he noted the skin of Lisa's face; it shone immaculate and golden. Her body had become a lantern with a flame flickering inside. He crossed to her, gently moved her right shoulder to angle backward, then eased her chin in the opposite direction. Contrapposto. Interesting.

She settled into the position, rested her right hand atop the left. "I want to breathe again," she said simply.

He nodded and waited patiently for her to go on.

"Eight years married to a man twice my age. Five children. My daughter Piera dead."

He saw that she was speaking these words for the first time, pushing them out of her as if they were poison, something she needed to let go of, like judgment and shame.

Chapter 29

Suffering slowed her down. So did thinking about her suffering and how she wanted to stop thinking about it. She needed to escape her weary thoughts. Take an axe to the bark of a tree and hack away the hungry worms.

At the edge of Agnella's village plot, Beatrice found solace in a thicket of red raspberries. In the evening, when the winds lifted and the sky deepened to a polished black, she would sit on the dirt and examine the shape of the leaves, the hoary thorns running the length of the stems. Imagining herself as a bee, she would taste the bitter white berries before hovering her mouth over the tender ripe ones, nipping them free with her teeth, allowing them to melt on her tongue.

Someday, when it was safe again to leave Agnella's home in Settignano for Florence, when Pisan marauders finally tired of wrecking people's homes, she would take a raspberry branch to Leonardo. "Something you might like to draw," she would say to him, handing him the branch, with its difficult textures.

Agnella and Michelangelo had tried to heal her with soap and their easy banter. She liked being with them; she liked how they poured water into each other's cups, and their gentle silences within the imperfect stone walls. From her corner piled with sheepskins, she took pleasure in watching Michelangelo, the breadth of his shoulders, the deep worry lines between his eyebrows.

One evening at dusk, the moon not yet visible in the sky, Agnella brought her a bowl of chicken soup. Crossing her legs, Beatrice took the broth and asked, "Can I have salt?" Michelangelo rose from his seat on the bench and delivered the pinch bowl to her. "Is there no bread to dip in my soup?" she complained. She was feeling petulant and wanted to test her friends to see how far she could push them before they would break. They ignored her and sat back down on the bench. "I liked myself better when I was younger," she said, louder than was necessary. "Before the troubles. The Pisans. My father."

"Hard times," said Michelangelo, and she heard him shifting his weight, dragging his boots against the floor.

"Then my mother. I think I was thirteen when she left."

"No longer a child," he murmured, leaning over his drawings.

"That's when my childhood ended," said Beatrice, sighing deeply, quite aware that Agnella and Michelangelo were exchanging exasperated glances. Rising to her feet, she placed her soup bowl quietly on the wooden table. "I'm sorry," she said. "It's time. I would kick me out of here if I were you."

Agnella's irises flicked purple in the darkening room. "Let me tell you something, Beatrice," she said. She sipped from her own bowl of soup. "Michelangelo and I do not agree on everything."

"Dead right," said Michelangelo. He scuffed his boots on

the floor. "But we agree on certain things. One is, knock before coming into my studio."

"The other is that it's easy to get to know somebody's lightness," said Agnella. Michelangelo looked up from his drawing. "But it's far more interesting to understand their darkness."

"Without the darkness, my art would be dead," said Michelangelo. He pointed a finger at Beatrice. "Same for yours."

She felt the truth in his words, for she had already traveled more than once into deep sadness. "I think I'll do some drawing," she said, sidling up to the table and slowly arranging her skirts on the bench.

Michelangelo and Beatrice often sat at the end of the wooden table, hunched over their drawings. He had presented her with a quill pen that Agnella had cut from a goose feather, and shown her how to tip black ink into it. Although it was unspoken, he had become her artistic mentor. He was training her on drawing the folds of cloth wrapped around people or angels, something he insisted she master before moving on to figure drawing. She liked deepening the shadows by darkening the crosshatching with fine lines drawn with her new pen. He would lean over and borrow the quill to show her how to deepen or extend the strokes of a figure wrapped in drapery. When he returned the quill, he slipped it back between her fingers and closed them gently around its slender tip. They were divided by culture—he of a noble name, she of refugee parents—and separated by age, Michelangelo being nearly twelve years older. But his kindness, and his body, made her long badly for him, and she found herself staring at him while slowly caressing her neck with the white feather. If he looked up from his drawing, she would be forced to leave the table and go outside to throw rocks at the sky. This happened several times every day.

Agnella stood to clear their soup bowls. "You need to set aside some of your wildness," she advised, scooping slop from the day's meals into an iron pail for the hens.

"My wildness? It's the warrior in me that keeps me alive." Beatrice's thoughts darkened, clouding with the faces of men preying on her in the piazzas of the city, touching her, clawing at her clothing.

"Your recklessness might have killed you many times over. It's a wonder you're still standing."

"All those men who like to hate. They get to be the heroes and I have to cower."

Agnella moved from the slop pail to grind olives into a paste. She threw some thyme into the mix and spread the black tapenade onto a slice of bread, still warm from the wood-burning fire.

Beatrice took the offering and bit into it, moaning loudly with pleasure. "I need a long cutting knife to defend myself," she said through her stuffed mouth. Her eyes pleaded with Agnella. "Why not give me one? I need it more than I need your fancy clothes." Agnella had found her a new *guarnello* to replace her ripped and faded dress, and had given her one of her own embroidered linen cloaks, retiring Beatrice's old quilted gambeson to the cellar for safekeeping.

"I'm afraid you'll have to be less independent. These unsettled times demand it. Stay close to me or Michelangelo."

"You think of me as a child." And she turned away to pout, hunched over her drawing, shutting down further conversation.

❖

She gave herself tests for walking out beyond the house, down the road, past the church, and back again to the safety of Agnella's refuge. At first, that was all the courage she owned. Michelangelo accompanied her on the farther walks, nodding to the locals and asking about their families, their children, the rates for their stonework. Unbidden, he would hum a tune, singing a simple melody, usually the same one, with a sprinkling of words such as "*La pietra serena brilla*" or "*La Madre e Il Bambino*." She could not believe they actually belonged to a song. More likely he was thinking about the sculpting that awaited him back in Florence. But his half-verbal songs were oddly comforting, and so she found herself humming along, singing the words a few seconds after he did.

One day, they scrambled through the dense oak forest, ferns and periwinkles grazing their legs, and descended to the riverbank so she could show him the clearing she loved, where she caught fish with her hands and admired the streaks of color reflecting from the stones. "Will you swim?" she asked, looking at him with a wicked half smile. Without answering, he dropped his clothes and, naked, walked into the river. She protested at first, erupting in nervous laughter, shocked that he had taken up her dare. But then she found herself standing naked next to him. Suddenly, she wanted everything she had repressed for days living together under the same roof. She wanted to explore his tongue and touch him the way she had the peasant boys, under cover of vines cascading from the trees. Nobody would know. Not even Agnella. She would take her chances with him, this man who liked her, who liked men, too.

Gripping his shoulders, feeling wonderfully, wildly, no longer like a child, she held steady against the current of the river and kissed him fully on the mouth. She felt his need, his hunger, liked the way he lifted her up against his pelvis as if to test their faith. The moment felt suspended in the air; they were both breathing hard, and they clung to each other, their naked bodies slick. But then his hardness went soft and she removed her mouth. They dressed on the bank of the river in awkward silence. Never again, she thought. She had seen him with the naked model behind the canvas curtain. He liked her to a point, but not the way he enjoyed other men.

They returned to Agnella's and hid their intimacy—and their shame—by being extra helpful with the chores. She eyed them suspiciously, then looked at her bracelets and seemed to be muttering a long, repeating prayer.

"I am traveling to Florence in a few days," she announced over dinner, looking from Michelangelo to Beatrice. "Work demands it and so does my pocketbook. I can take you with me." She looked directly at Beatrice. "Now, let's see to getting the knots out of your hair."

So it was that weeks after discovering the charred mattress in her battered family home, Beatrice agreed to return to Florence. They rode together in the wagon, the three of them, Michelangelo jumping out near the Duomo while Agnella and Beatrice traveled on to the Convent of San Jacopo di Ripoli. Beatrice had sold jars of olive oil to the nuns before, and she knew that the women operated a celebrated printing press, the second to be started in Florence. Two Dominican brothers supervised, Agnella had told her, but all the talent rested with the women. "Their elegant *stenti* attracts a dedicated and sophisticated following," she said, helping Beatrice down from the cart. "They set type for works by Plutarch, Plato, Augustine and Petrarch."

Even with a heavy basket hoisted on her hip, Beatrice stopped to look over the convent. She felt as if she was seeing it for the first time. It was built of local stone, its oak doors the only interruption of texture in its broad, austere facade. She had never paid attention to that before. Maybe, she thought, buildings expressed rhythms the way musical compositions did. Next to the convent stood the Church of San Jacopo di Ripoli, a genteel work of architecture, welcoming to all, its three archways framing a generous portico. A large cobblestoned courtyard introduced the set piece of architecture like a magnificent carpet rolled out to the public. Seeing it all together, she felt a sense of calm come over her, and she was glad to be back within the glorious city.

Beatrice put a hand behind her back and waved Agnella away. She was an olive oil vendor, all business—no need for a chaperone. Her hair shone below her freshly made garland of olive leaves and pink roses.

A big woman with florid coloring greeted her at the front door of the convent. She was wearing a long linen *gamurra* dyed in a modest earthy brown. "Beatrice," said Sister Francesca, the abbess, beaming a smile at her. "It has been a long time. Come in. Shut the door."

"Abbess!" a voice called out from somewhere inside the convent.

"That will be Sister Camilla," said the abbess. "We're putting the final touches on Boccaccio's *Decameron*." She cast a glance heavenward. "Camilla is obsessively, compulsively detailed." She looked again at Beatrice. "You have changed. I barely recognized you. You look fine today."

Beatrice looked at the floor, feeling shy. She was suddenly pleased that her ragged *guarnello* and her father's old jacket had been replaced by a linen dress dyed *azzurro*, the color of a clear blue sky. One of her hands rested on the pleats below her breasts. She caught the ribbon between her fingers, glad for its color, the pale yellow of parsnips.

"What treats have you brought us today?" asked the abbess.

"Lemons as sweet as oranges. Olive oil, apricot oil, lavender oil." She gestured to the basket with her free hand. "I pressed them with my neighbor." This meant Agnella. During their days together in Settignano, she had inspired Beatrice to offer more variety to her customers, and had shown her ways to perfume her olive oils.

Agnella had taught her something else: the difference between grieving and mourning. At least, Agnella saw a difference: "Grieving is a boat filled with water that's about to sink. Always on the brink of tipping over." Beatrice had been helping to feed the chickens, patting each one as they tottered forward to eat kitchen scraps from the palm of her hand. She might have looked only half-interested, dipping her head to receive feathered tickles from the birds, but she was paying careful attention to the healer's words. "Mourning is a boat that's already overturned so that everybody can see the ruin. The people you trust can help right it again."

"I will purchase one of each, Beatrice," the abbess said now. "But come with me." She motioned inside the convent. "Have you ever seen what we do here?"

Beatrice had not. She had never before been invited to. Perhaps a fresh change of clothing helped people improve on their kindness. She followed the woman into the dark corridor, with its polished terrazzo floors. The stone walls glowed with a scrubbed, soapy finish. She closed her eyes and enjoyed the sound of Sister Francesca's long *gamurra* dragging on the stones. It was a relief to step inside, away from the smells of the city and the morning sun beating down on the cobbles.

From the far side of the printing room, the abbess and Beatrice watched Sister Camilla at work. Her hands floated above the metal letters, looking for signs of imperfection. She leaned closer, making delicate adjustments to the blocks set within a shallow bed of saffron-colored sawdust. Natural light from south-facing windows flooded the room. Two other nuns, grim-faced and sweating, held a large oiled sheet, the tympan, to weigh down the letters.

The abbess approached and leaned carefully over the iron hand press.

"Final approval?" whispered Sister Camilla.

"I've given you that three times already, Sister Camilla."

"Yes, but the final approval is always the most painful."

Sister Francesca peered intently at the work. A minute passed.

Then another. Nobody spoke. A length of blond hair escaped from her cotton coif, and she pushed it away impatiently. Finally, she said, "Bless this, our humble offering lifted up to you." She and the other nuns crossed themselves, kissed their fingers and swept their hands heavenward.

"Press run of five hundred?" asked Sister Camilla.

"Yes, five hundred and be done with it. If there's a furor, we can reprint."

Sister Francesca turned her attention back to Beatrice. "We had grown accustomed to printing biblical pamphlets—thirty pages for every broadsheet. Setting type for *The Decameron* has allowed us to invent new forms of italics." She looked around the room furtively and leaned in, as if delivering some whorish gossip. "The type for this publication is lacy and organic." Her eyes widened. "Intentionally so."

The abbess moved away from the press. "Come, I'll show you the studio where we keep the paper." They ascended the stairs of stone slabs and entered a room bathed in sunlight. Colored inks in glass jars lined the shelves. Rolls of paper—French hemp and Italian flax, of varying weights and shades of cream and gray—were stacked up to the ceiling. Beatrice could read some of the labels: Fabriano, Prato, Coll.

Heavy footsteps on the stairs announced visitors. Beatrice recognized both of them from Leonardo's studio.

"Gentlemen, come in," said the abbess. "I was expecting you. You have come for drawing paper?"

"Give us your best price for Dutch-made," said Salaì. "And some wine if you have it."

Beatrice observed his energy, his jiggling feet. He seemed corked from a night of heavy drinking.

His companion, Giovanni Antonio Boltraffio, looked older and wiser. "The devil moves inside you this morning." He spoke with a harsh Milanese accent, without the luxury of vowels. He turned to the abbess. "We'll need enough to cover a wall measuring sixty by thirty feet. He wants the very best. *Carta bambagina* or finer, if it can be found. And not yellow—"

"He's looking for creamy white," said Salaì.

"No need for secrets between colleagues," said the abbess, wiping her brow with a linen cloth. She patted the bench beside her, gesturing for the men to sit down. "Am I correct to assume that this paper is for Leonardo's preparatory cartoon of *The Battle of Anghiari*?"

"Olive oil girl, I recognize you," said Salaì, ignoring the abbess and sliding his gaze over to Beatrice.

"And I recognize you, and your wild eyes. Like a hunter about to snare a rabbit," she said curtly, her cheeks growing hot. She remembered his kindness in Leonardo's studio when he wrapped his arms around her so tightly she could smell his sweat from his *baletta* game. That was then; this was now. She would not stoop to remind him of her name. He knew it well enough.

"My understanding is that Leonardo is obsessed these days with geometry," the abbess interrupted, "being most disgruntled with the brush. And yet here you are!" She looked at the gathered trio. "So Leonardo is preparing to paint again. Thanks be to God."

"My father," said Beatrice, looking at the abbess for encouragement, "loved Signore da Vinci's portrait of a girl called Ginevra." In fact, Leonardo had told her that the girl, who looked straight out at the world without fear, reminded him of her. "*Papà* described it to me so often I knew it as if it were hung in our house."

"When had he seen the portrait?" asked the abbess.

"Oh, he did not see it for himself! He heard about it from a priest at Santa Maria Novella." The memory made her eyes sting. She set down her basket and recovered herself. "He used to stand me in front of our juniper bush as his own Ginevra."

"As his own Ginevra," said Salaì, clapping his hands and leaping to his feet. "This is a revelation. It makes me think that all people should be able to see Leonardo's work." He gestured to Beatrice. "A peasant can enjoy it—here is proof. We should make his work public." His eyes darted between Giovanni and the abbess. "The preliminary drawing at the monastery where we're staying. The Virgin, the Child, Saint Anne and Saint John. Take it out from behind closed doors. Why not show Leonardo's genius to the public?"

"You can't be serious," said Giovanni.

"It is stunningly beautiful—so dark and haunting—full of humanity," said Salaì.

Beatrice didn't trust Salaì. He was selfish, always thinking of himself and whining to Leonardo about everything wrong in life. Maybe she was jealous of him. But this idea of his intrigued her.

"Abbess, you will be moved to tears. Imagine the most intimate moment between mother and daughter," said Salaì, bouncing on his toes. "The Virgin sitting on Anne's knees, their bodies pressed so easily together."

"Is it finished?" asked Giovanni.

"No, it is not, but what of it?"

"I would be most interested to see it," said the abbess.

"You will understand what I mean," said Salaì to the nun. "Leonardo has captured pure love. It is daring and brave, like an explorer discovering land for the first time. Leonardo as our Columbus!"

"I don't know who Columbus is," said Beatrice, her shoulders thrown back. "Perhaps he has discovered what has already been lived by other people long before him." Her words tumbled out, but she did not speak all of her thoughts. She was mostly remembering the feeling of being loved by her mother. It was inconceivable that all that nurturing had been taken away from her, though she was far from being done with it. She dared herself to speak again: "Sister, I have something to ask."

The nun folded her hands patiently together and waited in her gentle, pious way.

"I've been looking everywhere for my mother. She has been gone for almost four years. Maybe you could help me?"

Salaì was pacing the floor impatiently. "*Grazie, grazie.* We are all looking for someone. Did you know I'm an orphan, too? Leonardo never knew his mother. At least, he's never mentioned her to me. This is a culture of illegitimates, I'm afraid. Get used to it."

"Thank you, Salaì," the abbess said, cutting his observations short. "Have you tried the charities that care for homeless women, Beatrice? Finding missing people isn't my expertise."

"She has auburn hair and a long, beautiful neck!" Beatrice said, loudly and insistently. "Leonardo drew her. Please help me."

The abbess dropped some quattrini into Beatrice's hands and waved her toward the corridor. "It is in God's hands. But do come visit another day."

As Beatrice left the room, looking beseechingly back over her shoulder, Salaì was holding forth. "We must invite the gonfalonier, the priori, the guildsmen, the city's leading artists and navigators," he said, bouncing on his feet. "Invite Florentines young and old. And most definitely invite her," he said, pointing at Beatrice, "to represent the *popolo minuto.*"

Chapter 30

"It's a cool evening, but the stars will warm us," said Leonardo, his face sun-kissed from a day spent in the hills, sketching cypress and poplar trees and watching the flight of the red kite birds. Under the cover of night, they had walked through the streets from Leonardo's studio to Santa Maria Novella, using his thick iron key to let themselves into one of the private courtyards of the church.

"How would you paint the stars?" Lisa stopped to breathe in the space. The air had a November chill to it and she gathered her long wool cape tightly around her.

"They are unknowable. To represent them on a board might be an awful vulgarity." Leonardo spread a damask coverlet on the grass. There was daring in their decision to walk through the streets, hoods pulled over their faces, while Lisa's husband was away hunting bear in the north, her children tended by a houseful of servants.

"How are you doing tonight? These days?" he asked.

She looked at him seriously. "Free. Free as a man."

He raised a hand to the sky. "Could you paint them?"

"Can you believe I have never painted anything?"

"But if you did?"

"Well, then," she said, grazing her shoulder against his. "I would paint them the way I'd paint my soul."

"I like that," he said. He sat down and rummaged in his leather bag. "In my experience, with careful study and considerable patience, you can make a start of knowing the unknowable. As for the stars," he counseled, holding up a sliver of metal, "they have character and moods. Here, look through this. Hold it close to your own eye and look at these stars that appear so minute it seems nothing could be smaller."

She took the metal and sat beside him, arranging her skirts, then squinted to see.

"It is, in fact, the great distance that causes their diminution, for many of them are very many times larger than the star that is our Earth."

"If what you are saying is true, Leonardo, the sky is full of stars that are bigger and much older than the one we are on right now."

"I believe this to be true."

"What does one do with this knowledge?"

He drank from his wineskin and passed it to Lisa. "Live," he said at last. "Try to live honorably."

"You sound like the pope. I imagine he might say that to a crowd and do otherwise in his private rooms." She sighed deeply and took another sip, leaning closer to Leonardo. "Compared to those stars, we are very, very small. There was a time when all I wanted was to survive. But now?" Her thoughts seemed to travel. "It doesn't seem enough anymore," she said softly.

"Think beyond yourself. Once you begin to do so, you can observe much that most people ignore."

"Such as?"

"The air moves like a river and carries the clouds with it," said Leonardo. "Just as running water carries all the things that float upon it." He had put these thoughts down—writing right to left—in one of his notebooks, but it felt more satisfying to speak them aloud to her.

She reached over and gripped his hand, their warm fingers entwined. "My dear friend, Leonardo, I have come to depend on you."

He noticed that her eyes flickered with delight, but there was doubt lurking there, too. To be alone within the courtyard, as if they were children discovering a secret garden, was enchanting, but it wasn't enough for her. Her suffering still moved like heaviness across her eyes; sadness tugged at the corners of her mouth.

"Does anything bother you?" she asked him. "Make you sad, rile you?"

There it was again: a spark of interest to cover what lay behind.

"I'm human, just like you," he said. But he was observing her closely, thinking about her portrait. Watching her, he decided he must honor her shifting, layered emotions. To do otherwise would be to create a wooden puppet. It would mean layering pigmented glazes, countless times, achieving transparency, not hard lines; this great lady was no battle soldier with howling crease lines. Neither was she a Florentine lady given to dramatic swooning. If he could take his time, he could do her justice. Around the eyes and the mouth, he would paint her as she truly was: a woman in motion, with a veil of ambiguity.

"Go on," she urged.

"I have been mulling something over for a while," he said, speaking softly.

"I'm listening."

"This Earth." He paused and looked past Lisa to the cypress trees and the stone wall beyond. "It's in flux all the time, as you are."

"Me?"

"As you and I are." he said. "Its flesh is the soil; its bones are the strata of the rocks that form the mountains. Its cartilage is the tufa stone. Its blood the springs of the waters."

"Yes," she said, taking the wine, looking up at the sky. "Our bodies are like worlds unto themselves."

"It is my opinion that the veins that feed the human body are very much like the streams and rivers that feed the lakes and the oceans."

"What else?"

"In your portrait," he began, "I am trying to paint the fullness of your being." He decided against telling her the whole truth: that he wanted to paint the meandering curve of a river floodplain into the detail of her sleeves, and hint at rippling streams in the fine curls of her hair. He had finally settled on the background of the painting. The details still had to be worked out, but it would acknowledge the ancient dramatic shifting of land, mountains falling down, ice collapsing, rivers dammed, the creation of new lakes.

He changed tack. "I tell you, my dear Lisa, I am poorly schooled. I do not write Latin, never studied law."

"But you know more than all the citizens of Florence," she said, shaking her head. "Tell me something else you know."

"Well," he said, lying back on the blanket. "I have held a man's brain in my hands; I know the weight of a brain, its depth and structural intricacies. It is capable of delivering galaxies of experience! And it's an honor to feel that." He kissed the palm of her hand, happy in the telling. "Life is to be lived as a series of experiments. Cherished. Understood. Protected. Defending the city from the enemy. Defending people from plagues and pestilence by separating the city into safe zones. I have wanted to tell my father exactly this, many times—"

"Your father is alive, Leonardo?"

"He is."

"*Allora* . . . go to him," she said, pressing a hand to his shoulder. "Tell him of your life, what you have learned—"

"He measures success by the number of documents negotiated and signed, not sketches of old men, or horses whose eyes scream with terror."

"But your notebooks are your life."

"I wonder whether he is correct. 'Such mad scribblings,' he would say, and I would have to agree."

"Surely you have a memory of him that is not so dark?" she asked.

"I see what you're doing," he said, smiling over at her, sitting up. "Did I not ask you the same the other day during your sitting?"

"One-way conversations are dull. I've attended enough parties at the grand palazzi to know that."

"My father is Ser Piero da Vinci. Notary at the Palazzo del Popolo. Father of ten sons and two daughters. Four wives, two of them younger than I. Also, I'm illegitimate. He helped me to get three of my painting commissions." He shrugged. "Not much else to tell."

"Soon you will begin drawing the cartoon for a great battle scene here," she said, pointing to the arcaded cloister and the Hall of the Pope. "Will that not make him proud?"

He settled back on the blanket and motioned Lisa toward him. She placed her head on his chest, and he was surprised and secretly delighted by the kindness of her physical touch.

"What would you rather?" she asked. "Paint a portrait that only a few will ever lay their eyes on? Or create a work for all to see?"

"What do they pay?"

She pinched him, and his laughter echoed in the air.

"Do you care that my portrait will hang in our salon on Via della Stufa to be enjoyed merely by my friends?"

"The ones who paint their teeth? Now, that is disturbing." They laughed softly.

"When I painted the mural of *The Last Supper* in Milan, it was for a dining hall in a monastery. Have you ever seen what monks eat in a refectory? Mostly bean gruel. Mouths to coarse earthenware bowls, ladling it back, thinking about their next meal. I doubt any of them have looked seriously at my fresco."

"But maybe the magic was in the making?"

"The prior in charge would hound me every day, check on my progress, as if I were making spokes for a wheel."

"Leonardo the wheelwright. I can imagine it," she said.

"Lisa, a jester from the wrong side of town," he teased back.

"Fine by me," she said, clicking the heels of her leather boots together. "Beatrice said she liked my feet."

"She has a keen eye, that girl. Brought me a raspberry branch. I drew it the same day. She looked directly at me and declared: 'Signore, it doesn't take much to create art. The light of the paper, the shadows from a pencil.'" He smiled and shook his head. "Her hands were scratched from the prickles, her lips bright as a rose, ready for a bee to come down and pollinate. Maybe I should have thought more of her, but she spoke the truth."

"She's daring. I like that about her. Aspires to be an artist." She sat up. "Michelangelo has been tutoring her."

On hearing Michelangelo's name, he felt unsettled, as if the young sculptor was interrupting his peace of mind. Let him teach Beatrice. That was fine. But why hadn't she asked him to do the same? He stood up and brushed the grass from his cape.

"I suppose . . ." said Lisa.

"Yes, the city is quiet. All the actors gone from the stage. The servants will be sending the Office of the Night after us!" Offering his hand, he helped Lisa to her feet and waited patiently for her to dust her skirts. He took the iron key from his satchel, and they walked together to the gate, arms linked, holding on to their peace.

Chapter 31

The midday bells of the Duomo chimed: bright, clanging dissonance. Michelangelo had worked the leather buff back and forth across the planes of marble, smoothing the youth's cheekbones to a fine luster. The commission was nearly done. His father would be pleased to hear that the final payment was forthcoming: there were repairs to be made on their rental house over on Via San Procolo. "The roof is leaking—the servants have buckets on the table where we eat," his youngest brother had complained, loudly, to him. They rarely visited him in the studio, and when they did, it was with hands outstretched, eyes trained on his leather purse.

He skipped the buff over the surface of *David*'s curls, causing brilliance to leap from the marble onto the thick tresses. His feet shuffled slightly on the wooden platform, inching forward so that he could reach his arms partly around the muscular chest of his colossus. Dissections at Santo Spirito had shown him the red rivers of muscles and blue streams of veins that ran through the body. He set his head gently on the sculpture's left arm. The marble biceps bulged cold below his cheek.

Michelangelo gazed intently at the left side of the face, the warrior revealed by the fierce glint of the eye and the flared nostril. He reached his hand up and traced his fingers along the chiseled mouth. The lips were fleshy, young and boyishly impulsive. He put both hands around the sculpted head and examined its Janus face, for in every face, in every *body*, he believed, there was a double personality.

He liked her well enough, Beatrice, had enjoyed kissing her that time in the river. They had resumed their friendship and it seemed better, as if it had aged and matured in an oak barrel. "You, the maker of the giant-man," she teased him these days, when she switched his old olive oil carafes for new ones and stayed for long visits afterward. One afternoon, they sat outside the workshop on blocks of marble and watched the sun drop into the western sky. Her skin shone in the golden light. To sit and drink as if neither of them had a care in the world was a rare gift. He passed her the jug of wine, offered her some *salame* and *pane* and looked over at her. She seemed more at peace now, though he knew the wound of her mother's desertion would not easily heal. There was something about Beatrice that made him relax, less likely to growl and fight.

"I've never seen you smile wide before," she said, bending down to draw on the Duomo's foundation wall with red chalk.

"You think I'm all hard work? Your insult wounds me deeply." He made a ghoulish face with bulging eyes like a medieval gargoyle. She shook her head at him, snorted her laughter.

He knew he had grown too serious. He wanted to be open-hearted like Granacci, or irreverent like Rustici. He wanted to mesmerize like Leonardo. But he could not find the words. The weeks they had spent together in Settignano at Agnella's home, he had found himself glad to be with her, singing old folk songs badly, terribly off-key. He sat silent, stared at the ground.

"There's a special council," she said, filling the silence, no doubt tired of his brooding. "Leonardo will be one of the invited members. Your enemy, I guess. He and a bunch of old men. To decide where to locate your *David*."

He looked at her, wounded. Was she speaking the truth?

"It was meant for one of the buttresses of the Duomo," he said. "But now it's too big, too heavy."

"Where do you want it?"

"Leonardo will want it hidden away, no doubt of that."

"But what do you want?" she shot back.

He appreciated her directness. Forcing him to speak. She helped herself to more wine. He mixed it with water.

"I can't say. It's for others to decide."

"I say it should go to the best part of the city. The main piazza."

"It will have to be—" He looked all ripped apart.

"Perfect? Good to know. Because it is."

He looked at her and considered, felt their bond, decided he could trust her. "There is talk that its size, the size of everything, is wrong, that it points to a sickness," he said, standing up, hands to his head, pacing in front of her. "The Greeks and Romans sculpted nudes to celebrate the human form, its strength and beauty—I studied them when I was an apprentice at the Medici Garden."

"Lucky you. I study how to stay alive."

"Now there is talk that the Office of the Night is tracking me, watching my friends. The *David*, they say, is too much, too naked, too male."

"For women or men?"

"Anyway, that's why I went to Settignano, to stay away."

"That's why you went to Agnella's? I thought it was because I—"

"No. Yes. Of course. I wanted to be there with you. But the officers have been hunting."

"Hunting for what?"

"Evidence of, you know, men, being together."

For a long time, Beatrice did not speak. Then, "Fuck them," she said, standing, arms thrown into the air.

He stopped pacing and looked at her, this rebel girl.

"Fuck them," she said again. "Let them come and arrest you for your love of men, go ahead. You think they're going to hurt the genius who created the *David*? Wait until they see it. *David* will be the hero Florence has been waiting for. The rich need *David*, the poor need him; Madonna Lisa Gherardini could certainly learn from him, as could my crazy mother, wherever she is. Me? I need him, too. We all do. This naked boy of humble birth. He belongs to all of us."

He looked away from her, the hot prickle of tears threatening.

"Michelangelo, you are sculpting emotion in three glorious dimensions. Pure emotion, every inch of it."

Michelangelo shrugged and smiled at her torrent of words. Beatrice was a strange bird, but she had a way of expressing the truth that hit him squarely.

"You think so?"

"Don't live like this, never trusting," she said. "Keep on being. Keep doing." She pushed him on the chest to emphasize her point and looked directly at him, forcing his gaze to rest quietly on her own.

He grabbed her arm and pulled her into an embrace, and was surprised by how magnificent it felt. Their bodies pressed and relaxed into each other. He smelled her hair, perfumed with lavender. "Beatrice, my olive oil girl," he whispered into her ear. He thought about all the sweetbriar pricking the hills of Settignano, its wild red roses bursting from stems of tiny, vicious thorns.

Chapter 32

M y recommendation is that the *David* face the Baptistery of San Giovanni," said Botticelli. "Set him by the left side of the Duomo." The senior artist coughed, then took a moment to clear his throat before offering: "It would serve as a blessing to all newborns baptized and bathed there in the holy water."

Ten of the city's greatest artists had been called together in the new year to decide where to permanently locate the *David*. They shifted in their oak chairs in the Great Council Hall, moving their feet below the cold marble table toward the warming braziers.

"Maestro, you raise an interesting point," said a prominent goldsmith. He wrapped his gold-filigreed scarf around his neck to better ward off the bone-chilling January air and leaned forward. "And I would agree with you if what we were considering was a work of perfection. But the stone is *imperfect*, and the proportions of *David*'s hands are wrong."

"Nobody should argue with the earnest attempt at creating an emotional work of art," said Leonardo, pushing his chair back and standing to better address the gathering. "Michelangelo pulls on our heartstrings. He wants us to feel that his *David* is not merely going to battle, but going to battle for us."

Murmured agreement, nodded heads.

"Truly this exemplifies a noble and virtuous man," interjected Machiavelli. "To serve not only yourself but also the republic is the most honorable course of action."

"Wise words from the republic's great sage and second chancellor," said Leonardo. "We are all honored to be here in service of this great republic." He pulled his beard thoughtfully and nodded at the governor, seated at the head of the table. "Our task is not to be taken lightly, for, as my esteemed colleagues surely know, the decision we make now, in 1504, as to where to locate the *David* will have repercussions far into the future."

Some of the men pounded their fists on the table.

"David was a great biblical hero," said Leonardo, walking around the table, sweeping his eyes from one man to the next. "The shepherd clothed in modest garments who dared to battle a giant."

There was more thumping of hands.

"Though his wrappings were made of the roughest flax, his manhood was, indeed, covered, as befit a man who was interested in doing right by others." Leonardo bowed his head and stroked the length of his long, elegant beard. Speaking to the distinguished cultural leaders of the city pleased him, and he felt the weight of the moment, that finally he had arrived to claim his rightful place as the city's cultural titan. "David was a gentleman," he continued, striding slowly around the grand oak table, looking to the floor and back to the gathered council. "He spoke to the people, and to the ambition of the republic."

"David was of the republic, for the republic," exclaimed Machiavelli.

"Sir, he was indeed. David was of the republic, for the republic," said Leonardo, bowing slightly to Machiavelli, mirroring the chancellor and repeating his words to pacify him so that he might continue with his own speech. "Yet it must be acknowledged that he was clothed. And so, I believe we must all ask ourselves, why should this particular *David* be rendered immodestly, genitals exposed with flagrance to all citizen Florentines?" He stopped behind the governor and set his hands on his shoulders. "Is this not a most indelicate interpretation of the benevolent and modest David?"

The room went silent. Only songbirds outside the windows of the great hall could be heard.

"With respect, I . . ." The governor rubbed his hands to warm them and muttered a curse to his gout. "I have seen the *David*. At Michelangelo's studio with the second chancellor." He cleared his throat. "A work of remarkable beauty. Actually, I consider it to be more than what we have become accustomed to—" He glanced at Leonardo. "Present company excepted."

Leonardo returned to his chair and took his time sitting down.

"As to its immodesty, I appreciate the concern of Leonardo da Vinci, honored Master of the Arts. But I do not think it a sacrilege to the republic. If we look to the great works produced by the Greeks and the Romans, the nude was glorified—indeed, celebrated. I do not think we can attribute any shame to wanting that for ourselves and our own fledgling republic."

"There is much to admire about antiquity," said Leonardo, offering his words like perfectly ripe fruit, "yet there is also much about its hedonistic ways that some of us find to be repulsive." He looked at Botticelli, whom he knew to be deeply religious.

"Your recommendation, honored sir?" said Botticelli, urging him on.

"Place the *David* under cover within the Loggia dei Lanzi of the Piazza della Signoria. Place it within a black niche against the far wall, where they hang the tapestries, with *ornamento decente*, and in a way that will not spoil the ceremonies of the officials."

"Hide it away, in other words?" retorted the governor, and his words contained a measure of bluster. "Here is a dish of bitter pie!"

"Not bitter, no," said Leonardo solemnly. "I am only advising that we act with caution. To erect a naked giant that stands some seventeen feet is to impose a monstrous phallus, testicles and corona of pubic hair on all Florentines."

"Sir, what do you mean by decent ornament?" asked Machiavelli.

"An undergarment," said Leonardo. Some of the gathered hooted, and he overheard Machiavelli's loud whisper to his seatmate, the painter Cosimo Rosselli: "I'm not surprised that a prudish recommendation comes from Leonardo, one of our city's accused sodomizers. Naturally, it's in his interest to deflect the appetite for the male body to his young rival."

Finally, amid repeated calls for order, the crowd quieted down.

"Something elegant," continued Leonardo, sweat prickling on the back of his neck from the humiliation. "Perhaps a garland in bronze."

"If I dared to change the position of Christ's hand in *The Last Supper*," challenged Machiavelli, "would that not offend your individual right as an artist?"

"I paint people with their clothes on, and they are beautifully draped."

Machiavelli shook his head and sat back down.

"Gentlemen, may I suggest we cast our ballots so that we may determine a course of action?" said the governor.

Leonardo rose from his seat, pleased with his performance, for art was as much about the cult of the personality as it was about the work, even if the work remained unfinished. What he admired about Michelangelo had very little to do with the *David*, with or without decent ornament. He admired his guts. For he was about to expose his very soul to the adoration and wrath of the fickle public.

Chapter 33

He watched as she half walked, half floated across the court-yard. His shoulder ached from hours of painting, and still he stood at the window for a long time, his arm raised in a gesture of farewell. The driver whistled sharply to the team of horses and the carriage drove off, and she never looked back. Leonardo lowered his arm. Night descended, shuttering the daylight, darkening the poplar board propped on the easel, the brushes still glistening next to the palette of oils.

That afternoon, when they had been together, after the musicians had packed up their instruments, he had felt the kindness, the abundance of time, with vast horizons and no shoreline. Now he felt its devouring pulse and he gave himself over to troubled thoughts: I am without son or daughter. I lie down with a beautiful creature who is more child than man. And, something he would never write down in a notebook: This woman, Mona Lisa, transfixes me.

She had arrived late in the afternoon when rainclouds lay like skeins of wool pulled over the sky. He preferred to paint portraits in gloomy weather, when it was possible to discern grace and sweetness in the faces of men and women. It was raining lightly when she asked him what he wanted from her portrait. "Am I to become just another Florentine lady that the great Leonardo has painted?"

"Just another Florentine lady?" He wasn't sure he appreciated the tone of her voice.

"Leonardo, I mean no offence. I'm only wondering how far you will go with this painting."

She had surprised him by knowing about some of his earlier work, his *Lady with an Ermine* ("That girl looks icy to the touch"), his *Madonna of the Yarnwinder* ("Your Christ child was a stubborn one"). Because she and her husband, Francesco, occupied elite social circles in Florence, her knowledge was more reliable than common gossip.

"My friends tell me the marchioness of Mantua is growing impatient waiting for her young Christ," she had said, wagging a finger at him. "But I also know that your drawing of Neptune has pleased one of Botticelli's patrons."

He left the window and walked back to the easel. Her words—"just another Florentine lady"—came floating back to him. In the painting, he had placed Lisa sitting high on a balcony, with a vast emptiness behind her. He needed to begin the landscape in the background. To honor a woman with emotional depth, who would listen but not tell and, finally, also reveal. Had she been a quilter, she would have ripped up a length of tattered silk and patched it with hemp and linen to make it new again. His left hand reached for a brush, which he dipped into lake white, then into a glaze of walnut oil. He tapped away the excess liquid and pressed the brush against the wooden palette. In the top right corner of the poplar board he began to paint a monumental range of mountains belonging to an ancient, frozen time. Moving quickly, seized by inspiration, he dropped the brush and picked up another with thicker, horse-mane bristles. Now he traced a shimmering aqua lake beneath the mountain, with a rugged cliff and valley falling away below it, time itself eroding, thousands of years swept away, leaving a landscape transformed. To the left of the great lady, he sketched another vast body of water, belonging to another geography and era, with a river curving mightily, its watercourses mirrored in the sinuous patterns of the woman's sleeves. He wanted to signal an earth in flux, the way it shifted and morphed, just as people might walk through fire and emerge to see the light— maybe, ultimately, becoming the light. No detail. Not yet. Not for a long time.

The studio was cast in velvety shadows by the time he set down his brush. From across the commons came the clop of hooves as donkeys pulled home market carts, the bleating of lambs going to slaughter, the trill of birdsong, two monks pruning trees in the garden below. He felt his own silence, the weight of his body. Dear old Leonardo da Vinci, how useless and cumbersome you have become. As compared to the light efficiency of a bird. Aged fool, he thought. How to explain his desire to make something to outlast him? A painting for the ages; an understanding of how to fly.

And for what? To buy ongoing admiration? Or to stave off death, as if he—not God—could decide his own mortality? "*La vita*," he whispered. Pressing his hands on the cold stone of the windowsill, he turned his face toward the indigo-blue sky. Far above him, he saw in the clouds the delicate curves of a horse's head, the arched wings of a swan, lifting, defending its territory.

Chapter 34

The weavers deposited the woolen blankets gently at the foot of the *David* as if they were bearing gifts for the Holy Child. Stepping back, they made room for the Sangallo brothers, architects of renown, who unfurled the drawings of the mobile scaffold they had designed for the transport of the *David*. The conveyance would be pulled, they explained, huddling in close to Michelangelo, "by men moving at the delicate pace of caterpillars."

Giuliano, the elder Sangallo, wiping his brow in the warm spring sun, added that it would likely take four days to travel the half mile to the *David*'s place of honor in front of the Palazzo Vecchio, from which Donatello's *Judith and Holofernes* had been moved. Michelangelo had learned of the designated site by way of a messenger on horseback who, days earlier, had trotted his mount along the artists' back lane, handing him the message without bothering to dismount.

Leonardo's opinion, as he had heard it, had not held sway.

At least, not entirely.

The message on the parchment also indicated that the *David* would be required to wear twenty-eight copper leaves to cover his genitals. As if the body were blasphemous. The dictate was like a punch in the face, and Michelangelo had looked desperately for a friend in the lane, longing for somebody—Granacci, Attilio, Beatrice—to save him from collapse. He'd staggered back alone into his studio, and kicked the door shut.

"Horses cannot be trusted," said the younger Sangallo, eyeing the *David*. "One nervous lurch and the colossus might topple."

Forty men had been enlisted to pull and push the statue, housed in its wooden cage on rolling logs, through the streets. The men were assigned to shifts: two hours on, two hours off, hauling day and night, under heavy guard.

"*Va bene*," said Michelangelo grimly, nodding his approval. His stomach clenched in anxiety; he had barely eaten over the last two days.

Six men raised sledgehammers and waited for the command to expand the opening of the workshop. One hour later, the prior appeared, swinging a vessel of frankincense. Smoke wafted out of the newly created gaping hole.

The Sangallos were already wrapping the *David* in protective blankets, binding the wool covers together with rope, building a massive wooden crate around the sculpture, as if forcing the giant into prison.

So much conspired against the safe arrival of his sculpture, its elephantine weight supported by bone-thin ankles. Michelangelo joined the entourage as the first men inched the wagon along, sucking in his breath with every surge of the team, and with the horrible rocking of the *David*.

By midnight, the colossus loomed above the street, his eyes the height of the second-story rooms of the Convent of Santa Caterina. A crowd was forming around the conveyance, more and more people appearing from side streets, candles held aloft, to join the procession. Michelangelo shrank back into the inky shadows, preferring to bear witness. The candles grew to a blur of flames, a river of fire running above the streets.

He saw Agnella coming out of the convent, palms pressed together in a blessing. He nodded to her. The men groaned under the weight of the ropes, the smell of their sweat mixed with the perfume of the lilac blossoms wafting heavily in the gentle May air. He and Agnella walked slowly together, not speaking, the cocks calling, the street dogs skittish, setting to barking.

The conveyance was ordered to halt, and the men readied to turn a corner. They were near the back-lane studios where Michelangelo had first modeled his boy hero in clay. Skins of fortifying wine were passed to the men by the gathering crowd.

Agnella reached for Michelangelo's hand and pressed it into her own. "I remember when your father brought you to my house."

"Full of airs and ridiculous pomp, I imagine."

"Of course. He strutted into our little well-swept home, ordering his livery boy to check the cupboards for mice droppings and my own glistening hair for lice. Finally, he handed me a basket with a bawling baby inside. I wished it might have been different for you. Not the way I raised you—"

"Pure perfection, of course," teased Michelangelo, glad to be walking with Agnella through the night.

"Only that I wished your father could have seen you for who you truly are."

"Incapable, I'm afraid."

"Well, now, all of this is for you," she said. She pulled the hood of her cape up and over her head, her eyes deepening to midnight blue. "Let go of all your torments and be glad for this." Pride flooded her face. She also looked assured, as if she believed now the governor would surely see his worth and offer him protection. She spelled it out for him: "All of these people have come to pay homage to you and what you have created, your glorious *David*."

"If you say so," he said, sounding unsure, clasping his hands together to hide their trembling. "It needs to arrive without crashing."

"I'm praying for its safe passage."

He was still sickened by the sight of the copper leaves defacing his sculpture. But there was nothing he could do about it, except to pray for strength.

They shuffled along with the procession, listening to the low murmur of the crowd, the occasional squeal and laughter from a child allowed to stay up late to witness the parade.

"I am staying full-time at the convent these days," Agnella told him. "Many women need my healing—"

"Where is Beatrice?"

"Back in Settignano, replenishing supplies. Her clients demand more and more of her products. It's hard to keep up! You'll see her soon." She squeezed Michelangelo's hand and smiled. He saw in her expression that she dreamed of more for him and Beatrice, more than he could possibly give her.

She turned to walk briskly back to the convent. He walked on, alone with the crowd. Moving at the pace of a caterpillar with the rest of the entourage, he found himself tingling with life even as he was lulled back in time.

He had been out late with Granacci, running through pounding rain and stopping to catch their breath at the San Marco monastery. Savonarola had presided over it at the time, and Michelangelo felt comfortable seeking temporary refuge. He also felt *malinconia*, had wanted to be alone and stay the night within the hallowed halls. Granacci, starving, wanted to push through the rain to his room near Ghirlandaio's studio, a few blocks away. "All right, with your blessing, I'll go," he said, shaking his head at Michelangelo before he ran back out into the pouring rain.

There was a stone bench in the San Marco foyer, cool to the touch, and Michelangelo had lain down on it and fallen asleep with the kind of delicious abandon that adults long for but seldom achieve. He was never sure what woke him from that deepest of slumbers, what betrayed the still, sweet black of the night: a softening of twilight, the chill of the damp shirt still tied around his neck, or the voice that sang in curves and figure eights and climbed vertically, taking Michelangelo's heart with it, even before he opened his eyes:

Broken and thrown to the wind is all hope.
I have seen Heaven turn me to weeping.

Behind this voice were others, a chorus of men; Michelangelo could hear that now, though he had no idea why or how so many people had entered his family home. That was when he startled; his eyes open, he sat up.

The voice belonged to a young Dominican carrying a trowel, the better to dig up new soil and encourage the rosemary growing in the herb garden of the San Marco courtyard. "The bells toll five," he said. His cheeks were flushed with an unbroken night's sleep, and he was wearing the black cloak with white cotton rope tied around the waist that all Dominicans wore. His hood was down.

Michelangelo studied the double knot of the rope and looked at the young man with the beautiful voice.

"Morning prayer," the novice added, nodding toward the courtyard and the chapel beyond. "Forty-three men, singing together."

Looking past the arcaded hall, Michelangelo imagined the men, half-awake, half-aroused, torn from the blanketed secrets of their beds, singing in grudging unison. They sang together to repress the desires of the flesh, to eradicate the memory of being spurned by the daughters of their neighbors, to give themselves over to poverty, humility, chastity—and God. He knew their stone rooms were designed as cells of contemplation. In every room at San Marco, an arched window overlooked the cloister and a large courtyard of greenery, with a stone kneeler for sustained prayer. Every cell was an essay of minimalism, but for a luminous artwork by their Dominican brother Fra Angelico to inspire their enlightenment.

The monks sang a low, melodic line with the solemnity of an army beaten and retreating. The storm of their music built the space between dawn and sunrise. Not even the cocks crowed. I should leave, thought Michelangelo. But he seemed unable to move.

That voice—that voice rose again in song, finding tenor notes that Michelangelo never knew existed, inventing pure joy against the bleakness of the men's chorus. It was like freeing a man from a stone block and watching him dance away. Directly before him, the novice sang, in Latin, eyes closed, voice reaching and soaring, while, in the chapel across the courtyard, the men sang a somber prayer:

> *I was wounded,*
> *but in my sorrow I called upon Thee.*
> *O Lord did I hope*

The song ended. The young man drew his *cappuccio* around his blushing face; his green eyes were heavily framed by black lashes.

Michelangelo felt larger than his sixteen-year-old body. He stood and bowed to the singer. It didn't matter that he was half-naked. "I've never heard anything like that before," he said.

"It's new. I'm hoping you didn't mind the liberties I took . . ." He made large curving gestures with his hand and laughed. His eyes shone. The room, stone-vaulted, shadowy, allowed only the outline of his mouth and the whites of his teeth. "Josquin Desprez. A composer from France," he added, motioning to the other side of the monastery. "My home country. And an admirer of our great leader, Savonarola."

I want to kiss him, Michelangelo thought. Instead, barely moving his lips, he said, "He inspires us all in his devotion."

"He so loves the poor, and so hates corruption," agreed the monk.

Michelangelo remembered feeling all-powerful then, as if the moment was his to own, and he stepped forward and kissed the monk fully on the mouth. He clung to the white habit inside the black cloak, felt the man's hands pressing against his own bare back. In a few scant moments, Michelangelo learned everything about him: the smell of the earth on his linen cloak, the heat of the soaring notes on his tongue. Then the moment of crossing from ordinary to extraordinary was over. Wanting more, Michelangelo explored hungrily with his tongue until finally the novice pushed him away. He drew his black *cappuccio* down low over his head and heaved the oak door open, stepping into the gloaming of the garden.

Michelangelo never saw him again—though he never looked for him, either.

Emerging from his memory, Michelangelo heard the low murmur of the crowd pressing around him, the laborers hauling *David* grunting in unison as they heaved against the braided ropes. Progress was slow.

Seeing the *David* actually in motion held particular power for some of the crowd, and men and women fell to their knees, pressing their foreheads to the ground as if God had come down to their cobbled streets.

The night was edging toward dawn, its blackened husk peeling away for the fruit of sunrise, and the great sculpture continued moving forward, bound and tethered on its conveyance, pulled by a shift of fresh laborers. It moved for days through the city, and always *David* was blessed by a river of candles, staying upright on a prayer, caressed by a flickering glow.

Chapter 35

The Piazza Santo Spirito had been transformed into a mid-summer festival of color honoring the Feast of Saint John. Banners made from strips of wool hung down all four stories of the stone buildings. Let the rest of Florence be draped in silk, huffed the wives of the dyers who had stitched the thick flags; all the florins in the world could not convince them to trade their woolen standards for a vulgar show of silk.

Iron cauldrons of hot vegetable soup stood at the ready, along with loaves of bread stuffed with chestnuts and honey. A pig with an apple in its mouth roasted over a fire nearby. Prior Bichiellini stepped next to Beatrice and jabbed his knife into the beast. "Cooked through," he said. "Your thoughts, Beatrice?"

She bent forward and inspected the juices running clear. "Ready to serve, Prior."

A dozen children running through the sweet-smelling smoke

came to an immediate halt. "Time to eat!" they shouted, clapping their hands. "*Mangiamo!*"

More than a hundred people rushed toward the feasting tables. They took their faith seriously and attended Mass to pray on their knees almost every day of the week. But the Feast of Saint John celebrated the miracle of bounty. No tickets, no requirement for penance or prayer.

"Women and children, step up!" called Michelangelo. It was the third year that he and the prior had organized this community event for Santo Spirito, and this time they had arranged to roast a prize pig selected from Settignano. The prior and his monks had made dozens of cheese tarts sprinkled with herbs, saffron and ginger. Naturally, there was an abundance of wine and mead.

Michelangelo handed a plate of giblets to Giovanna and Lucia, the sisters who were once beggars. Now they studied Latin and embroidery at the Ripoli convent. "Take this plate to the prior and make sure he eats. He needs to fatten his belly like Pope Julius!"

Picking up an empty platter, he turned to the roasting pit, elated by the chaos and joy swirling all around him. He smiled at Beatrice and she nodded back at him. Maybe tomorrow the wolves would circle. But at the moment, all seemed right in the world.

"Michelangelo, you've become a holy man."

He turned to face Leonardo da Vinci, who stood before him, lavishly clothed in a purple silk cape and a rose-pink cap. His pretty boy stood next to him. "Delicious," said Salaì, stuffing his mouth with strips of roasted pig.

Michelangelo felt his back stiffen. Here was the man who had insulted him in public and demanded that his *David* be covered up. The Feast of Saint John belonged to Santo Spirito, to the people of Oltrarno, where the wool laborers had toiled for two hundred years—not to Leonardo. He watched as the old man surveyed the crowd, his rich cape rustling in the wind. What business did he have here?

"Leonardo da Vinci, welcome to Santo Spirito!" The prior stepped forward and grasped Leonardo's hands with both of his. Beatrice moved next to Leonardo and offered him a bowl of soup.

"The pleasure is mine. Your festival would make any member of the priory green with envy," said Leonardo lightly. He smiled at the colorful humanity in the piazza, the beautiful, hand-crafted banners, and gulped back half of the soup. "It feels like a village," he said, looking at Beatrice, acknowledging her with a bow. "Something all cities need to cultivate more often."

Michelangelo scoffed and turned back to tend the fire.

"You must be pleased with yourself," said Leonardo, leaning in to Michelangelo the moment the prior excused himself. "Winning so many commissions you can now afford to feed the poor? Does Soderini provide you with meat from his private butcher?"

"I'm surprised you troubled yourself with a trip across the river. Why leave your patrons and dukes of indulgence to dine with the unwashed?" Michelangelo grabbed the poker and stabbed angrily at the fire.

"Your ego knows no bounds. Your *David* takes up prime real estate—"

"You insisted on slapping a diaper on my shepherd boy. For a court artist, you have no class, except among swine." He pointed the poker at Leonardo.

"You want to own every corner of this city," said Leonardo, suddenly grinning. He appeared friendly to the crowd, but those close by no doubt heard the venom: "A dog pissing to mark his territory."

"That's enough," Beatrice said, moving to stand between him and Leonardo. "Stop this now. You sound like two little boys arguing over a lost ball. This city has work enough for you both. Though I can't say there's room enough for your big fat heads. You may be exceptional artists, but you are lousy men. Once I admired you both." She yanked the poker from Michelangelo and threw it onto the fire, sending ashes into the air.

The prior returned from the grill. He looked at Leonardo and then at Michelangelo, clearly sensing the simmering hostility. "Even if we are on the rotten side of the river," he said to Leonardo, changing the subject, "our library has more books than I'll ever read in my lifetime. It is yours to explore at any time."

Leonardo bowed graciously to the prior as a knot of children gathered around Michelangelo and pulled him forward, begging him to watch the juggling entertainments in the piazza. He was glad for the excuse to step away from Leonardo. Somebody threw him a lemon, then another and another. Soon enough, he was juggling while jesters threw burning torches high into the air and caught them effortlessly in their bare hands.

Trumpets blared. A carriage pulled by a pair of horses was crossing Piazza Santo Spirito at a trot. Everybody knew by the sound of the trumpets and the high polish of its leather and iron exterior that the cart belonged to Governor Soderini. Little boys squirmed free of their mothers to get a better view. The governor stepped from the carriage and Machiavelli appeared by his side, wearing high leather boots.

"Brother," said Soderini, grasping Michelangelo's hands in his own. "I am very glad to find you here." He seemed unusually effusive. Michelangelo wondered if it was because he'd consumed too much wine.

Machiavelli was now strutting around the plaza, addressing the people. "It gives us great pleasure to find ourselves in the community of Santo Spirito, among its industrious people." The crowd applauded loudly. He pointed to Leonardo and doffed his cap, then bowed low. "Master of the Arts, Leonardo da Vinci." Polite applause as the crowd looked with interest at the man with the mane of white hair and richly endowed clothes.

"Maestro da Vinci has been commissioned to paint a fresco of the Battle of Anghiari inside the Great Council Hall at the Palazzo Vecchio," said Soderini to the crowd that had gathered around him. "But Florence is a city of many riches, which is why we have come here, to your celebration: to invite a man you know and admire, a man who has earned your affection"—he stepped next to Michelangelo—"to apply his great talents to our beloved city hall as well!"

There was a burst of thunderous applause and shouting.

Michelangelo was still holding three lemons. He handed them to a man standing nearby and straightened his vest. He turned to Soderini for clarification. "Gonfalonier?" he said, eyes questioning.

Soderini looked meaningfully at the crowd. "Michelangelo has given you the *David*, a monumental hero for you, the people, standing proud in front of our great Palazzo Vecchio." The crowd shouted its delight for several minutes. "He gave the *Pietà* to the pope, and all Romans." More cheering. Soderini stepped in close, placing a hand on Michelangelo's head as if blessing him. "Now our beloved son will paint another great Florentine triumph." The crowd went wild with applause and wolf whistles.

Machiavelli stepped in front of the governor and waved both hands for silence. "Our city will see the battle of two geniuses!"

"Michelangelo," Soderini said, finally turning to face him. "You are officially commissioned to paint the east wall next to your elder, Leonardo da Vinci."

The crowd roared and threw chestnuts in the air. Michelangelo looked at his boots and up to the sky. He felt unable to move.

Beatrice stepped to his side and hissed in his ear: "It's an honor. Are you daft? Show your thanks." Hand on his back, she pushed him forward.

Michelangelo looked over at Leonardo, whose chin was lifted defiantly even as his eyes shone. He seemed to be enjoying the moment. Their rivalry and public squabbles had come to something real: a competition between the young upstart and the old master to see who might prove to be superior. They were officially pitted against each other.

Overwhelmed, fearful, Michelangelo knelt at the governor's feet, pressed his hands in prayer and wept. The competition was on.

Chapter 36

H e rose before sunrise and rinsed in silence at the washing bowl. Paolo stood beside him, linen towel at the ready. Quietly, Leonardo shuffled from the sink to breakfast—a plate of beans with cabbage grown in the monastery garden, doused with olive oil warmed with rosemary and mint.

Already he had received warning from Soderini's office that his wall painting required attention. Further delays would mean calling off the commission and ceding the great room in the Palazzo Vecchio to Michelangelo.

Paolo helped Leonardo dress, handing him clothes with ceremonial care, as if they were artifacts belonging to the Etruscans: leggings the color of eggplant, a white silk blouse, a linen gambeson—rejected: "not today, too constricting"—a favorite tunic ("the rose-pink one"), hand-stitched leather shoes with three buckles. Then out of the bedroom to the hallway, past the kitchen, toward the back stairs, avoiding the other workrooms.

None of his apprentices said it out loud, though he knew they all thought it. It was why Paolo had taken it upon himself to hide his sketches of flying machines. They were in favor of Machiavelli's strategy; it ensured *The Battle of Anghiari* cartoon would be completed. The deadline was only months away.

Rarely did his new morning ritual feel ethical or right. For who could say that his time sketching peasants in the marketplace, freeing birds from their cages, sitting on stone benches with vagrants, was wasted? His wanderings produced images of the real and wretched who populated the earth. There was beauty in the line of a thieving prostitute's long neck, a drawing he continued to deepen and detail. His dissections of the muscles around an old man's mouth and lips, turned stone gray with death, showed him how to authentically draw somebody howling in pain or softly smiling.

"Very good, very good, yes, this way, here we go!" Paolo chirped like a bird as Leonardo appeared in the back hall. "The boys are downstairs, Master."

Giovanni and Ferrando had been tasked with escorting him west to the studio, the Hall of the Pope at the Santa Maria Novella church complex. The old dwelling place for visiting popes was rarely used, but it was magnificent and grand enough to accommodate the monumental preparatory drawing.

Leonardo hesitated at Raffaello and Zoroastro's room, where his colors were expertly prepared, ground to fine powders, and where he was making a drawing of Neptune. Thinking of it, his mind pounded with the waves of an ocean, the sound of the sea spray filling his ears. He yearned to pick up a stick of black chalk to begin detailing the chariot churning through the deep waters.

Paolo, anticipating where his mind had wandered, began to urge him along. Leonardo sighed, then stopped to absorb a flash of color just ahead: two birds frescoed on the wall. So this is what happens when I am gone, he thought. "Zoroastro! Raffaello!"

"Likely still sleeping, those two," said Paolo, unwilling to be delayed. "I'll have them paint over it," he said, gesturing to the wall. "Shall we?"

"Boys?" Leonardo stepped closer to the fresco. He put a hand on one of the birds and withdrew it hastily. "You reduce both of these creatures to floating and sitting," he said, not bothering to acknowledge the apprentices who had arrived half-dressed from their rooms. "Paint a third that dives with the speed of a cannon-ball, straight down to the earth."

He took some conté from his pocket and curved three vertical lines down the wall, adding a flourish at the bottom to indicate a bird's head. "Like that," he said. The young men stepped closer to examine Leonardo's sketch. They nodded slowly.

"Well, then," said Leonardo. "Paolo, shall we meet the others?"

"Right behind you," said Paolo, delivering his master to the studio assistants.

Waiting patiently by the carriage, Ferrando and Giovanni greeted their master with encouraging smiles. "Today we will leave the wheels behind," said Leonardo, stepping past them toward a low-slung stone building. "It's a good day to ride."

In the stable, Leonardo kept three horses. Before being thrust into this battle of painters, he had enjoyed riding in the mornings along the banks of the Arno, winding among the willow trees, picking his way past the boys who fished in the river.

A stable novice in a Dominican cloak emerged from the shadows. He held up a clutch of rope halters without iron mouth bits. "Is everybody at ease with bareback?"

"Halters will be sufficient. It's a magnificent day," Leonardo said, observing the blue sky. "Let's ride to the river first." He stepped forward and stood perfectly still, his hands at his side, waiting for the horses. Ropes dangling, they trotted toward him. Only when he could feel their velvet nostrils touch his face did he feed them apples pulled from his satchel. He stroked their long, chiseled heads and stared directly into their massive, shining eyes.

"Let's go," he finally said.

Ferrando, an athletic rider, climbed lightly onto the back of a silver-gray Andalusian. Giovanni—a city boy from Milan— heaved with both hands until he managed to hoist himself onto a spindly Caspian.

"To the Arno," said Leonardo, sitting easily on a big black gelding. The horse flattened its ears and pranced in circles. Leonardo turned his mount with a gentle pull on the lead rope and led the others across the cobblestones.

The river plain was scattered with marsh grass and juniper, and the thistles were beginning to blossom pink and lavender. Leonardo skirted the Ponte Vecchio and allowed his horse to run free on the muddy flats. The others followed, though Giovanni's horse quickly wandered to a grove of willows and began pawing at a dead fish rotting on the banks. Giovanni gripped tight to his horse's mane. Ferrando came up alongside him, took the halter rope and walked the horses to Leonardo, who was now standing on a bank of shale. The ground was slippery, and the horses shifted uncomfortably on the rocks, ears pinned back, tails swishing.

"Bring your horses close," Leonardo said, leaning forward to insert his fingers into the mouth of his gelding. He pulled up the lips of his black beast, revealing teeth.

"Should we be getting to the cloister," said Giovanni, shamelessly hugging the neck of his horse, "to sketch the battle?" Leonardo had overheard him complaining that pasting together hundreds of sheets of royal folio paper with flour, then lining the lot with Florentine linen, had left him with a sore body. Sitting a horse bareback was no doubt making the pain worse.

"This *is* the battle," said Leonardo. "Hold tight." He leaned forward and gripped the gelding's mane with both hands. Trotting forward, he brought his horse alongside Giovanni's so that their muzzles touched. Instantly, the animals flattened their ears. Ferrando's horse let out a high-pitched whinny and pawed the ground. "Bring him in, too," instructed Leonardo.

The third horse was led into the knot, and the men yanked hard on the lead ropes to keep the animals bunched. Leonardo handed his lead to Ferrando. "Hold them," he said, bouncing on the gelding's back and kicking it forward. The eyes of the horses rolled in their heads. This time, the gelding bared its teeth and lunged forward at the other horses. Leonardo kicked again, wanting to feel the intensity of battle when soldiers lunged for the flag, piercing the bellies of their enemy with long swords.

Leonardo drove his horse forward, provoking the others to fight. He felt himself freefalling to his days as a young blood. There was a time when he had indulged his body boldly and freely, and felt no shame. Until one night there was loud banging on his door and the Officers of the Night burst into his studio to find him in bed with one of his lovers, a seventeen-year-old boy. He remembered the humiliation of being half-dressed, turning away from the young Jacopo, the officers spitting their disgust on the stone floor, tying his hands with rope, pushing him out into the streets. He had been accused of sodomy, the *tamburazione* written on a slip of paper and deposited anonymously into one of the holes of truth.

"Again!" shouted Leonardo, heat gathering behind his eyes. He reversed his mount, gave a swift kick and felt it transformed into a raging beast. Giovanni's Caspian was wild with fear, its head bobbing frantically. Ferrando, understanding what his master was after, grabbed a long willow stick and threw it to Leonardo. "The standard!" he shouted. "Warriors and horses fighting for it! Horses biting each other—"

"I want it," said Leonardo, in a voice so dark with malevolence it truly frightened his assistants. They watched as he curled his body to grasp the willow stick, how his horse flexed its entire side to match his movement. The other two animals bowed their necks in warning; Ferrando's strained its head forward, bared its teeth and bit down hard.

Finally, his heart racing, sweat clinging to his body, Leonardo swerved his black gelding away. "That's enough," he said. He rode his horse to the bank of the Arno and allowed it to drink its fill. The others followed, swishing flies from their backsides with their tails, the scene transformed to a bucolic, peaceful landscape.

"The fury of slaughter. Men and horses swirling. A desperate, endless circle of violence," Leonardo called to his assistants over his shoulders. "Well done, you two."

❖

Leonardo took his time fishing the keys from his bag while his assistants wiped down the horses and roped the halters to iron rings on the walls outside Santa Maria Novella. They walked along the Great Cloister and pushed into the vast Hall of the Pope, admiring again its vaulted ceiling and two rows of thin, elegant pillars marching down the length of the monumental room. Through the windows, light fell in a series of slashes on the stone floor.

Although their clothes were soiled by the violence along the river, the mood of the artists had softened and turned reflective.

Leonardo eyed the preparatory cartoon, measuring some sixty feet long on the wall. The figures—four cavalrymen waging war on their horses, other men fallen and being trampled, the horses themselves biting and tearing at each other—were far too rigid; he could see that now. He needed to make them light and agile, not weighed down like knights in heavy plate armor.

Giovanni walked to the large scaffold they had built, an accordion on movable wheels. When adjusted on a scissor lift, it could be raised to create a sturdy platform some fifteen feet in the air.

Ferrando picked up the willow stick they had brought from the river's edge. "And the flag—the standard—does it actually break in the struggle?"

"I think so," said Giovanni.

"In two places," Leonardo agreed.

Just then the doors swung open and Beatrice stepped inside the great hall. She nodded curtly at the artists and set a basket heavy with offerings on the table next to their drawing materials.

Leonardo bowed and smiled at her, though his thoughts turned sharply to the moment when she had intervened during his petty, dog-pissing argument with Michelangelo, shortly before Soderini and Machiavelli had loudly announced a battle of painters.

"Madonna Lisa sent me with enough food to feed all the mercenary soldiers of the land." Beatrice looked at her boots and over to the artists. "I'll stay quiet," she said, her long black hair falling over one shoulder. "I only want to learn."

"Well, then, I'll try to keep my ego quiet," said Leonardo, bowing slightly. He strode to the far side of the mural and marked the lower edge of the paper, then returned to the other edge to leave another scratch. He motioned for the scaffold. Ferrando and Giovanni pushed over the machine on groaning wheels, and he climbed to the second-story platform. Homing in on the central battle scene, drawing with his left hand, he shaded with rapid crosshatched lines, heightening the muscular power of the Florentine calvary chasing down the Milanese enemy.

"I like the horse he's riding," he said, pointing to the animal collapsing on its hind legs. "Let's work on mirroring that collapsing action of the horse on the far right of the mural." The artists hustled to gather black chalk.

"Will you shield the beasts in armor—chamfrons, crinets, peytrals, flanchards?" asked Ferrando.

"No, let them be as naked as their fear. For the soldiers, no hose or footwear. But wearing fantastical armor. I'm imagining one of the Milanese horsemen wearing a ram's head for a breastplate." He paused, surveying the emerging scene of violence. "All right then, send up the white."

Giovanni gathered a fistful of white conté, but Beatrice snatched it from him and climbed the scaffold effortlessly. "Make the ass a brilliant, glossy white," instructed Leonardo, apparently oblivious to her presence. "Lift the tail high and darken underneath." The girl bent to the drawing and did exactly as instructed.

Leonardo stepped sideways and focused his attention on the bare-footed soldier—the Milanese enemy—riding the horse. He paused for a moment, peering at the paper, then boldly shadowed the twisted curve of the rider's back in black conté. Five minutes later, he had deepened the crosshatching of an arm twisting at a deranged angle, desperate to extend far enough to hold on to the shaft of the tattered Milanese flag that the Florentines had seized. The Florentine cavalry was riding them down, and he needed to show the terrible fear and fury of the moment.

After an hour of working next to Beatrice, he lowered his arm and stepped off the scaffold. The face of an old soldier with a curved sword raised high had taken on an intensity that pleased Leonardo. He liked how the man cried out, his mouth a darkened cave, his eyes inked with hatred and a knowledge that he was at the end of his life. He had not been given the commission to transform the coveted massive slab of Carrara marble into a biblical hero by the name of David. But he would astound the world with his *Battle of Anghiari* and his antihero. Leonardo—not Michelangelo—had witnessed the cruelty of men warring against each other, the hideous slaughter of men, the blood of young and old staining the ground. There would be no limits to their malignity; an antihero was what war demanded.

As for Beatrice, he had always thought of her as an artist. She had an eye, and an irreverence, and an ability to look laterally at the world. Now, looking at the horse she had partly completed on the mural, he could see that she had a talent for drawing, as well.

"Looks fine, very fine," he said, reaching for Beatrice's hand. "Let's have a look from the floor. And then we'll see what Lisa has arranged for our afternoon meal. Giovanni, Ferrando, lay some blankets outside in the courtyard for our banquet! Enough of this war."

Chapter 37

She felt a little drunk on herself. Her success in business, her friendships with powerful Florentines, her ability to learn from Michelangelo and Leonardo while showing them their petty, competitive ways—all of it made her swoon with joy, a feeling she had not thought possible in these last years. True, the guards at the city gates seemed to be on high alert for her, jostling among each other to harass her, an eighteen-year-old unmarried girl from the village, eyeing her boots, pawing through her fancy cape (also gifted from Madonna Lisa), doubling and tripling her toll payment before allowing her to pass. She ignored them, daring to look defiantly in their eyes. Let fear curse others, not her.

Outside the city gates, the dawn sky lightening to the gray-blue of a snail's shell, she stood tall—taller than most of the villagers, who hunched protectively over their carts and baskets. She cast her eyes over the miserable crowd, snagging the lines and angles of the hardened faces to sketch later on. She no longer saw the crowd as an unknowable, seething mass but as many individuals gathered tightly in a desperate knot. Some of them had offered her food, or warmed her shivering body with a nod and a smile. Over the years, she had come to know many of their names and some of the details of their hard lives. Their kindness had helped her feel whole again.

Today, a boy caught her attention. His hair was the color of a freshly harvested pumpkin. She knew him as a child from the squatter camp, where beggars slept below their shanty roofs, some with only battered grass weavings separating them from the elements. When he found her in the predawn, his fingers would immediately seek hers, and she would allow it. Once he had given her some golden acorns from a cypress tree. She watched as he ran hard toward her. Beatrice noted that he'd lost his cap. He had something clutched under his arm.

Yes, it was time, she mused. Time to offer this sweet orphan boy a job helping to carry her baskets of goods to the artists. In time, she imagined purchasing a wagon and a donkey so they could ride across the city in style.

She wondered why he was moving so desperately through the crowd. He was running, not skipping, as he usually did. She registered a memory, the voice of her father: "Do not become useless to yourself."

A pair of hands clapped once, twice, three times and panic slashed through her. A massive sentry—as big as a monster— leapt from the city gates into the recoiling crowd, a path opening to allow him clean passage. Toward the boy. Toward her. Let him come. I will protect this child, she thought, and stand my ground.

She stepped away from her cart and tucked the boy under her long skirts the color of a faded pink rose. She felt his scrawny arms, his hot mouth and his cheek wet with tears pressed against her naked thigh. His hands gripped her leather boots. The loaf of bread the child must have stolen—the bakers were always earliest at the gates—felt warm and comforting against her leg.

She stood tall in her boots, pleased with her plan for growing her business, looking forward to the telling of the story when she saw Michelangelo and Agnella, who had spent the night in the city at the Santa Caterina hospice.

Beatrice often imagined Hell to be a scorched and ruined land where olive trees collapsed into the maw of sinkholes. But there was another kind of Hell, and it clawed at her from all sides. The guard bashed his way forward, sending birdcages flying in his search for the thief. Head down, she commanded herself. The crowd tensed around her. Even the roosters seemed silenced by fear. She dared not look up. Soon, she hoped, she would be allowed to pass through the city gates.

She could feel the boy's hands ripping bread from the loaf and stuffing it into his mouth. My little redheaded friend, I will repay you for the golden acorns. She was offering him protection and, coming up, a new way to live. Maybe there was some sense to giving love freely.

The guard now towered above her. Could he smell the bread? Head bowed, linen hood pulled low, she fixed her eyes on the intricate weave of his iron vest and the tufts of black hair that grew in patches on his thick arms. How could one man grow so large while others grew small from starvation?

Slowly, carefully, she emptied her leather satchel and extended her coin. "Payment to enter your city, so beautiful," she said automatically. The boy was rigid with panic below her skirts. "May Florence be ever golden."

She said the words obediently, but she did not feel obedient. The people around her, dressed in rags, crazed with hunger, looked ripped apart. They stank of onions and poverty. The air here felt unclean; the dawn itself looked torn asunder. Her throat tightened. She found it difficult to breathe.

She felt a brief, crazed scuttling and the boy pushed out, sending her skirts billowing. The guard turned to chase him, but she pointed defiantly at him and ordered him to stop, even as her stomach contracted with fear. She felt strong enough to defend the weak. "Leave that boy! He is hungry. Let him be, you ugly toad!"

The man stopped, momentarily dazed by her stupid show of bravery.

"Will we deny him that?" she added, turning to the crowd. "Who else is brave enough to join me?"

But it was too late. She heard the roar of the giant and felt a blow to her head. She crumpled against her cart, rattling her clay carafes, and mumbled a furtive prayer that they would not be broken.

A garland of fear wound its way through the crowd. Bystanders watched with curiosity—this guard was the embodiment of the animal that lurked inside all of them. What lay in store for her offered a narrative with suspense and just desserts.

"Hiding a thief. Inciting a rebellion. You will be beaten for this." He looked at her with angry, rheumy eyes. Beatrice could smell the oily stink of his unwashed skin.

"My customers wait for me inside," she said weakly, feeling ridiculous and worthless.

He had an iron grip on her wrist and was hauling her away. The crowd sounded a ragged chorus.

She twisted around to see her cart, abandoned, strangers backing away from it as if touching it might infect them. A rooster crowed, beating its wings against a wooden cage. Would anybody help her?

He dragged her past the tollgate, past the other guards, one of them jumping with glee. She struggled, but he yanked her arm hard, sending her to the cobblestones. He yanked her up again; she felt her limbs might come apart like a wooden puppet. Now he pushed her to the right, down an alley, a route she did not know. It led to a dead end, where a park had been closed off to the public. She felt brambles scratching her legs and saw a hastily erected stone wall and a makeshift wooden door. Shrubs grew thick around it. She could still hear the clatter of the vendors pushing their carts nearby. She wanted him to finish whatever he had planned for her quickly. He was breathing hard, the breath of an ox hauling logs up a hill, opening the door with a large iron key. Her wrist was on fire, and she thought of her mother gently hanging beeswax candles on wooden racks, the game of dipping her hands into bowls of wax, feeling the sudden, alarming burn, then the soothing, silky warmth.

The door lurched open and the guard pushed her across the threshold and into the secret green. This is another world, she thought, stunned by the lush foliage allowed to grow everywhere along a long, narrow track, once a place of heavy traffic between two tollgates, the Porta alla Croce and the Porta a Pinti.

She remembered how the vendors often complained about the decree from the Medici family that had closed a busy public thoroughfare so that the ruling elite might enjoy long, uninterrupted horseback rides.

The guard released her wrist and pushed her forward. She immediately ran, and he caught her with two leaps. One of his hands held both of her wrists behind her back. How strange it was to walk together down the abandoned road, past rosebushes and cherry trees, sweetness filling her senses and the dread of what was to come churning her stomach. She looked over at him and saw his face lined with wickedness.

He punched Beatrice hard on the back of her head, and she fell to the grass, her ears ringing with pain. She screamed, scrambling to her knees, until he grabbed a mound of grass and stuffed it in her mouth. Then he picked up a rock and she growled, pushing out resistance from the back of her throat. The rock came down hard on the side of her head, and the ringing in her ears became pounding—she felt herself fading in and out of consciousness. The pounding grew louder until it seemed it was both inside and outside her head. She could feel his hands grappling with the cloth bandages binding her breasts, but she had tied them so well and so tightly, his swollen fingers could not manage to undo the intricate knot. Cursing, he busied himself with ripping the clothes from her hips. Her skirts lifted, and the chain mail of his vest pressed hard on her face. She stopped moving as his massive weight came down upon her. The ringing in her ears grew loud and overwhelming, a monastery of monks shaking tiny silver bells, and her mind traveled in their direction, toward the relentless vibrations.

❖

"What's this?"

From far away, Beatrice registered the voice. Her face felt wet and sticky—slowly, she wiped away the liquid so that her eyes could squint open. She saw a man with a lean, ugly face sitting high on his horse, his black tunic floating around him. Somebody she recognized. His figure was slight and his cheeks sullen. He looked to be barely thirty years old, yet he held himself easily, with the bravado of an old warrior. Yes, thought Beatrice groggily, it is he. A government official. Her mind attempted to latch on to his name in her memory. He carried a jousting lance by his side and raised it to thrust hard at the sentry's chest. "What's this?" he said again.

"My lord, if you please, she's a thieving villager," answered the guard. His voice cracked with interrupted lust.

"All women respond best to rough handling," said the official, with a thin-lipped smile. "If she is to be submissive, it is necessary to beat and coerce her."

The ringing filled Beatrice's head; she watched how the guard grinned, as if he'd experienced delightful complicity, how he shook his hand in the air triumphantly.

"Animals, all of us, that's what we are," said the man on the horse. "My father introduced me to books. Livy's history of Rome, an excellent, classic resource. I read it all the time; when other boys were out running races in the fields, there I was, alone with the words of Livy. And, the Roman philosophers—when I was a young man, barely married, I adored the words of Lucretius, who spoke of banishing superstitions and favoring the will of a man. That spoke to me, and do you know what?"

The guard looked confused by the official's long speech.

"I copied the book out, all seven hundred pages."

"There's no place for the peasant scum in Florence," said the guard, interrupting. "Though I'd be glad to have my way with her."

The official looked down on him. "You left your post at the toll-gate," he said, his tone icy. He stepped his horse closer. "You have failed the republic and dishonored its *virtù*." He aimed another thrust of his oak lance.

"He has long terrorized us." A third voice, this one with a rich timbre belonging to a woman. Through the fog filling her head, Beatrice thought she recognized Agnella. "Chancellor Machiavelli, my lord, humble servants of the republic count on you to punish those who weaken the state."

"I do not know you," said Machiavelli, stepping his great white horse toward her.

"I know you to be a fair advisor to our Gonfalonier Soderini, and greatly skilled in negotiation with leaders of foreign states." Agnella was an expert at preening and placating; the words slid smoothly from her mouth.

"Naturally, I am pleased with your political assessment," said Machiavelli, leaning forward in his saddle.

"Your battle of painters between Leonardo and Michelangelo is a stroke of genius."

The second chancellor nodded, bathing in his own brilliance. "You know this girl?" he asked, finally.

"I shall take her to the noble doctors of medicine at the Ospedale di Santa Maria Nuova," said Agnella.

Beatrice felt the side of her head ooze blood, and the twinge of purple bruises distorting her face. Agnella brushed a hand gently over her cheeks.

Machiavelli tossed a rope around the guard and pulled tight, saying, "This man disrespects himself and the republic." He turned his horse, and the guard lurched painfully forward. "The government is soon to reopen this greenway to citizens," Machiavelli added as an afterthought, looking appreciatively at the lush garden. "I shall advise the governor to hasten the project. Though I shall miss it for my jousting practice."

Beatrice was fighting to stay conscious. Everything around her sounded extra loud—the pawing of the horse's hooves, Machiavelli's voice, the shaking of the silver bells inside her head. She tried to speak, but her mouth seemed locked.

"Your devotion to the betterment of the city is a model for us all," called Agnella after him, sounding every bit the obedient subject his kind enjoyed. "God make you happy," she added.

Agnella waited only long enough to see the guard hauled away before spitting on the ground where Machiavelli's horse had stood. Working fast, her fingers flying, she lifted one of her underskirts and tore free a clean patch, pressing the compress against the gaping wound on Beatrice's head. Beatrice gasped, struggling to keep her eyes open.

Two villagers Beatrice knew from Settignano came fast across the green to her. They must have run the news of her abduction to Agnella at the hospice.

"We have a cart waiting for you and the girl," said one woman.

"Just outside the wooden door. How is she? Will she live?" asked the other.

"She will live, yes," said Agnella. "I think Machiavelli's jousting practice might have saved her life. I told him I'd bring her to the big city hospital; it wasn't the time to convince him of the value of the women's hospice; a man such as him probably believes it is run by witches."

Softly, sternly, she instructed: "Stay awake for me, Beatrice. Do not follow the ringing." She tore another long length from her skirt and wrapped Beatrice's head several times until the blood was staunched. Her hands ran gingerly down the length of Beatrice's body, muttering to herself: "One broken wrist, two broken ribs. The head—it's too early to know." She straightened Beatrice's skirts and hoisted her up. "Stay with me, Beatrice. Listen to my voice," she soothed. "No sleeping. No following the ringing. Right here, with me."

The women lifted Beatrice and carried her across the green. They brought her through the mouth of the gate and stepped into the street. Word had traveled fast outside and within the city. A crowd closed a tight circle around Agnella and Beatrice, but it was Michelangelo who pushed past to lift Beatrice in his arms and place her onto a waiting wagon.

"Michel, we'll take her to the hospice at Santa Caterina, where I can tend to her," said Agnella. "Roll forward carefully; avoid the ruts in the road as best you can."

Beatrice heard Michelangelo giving grim approval, then felt movement, the sound of horses stepping forward. From there, she knew no more.

Chapter 38

The Santa Caterina hospice had four small rooms, each of them occupied by women. Two were victims of domestic abuse, both with lacerations to the face and broken fingers. One patient believed that a demon lived inside the bulging knot of her right thigh. Another had fallen sick from the hex of her husband; he preferred his younger mistress.

Not all of the patients were destitute. Several from wealthy families were sharing beds with their sisters who, without the promise of suitable suitors, had been pressed into service within the convent. Their rooms were located farther down the hall. These women sometimes demanded tincture of opium and gold leaf, for amusement and pleasure; Agnella always listened to their stories and declined their requests, politely. She saved the mixture for patients who truly needed it: Beatrice was one.

Agnella cauterized the gash in Beatrice's head with a salve of rose oil and turpentine mixed with warm egg yolks. Two nuns wrapped her head in a turban of white gauze. Their mentor—whom they respected as a doctor—secured wraps around her ribs. The girl's skin had turned gray; the veil of death hung near. Tomorrow they would know whether she would turn away from the ringing and return fully to the earth.

Agnella pointed to Beatrice's broken wrist, badly swollen and already the color of a thunderstorm. "Tomorrow, if she is still with us, we'll set it with laudanum."

"Pimpernel, to help her sleep?"

"Yes, she can sleep safely now. A dose of pimpernel, fine. But wash her first," said Agnella. "Then massage sweet chestnut oil into her feet and legs. Use a little honey and sage. You have the oil in your apothecary?"

"Enough, though we could use more." The second nun spoke crisply. "She is a beauty, and so young. Who would do such a thing?" The women let the comment hang in the air. Then: "I'll fetch some." She left the treatment room, but not before tears sprang to her eyes. Patting a linen across her face, she inhaled deeply, lifted her chin and ran to the apothecary.

There was another patient at the hospice who benefited greatly from opium—a woman Agnella had recognized. This patient had arrived days before Beatrice; she had called herself La Riccia. Since then, she had lain on a bed without speaking, the blood weak in her body, her skin dull as limestone. Because she seemed confused and disoriented, she was kept for a week in an airy private room to steady her pulses. The nurses bathed her with warm water infused with lavender. Agnella sat on a wooden stool by her bed, reading long passages of poetry to her. "'Beauty and Duty in my soul keep strife.'"

Does she remember, Agnella wondered, that her true name is Leda? That they had once been neighbors? She feared the worst about the state of Leda's mind, that a series of assaults—and, possibly, brothel poisons—had created terrible, disorienting trauma.

When color started returning to Leda's cheeks and her muttering had quieted, Agnella asked that Beatrice be placed in a bed next to her. The nurses did not question this instruction. Beatrice and Leda lay beside each other, beneath their white linen sheets, and slept for another two days.

"'And 'twixt the two ladies hold its love complete,'" Agnella read, sitting between the beds, a book in front of her, legs wide, leather boots rising above her knees. "'The fount of gentle speech yields answer meet, That Beauty may be loved for gladness' sake, And Duty in the lofty ends of life.'"

Chapter 39

The sound of moaning. A lament from another, faraway time. A human cry. Beatrice wished the keening would stop. If only she could find a way to undo the knots of pain, she might begin to heal the anguish coiled through her head and her body. Thinking about it only seemed to tighten the knots until she fairly pulsated with pain. She clenched her eyes and heard a moan gather in the back of her throat, an animal agony leaping past her tongue.

If she could get out of bed, she might be able to outrun the sound of tiny shaking bells. It was hard to breathe, and she felt faint. Something pungent in her nose, the smell of pimpernel. Immobilized, her thoughts raced in all directions. She missed the olive tree, the ancient one with its massive trunk and gnarly arm that towered above the rest of the grove. Its flowers were powerfully shaped; she liked the way their sweet perfume, similar to the scent in her nose now, cleared her head. When she was a child, she would climb up its rough bark, chiseled and scarred all over by time. Even when the sun dropped low on the horizon in November and the winds from the Apennines blew unkindly over the land, there was a warmth to the olive bark. When it was time to harvest the great tree's black olives, she would place a wreath of its silver leaves around her head, climb to its highest branches and speak of her wish to shake the branches so they might kindly release their fruit onto the blankets below.

"There she is. Our pride! The olive girl!" her *papà* and *mamma* would say, pointing to their daughter half hidden by the branches.

Agnella was always there, among the other villagers, and there were bottles of red wine and smoked boar layered in thin slices onto loaves of tough Tuscan bread. Beatrice would make a pretty speech that was long-winded and amusing. Nobody was allowed to interrupt. There was a lot of gesturing, with her arms reaching up to the sky and pointing dramatically to the earth, as she balanced in a crutch of the old tree, her black hair tumbling down her back. Sometimes she would stand up and bounce on a thick arm of the tree, and the fruit would rain a blessed bounty to the ground. Everybody harvesting would yell up their thanks to the tree, using the nickname—"Grandfather"—that her family had given it: "*Grazie, Nonno!*"

The memory dimmed until it was extinguished by the pain climbing out of her throat. "Mamma!" she cried.

As if looking dully through a linen sheet, Beatrice was vaguely aware of the night nurse who bent over her to administer more pimpernel into her nostrils. She felt something around her wrists, something painful in her bones, and wondered whether the guard's hands were still gripping her there. The nurse checked her pulse, muttered something about it being weak, and something else about ice-cold feet. How could the nurse *and* her attacker both be there? She yearned for him to get off her, for more blankets, for another rubbing with chestnut oil. She heard the nurse leave, wooden clogs slapping on the stone floors, linen skirts swishing. Why was she leaving Beatrice alone with the guard?

In the bed next to Beatrice, a patient stirred. A woman's hand appeared, emerging from below the pile of blankets. Feet flexing, legs bending to form the peak of a rooftop. The woman rubbed her face slowly with her free hand. Through a slit in her eye, Beatrice watched the other patient, allowing her vision to slowly adjust to the dark. It was as if the sheet had lifted and she could see more clearly. The patient's forehead was slick with sweat, and goose bumps were rising on her arms. Beatrice listened to the woman's slow, irregular breathing. Her hand jerked to her neck, and Beatrice could see the outline of bruising there.

A voice—her own?—called out in pain: "Mamma."

The same voice: "Mamma."

"Beatrice?" the patient asked. The question was followed by a declaration: "Beatrice."

She did not stir. But the woman did. Beatrice heard blankets pushed aside, saw legs toppling, sliding to one side, feet appearing at the edge of the bed. Hands braced against the mattress, reaching toward her, fingers piercing the dark, finally landing on her bed. "Beatrice, I am here."

The nurse appeared at the door with the oil, carrying a burning tallow in her free hand. "Signora," she said, alarmed by the sight of the patient standing on her own. "Into bed with you."

The patient put up a hand to silence the nurse. "Leave us," she said, breathing hard now. "I can care for this girl. I have the right."

"No, signora, you don't. Not on my watch." The nurse swept in to intervene.

The woman lifted her chin. Beatrice saw how her face trembled, and how she mustered the energy to speak defiantly: "Ask Agnella." Gasping for breath. "I am Leda, mother of this girl."

Another patient was wailing from down the hall. The nurse let out an exasperated sigh, crossed herself and set down the chestnut oil. "Rub her feet with this, if you like. I'll be back before you can do any harm."

Beatrice tried to make sense of what she had heard. Her vision was blurred again. She watched as the woman who called herself Leda collapsed to the floor and lay there awhile. It was impossible that this was her mother. The woman looked nothing like her, except for the auburn hair and the long neck. She watched as the patient hauled herself up by the bedsheets, arms shaking from the effort. Beatrice looked at her closely as she knelt by the edge of the bed. The woman floated her fingers above Beatrice's face, above the gash, above the bruises. Her fingers were shaking, and still she held them above the horizontal marks on Beatrice's neck, the outline of a man's hand. She tracked the cuts on Beatrice's arm, her wrist bandaged in a linen and plaster cast. "They've done a good job," said the woman. "These strips of white linen around your chest are delicately, carefully arranged. They will help you heal, Beatrice."

It was only when the patient said her name again that she recognized her mother's voice. Leda had a particular way of extending the *ch* sound at the end of her name by pushing out her lips so that it sounded like Beatrishhhhay.

Beatrice felt very tired and agreeable to whatever came her way. Somebody had started to rub her feet, which was a great kindness. How warm the hands were! She remembered sleepily how she would bounce her feet on the branches of the great olive tree. She remembered the joy on everybody's faces, the cascade of olives as black as ebony falling down into the big gathering circle of hemp blankets.

When the nurse came back and saw the woman rubbing Beatrice's feet, she nodded approvingly. "That's good," she said.

Beatrice noticed how the patient looked over at the nurse, with eyes weary of life, as she slumped back to her bed. "I feel the opium scratching here," said the patient, lifting a tired hand, "at the back of my eyes."

"It's a difficult time, to be sure," said the nurse, with some softness in her voice.

"I gave myself over to the darkest of evils. I lay down with strangers to lose my mind—to destroy the pain. That's the truth of the whore I became."

Beatrice was having a hard time following. Was this woman really her mother?

"God will forgive you."

"But I abandoned my child. I'll be judged forever for my weakness."

"There are plenty of us who were forced into the brothel to service the elites of the city," said the nurse. "And who succumbed to the addiction of laudanum. Myself included. Do not think yourself an original." The nurse moved beside Beatrice's bed. "You want your daughter to live?"

"I do," said the patient, and Beatrice watched her scratching at her arm.

"*Allora*, signora, do your best," said the nurse. "A girl needs her mother."

These were true, wise words, thought Beatrice. She felt regret when the nurse clogged away from her bed and out of the room.

Beatrice lay still for a long time, hearing the patient's rhythmic scratching on her arms. She wondered why she was scratching and hoped Agnella could find a salve to help her heal. She heard the patient push aside her sheets and crawl out of her bed, then into bed with Beatrice. The woman moved carefully, so as not to place any pressure on Beatrice's wounds, which was kind.

"Beatrishhhhay," the woman said, and she cradled Beatrice's fingers with her own, doing the holding for both of them.

Later that night—it must have been near dawn—a rooster crowed powerfully, and then another, until it seemed like all the roosters in the city had joined together in a fearsome chorus.

When she woke at dawn, Beatrice's hand was warm, and it was doing some of the holding.

"Mamma," she whispered, eyes closed, lips moving. "There you are," she said. "I was looking everywhere for you."

Chapter 40

Leonardo had gone to the Palazzo Vecchio to pick up his latest payment for his work preparing the battle scene. Fifteen gold florins a month for his labor. The city treasurer had treated him with disdain and paid much of his fee with quattrini, as if he were nothing but a penny painter. Machiavelli had also been on him, threatening to withhold payment if Leonardo missed the next deadline. Dazed and humiliated, he headed into the vast Piazza della Signoria. He pushed past the massive crowd gathered around the *David*, past the carriages of the rich that formed a circle around the sculpture, the better to enjoy a view of the colossus from the comfort of their leather seats. It was his first time truly looking at the statue. The copper leaves created an elegant covering of the bulge, he thought, and saved the women permitted into the streets from the alarming sight of male genitalia.

He took his time assessing the figure, walking from side to side, allowing his thoughts to brew. He studied the feet, the ankle bones, the muscular calves. He turned his back on the *David* and walked away from it, finally turning to face the sculpture from the edge of the loggia. All these months he had heard about this naked man, had discussed it, disparaged it, listened to others heap praise upon its grand, audacious scale. But this? This was art at its most fearless. It was sublime and monumental and wicked of Michelangelo to impose the colossus on the populace. This was subversion rendered in marble! Florence had been remade. It would never again be complete without the *David*. Looking at the crowd mesmerized by the sculpture, he realized that art had the power to elevate the way people thought about their city.

But there was something else crowding into his mind. He dropped his eyes to the piazza. The circle of carriages made him think of Hippocrates and his methods for squaring the circle. The math was difficult to follow. Leonardo had studied it and found a way: he had sliced the circle into thin triangular wedges. He had unrolled the circumference to discover its length, until he had come to an approximation of a circle squared. Over many years, he had devised 169 formulas for squaring a circular shape. But he could not square what had happened at the community picnic in Oltrarno. He understood that Michelangelo was now officially commissioned to paint a battle scene on the wall next to his own painting. His brain understood that well enough. But these last weeks he had been poking at an old abscess that he'd discovered was still inflamed and terribly painful. He found himself obsessing over the past, going back to his childhood, of being given up by his mother and labeled as illegitimate by his father. And later, of being charged by police for being a sodomizer, of failing to produce workable war inventions and cast a proper equestrian monument. He even chided himself for *The Last Supper* fresco that refused to stick to the wall. Standing there on the piazza, Leonardo struggled with this question: Why was he not enough?

Shouldering his way through the crowd, he turned blindly down a side street. The sun was low in the sky, and the tallow had been lit within the front windows of some of the shops. Machiavelli's rodent face floated in front of him. Being bullied by the chancellor and the treasurer. Leonardo felt the breath go out of him. He was too old to weather this.

He took the steps down to a tavern. It was dark inside and smelled of piss and crow pie left to rot in the sun. He bullied his way to the front of the bar and ordered some fortified wine. The crowd was a greasy lot, some of them bare-chested, with black leather jerkins. He had wandered into the Buco. His balls, not his brain, had led him there, and that was perfect for the moment. He ordered another glass. A battle of the lions. Was Soderini not a friend of Michelangelo's family? Had he insisted on this competition of painters as revenge for making Michelangelo put a diaper on the *David*?

"*Guarda!*" The crowd was braying loudly, and with surprise Leonardo noted that Salaì was also at the Buco. A group of men were lifting him like an angel of desire, his luscious curls falling about his face. "Master. Be my master!" bellowed Salaì.

A serving wench approached, the pleats of her *camicia* pulled low against her breasts, then neatly stepped aside, her wooden clogs saving her feet from touching the beer and piss puddling on the floor. Somebody yelled: "Don't spit on the table, spit on the floor!"

As Leonardo watched, Salaì was placed back on the ground, one man tucked hard in front of him and another right behind. The dance of the *florenzer*—as the Germans liked to sneer—began, all three men gyrating and grinding.

Leonardo looked away from the stinking, fetid chaos, and lifted an edge of his cape to wipe his brow. He swayed, considered puking, something vile catching in his throat. He signaled for another drink as the crowd pressed in closer.

Part III

1504–1505

The soul operates principally in two places . . . in the eyes
and in the mouth—it adorns these most of all and directs its full
attention to creating beauty there, as far as possible. It is in these
two places that I maintain these delights appear, saying in her
eyes and in her sweet smile.

These two places may be called, by way of a charming metaphor,
the balconies of the lady who dwells in the edifice of the body,
which is to say the soul, because here, though in a veiled
manner, she often reveals herself.

—Dante Alighieri, *The Convivio*

Chapter 41

Michelangelo visited Beatrice at the hospice often. When he learned that Leda had been found, he beat his chest hard, shouting, "Hallelujah!" A nurse appeared and told him to quiet down or face Agnella's wrath, which made him hang his head and smile. As Beatrice floated in and out of consciousness during those first terrible days, he would sit on a wooden stool beside her and sketch versions of the girl standing up tall, holding a goldfinch in her hand. Other times, thinking on the battle scene he was commissioned to paint, he would press his pencil to paper and conjure a series of naked men by the edge of a river, making their fear of the enemy palpable, their eyes wild as they rushed to haul themselves out of the river and prepare for battle. Many of the women in the hospice, he realized, were doing the same: they were convalescing before having to face the world again.

"Why don't you talk to her?" Agnella said one day, checking

Beatrice's pulse and gently lifting her eyelids to see how the healing was progressing.

"Talk to her? She's sleeping. She can't hear me."

"How do you know for sure?"

He waited until Agnella had taken Leda for a slow promenade down the hallway before clearing his throat and starting to speak: "Beatrice, it's time to wake up. For one thing, my olive oil has gone dry. For another, you're a good artist and need to keep drawing. And you make me laugh when I start to act like an old crank. Actually, you help me to stay human."

A couple of days later, when he was bent over his notebook singing one of his atonal songs, a voice, barely audible, joined his. It was Beatrice, looking over at him. "There you are," he said, jumping to his feet. He kissed her on both cheeks and beamed a smile at her.

"Were you singing?" she asked.

"I might have been."

"You have a terrible voice."

The next day, when she was able to sit up, he spread a samite cloth over her legs and pulled a walnut and raisin pie from its paper wrapping. They called it "the picnic without a riverside." She seemed to relish that morning, just the two of them.

"Talk to me," said Beatrice, speaking hoarsely. All these weeks later, her throat was still raw from the strangling by the sentry.

"I'm working on the preparatory drawing for the Battle of Cascina."

She nodded at him and lifted her eyebrows, signaling that he should go on.

"I've decided to draw the soldiers not in battle, but in the moments beforehand. It's a hot day in July 1364, and they've removed all their armor. They are bathing and resting on the shores of the Arno when one of the soldiers sees the Pisans approaching and calls out: 'We are lost!'"

"We are all lost," whispered Beatrice, no doubt thinking of her murdered father, and the attack that might have killed her.

"When I draw or sculpt, I'm trying to think about all the energy that is burning inside a person," Michelangelo said, leaning toward Beatrice. "Remember my *David*? His entire right arm hangs down passively, but I wanted to carve veins as if they were pulsing with life on the backs of his hands. His muscles are flexing in his right thigh. So that you believe in the potential of his power. It's there, ready to be unleashed, but only at the crucial moment."

Her eyes glittered with understanding.

"I'll try to do that with the soldiers, as well. I know it's the Battle of Cascina, but I'm calling it *The Bathers*. Their bodies will be twisting; they'll look panicked, trying to buckle on their armor as they hear the trumpet blaring and shouts that the Pisans are nearly upon them."

"Nude warriors?"

"Crossbowmen, soldiers, captains of the army."

"They're all naked?" Her voice was raspy, but her mouth twitched with amusement.

"As God designed us."

"Leonardo is drawing, too."

"His will be great."

"A battle with horsemen," she said, with a slight shrug of the shoulders. "You. Go work."

"Are you all right?"

"She is tired," said Leda, scratching one of her arms in the next bed over. "So am I."

"They want the cartoon up on the wall in the next month."

"Go," Beatrice said. "Go work. I need to rest anyway, and so does my mother."

He held her hand and nodded. But only when she closed her eyes and fell into a deep slumber did he leave her to walk back to his studio.

Chapter 42

There was another golden day when Leonardo walked into the hospice wearing rose-pink hose and his matching cap and handed posies of blushing roses to each of the nurses. Then he surprised Beatrice and her mother in their shared room, with its whitewashed walls and dark timbers crossing the ceiling overhead. Leda was hand-stitching cotton bolsters for other patients, and Beatrice was stuffing the pillows with goose down. "Come see," he said, beckoning them to the window. He opened the pane and whistled low. A silver-gray horse appeared and thrust its noble head through the opening. Leonardo handed Beatrice a small apple. When it had been inhaled from her palm into the Andalusian's velvety mouth, he produced another for Leda. They laughed every time another apple was devoured.

By then, other patients and nurses had gathered, and Leonardo seized the opportunity to entertain them with a small spectacle. He crossed the hall and thrust his hands into the basket of goose down. "Ladies, I present to you a bird of paradise," he said, surprising everybody by flinging the feathers into the air.

Beatrice reached into the basket and threw more feathers into the air. Soon, everybody was laughing and digging into the basket. Beatrice said, "Mamma, come see," but her mother had retreated to her stitching.

Later that day, when the falling sun pierced the windows of the hospice, Leda and Beatrice sat on a stone bench next to each other and bathed in the dazzling light, saying nothing. In the stillness, Beatrice allowed herself to hope for a life of modest means and simple pleasures at their farm in Settignano. They could rebuild their family, she dreamed, leaning back on the warm stone wall. She would have a mother again.

Her mother sniffed and shifted beside her on the bench. After running from the brothel and leaving her regular supply of opium, Leda felt sick much of the time. Stitching one pillow a day was all she could manage before succumbing to nausea. Beatrice had to keep their conversations simple or be blamed for making her mother's withdrawal worse. But that day, with the horse at the window, Leonardo had made her mother laugh. And she had smiled and shaken her head when he handed her the portrait he had sketched of her on the steps of the Piazza della Santissima Annunziata.

"I don't think I deserve as much: a drawing from you, the great artist."

"Please, signora, take it. It belongs to you, as you told me back when we first met."

"My eyes, the dark shadows," she said, dipping her face to try to understand the portrait. "I don't recognize myself."

"Ever a beauty," he said, bowing. "As holds true for your daughter." He took his leave with athletic grace.

"Always one for grand entrances and exits," said Beatrice, feeling suddenly deflated.

"'Ever a beauty,'" scoffed Leda, watching the artist walk away. "I could have done without ruining my life."

Beatrice decided to risk asking the question. "Mamma, I need to know," she began, head down, looking at her hands, clenched angrily in her lap.

"Beatrice, don't start. Look at my skin. All the hideous bumps."

"I see them, Mamma. Goose bumps. One of the signs that you are—that you were—using too much laudanum." She turned to face her mother, who was twisting on the bench, growing irritable, wiping strands of hair from her face. The addiction had wrecked Leda; Beatrice could see that. But a quiet rage was building inside her: all of this might have been prevented if only her mother had not abandoned her in the first place.

"Clear your head for a moment," Beatrice pleaded. "Can you do that for me?"

Her mother straightened her back and slowly looked over at her.

Beatrice wanted to shake her. Instead, her voice low, she said: "I need to know."

"I never liked that farm. It was lonely and isolated. Your grandparents liked it, and your father did, too. He said it calmed him, after losing Constantinople. It appealed to his poetic side." Leda was hunching her shoulders up to her ears, her voice getting louder. "He went out to check on the hens. You remember?"

"Of course I do," snapped Beatrice.

"I was stitching. I should have gone with him. Then he was dead, broken by their shovels and pitchforks. After that, no more breathing for me."

"But you left me."

The accusation hung in the air for a long time.

Leda dragged an arm across her face. "Crazy. I went crazy," she whispered.

"Mamma," said Beatrice. "You . . . you never came back for me."

They sat silent.

Leda looked out the window where the horse had nuzzled their hands that morning. "You see the pear tree with its fruit and greenery?" Beatrice glanced out through the glass, and her mother continued: "Once that was me. But then I was a tree without any leaves, and my branches grew thin and brittle, easy to break. I broke—that is what happened. I broke and I escaped." She ran her restless fingers up and down her bodice.

Beatrice reached an arm around her mother. Once Leda had been her guardian angel; now she was Leda's caregiver.

"You are better than this. Than me," said Leda, flapping a hand in the air.

"No, Mamma. Don't speak like that. We have each other. I am grateful for that."

Even as she said these words, Beatrice longed for something more, something she could not ask for: an apology.

Chapter 43

Agnella had given her a walking stick crafted from an olive branch. She wanted to hurl it through the air and curse the gods for what had happened to her. For making her a girl. For making her a nothing. For making her the daughter of a whore.

Angrily, Beatrice grasped the stick and steadied herself. She fixed her wreath of oak leaves carefully over the stitching on the side of her head. Gone was the mother who had once brushed her hair and taught her to make garlands of olive leaves and roses. Beatrice had found her, yet she was never coming back. Whatever kindness existed for her was unlikely to be found in Settignano. Even their little stone hut had been destroyed. Her mother had lost the ability to care for her. Love? Leda loved opium more than Beatrice. That knowledge no longer made her eyes sting with tears. It felt good to be clear about where she stood; it strengthened her resolve. Slowly, chin lifted, she started walking along Via della Stufa toward the artists' laneway.

She knocked at Michelangelo's door and discovered him hunched over the table, a piece of black conté in his hand. He jumped to his feet, rushing to hold the door open for her.

"May I?" she said, nodding her head toward the sole chair in his studio.

He picked up a deerskin, settling the hide and some dusty pillows on the chair, and motioned for her to sit down. "Are you well enough? Agnella threw you out of the hospice?"

Beatrice offered a smile and set her cane to the side of Michelangelo's table. Displayed on its surface were naked men, examined from every side, from every angle, every muscle of the legs, arms and stomach twisting and turning to show her another piece of flesh. There were so many she looked away, embarrassed.

"All your devotion," she said, gesturing with her chin to his sketchbook. In his company, she felt her anger easing.

"What do you mean?"

Beatrice was not fool enough to believe he would be content to stay in Florence. His genius would outgrow the glittering city. Venice or Milan would send him invitations. Or there would be commissions from the papacy in Rome. They never spoke of it, but they both knew that Michelangelo's destiny was larger than what kinship lay between them.

"What do you mean?" asked Michelangelo again, seeming intrigued by her statement.

"Can't you see how much you love them all? If men devoted this kind of attention to their wives, I believe Florentines would be a happier lot."

He smiled, and his eyes seemed to deepen in color. "We have

only one shot at living. These men are giving it their very best. They're all of them heroes."

Beatrice looked back at him. "They are. They seem alive to me. I fear for their lives just now. I want them to hurry up and put on their armor before the enemy arrives."

"Beatrice, do you think Leonardo is in love with the people he paints?" Michelangelo looked at his hands and rubbed some charcoal from his fingers.

"Not in the same way as you. Your art honors the flesh and blood of the hero. Leonardo makes us see the force of nature, the flow of rivers, even our inner thoughts"—she pounded her chest with a fist—"the way we think and feel. There's always something trembling right behind the eyes. A mix of fear and wisdom, I guess." She settled back on the chair and hesitated before half whispering: "I saw that with his portrait of my own mother, and his sketches of the warriors. Strange. I saw that look even in the wild eyes of the horses fighting for their lives in his big battle scene."

"I want my soldiers to seem alive."

"They do—to me they are. Always moving and twisting, the better to show off their muscles." She smiled, then reached for his sketchbook. She pointed to a drawing of a man with fear in his eyes, turning his body as if to escape his own terror. "They seem strong enough to fly like hawks."

"Like you," he said. He slid the chalk over to her. "Draw what you like."

She did not look at him but moved the book closer and removed a blank sheet of papyrus. Moving quickly, as was her custom when secretly staining the walls of the city, she sketched an angel with a child's innocence and wings splayed out beyond her robes. Her lines were rough and coarse, but she took time with careful hatching, showing through the dark lines of her pencil that this angel's arms were lithe and muscular, capable of lifting off the page.

Michelangelo studied the papyrus and nodded. "Good. This is a good start. You need to be more convincing with your shading, though. More detailed and delicate. Be patient. For instance, here." He rolled his shirt back to reveal his right forearm. "Draw my arm."

Thinking he might be joking, she rolled her eyes at him. But he had already begun sketching in his notebook with his left hand while holding his right arm completely still for her. She eased the papyrus back in front of her and selected a fresh red conté.

"That's for later," he said, taking the conté from her. "Start working in black graphite first. The tip is finer."

The air in the studio grew still. She bent over the paper and drew the length of his fingers, the boxy shape of his knuckles, the incline of his wrist. With fine crisscrosses of the graphite, she darkened areas to indicate the muscles that traveled along the inside and outside of his forearm. She pressed down to show the crook of his elbow.

An hour had passed and she was still drawing when she sensed his eyes on her.

"That's enough for today," he said. "But you must practice."

She was annoyed that he was treating her like a child, but held her tongue. "I will. I want to become an artist. Not only in secret. I'm eighteen years old. I need to think about what I will do with my life."

"It's a dream," he said. She braced herself to hear that she should abandon her aspirations. Instead, he added: "It's a good dream."

"The nuns at the Ripoli convent showed me women can be artists, too. People are paying for their work. I'd like that. To sell my drawings. To exhibit them. I don't only want to draw in secret on the city walls."

"If you practice, something will come of your art. I promise. But for now, I have to focus on my battle scene. Rumor has it that Leonardo is finally hard at work on his cartoon of *The Battle of Anghiari*. Machiavelli imposed a strict deadline. Failure to honor the contract means we have to repay all the money or hand over the completed portion of the cartoon so that another artist can finish it!"

"I'd happily volunteer," said Beatrice.

"Only two weeks to go." He glanced at his sketch of three young soldiers, panicked by the coming attack, leaping out of the River Arno, all of them tormented souls, the way he liked to depict his subjects. "I wonder if the governor and Machiavelli will insist on a devil's agreement to have Leonardo halt progress until we can both paint simultaneously like gladiators in the Coliseum." He picked up the black chalk and deepened the shadow on the legs of a naked warrior crawling from the river.

"You need space to make your cartoon," she said, looking around at the small studio.

"They have me over at one of the big rooms at the hospital of the wool dyers in Sant'Onofrio. Smells like wool, mildew and death. Actually, to be honest, it smells like death wrapped in mildewy wool."

She shook her head and laughed. "I shouldn't tell you, but Leonardo's working in a palatial space usually offered to popes!"

Michelangelo gave a crooked, bitter smile. "Compared to Leonardo, I'm receiving far fewer florins, and I've been given mere months—not years—to complete my cartoon of the battle."

She nodded but stayed silent. They sketched together and sang one of his nonsensical songs.

"I have been staying this last while with Madonna Lisa," said Beatrice.

Michelangelo paused to consider. "Is Leonardo still painting her portrait?" He had heard gossip about the commission. "He hasn't completed such a small thing yet?"

"She is a great Florentine lady and very kind," she said, ignoring the jab. "She has offered me the old garden shed. It has little windows set in the stone walls and views to the courtyard and a garden of lemon and pear trees." She saw Michelangelo's brow growing dark, but continued: "Madonna Lisa insists that I can move in and stay as long as it pleases me."

"What will you do all day?" he asked, setting his face to brooding.

"Why do you care how I spend my time?"

"It's only that . . ." He looked at his boots, then to the timbers of his studio. "If you're living in high society, you won't want to mix with the likes of me."

"I'll spend my days storytelling and teaching the children how to climb a cypress tree fast—or how to dry your body after a river swim by lying on the back of a pig." She started to laugh and squeezed her sides. Her ribs ached. "And I'll be selling olive oil just like before." She smiled at him and tapped her cane lightly on the floor. She had suffered and survived; now she was ready to get on with life. "You have my cart?"

He indicated a shape across the room, covered with a piece of silk. He rolled it over. Then, changing his mind, he motioned for her to join him outside. "*Vieni*. For the light."

She saw new copper edging, the sides sanded smooth. He had painted the cart with angels, some gripping trumpets, others with harps cradled in their rosy arms. At the front was a carved rondel of a girl's head, hair flowing to the sides, a wreath of mountain flowers delicately painted in white and pink. The handles had been bound in leather strapping.

"Did you sculpt my cart?" she exclaimed. She lifted the handles and automatically pressed her right hip forward to correct the broken wheel. The cart glided easily away from her and, with a shriek of delight, she walked quickly to catch up with it, pain shooting through her chest. "The wheel is fixed!" she called, holding her ribs and trying not to laugh. "It's good enough for a Medici!"

A small crowd of men from the laneway had gathered around Michelangelo. They stood shyly, arms folded across their chests.

"She likes it, I think," said the coppersmith who had welded the edging to the cart.

"Of course she does," said the ironsmith, shrugging his shoulders as if that much was obvious. He seemed proud of the new wooden wheels and iron axle he had fitted for the cart.

With a mere touch of the handles, the cart rolled smoothly in front of her. Beatrice pulled up in front of the men and smiled her thanks. Her head throbbed, but she felt like she was in a blissful dream. They looked seriously at her, not wanting to acknowledge their role, wanting the moment to be owned by Michelangelo, the lion in the laneway, whom they adored.

"Well, then," she said, shrugging her shoulders. "I thank all of you with all my heart."

She gazed at her earthenware jars, which were settled in a bed of juniper branches, blue berries still intact.

"Eat those berries—heals snakebite," said Michelangelo. "Agnella's touch, of course."

Back inside the studio, she curled and uncurled her fingers and looked at his many wall paintings. The girl who was flying—it was as if she was seeing the drawing for the first time. "Who is that?" she asked, bending forward.

Michelangelo looked to the ceiling timbers and shuffled his boots on the floor. "That was a long time ago."

She looked from him to the wall sketch and waited.

"It was after I met you for the first time in Settignano, when you raised your arms above your father. Like you were blessing him. That image stayed with me. The strength you had inside you."

She nodded, felt the sting of tears, and wiped them away quickly. The pain in her limbs eased. She wanted to tell him something. "Everybody admires your *David*. Lisa and Francesco, the servants, the vendors."

He looked at her seriously and nodded to show that he understood.

"But now," she said, tugging at his tunic, "watch out, because everybody will be admiring my cart!"

"Well," Michelangelo said, "thank you for helping me with *David*, and for calling me an *idiota*."

They laughed awkwardly. He reached for her hands, searching her eyes as if asking a question. He kissed each of her palms, traced his lips on both of her wrists, then let go, as if in farewell.

Chapter 44

That June, the summer of 1505, the humidity lay thick on the air. Reluctantly, Leonardo pulled on his purple wool stockings and threw a red silk cape over a white blouson, a costume of victory, he supposed, or some kind of good-luck witchery. By the time he reached the political heart of the city, his heart was racing and his hands felt clammy. He nodded at the guards at the front entrance of the Palazzo Vecchio. The massive wooden doors were pushed open, and he walked through into the darkness of the vaulted entrance hall. He tore the cape from his throat—even the light silk was too confining in the morning heat—and put a hand on the cold stone wall to find a measure of comfort.

Leonardo had resisted this moment to the last; he reached a landing, turned a corner, then ascended another flight of stairs, aware of the trembling of his hands.

Oils, he had decided, not watercolors. Oils would deliver rich, lustrous tones. His assistants could dry them on the wall with torches. Experiments on his studio wall at the Hall of the Pope had proven the technique.

He stepped into the upper hallway and walked ten paces to the looming doors of the Great Council Hall. He heaved his body against one of the doors, but it remained firm. Giovanni and Ferrando would arrive soon enough; still, he wanted badly to be inside now, to confront the monumental scale of the wall, the void that needed to be filled with his battle scene. A braccio was an arm's length; the hall measured 104 braccia long by 40 wide.

"It's lonely in the dark."

He turned to see Governor Soderini, half-dressed, blouson untucked.

"Though my thoughts are my constant companion," Soderini continued. "Better to get up and walk them around than let them fester while sleepless and horizontal."

Unwashed, breath stinking of yeast, and with an amazing capacity for early-morning chatter, thought Leonardo. "Before the rest arrive," he said, "I want to—"

"Exactly right. Up before dawn. I am myself, most mornings, in fact." Soderini produced a large ring heavy with bronze keys and punched one of them into the door. "Best time to see the people, see how they should be governed." He maneuvered the key and the lock clicked open. "Before the breaking of dawn, I look out onto the piazza, into the emptiness."

"The city at its most hopeful."

"No mess, no rooster testicles for sale, just a man alone—"

"Wanting to fly."

Soderini looked at Leonardo as if seeing him for the first time.

The door swung open and they walked into the giant room, where the heat compressed and solidified. Leonardo dropped his cape on the floor and walked to the daunting emptiness of the east wall, wiping sweat from his brow. He had worked on the commission for more than two years: its concept, its design, the preparatory drawing. Earlier in the spring, his assistants had received eighty-eight pounds of sifted white flour to make a paste to glue the paper cartoon to a linen backing. Workmen had recently hauled bags of sand into the Palazzo Vecchio. They'd laid the sand next to buckets of wet lime putty, mixed them together and applied a smooth intonaco. After waiting for it to dry, Ferrando and Giovanni had filled small cotton bags with charcoal to pounce the outlines of the cartoon over the immense wall. The charcoal transferred neatly through tiny pinpricks in the preparatory drawing, following every stroke. It had taken them days of work, but ultimately they had reproduced the central battle scene, horses and humans in furious combat, fighting for their lives. Now it was time to paint.

Boots on the stone stairs: the sound of Leonardo's assistants arriving. Machiavelli was right behind them, as if chasing them into the council hall.

"Gentlemen, welcome," said Soderini. "I've waited for this moment for years. Tell me, what work will you be doing?" He was kneading his hands nervously as he looked from Leonardo to the faces of the gathered studio assistants.

It was Giovanni who broke the awkward silence. "As you can see, the rough coat has already been troweled onto the wall. We applied a smooth primer coat of white lead and tapped the outline of the cartoon onto the prepared surface."

"Yes, very good, very good." Soderini rubbed his hands together. He looked at the scaffolding that Leonardo had invented, at the trestle tables laden with colors and earthenware vessels for preparing pigments, at the small glass jars filled with linseed oil.

"Leonardo will be painting with oils, working *a secco* on a dry surface, to honor the encaustic technique of antiquity, which we all admire—"

"Oils?"

"There's no need to be alarmed," said Leonardo, understanding that their innovation had set off alarm bells. "We tested our ideas in the studio. I can assure you that painting in this manner produces highly satisfying results, deeper colors and nuances of form without having to rush the process. Fresco means painting fast all the time."

"Pigment and oils provide all the lush earth tones of—" Giovanni was about to reference *The Last Supper*, but thought better of referring to that fading experiment.

"But surely there are earthy tones to be found with tempera, letting all the color sink into the wet plaster?" Soderini asked. Machiavelli started to pace in small, tight circles. "Think of all the fresco artists—Masaccio, Fra Angelico, Giotto—they all worked their watercolors into wet surfaces."

Leonardo raised his eyebrows ever so slightly at his assistants. Soothing the client was a job he loathed. He put a hand on Soderini's shoulder. "We'll review all the pouncing of the cartoon on the wall and be painting soon enough. Pure pigments mixed in linseed oil."

As far as he was concerned, the conversation with the client was completed, and his thoughts wandered. On Saturday he would walk over to Via della Stufa and join Lisa for a celebration. Many moons had passed since they had seen each other, and he needed to apologize for neglecting the portrait. He took off his jacket and rolled up his sleeves. The humidity was thick enough to cut with a dagger. He was sure it would rain.

"How is Michelangelo progressing, do we know?" asked Soderini.

There was another awkward silence. Leonardo brushed back his hair and betrayed no emotion.

"Michelangelo di Buonarroti?" asked Giovanni, as if hearing the name for the first time.

"Very well, I am sure," said Leonardo smoothly. His shirt was soaked through with sweat, and now he felt light-headed. "I'd wager that we will see the imminent destruction of beauty. Including an army of naked men, his signature."

Soderini laughed loudly. Then came the slam of a door and the pounding of footsteps across the floor.

"Well spoken, Leonardo. If I may continue your thoughts?" It was Michelangelo, his face swarthy and sun-bronzed. He approached the group with a confident swagger. "They are young men," he said. "My age," he added smugly. "And they are caught off guard, barely awake from a long, deep sleep on the banks of the Arno. They're brave and they're beautiful and they're willing to give up their lives in battle."

"Well, then, let the blood battle begin," said Machiavelli, clapping his hands as if signaling the start of a horse race.

"Boys, set the scaffold and prepare the linseed oil," said Leonardo. He rolled up his sleeves.

Michelangelo approached Soderini and bowed. "If it pleases the governor, I would ask that Leonardo be given time to paint his fresco at his leisure. I will follow with my own at a later date."

Soderini nodded kindly. "Machiavelli? Leonardo? Are we all in agreement?"

They agreed and Michelangelo took his leave.

Leonardo's wall painting had begun well enough, despite the extraordinary heat. Standing back in the enormous, airless hall, looking at the lines of the elaborate, entwined horsemen fighting for the flag, Leonardo was almost frightened by what he had created: the horror of war.

The problems began later that week when he started painting the intonaco with the oils. Leonardo had not anticipated the extreme heat. Nobody could have. The oils started sliding down the wall. At first, Ferrando reassured him and pressed more linseed and colored pigments at him. They had to double, then triple, the amount he was accustomed to using. The writhing horses started to melt into the soldiers, the outlines of their faces blurred into unrecognizable shapes.

In the early afternoon, the heavy clouds ripped open and torrential rain pounded down on the rooftops of Florence, punishing the brick *cupolone* of the Duomo and flooding the streets. A howling wind drove the rain sideways across the city and through the open windows of the council hall. The summer skies had turned dark as night.

"Bring the braziers!" Leonardo shouted over the deafening

winds. "Stiffen the oils!" They set three braziers on the floor and waited to see if the oils would dry in place. The wind howled and shutters on the south windows banged open and shut. "Get me a torch," said Leonardo. "More than one if you can find them."

Ferrando ran out of the hall and down the spiral stairs, but many precious moments were lost in finding guardsmen, explaining the crisis and securing permission to free one of the torches from the palazzo's massive stone wall. At last, torch in hand, Leonardo brought the flame close to his wall painting. He had envisioned a mural that would be defined by insane violence, yes, but also a whirling moment of dazzling movement and fantastical allusions to faraway exotic worlds. He was trying desperately to retain the helmet of one of the warriors, designed as an enormous deep-water mollusk and, lower down, a ram's head as a breastplate. On the soldier's shoulders were spiky encrustations, as if starfish with a skin of brass tacks had crawled onto them. "Because in war you can believe in anything," he had once instructed his assistants. Now his dream was slipping away, leaving a trail of humiliation on the wall.

All of the subtle undertones that he had imagined and drawn for more than two years had turned into black smudges.

Salaì rushed into the room carrying another brazier. "Found it in the governor's private rooms!" But it was too late. Leonardo shook his head. Exhausted, near tears, Giovanni and Ferrando sat on the floor, their backs to the ruined painting. Leonardo walked to the opposite wall and gazed at the massive room, all of him broken. Bowing to his assistants, he walked slowly out of the Palazzo Vecchio, vowing he would never go back.

Chapter 45

It was late in the evening by the time Leonardo reached Via della Stufa. He walked slowly, head down, red paint smeared over his white blouson. At the entrance doors, a night watchman stepped out from the shadows, his hand on his leather scabbard.

"Signore? State your name."

Leonardo noted the festoons of roses, the gilliflowers and trailing ivy overflowing from the mouths of marble lions. He was at the front entrance of a palazzo, the tall wooden doors finely decorated with bronze foliage. He needed to knock and go in.

"Signore, your name?" The guard had stepped in front of him. He was a big fellow, young, and his unlined face shone with sweat. Despite the afternoon downpour, the humidity had only intensified over the course of the day; now, the nighttime sky had burned to the color of ash.

"My name? That depends on the day, doesn't it?" The guard stared at him as if he might be confused, or possibly drunk.

Leonardo elaborated: "It could be Master of the Arts, or simply Master. It could be Honored Son of Florence—"

"All right, old man, it's time you went on your way." The guard gripped Leonardo's arms and turned him forcefully from the door.

"No, no, I must go in," protested Leonardo. The heat was suffocating. "They are expecting me," he said. "Tell them Leonardo da Vinci is here."

He saw a hideous face: bulging monster eyes, roiling tongue. Imagined or real? He could hear voices in the distance, his name being whispered. The sight of the grotesquerie sent his mind back to the events of the day. The problems had begun when he'd started painting the richly colored oils over the dry plaster surface. He had not anticipated the extreme heat. The linseed oil seemed bad. Had his supplier cheated him by selling him weak liquid, lacking concentration? The color had slid down the wall. Even his most experienced assistants could do nothing to stiffen the oils and save his wall painting.

He had walked out of the Palazzo Vecchio. He would never go back. In his defeat, he could not stay in Florence—he would find a new patron in another city and grow soft whiling away the years.

A sound of clanging metal and the doors swung open. A bright-faced housemaid peered into the evening, beckoning to Leonardo with both arms. She scowled at the night watchman before shutting the doors with precision. Her leather boots clicked smartly on the marble tile floor.

Inside, the stifling heat dissipated. Leonardo stepped into a cool green oasis afforded by an interior courtyard planted with blossoming night flowers.

"Leonardo, so good of you to come!" It was the silk merchant. Mona Lisa's husband. "Friends, Leonardo da Vinci has graced our home! He needs no reproduction. I mean, introduction." The man had obviously had too much to drink.

Leonardo saw women with lead-painted teeth, dressed in brilliant, gaudy colors. They were perched at a grand white marble table and watching him with amusement. Other guests sat below an arbor of blooming roses and linden branches, slapping their legs in laughter with jewel-encrusted hands. The sound of water gushing from a small army of water nymphs overwhelmed his ears. Bankers, lenders and government officials—he recognized many of them—lounged comfortably on long benches of turf.

"Have a seat, dear friend. You don't mind our rustic experiment?" The silk merchant again, now whispering in his ear. "They call these *exedra*, the latest furniture art from Venice! Benches made out of grass."

The sound of laughter was the braying of donkeys.

"Francesco, you are monopolizing our guest." A gentle hand on his shoulder, the familiar smell of apricot oil. Mona Lisa flitted her fingers at her husband as if to say "Run along."

"The air is painfully heavy," she said, handing Leonardo a cup of chilled vin santo and walking him away from the crowded salon.

A servant opened a carved wooden door and they stepped out into the courtyard. The moon hung low in the sky, enormous, a disc of ocher. "I was looking for privacy, but that thing," she said, gesturing to the sky, "is very demanding."

"Dazzling to see it. Covered over with water. Maybe they're golden lakes, reflected back to us like a mirror," he replied, his voice heavy with exhaustion, bending his hand in a convex shape.

She dared to press her hand against his. They were alone, away from the crowd. "You've been working very hard today. I see you are tired." She led him into the garden and breathed deeply. "Tell me of the fresco, the painting of it at the Palazzo Vecchio. Are you pleased?"

He stepped away from her, unable to speak.

Sensing the mural had not yet achieved his ideal of perfection, she changed the subject. "Beyond your work, my husband has informed me today that your father is very ill." Francesco and Ser Piero had long contributed to the funds at the Santissima Annunziata; they often met over legal matters.

He nodded and kept looking up at the moon.

"Leonardo, you must go, you must see him on his deathbed. Allow for reconciliation. Perhaps in your heart you will find forgiveness?" She stepped in front of him, forcing him to look at her. "You can't deny him your presence, his firstborn, in his last hours."

"I have been an annoyance to him all of my life."

"I don't believe that. Why else would he recommend you to Francesco, and the church commissions, if he did not believe in the greatness of your talent?"

Leonardo shook his head and took a few more paces away from Lisa. He had been working on her portrait, layering a pigmented glaze over the painting with obsessive patience. It might take him years to achieve the appearance of inner radiance, but there was no other way to pay tribute to her. The portrait of Lisa occupied his thoughts just as solving the problem of flight did. Maybe the way he was painting her had the power to eclipse the business of portraits to something much bigger, more timeless.

"Is it so easy for you to deny yourself emotion—to feel pain or even love?" She reached out, snatching at the side of his cape. "I look at you, dear Leonardo, and I see a great scientist, an engineer, even a magnificent painter. But what of your emotions? Do you ever write in your many notebooks of your feelings for me, or for Salaì or Beatrice? Or are all your scribblings tributes to your inventions?"

"I'm not a piece of dead wood, signora, if that is what you are suggesting."

"I know we have shared so much, and you have brought me back to myself. But, your father on his deathbed—"

"Leave me to my thoughts," he interrupted. "Go back to your friends." He pulled his cape from her fingers. The failure of his fresco sat heavily in the pit of his stomach, and he cursed the way he had sullied his name.

She hesitated behind him; there was a sweetness in the air: lavender and lilacs. But Lisa turned back to the party.

In the courtyard, he stumbled and, feeling disinclined to walk on, he shook off his cape and lay down on the grass. He felt very hot and thirsty, and was glad to surrender. Exhaustion was a heavy, wonderful blanket. His body sank to the earth.

He allowed himself a memory, something from his childhood: how he trod his pudgy little-boy feet through the forest, brandishing a stick, his warrior sword. Four or five years old he might have been at the time. When he came to the river next to the town of Vinci, he tested its depths, then plunged it into the still waters, triggering a tiny vortex of action. He still remembered the tug of joy when he realized that everything in nature curved—nowhere was there a straight line to be found, not even in his powerful stick.

Adults might aspire to solve wars between the Italian states or build a cathedral with a monumental dome. His aspirations at the time were as small as his tiny hands. He might pick up a stone and hold it, feel its weight, wonder at its round shape. He never thought about time—its significance, the measurement of one minute becoming an hour, becoming a day. He scrambled his way up the boulders, past the meadows that spread wide behind his house and into the forest that shimmered with shadows and promise. He was occupying space, not time. Picking up a rock that seemed to want him, that fit into his hand as a goldfinch might, that he could warm with his touch. He remembered how he would stand still, bare feet nestled in the grasses, listening to the sounds of nature: the alarming birdcalls, the rustling of cypress branches, the groaning of tree trunks. All of it amused him, inspiring him to shout back at the forest: "*Buon giorno!*"

Other times, he would whisper to his rock friend, tickling it with his voice like a feather. The little stone in the sweaty palm of his hand. That moment of gladness, a tentative conversation, not sure about each other, and then, by the time morning had turned into afternoon, the blossoming of trust.

His mother, Caterina—where was she during those languid days of childhood play? Likely out somewhere in the fields, pulling rocks from the soil, picking lemons, planting olive trees, hoping to find enough food to feed them at night. Even as a little boy, he understood that they could not be together by day. He accepted as fact her daily disappearance. When he woke in the morning, he walked sleepily to the cup of goat's milk and the bread set out for him on the table. Despite his hunger, he never finished the bread entirely. Maybe he wanted to leave proof that she had been there. Maybe it comforted him somehow.

What was certain was that his mother loved him. When he found her in their stone hut at the end of the day, she would bend down and hug him, and take her shawl from her shoulders and wrap it around both of them, as though they were bandaged together, and he could taste the salt on her neck and breathe the rosemary oil she pressed like melancholy into her thick black hair.

He supposed, on looking back, that he was learning to be patient. Or learning to be a student of the world. When he sat in the apple tree, he watched the cows closely. Their tails would whisk up into the air and slap down hard on their backsides. At first, he thought this was a signal to him. An adult, such as his grandfather, would say he was studying the cows. What he was doing was watching them. One long, languid afternoon, when the cicadas were buzzing so loudly they seemed to be inside his head, he looked closely at the cows. It grew hot and still. He stayed quietly in the branches for the entire afternoon. As the sun dropped low toward the earth and the evening breezes rustled the branches of his apple tree, that's when he realized the cows were not signaling to him; they were merely flicking the flies off their backs. He felt a hollow loneliness then—and even now, he still felt it as a memory.

An ache in his heart. Leonardo from Vinci—a man without a respectable family lineage or even a last name. He shifted, feeling empty, and he felt sorry for the child with the tiny hands and the bonnet rough and dirty on his head. People liked to believe they would never forget the face of a loved one, but that was not true. Flesh, left unseen, untouched, unloved for long enough, dissolved and floated away like mist. With time, his mother's soft adolescent face had disappeared entirely from his mind. He remembered thinking how curious it was that he could no longer remember her face, though he was not a callous child. Even the color of her eyes, so young and shot through with a shining faith, faded from black to gray to nothingness. Her figure, thin and muscular, which once held him with such strength, receded into the fog until he could no longer feel her arms.

Memories can hang low in the brain like fish sliding through silt at the bottom of a river. Something surfaced while he was a student apprentice at Verrocchio's studio. His mother was startled back into existence. He was sculpting small figures from clay: wet the ball of red into something warm and malleable, then pinch it into a perfectly proportioned human being several inches tall before laying the blade of a sculpting knife to the body. It was satisfying work—better than making paintbrushes for the studio or sweeping the floor—but with its own challenges. Try as he might to breathe the fire of his imagination into the form, the clay resisted.

Verrocchio and some of the older boys, Ghirlandaio, Perugino and Botticelli, had rushed out after lunch to supervise the installation of a piscina over at the Old Sacristy of San Lorenzo. Being made of marble, it was a delicate washing basin, and the boys didn't trust the men on the installation crew. There Leonardo was, in a rare moment of quiet at the studio, just himself and his dead ball of clay. Beyond the open doors of the studio, children were shouting loudly and playing hoops, and he could smell meat roasting, likely the goat that had been dragged on a rope past the studio earlier that morning. It was starting to rain and he felt lazy. He spied a roll of linen resting on one of the tables, fine cloth ready to be stretched as canvas. (Verrocchio told him sternly later on that it was the very best linen from Rheims.) He liked the weight of it in his hand, and suddenly, in one gesture, he had slipped out his knife and cut a length. What he wanted was to bring that dull little figure to life. He dipped the linen in a pail of wet clay and softened it with the mud. He worked the cloth around his sculpture, draping it generously over the shoulders, pleating it at the waist and allowing it to fall all around the feet.

Now he could draw what he had sculpted.

It was raining hard by the time he found his silverpoint and prepared a wooden tablet to draw on. He mixed some bone ash with his saliva to rub over the surface and held the pen tightly in his left hand. He wasn't sure if what he was drawing was an angel or a human—the draped cloth seemed to invest his lines with something imaginary and immortal. He liked the feeling of silverpoint on the abrasive board, the invented movement, and he was thinking that this was the way to challenge the Flemish pictures with their perfectly round trees dotted on the landscape. He shaded the deep creases of the fabric by building a density of lines and, with a single stroke, traced the line where the cloak fell from her breast to her knee to the earth. The figure, formless and lifeless, became a young woman. And suddenly he thought of the blanket he used to wear at night as a little boy in Anchiano. He felt the weight across his shoulders, and he remembered his mother—

her olive skin, her eyes black as stallions. The drawing was still wet, and he remembered everything. She spoke to him: "Don't go."

All those years of gradually erasing her voice from his mind. That day in the studio, her words came hurtling back to him. He could feel her fingers gripping his arm, their cheeks pressed together, and he could hear the way she kept repeating: "Don't go. Don't go."

He wished now that he might speak of his wall painting—his failure—to his mother. She might wrap him in a coarse blanket and soothe him. His beard felt wet and he didn't like that feeling.

He opened his eyes and he was back on the grass, a young woman bending over him.

"Can you let go of my wrists?" she said.

It was the olive oil girl. Beatrice. He released his grip.

The evening came back to him. The sound of laughter from inside: more braying of donkeys. He pulled tufts of grass from the ground and held them to his nose. They were sweet and cool to the touch. Where would he go now? And Michelangelo? The young, brilliant bastard. Without a doubt, he would triumph and carry on. He would seek work in Rome. Maybe Pope Julius could arrange a grand commission for him. There had been talk of refashioning the dull interior of the Sistine Chapel. But he, Leonardo, what of him? "Must I toil for fresh laurels?"

"My lord, you are unwell."

He smiled at Beatrice and reached for her hand. She leaned close, smelling like springtime. Touching his forehead, burning up with fever: "Water, to begin with." She returned with a large carafe from her garden cottage and helped him to sit up. He drank long from the jug and, after she had patted his face with a cool cloth, lay down again, resting comfortably, spreading his hands over his heart.

At last, he eased himself up on one elbow and turned to Beatrice. The water filled his body with goodness, clearing his senses, clarifying his thoughts. He had forgotten to drink anything during the stifling hot day. Looking up at the stars, he raised a hand to the sky. "The heat will lift, and they'll brighten as the night goes on." He patted the ground beside him, ever the elegant host. "Come see for yourself. Tell me, are you fully recovered now?"

She lay down on the cape beside him, smoothing her skirts over the grass. "I am," she said. "As well as can be."

The velvet dark eased the patter of his heart. They lay still for a long time, gazing at the stars. A slight breeze, imperceptible at first, blew across the courtyard, bringing some relief from the stifling heat. He felt his body relax against the moist ground.

"Do you remember when you taught me about juniper?" he asked. The deep timbre of his voice recalled their first meeting at the city gates.

She smiled in the darkness. "Let me remember this," she said. "The year 1505. When Leonardo da Vinci told me that I, Beatrice from Settignano, had taught him something."

"You taught me that we are all cut from the same tree," said Leonardo, rummaging through his leather satchel to fish out a dried sprig of juniper. "That the tallest trees are made up of their branches, and their branches are made up of tiny, feathery needles. All of the patterns repeat in nature, as in life."

"Go on," she said.

He held up the juniper, a little withered but still holding its feathery shape, for Beatrice to see. "I am the father and Michelangelo is my brother. Isn't that what you said? We may not be the same. We may be broken pieces. But we are all a part of each other."

She nodded and smiled again. "Leonardo, may I ask you something?"

"So long as it has nothing to do with painting a very long wall."

"What do you do with all of your knowledge?"

Another breeze, stronger and cooler, passed over them. He was reminded of a similar conversation with Lisa. She had accused him of sounding like the pope after he had declared it important to live honorably.

"Beatrice, you tell me. What do you want to do with it?"

She sighed deeply. "Signore, I would say that, compared to those stars, we are as tiny as ants."

A dog barked, setting off a rooster that shrieked in the night. Loud voices and laughter drifted out from the party. The guests were only across the courtyard, inside Mona Lisa's palazzo, but they seemed as far away as the heavens above.

"Have you ever loved someone?"

He was relieved she had asked the question. "Yes," he said. "My mother."

"This is the first I have heard you speak of her," said Beatrice. Perhaps she had expected a clever answer about the flowing river or the greatness of the stars. "Does she live here in Florence?"

"I don't know. But I will have to find out." He sighed and was cheered by the thought. "And, you, dear Beatrice? Have you loved somebody?"

"Such a big word," she said, scoffing, pulling out a handful of grass and throwing it back down. "Yes, I have," she added at last. "Very much, though it hasn't always been easy."

He waited for her to go on.

"I have been thinking recently of my father. He would set me against the juniper bush, writing poetry in the dirt by our hut. And my mother. The other day, when I visited her at the hospice, she had plucked a lemon and held it to her nose. With every day, her clarity has been returning. Perhaps she can soon return to Settignano. We will rebuild our little home and prune the gnarly olive branches. Return to our ordinary lives."

They were quiet for a moment. She noticed a brooding around his lower lip, the jutting of the chin like the old men in the market.

He took another deep drink of water. Wiped his mouth with a patch of linen. "Don't lose yourself in all of this splendor," he said, gazing across the courtyard to the palazzo. "The city can be confusing. I came here as a refugee from Milan and, though this is my hometown, I've never really felt at home here. Go back to your village when you feel homesick, whenever you need to feel that you belong. Keep your mother close, in a way I was not allowed to."

He eased himself to standing. She shut her eyes for a moment, as if not wanting him to go, and listened as he brushed the grass from his clothes.

"I have grown old, but you have time on your side. Use it well," he said.

He straightened, looked slowly to the stars in the sky and walked toward the gate of the courtyard. But then he lifted a hand in the air, as if to signal that he had forgotten something. Not his cape or his satchel, but words he wanted to say. "And *grazie mille*, my friend. I believe you will achieve much in your life. Into the wolf's mouth you go." He smiled. "That's what Florentines say for good luck."

Without missing a beat, Beatrice gave the traditional response: "*Crepi il lupo!*" May it die.

Chapter 46

He placed the Communion host on his tongue and bowed low in front of the priest, thinking: There, done with the old man. Piero Fruosino di Antonio da Vinci, the Florentine notary. My father.

Incense and smoke, the glow of the wax figures crowding around the Virgin Mary, melting slowly, the drone of the liturgy. Leonardo looked around at the faces aligned in steely expression, men and women, high society, people on their feet. He stepped back from the altar, nodding grimly at his seven half-brothers, seeing his uncle next to Salaì and Paolo, his studio assistants shuffling anxiously on their feet, hot and uncomfortable. All of the concerned, Lisa and Francesco, the curious and the disinterested, snapped into focus in one all-seeing moment. He walked with head held high. His father had left him nothing from his estate. That sealed the tragic nature of their relationship. Actually, it allowed for an unbroken line of disappointment.

He had never gone to his father's deathbed. It seemed unforgivable to some, to want to be separated in their last hours, and Lisa had begged him to reconsider. Death was not something to dance around; it needed to be seized, drawn inside the body. How she had clung to Piera as she passed from Earth to a better place in Heaven!

Beatrice stood in a niche by a side altar, observing the crowd. He could see it written all over her face: the shame, the anguish, the pain of erasing pain. Did she hear it, too? The sound, the splitting, the opening, the crack down the middle of an ancient oak tree. He watched as she put a hand on her father's old jacket, which she had switched for her cape today, clearly finding a measure of comfort in its threadbare quilting. Maybe she was losing her father all over again. Reliving her lonely treks to the city at dawn. The scourge of being an outsider. The assault. God, give her peace. Let it all wash away.

Released from my duty as grieving son, he thought, picking out familiar faces in the assembled crowd at the Basilica of Santissima Annunziata. There were his business acquaintances, clients, all of them gazing at him, beseeching him to remember the work he had promised to do; Machiavelli raising up his arms, as if to launch into a speech, and Soderini pulling on his cape to subdue the urge. Leonardo breathed in the heady frankincense, devoured the perfumed smoke in his mouth and staggered from the church.

The sun was hanging low, clouds bruised, any sign of the morning's first blush obliterated. What he thought of then were blackberries and flowering anemones, chartreuse against the purple hues of rushes and reeds. He remembered his chalk drawings of star of Bethlehem and Job's tears—simple, tender sketches with red conté—and the love he felt not for his father, but for the meadows and woods that edged his village of Vinci. He felt the blessing of his mother. The shadow of loss.

He walked into anonymity in the crowd at the Piazza della Santissima Annunziata. He crossed to his familiar seat on the stone steps next to the Ospedale degli Innocenti, sat down heavily and put his face in his hands. Pathetic, he thought. I am a grown man and yet I feel like a child, mourning—not his loss, no, but the scorn.

The arrival of men pushing toward a crowd gathered for a cock-fight made him rise. A short walk along the cobblestones to the hospital of Santa Maria Nuova, and he retreated inside, moving past patients tottering uneasily on their feet, babies screeching, the hoarse scream of a young woman, down, down the steps to the subterranean cave of the hospital.

"My lord!" a voice called out. "Maestro! It was too much to bear. The church filled with stink and heat. All those people."

Leonardo turned and saw a strange apparition: Michelangelo. He wiped his eyes and looked again.

"I don't blame you for hiding."

"*Salve*, Michelangelo. Welcome to my secret world," said Leonardo. "I'm sure you have one of your own." He opened a heavy wooden door and lit two large tallows. A windowless room, stripped naked, came into view; its only furnishings were a wooden table and a large ceramic basin set on the floor. The bare minimum—no art, no artifice.

The familiar smell of old blood assaulted their noses.

"Dissections?" Michelangelo asked.

"Whenever somebody is volunteered."

They looked at each other, treading uncertain ground.

"You walk here unnoticed at night, do the work and return before sunrise."

"Yours?"

"Across the bridge at Santo Spirito. The friar obliges."

"An excellent library," said Leonardo, remembering. What the hell was Michelangelo doing here? He was aware of the stink of the airless room. White cotton soaked in ammonia. He looked down at the basin. Old, hardened blood.

"I saw you rush from the funeral," Michelangelo began. "It's not my style to stalk people. My legs just started moving in your direction."

"Full moon, I suppose."

They looked at each other again. There was no room for a quarrel.

"It is hard, isn't it?" Michelangelo's eyes shone with grief.

Exposing himself, thought Leonardo—there's a brave man. Drunk or pumped high with opium? "To be an artist? Always."

"Every gesture requires . . ." Michelangelo looked at his hands. "You have to risk everything to make a work of art matter."

Leonardo felt a crack of empathy, lightness. The dark, mysterious room at the bottom of Florence invited him to leave behind insults and humiliations. "Trust what's coming out of your head. If young artists can't do that, well, then—"

"I want to speak with my heart, and stop the battle of words," said Michelangelo. "I didn't welcome you home to Florence and that was wrong of me."

"I was an arrogant ass." Leonardo crouched and then lay down fully on the stone floor, relishing the cold of the vault. "I feel exhausted. Today was my father's funeral, and nothing I could do ever made him proud."

"My father cares only about how much I earn."

"Your mother died in childbirth?"

"When I was six."

"Mine abandoned me—or my father stole me. My father specialized in the drafting of wills," said Leonardo, looking up at the old timbered ceiling. "With a stroke of his pen he might have allowed recognition that I was his son."

"He was a *capone*, a fathead," said Michelangelo. Then, "How am I to produce something worthy to fresco? You have a thirty-year lead on me."

He said the words as though he was a victim, but Leonardo suspected he did not feel that way at all. The rumor was that his preparatory drawing for the Battle of Cascina was nearly done, ready to be transferred by pinpricks to the wall of the Great Council Hall.

Leonardo looked over at the younger man and felt a tiny thrill claw through him. Should he seize on that vulnerable look in Michelangelo's dark eyes and twist it to his advantage? He thought of the woodpecker bashing its head repeatedly against tree trunks to seize tiny insects. Over many days of study, he had discovered that the tongue of the bird measured three times the length of its bill, allowing it to retract into a soft bolster to protect the bird's brain whenever the pounding began. To any other creature—to a human being—the force exerted on the head would be lethal. All of this he had written down in one of his notebooks.

The very thought of it, the thought of banging heads with Michelangelo, exhausted him. He did not have a soft bolster to cushion the blows. "You have youth on your side. Take a risk; the battle is what you imagine it to be, what you fear most." He wrapped his cape around his knees to fend off the stale damp of the morgue. "There doesn't have to be a beginning, or an end. One remarkable moment. That's all."

There, he had offered a truce. Words of encouragement. Had he imagined that this young talent represented the enemy? This conversation could never happen again. "There are many who possess technical skills. But rare is the man who can invent something new."

His mind flitted to the hills and valleys of Caprese, where his first flying machine had already been tested. He must return to paring down the weight of his mechanical bird, to be certain it could fly free in the air when pushed from the ground. Flying. My God, he obsessed over it, scribbled in secret, mirrored script, desperate to test that a substance offers as much resistance to the air as the air to the substance. There was still life in him yet. He needed to remember that.

Leonardo rose to his feet, ignoring the stiffness in his knees, and extended a hand to Michelangelo. He wondered why the young sculptor had not mentioned Leonardo's failure with his wall painting. "Do what you feel is right. Too many people live the unlived life. They could have been someone." He looked at the plaster walls, stained yellow with age. "So could anyone."

He hesitated and looked over at the young artist, at his wild hair, his brow furrowed with obsessive thoughts. "The best thing about coming back to Florence?" The revelation came hurtling toward him. "Knowing you were here, biting at my heels, making me run when I'd tired of walking."

"A pain in the ass?"

Leonardo smiled. "In a pleasurable kind of way."

There, he had dared to speak the truth. No rehearsing of the words. But there was more that he needed to add. "Michelangelo, your *David* astounds me. It dazzles me. To be honest, it makes me jealous. But, my brother," he said, remembering Beatrice's wise words, "we are all cut from the same juniper bush."

Chapter 47

Sweetbriars in a vase; wicked thorns and tender pink blossoms. A table piled high with sketches and leather notebooks. A purple scarf thrown over a chair. It had been many months since she had last sat for him. Now she was alone in the studio, late-afternoon light falling over the wooden floors. All the dust exposed, coating the furniture in white, adding an extra dimension.

Lisa picked up the scarf and wrapped it around her neck. Walked behind the easel, where he always stood, assuming the position of artist. "Twist a little to the right, chin down, up again, look at me," she heard his voice from a faraway place. "Trust me, tell me about your life, your loss, your sorrows, your beliefs." She had been a willing captive, granting permission for him to do with her what he wanted, holding still on the chair, breathing through her nose, learning his words: "Contrapposto, sfumato, cross right hand over the left, a little more, that's fine."

She touched her hand to the naked skin of her neck. Cool—though it was a warm day, the winds becalmed, blue skies wrapped around the city. She had become one of his painted women, Ginevra, Cecilia, Mary, Saint Anne. See me, feel me, touch me, I am all yours. She looked at the board propped on the easel.

"There you are, Madonna Gherardini."

Leonardo strode athletically across the studio. "Riddle me this." Gripping her hands, kissing them gently. "Those who give light for divine service will be destroyed."

She tilted her head to one side, removed her hands, bristling at the formality with which he had addressed her. Did all their friendship amount to anything?

"Fireflies when day breaks," she said at last.

"Could be, though I had something else in mind." Eyebrows lifted, urging her on.

"The stars every morn."

"Intriguing. What else?"

"Leonardo, I cannot stay for long. We should discuss the portrait. My husband has been asking . . ." It wasn't exactly anger she felt. Or rather, she wouldn't allow that, knowing that Francesco's anger always ended in shame. She felt restless, yet pulled to this man; he transported her every time they met.

"The bees who make the wax for candles." He clapped his hands in delight, proud of his riddle. She noticed the wrinkles around his eyes, intelligent, curious, deep river waters.

"I'll remember that one," said Lisa, nodding, returning a smile. "I'm sure the children will be delighted." She looked at him and felt it again: the transparent glaze of walnut oil down her cheek. Horse hair, silky and strong, caressing her skin. She had memorized his every move, dipping the paintbrush into the translucent gold paint, then facing the board again. One stroke. Another, then another.

There was a sudden scampering, the sound of something bounding across the floor. A baby monkey dressed in a lacy white dress pounced onto the chair and sat very still, its enormous brown eyes staring intensely at the humans.

"Portrait of a lady, *una donna vera*," said Lisa. "Signed Leonardo da Vinci."

"I have something to show you," he said, laughing, sweeping her toward the door. She thought of the first time they had met at the studio, the weight of his hand on her arm, feeling they might sink together.

Into the moody shadows of the monastery stable, past the arched stone entrance, all sounds muffled by the straw on the ground. Leonardo clicked his tongue, calling gently to his horses, smiling at their snorted replies, the sound of hooves pawing heavy as iron against the ground. "Lisa, I've been called away to Milan," he said abruptly, turning to her. "I expect to be spending much time there."

And so this was happening, she thought. He was leaving behind the people who mattered. "What of your unfinished work, all that is still to be done here, the battle scene, my portrait?" She rattled off the list as if duty required it. Who was she, a poorly paid assistant to the governor? Besides, he was not listening—his head was lifted, mouth curled, and he was calling again to his horses.

The stable boy emerged from the darkness with a horse trailing behind him. It was the gray Andalusian, its silver mane wild and curly, a long forelock sweeping low over its face. The horse stepped forward, knocked its massive head against Leonardo.

"As you are a rider, with experience in the hills of Caprese, I am entrusting you with this noble creature," he said, wrapping his arms around the neck of the great beast. "Please indulge him. Take him for long rides in Tuscany or even here in the city. My understanding is that the governor has reopened the greenway near Porta alla Croce for all people—and riders such as yourself."

"Leonardo—" She started to speak, but was unsure as to how to respond. For how could he possibly conceive of a woman riding bareback in the city? He expected so much from her, had pushed her to think for herself, requiring her to stretch her brain in unseemly ways.

The horse snorted loudly and shifted on its feet. "He will require your devout attention," Leonardo said, producing a carrot from his satchel and feeding it from his hand.

Just then another stable boy emerged, leading the Caspian horse. It was not as tall as the other, but had filled out to a healthy size, treated well by the Dominicans within the Florentine stables.

"This one is for Beatrice," said Leonardo. He rubbed his hand down the flank of its neck. "Better behaved, and loyal to a fault. She'll transport the girl easily from Florence to Settignano whenever she needs to visit."

"Is this your way of saying my portrait is not yet finished?"

Leonardo looked up at the sky. Was he praying? "You, Madonna, are a woman of shifting light and darkness. To capture your being,

I discovered, is more difficult even than solving the problem of flight." He looked over at her, hoping for a smile. "I am required to ask for your continued patience."

She sighed and stepped away from the horses.

"Lisa, indulge me. I have dedicated a lifetime to studying how to truly see things. My notebooks are my attempt to record my drawings and discoveries, to patiently, carefully use my eyes, knowing how to see, *saper vedere*. I have discovered the golden waters on the moon, how to engineer a canal and map towns, how to breathe underwater with my apparatus. But I cannot yet say with satisfaction that I know how to complete a portrait worthy of you."

"Leonardo, please." She refused to address him formally, raised a hand in gentle protest. "Do not think of me as an impatient housewife, waiting breathlessly to hang my image on the wall of our salon."

"We'll leave that to your husband."

"Do you not know the rules?" she asked, impatience rising in her throat. "That ice will melt, that fire is hot, that women of the *grandi* class have no right to ride bareback through the city? You are oblivious to it all, the real world. This"—throwing her hands up into the air—"this is not some kind of fantasy."

"Start something new," he said blithely. "Rules are not to be feared, only blind obedience of them."

"You abandon Florence for Milan once again."

"The new governor has summoned me there." He shrugged. "It seems I am obliged. Milan has been good to me. I have been told that the French king would like to remove *The Last Supper* from its wall and haul it to France. Perhaps I will distract him by producing a new work."

"You abandon the people who love you here." She bowed her head, hiding her hands within the mane of the Andalusian. Her voice felt broken, and she could not bear the thought of being in the city without him.

"*Allora*, this is true," he said, finding her hands and gripping them tightly. "For my entire life, I have studied." He looked at her as if trying to piece together how to say what was necessary. "But mostly, I have been ignorant when it comes to knowing myself. I never had a teacher such as you."

"Will I see you again?"

"Madonna, I would be honored to see you at my exhibition. It will be open to all people, from both sides of the river."

"Beatrice?"

"She inspired it all."

Chapter 48

She arrived at the exhibition predawn, before the crowds started to arrive. Inside the walls of the Santissima Annunziata monastery, within a billowing tent of linen, Beatrice stared obsessively at Leonardo's drawing. It was the preparatory cartoon of the Virgin Mary, the Child, Saint Anne and Saint John. At first, the work seemed horrible, all black and dark; it smashed into her eyes like a fist. She knew it was unfinished, and yet it carried a terrible and raw beauty. Charcoal pressed hard into the paper, the figures surrounded by dark shadows, light shimmering from their faces. It felt timeless, as if it had found her after traveling for thousands of years.

The more she examined Leonardo's drawing, the more the streaks of white became blazes of light. She felt drawn—no, lured—into the picture. Mary and Anne seemed as authentic as women in Beatrice's village, supportive of each other while tenderly holding an infant child. It was as if Leonardo were revealing a path to the spiritual world and a human empathy that she had never imagined from him.

She felt an arm brush against her. "*Allora?*" she said, annoyed that her time alone in the tent had come to an end.

"Pleased to meet you," said an old man. "I am Sandro Botticelli." He tapped her arm with his knuckles. "I have lived a long life, but I've never seen anything like this." He bent toward the drawing.

She looked over at him, this aging man in fanciful silks and velvets. Lippi had once told her all about being apprenticed to him. "I wish I could draw even half as well as Leonardo," she said.

"You draw?" He looked quizzically at her, his eyes bright with intelligence.

Beatrice understood his disbelief; she was only a peasant, dressed in a rough linen tunic and a borrowed cape. A poor girl who had no right to art. Neither to view it, nor to make it.

"It's so real, the sweetness between mother and child," she whispered, ignoring his question. She saw pure love in the way Anne looked at her daughter, but also in the rings of charcoal around Anne's eyes, her passage from a life that was once carefree. Something caught in Beatrice's throat. She felt the absence of her own mother all over again, the way their love for each other had been chopped into ugly bits. "I used to sit on my mother's lap."

Her candor caught Botticelli's attention, and he poked her arm with a bony finger. "That's what happens. And then we all grow up and the troubles begin. Why do you think I paint worlds of fantasy? So that everybody can escape!"

She heard shouting and turned to see what the commotion was about. Hundreds of people were crowded outside the monastery, some of them waiting solemnly to enter the public exhibition, others growing impatient to get inside. Standing on tiptoes, she could see that the line now snaked its way along the wall of the monastery, turned a corner and disappeared toward the Duomo. The *maccheroni* vendors had lit their charcoal fires and set their pots to boil. A group of nuns—wealthy girls who had lost their freedom but not their florins—headed for the food carts, laughing as they pulled strands of goat cheese apart with their hands.

Beatrice waved at the women, beckoning to them and throwing some copper coins through the air, and a plate of *maccheroni* was handed across a dozen people to her. "Look at all of them," she said, laughing out loud. The crowd continue to swell. She saw passengers fling open their carriage doors and start arguing with the monks for line privileges. Two men dressed in double-breasted gambesons started pushing at each other. Monks stepped in to restore order.

"You'll have to wait," said the monk at the entrance. "We're at capacity."

"I'm the governor!"

"Art for all. First-come basis," replied the monk. "Salaì's orders."

"These people," protested Soderini, "eat pasta with their hands. Clear them out so we can have a look."

Another monk, bigger than the others, switched from Latin to *volgare*. "You. Wait in line," he said, crossing his arms across a vast chest.

Three women drifted past, their necks adorned with long garlands of lavender and orange blossoms. A heavily muscled man walked by with a pair of monkeys. The women offered a garland to Beatrice and bowed, hands pressed together in prayer.

"Making friends wherever you go."

Beatrice turned to see Michelangelo standing in front of her. "It's a *carnevale*!" she said into his ear, eating another mouthful of cheesy pasta.

Over the roar of the party, it was nearly impossible for her to hear Michelangelo's response. She thought he said something like "Can I have you for myself?" and she felt his hand around her waist, leading her away from the crowd. They walked together to a shadowed corner of the monastery, beyond the lemon trees. She jostled next to him, eating with wild delight, allowing her hands to fly through the air rather than keeping them pressed together primly like other women at fancy parties.

"Did you see all the people lined up on the street?" She put her lips against his ear—as much for her own pleasure as to see if it might trigger a vibration below his belly. Leaning closer, she inhaled his musky scent, the red wine on his tongue, and she moved to press a breast against his arm. She cherished his company, even if there was no hope for a love match. Not even to satisfy Agnella. Not even to keep him safe from the Office of the Night. But she could bring him food. Draw and paint next to him. Make him laugh when he grew too serious.

He stepped forward, caught her by the small of her back and traced his fingers lightly over her lips. "I like you," he said. "And I like that."

The blare of a trumpet pierced the air and interrupted their intimacy. Leonardo appeared, and the crowd parted to make room for him and Salaì. Salaì wore a pair of wooden wings on his back.

They were wider than he was tall, and each was detailed with feathers individually dipped in silver and gold.

"Look at his hair," said Beatrice, elbowing Michelangelo hard in the ribs, amazed by the way Salaì had streaked his face and hair with some glittering precious metal. He glowed like mirrors catching sunlight.

"Officials are arriving," said Michelangelo. "Too bad." He gestured to the main gates, where monks were lifting the male guests' leather jerkins, doublets and gambeson jackets, checking for weapons. It was Machiavelli and Soderini, with their entourage.

Beatrice drifted to the long walnut tables with wooden benches. By midday, guests were feasting with abandon at the banquet, their heads bowed over pewter bowls of fish stew or veal pies. Some dipped bread into aromatic soup. How strange and wonderful it was to see men and women, wealthy and poor, not divided but eating together, sharing platters of food, passing goblets and plates to each other.

Two women dressed in emerald-green caftans stepped toward the tables, black hair pulled into glistening braids. Platters of fruit stacked high on gold pedestals sat on top of their heads. A man in a silk turban approached and set a large clay jar on the ground. He gestured to his leather holster fitted with tiny porcelain teacups.

"This is a lovely surprise," said Soderini, admiring the women.

Beatrice chose a bowl of fish stew and stepped closer to the distinguished guests to listen to their conversation.

"Orientals," said Machiavelli. "Possibly from Java? I hear Magellan is hoping to make an expedition there. If Charles of Spain will indulge him."

Soderini shot him a defensive look; without the Medici, the Florentine Republic no longer had the funds to finance large expeditions abroad.

The men turned their attention to the large tent next to the lemon trees. Its walls of white linen breathed in and out. People inside were staring with feverish intensity at Leonardo's small drawing.

Beatrice caught a glimpse of Leonardo holding court the way he liked to, with a group of admirers fanned around him. His face was more handsome today than she remembered, his skin smooth and burnished. A man handed him a carafe of Chianti, and he bowed in dramatic gratitude, swirling a crimson velvet cape cut short to reveal his athletic legs. He drank, spilling some of the red wine onto his cloak.

A look of discomfort spread over Leonardo's face as the governor approached with his entourage. Soderini was talking loudly and gesturing with considerable bravado. She heard: "We need to insist on its completion—isn't that right, Machiavelli?"

She saw Machiavelli press his fingers on the artist's arm. "*The Battle of Anghiari* is a work of major significance for the republic. You must see it through to completion. Choose a less humid day and make the repairs." He crossed his arms and held steady.

Beatrice watched for Leonardo's reaction to the bullying. He seemed to be attempting to smile, but it looked more like a wince. She doubted he would give in to the harassment of these powerful patrons. Finishing did not interest him. Starting did.

She spotted Madonna Lisa in a corner of the billowing tent. Lisa was magnificent in a long cinnabar-red gown with billowing sleeves of bright-blue damask, a red cap pulled over her forehead as a man would wear it. Like everyone else in the crowd, she was sipping from an earthenware cup—thick, unrefined pottery, not at all like the fine porcelain Beatrice had seen at her mansion. She waved at Beatrice and smiled, showing naturally white teeth, none of them painted. Gone were the fussy adornments of her society friends. This woman once whipped by grief, who had crumpled to her knees and come back to stand as tall and straight as the Campanile. Her face shone with dignity and strength, and Beatrice thought of her as an entire being, whose beauty coursed through her like a mighty river.

As Beatrice made her way to Lisa's side, she was distracted by the sight of Michelangelo approaching the illustrious group, his black cap pulled low. He embraced the governor with both arms, then shook Machiavelli's hand, pumping it hard. Beatrice watched as Leonardo bowed to Michelangelo and the young artist bowed lower to the master. They seemed to have made an uneasy peace, which pleased her.

She turned sideways to allow room for Paolo and his undercooks to parade past with trays of food raised high above their heads. She had never seen such quantity and variety before: basins of olives, platters of roasted capons and pheasants dressed in herbs, baskets of tarts decorated with mint leaves and pomegranate seeds. The tables had been reset with fresh layers of white linen, candles set to glowing. Guests began seating themselves on the long wooden benches, ready to pour wine for each other and enjoy a formal dinner. Beatrice knew she should sit and pull out her cutlery case—the tiny fork and spoon everybody else seemed to have brought with them—but she had not thought to bring her own tableware. Instead, feeling bold and irreverent, she grabbed two tarts and pocketed some sugared nuts to take to her mother.

Ferrando angled by her, carrying a wooden cask of wine on each shoulder. "Gifts from patrons," he said, winking at her. "Meat at last, not just Leonardo's vegetables!"

There was barely enough room for her to extend an arm and find Lisa's hand. Together, they squeezed through the crowd to stand at Leonardo's side. Beatrice reached out to Michelangelo and linked an arm through his. Her cheeks glowed hot, and she felt giddy and loved. Leonardo looked kindly at her, then rested his eyes on others who had joined their circle.

Soderini's wife, chin lifted, gestured toward Leonardo with a long peacock feather. "Master of Arts," she said, curtsying deeply, "your fresco will pay tribute to the greatness of the Florentine people. You must return and complete it."

"You should try this—it's really, really delicious," interrupted Beatrice, her mouth stuffed with a generous portion of mushroom tart.

"May I present Beatrice, a good friend," said Leonardo, hugging her to his side. "And not merely an olive oil girl," he added.

"A fine artist, too," said Michelangelo.

"Exactly right." Leonardo nodded. "Plenty of talent and lots to teach all of us."

"Our Tuscan daughter," said Lisa.

There was an appreciative pause, and then, as if he had forgotten himself, Leonardo spoke with gladness: "Honored guests, may I present Madonna Gherardini del Giocondo. My dear, wise friend."

The governor and his wife hesitated and finally bowed to the women, then Soderini stepped toward Leonardo to insist again on the completion of the fresco.

God watch over you, thought Beatrice, and squeezed Leonardo's hand to steady his heart.

The blare of a trumpet pierced the air. In the courtyard, a group of musicians stepped forward playing viols, followed by others holding wooden cornetti to their lips. Monks lit candles within giant white lanterns—designed by Leonardo, she knew, and made by Salaì out of flax paper—and set them like moons touching the ground. Flowing from the exhibition tent, the crowd gathered to watch and be enthralled. A musician started playing a slow ballad on his lute and Salaì appeared, slightly stooped under the weight of his large wooden wings. They seemed too heavy to allow even the most modest flight, but Beatrice appreciated the spectacle—he looked like a silver and gold butterfly—and joined in the riotous applause. He lifted his arms and monks appeared in the fading light, carrying pillows covered in bright swaths of silk and inviting the elderly and women to sit upon them.

Beatrice stood up on her toes, the better to see the depth of the crowd. She had been at the exhibition all day, and still the entrance line showed no sign of ending. It looked like the party would go on all night. More long tables were being set up with shimmering lengths of linen and endless tallows.

Her head felt light from the wine she had drunk, and she wanted to share the strangeness of the moment, the lavender sky kissing the darkness of the earth. She wove through the crowd and found Michelangelo alone in the white tent, crouching in front of Leonardo's drawing. He had lit the tallow on his leather head strap and was peering at the sketch, one section at a time, sweeping the light slowly in front of the work. His hand reached forward and she thought—she feared—he might rip the paper from its frame. But what he did surprised her: he had curled his fingers together and was drawing in the air, tracing Leonardo's lines: delicate movements for Mary's face, followed by a fury of movement where the drapery of the women fell to the earth. Was he pretending to be Leonardo? Her heart went out to him then, and she loved him for his pure, unpolished heart.

"I have some charcoal," she joked, making to fish through her leather pouch. "In case you are planning on offering some improvements?"

Michelangelo stepped away from the work. "Not a chance. He's the Great One."

"Leonardo calls it humanity."

"He's making emotions real."

"If you like that kind of thing."

"I'd like to learn from him, think of him as my mentor. Do you think Leonardo can be trusted?"

"I do." She reached forward, drew her fingers lightly across Michelangelo's knuckles. With her other hand, she widened the leather pulls on his gambeson and pressed the charcoal stick against his skin, drawing the outline of an angel—face lifted, wings spread wide, the way she wanted him to feel. She breathed in his smell of damp wool and liked it all over again.

"Will you come with me back to the studio?" he asked.

"To do what?" She was thinking dark, sexual thoughts. Didn't everybody?

"We could be together and you could paint with me." He caught her in his arms and lifted her off the ground.

"I might, or I might not," she said, lifting her head to him, allowing the dark lengths of her hair to fall down past her neck. She pressed her mouth against his neck and kissed him lightly, tasting the salt of his skin, and the tent whispered behind her in the evening wind. Her wish was to touch this maker of beauty, who had made *David* a hero for the city.

"*Allora*," he said, bowing his head, gently setting her back down on the ground. They stood with their foreheads pressed together. Their flirting was no good. A white wedding—unconsummated, without sex—was a lie they could not bear to live.

He reached for her face and smoothed her brow with his rough, calloused fingers. She saw the apology in his eyes.

"Even if this . . ." He looked from her face to the deep-purple sky. "Promise me you'll keep working on your art," he said.

She nodded. Let the confusion between them be gone. Going forward, she would pursue clarity. She was nearly ready to take up Agnella's offer to exhibit her drawings in the hospice of Santa Caterina. She could imagine them in that place of healing, her cherubs and wild-eyed angels, her portraits of the leather-skinned village vendors who stood hunched outside the city gates.

Outside the tent, under the stars, monks and artists swirled together. Some of the artists were wearing colorful headdresses fashioned to look like swans and serpents, with patches of silk fabric for scales. The crowd let out a roar and the headdresses were removed and sent flying like kites into the air. The players were revealed: Benedetto! Gherardo! Giovanni! Dante! Arrigo! Bartolomeo! Ferrando! Each stepped forward and shouted out his name: they all worked in Leonardo's studio.

Salaì gestured and Leonardo stepped into the courtyard. He removed his white headdress, which curled like the horns of a ram. With a quick jerk, he hurled it into the air and the horns unfurled like a long white veil. Beatrice watched, mesmerized. She understood what was happening. This was Leonardo's way of saying goodbye.

The crowd surged and Beatrice was nearly knocked off her feet. She was reminded of swimming in the gentle current of the River Arno. Leonardo's sketch of mother, daughter and child had shown her that tenderness was possible for both the lowest and holiest of humans. Wait a minute, she thought, holding a plate of iced pears in one hand, a stick of charcoal in the other. I am feeling again. For Michelangelo. For Leonardo. For Agnella and Mona Lisa. For my mother. She wanted to take all of her emotions and throw them in a ball up high so they could stay, untouched, in Heaven. Maybe that was where enlightenment was found, right next to love and forgiveness.

There was something moving through the air. She felt a warm breeze and directed her gaze above the hundreds, possibly even thousands, who had gathered within the vast courtyard. The roar of the crowd disappeared. Beatrice looked up and trusted her eyes. *Saper vedere* is what Leonardo called it. Larks, nightingales, white parrots—it could be another exhibition—a flock of birds lifting off. She saw them clearly. Ascending.

Epilogue

A cockleshell!"

"Sketched on the paper?"

"Instead of your portrait you saw shells?"

"Just one."

"Long live the cockleshell!" said Agnella, raising her cup of mead and banging it hard against Lisa's.

"May it live on, that tiny sketch," said Beatrice, laughing, spilling some of her drink.

"As my portrait never will," said Lisa, setting her drink down.

They never tired of her story, the one where she was alone in Leonardo da Vinci's studio, just before he traded Florence for fresh fortune in Milan. She had walked over to the easel to finally glimpse the portrait he had never allowed her the privilege of seeing. But the wood panel was gone, replaced by a single sheet tacked to a fresh board. Then the monkey arrived and took up its chair—or did Leonardo bound into the room first? Master and animal caught in a fantasy world where everybody dressed up in fancy clothes and snacked on dates and bananas.

"All these years gone by and I have only seen him once," said Lisa, resting her hands on the table the way Agnella did. Beatrice knew she admired the way the healer arranged herself naturally, curved into space, rather than holding herself rigid as a measuring stick. "Francesco fixed a meeting at the Palazzo Vecchio in advance of Leonardo's legal hearing with the governor and his advisors. For quitting the battle commission, refusing to do it all over again. There he was, the great Leonardo, standing on the steps of the palazzo and caught by Francesco, who pressed him for details about when my portrait might be delivered. Naturally, he waxed on like the moon, avoiding anything real or specific."

"He was paid for his troubles?" Beatrice served herself a large piece of chestnut pie and put half of it into her mouth. Lisa handed her a linen napkin and took another sip of the honey wine.

"Francesco paid him from our first meeting in his bottega."

"I loved him from the moment I saw him, releasing that white parrot into the sky," said Beatrice, eyes shining. She felt shot through with elation, the way she had that day in the lineup outside the city gates. One of her drawings in the Santa Caterina exhibition showed a white bird racing for the sky, moving with such speed that some of its feathers ripped into the sky. That one was dedicated to Leonardo.

"You say it with such ease," said Lisa.

"What?"

"Love."

"Oh, that. Yes. Might as well. I was in love with Michelangelo. And he loved me, too, but not entirely, not that way. He loved his art even more." Her words galloped ahead of her. "I'm in love right now."

"Careful," advised Agnella.

"Iacopo—he came back from Romagna. Mercenary soldier no longer. He scolded me, though, for stealing eggs from his mother's hens." She stuffed the rest of the pie in her mouth.

Agnella and Lisa looked across at each other, absorbing the revelation, plainly thinking, Such a beautiful girl, still given to a wild spirit.

"Are you making plans?" asked Lisa nonchalantly.

"*Basta,*" Beatrice warned. "That's enough." She defiantly lifted her chin. "Maybe we are, maybe we aren't."

"Beatrice, don't dump all of your apples out of your cart. You need time for yourself, and you have your new exhibition to prepare for."

Nodding in agreement, growing serious, Beatrice considered the women she adored looking back at her. It was true that, after seeing her exhibition of bird drawings, Prior Bichiellini had requested that she display ten of her charcoal drawings in the Santo Spirito library. She had completed a series of cypress trees, black and thin, glinting like swords. And one other work, the most difficult: a portrait of *Il Papa*, her beloved rooster.

All their wisdom and kindness, given to her as gifts. Better than myrrh or frankincense.

"Iacopo is an honorable man," she said. She lifted red apples from the basket. "Can I give these to the horses?" They were roped outside, the Andalusian and the Caspian, chickens pecking at a safe distance in the yard. She stood to go outside, glad to escape the conversation.

"*Va bene*. She's all right," said Agnella, after Beatrice had departed. "Learning well at the convent. Nearly finished her training as a midwife. Transforms herself the moment she walks into a patient's room. All efficiency and expertise."

"She keeps long hours there—I think she likes it—and never seems too tired to dance in the courtyard when she comes home to Via della Stufa at night." Lisa looked around the room, at its whitewashed walls, gilliflowers spilling from clay pots near the window. Agnella's house was a refuge, simple and primitive, of the type favored by Savonarola for its honest construction, without gold or silver embellishments or even the brightly painted terracotta rondels so commonly found in Florence. On the wall was a single artwork, a carving of the Virgin and Child. Lisa studied the way Mary cupped the feet of baby Jesus in the palm of her hands, as a real mother would.

Agnella followed her admiring gaze. "That was made decades ago by one of my neighbors, a sculptor by the name of Rossellino. I like it, though it's growing old and dusty."

"I find your home an oasis," said Lisa.

Before he moved away to Rome, thought Agnella, this home was Michelangelo's oasis, where he could clear his mind and collapse into her caring. Each month, a young moon etched in the sky reminded him it was time to visit Settignano. Ever faithful, he had come back a year ago to tell her the news of an important commission to paint the Sistine Chapel for Pope Julius.

Beatrice came clattering back into the kitchen. "Horses are settled now. Shall we go? I want to see Leda before the sun goes down."

She called her mother by her first name these days; it seemed easier that way.

"Leda is an old Greek name," said Lisa.

"It means—" added Agnella, but Beatrice interrupted her.

"I know. Leda means happy."

"I believe Leonardo painted Leda with a swan. Beautiful, no doubt. Your mother suits her name more than ever these days," said Agnella.

"The goose bumps on her arms have been gone a long time. I think I'm learning to trust her again."

"Before you take your leave . . . Beatrice, Lisa, have you seen this?" Agnella rose from the wooden bench and walked to the fireplace. Sketched above the mantle was the figure of a man twisting head and body in contrapposto toward them. She remembered how Michelangelo had pulled a stub of charcoal from the fire, honed its edge to a fine point with his knife. This was when he was completing the *David*. She had been ladling soup into terracotta bowls. "I asked him whether there was a demon—somebody he feared." She saw in her mind how he'd traced the male figure, working with tiny movements of the hand, darkening the hatching on the wall to reveal a noble bearded face. The right arm of the man reached out, a billowing cloak floating grandly behind his torso.

"What did he say?" asked Beatrice.

"Of course he was reluctant to tell me. Finally, he said: 'The giant I face is older than I, and more talented. He's known by princes and paupers across the land.'"

"Leonardo," said Lisa.

"Yes," said Agnella, looking up at the sketch. "He said, 'My nemesis is the one I most admire.'"

"*Dio mio*, sounds like the Michelangelo I know," said Beatrice. "Obsessed and obsessive." She remembered the marble dust he left on her hands, the sound of the new word on her tongue: *scultore*. "I miss him. What he taught me." She hesitated, then lifted her gaze to look directly at the women at the table. "What we gave each other."

Author's Note

I never planned to write a novel about Michelangelo and Leonardo da Vinci. The idea emerged slowly during the time when I was an architecture critic writing about starchitects and powerful public artists who were rebranding twenty-first-century cities around the world. Turns out the trend didn't start with Frank Gehry or I. M. Pei, but hundreds of years ago in Florence. But that's not what hooked me. It was discovering that even superstars struggle with their own personal demons and harsh judgment. Then Beatrice showed up in my mind as an olive oil girl sent down from the hills to the city like a wise talisman. At that point, I couldn't let the story go.

Tuscan Daughter is my attempt at drawing back the curtain to reconsider history through a female gaze. As much as I was intrigued by an epic clash of titans, I felt compelled to give voice to strong female characters who were never given a chance to be seen or heard. How brave are the outsiders: artists, gays, women who had no rights and who claimed their own power outside the rules.

Writing a historic novel featuring two of the world's greatest art geniuses has been extraordinarily humbling and often overwhelming. It required years of heavy research and the courage to let much of the investigation go. In many ways, I needed to add layer upon layer of understanding, something that Leonardo called the process of addition *per via di porre*, but, ultimately, take away, something Michelangelo called *per forza di levare*. With the help of many, I learned that this was the only way to reveal the emotional track playing inside the heads of my characters. I had already imagined and written much of the character of Beatrice and her complex relationship with Michelangelo when I read in one of Charles de Tolnay's renowned biographies on Michelangelo that the artist did, in fact, mentor at least one female artist during his lifetime. She was Sofonisba Anguissola, who became a court painter and lady-in-waiting to the queen of Spain, and lived to the grand age of ninety-seven years old. At the same time, Leonardo painted women not in demure profile but gazing directly out into the world. I like to think of both Leonardo and Michelangelo as feminists ahead of their time.

Numerous reliable sources, including the Renaissance writings of Giorgio Vasari and Agostino Vespucci, further confirmed by Italian researcher Giuseppe Pallanti and British scholar Martin Kemp, prove that Lisa Gherardini del Giocondo was the subject of Leonardo da Vinci's enigmatic portrait *Mona Lisa*. Her husband, Florentine silk merchant Francesco del Giocondo, enlisted Leonardo da Vinci to paint her portrait in the early 1500s. As is meticulously detailed in Dianne Hales's *Mona Lisa: A Life Discovered*, Lisa was a Florentine and the mother of six children, though three had tragically died by the time she turned thirty-eight. She was destined to become celebrated around the world as Mona Lisa, but Lisa Gherardini died in obscurity in a Florentine convent. Her funeral was held not at her husband's church, but at Santo Spirito in Oltrarno, her childhood neighborhood.

During the years when they both lived in Florence, Leonardo da Vinci and Michelangelo were commissioned to paint epic murals on the east wall of the Great Council Hall in the Palazzo della Signoria, now commonly known as the Palazzo Vecchio; its contemporary name is used throughout *Tuscan Daughter* so as not to confuse the reader. Although Governor Soderini and the Signoria Council of the Florentine Republic demanded that Leonardo complete *The Battle of Anghiari*, he never did. Charles II d'Amboise, governor of Milan and marshal of France, intervened, requesting Leonardo's services in Milan, including a commission to design his suburban villa and garden. A drawing by Peter Paul Rubens reconstructs the central fight for the standard in *The Battle of Anghiari*. Michelangelo's cartoon of the Battle of Cascina was never tapped onto the wall of the Great Council Hall. A painting by Bastiano da Sangallo is the most complete surviving copy.

A list in one of Leonardo's notebooks itemizes all of the materials required and approved by the City of Florence to complete the monumental wall painting within the Great Council Hall: "260 pounds of wall plaster; 89 pounds eight ounces of Greek pitch for the painting; 343 pounds of Volterra plaster (sulphate of lime with size); 11 pounds 4 ounces of linseed oil; 20 pounds of Alexandrian white; 2 pounds 10 ounces of Venetian sponges." Recent research published by Martin Kemp indicates that Leonardo's central *Fight for the Standard*—the fight scene that was actually painted—would have measured 12.5 by 14 feet. Its soldiers would have been about 25 percent bigger than life-size.

In 1508, Pope Julius II commissioned Michelangelo to paint the ceiling at the Sistine Chapel. Michelangelo lived in Rome until his death in 1564, a few weeks shy of turning eighty-nine years old.

In 1519, at the age of sixty-seven, Leonardo died in the castle of Cloux, France, after serving for many years as *peintre du roi* for his patron, King Francis I. He left his painting of the Mona Lisa to his companion, Salaì, and it was purchased by the king. At the turn of the nineteenth century, it was installed in the Louvre Museum.

In 2012, art researchers and scientists sponsored by the U.S. National Geographic Society began chipping away at a frescoed wall by the sixteenth-century artist and biographer Giorgio Vasari that covered Leonardo's unfinished fresco in the Great Council Hall at Palazzo Vecchio. The project is currently known as the "Lost Leonardo."

In 2019, an exhibition at the Opera di Santa Maria del Fiore in Florence produced the transcripts of the distinguished committee convened to decide the location of Michelangelo's *David*. Leonardo's recommendation that the genitals of the colossus be covered and the giant sculpture tucked into a black niche of the loggia—*"che stia nella loggia"*—is part of the historic record.

Tuscan Daughter was carefully researched over many years,

which meant reading primary sources, interviewing Renaissance experts and attending numerous exhibitions honoring the work of Michelangelo and Leonardo da Vinci. I also conducted several research trips to Florence, to live there, to study the masterworks at the Uffizi Gallery, the Accademia Gallery, Casa Buonarroti, Santo Spirito church, the San Marco monastery museum and the Laurentian Library, and to trek the hill-town paths of Settignano. I visited the Santissima Annunziata cloister (now the Italian Geographic Institute), where Leonardo had been invited to stay by the Servites, and saw the artist's secret side entrance and the frescoed birds on the wall. Wall drawings and playful doodles in charcoal were often created by Michelangelo in his studios and at his family villa in Settignano, something New York Metropolitan Museum of Art curator Carmen Bambach has written about. To see original works by Michelangelo and Leonardo da Vinci outside of Florence, I traveled to the National Gallery of Art in Washington, the Louvre in Paris, Saint Peter's Basilica and the Apostolic Palace in Vatican City, the National Gallery in London and the Royal Library at Windsor Castle in England.

Many of the characters in *Tuscan Daughter* are well known to the reader, though the nuances of their personalities and motivations were entirely my creation. The rest of the characters are my inventions, but readers may be surprised to learn that Machiavelli did, in fact, have a long liaison with a prostitute by the name of La Riccia. Months and years that are relevant and historically accurate are noted. Elsewhere, I have taken some liberty with the timeline. Any errors are entirely mine. The only thing I can rely on is my imagination.

I revised and expanded the novel during the COVID-19 crisis, when my four children returned home with their partners and a new baby. The world went quiet, wildlife crept out from the woods and ideas blossomed.

Acknowledgments and Selected Bibliography

For believing in this book, I offer my heartfelt thanks to Harper-Collins and, especially, to my editor, Jennifer Lambert, for her outstanding insights and clarity. My agent, Hilary McMahon, a fearless, high-energy champion of authors, has always been on my side. For enlightening conversations on Mona Lisa, Leonardo and Michelangelo, I am indebted to the renowned art historian Martin Kemp, Oxford University Professor Emeritus and distinguished author. For welcoming me into their venerable institutions to discuss up close original works by Leonardo, I am grateful to Matthias Wivel, Curator of Sixteenth-Century Italian Paintings at the National Gallery in London, and to Martin Clayton, Head of Prints and Drawings at the Royal Collection Trust, Windsor Castle. My great thanks to University of Toronto Professor of History Nicholas Terpstra for his careful reading of the manuscript and for offering judicious comments as an Italian

Renaissance expert while deferring to my creative license. Many thanks also to the sharp-eyed and astute copy editor Sue Sumeraj, and to marble sculptor Carl Taçon for his insights into the technique and physical impacts of marble sculpting, as well as to University of Toronto Professor Emeritus Olga Pugliese-Zorzi, former chair of the Department of Italian Studies, for enlightening me on appropriate use of Renaissance-era Italian. For helping to nuance the novel, I thank John Paoletti, Professor of Art History Emeritus, Wesleyan University; Jacalyn Duffin, medical historian and hematologist, Queen's University; and Mark Jurdjevic, Professor and Chair of the Department of History at York University's Glendon Campus. Thanks also to Italian tutor and translator Elena Vassena and to Alison Woolley for teaching me the art of fresco in Florence in 2019 and for reviewing some technical details of the wall paintings by Leonardo and Michelangelo. It's one thing to write about fresco; it was another to mix sand and lime putty with my own hands.

I'm grateful to the readers, writers and editors who guided and encouraged me with generous insights along the way: Sarah MacLachlan, Allison McCabe, David Young, Jennifer Robson, Michael Ondaatje and Dianne Hales; to all of my loving family and to those who kindly agreed to read and comment on early drafts of the manuscript: Barbara Berson, Maria Scala, Douglas Lawrence, Janine Metcalfe, Sasha Rogers and her Summerhill book club; and to Rana Khan, Dale Mackey, Helen Hatzis, Monica Gutschi, Ginetta Peters, Carolyne Bayly, Paget Catania and all of the Beaches crew for offering sustaining companionship and laughter. Deep gratitude goes to my children Hannah,

Dylan, Alexander and Geneviève, for reading, for insights and for invaluable plot guidance. To my husband, John Terry, thank you for your unrelenting optimism and wisdom, and for always being my mountain guide.

The following resources were crucial during the writing of this novel:

Clayton, Martin, and Ron Philo. *Leonardo da Vinci: The Mechanics of Man*. London: Royal Collection Enterprises, 2010.

Condivi, Ascanio. *The Life of Michelangelo*. London: Pallas Athene, 2006 (first published in 1553).

Crum, Roger J., and John T. Paoletti. *Renaissance Florence: A Social History*. Cambridge: Cambridge University Press, 2006.

da Vinci, Leonardo. *Notebooks*. Selected by Irma A. Richter and edited with an introduction and notes by Thereza Wells. Oxford: Oxford University Press, 1952.

de Tolnay, Charles. *The Youth of Michelangelo*. Princeton, NJ: Princeton University Press, 1943. (All six volumes of de Tolnay's magnificent *Michelangelo* series were given to me by my husband for Christmas 2019, when I wanted to put my novel aside.)

Hales, Dianne. *Mona Lisa: A Life Discovered*. New York: Simon & Schuster, 2014.

Hartt, Frederick. *David: By the Hand of Michelangelo; The Original Model Discovered*. London: Thames and Hudson, 1987.

Isaacson, Walter. *Leonardo da Vinci*. New York: Simon & Schuster, 2017.

Jones, Jonathan. *The Lost Battles: Leonardo, Michelangelo and the Artistic Duel that Defined the Renaissance*. New York: Simon & Schuster, 2010.

Kemp, Martin. *Leonardo*. Oxford: Oxford University Press, 2004.

Kemp, Martin. *Leonardo da Vinci: The Marvellous Works of Nature and Man*. Oxford: Oxford University Press, 2006.

King, Ross. *Machiavelli: Philosopher of Power*. London: HarperPress, 2007.

Machiavelli, Niccolò. *The Prince*. New York: Knopf, 2006 (first published in 1513).

McCabe, Joseph. *New Light on Witchcraft*. Girard, KS: Haldeman-Julius, 1926.

McCarthy, Mary. *The Stones of Florence*. San Diego: Harcourt, 1963.

McIver, Katherine A. *Cooking and Eating in Renaissance Italy: From Kitchen to Table*. London: Rowman & Littlefield, 2015.

Stone, Irving. *The Agony and the Ecstasy*. New York: Doubleday, 1961.

Symonds, John Addington. *The Life of Michelangelo Buonarroti*. New York: The Modern Library, 1928. (An original leather-bound edition left on my dock at the cottage by a neighbor.)

Trexler, Richard C. *Public Life in Renaissance Florence*. Ithaca, NY: Cornell University Press, 1980.

Vasari, Giorgio. *The Lives of the Artists*. London: Penguin Books, 1965 (first published in 1568).